THE UNITED

A CULLING OF BLOOD AND MAGIC

K.M. RIVES

The United by K.M. Rives

Copyright© December 2022

Cover Art: Kiff Shaik @ Solidarity Squad

Editing: Kraken Communications

Proofing: Leticia Teixeira

This book is a work of fiction. Names, characters, places and incidents are either a product of the authors imagination or are used fictitiously. Any resemblance to actual persons, living or dead, or to actual events or locales is completely coincidental.

This book in its entirety and in portions is the sole property of K.M. Rives.

The United Copyright© 2021 by K.M. Rives. All rights reserved. No part of this publication may be reproduced, distributed, or transmitted in any form or by any means, including photocopying, recording, or other electronic or mechanical methods, without the prior written permission of the publisher, except in the case of brief quotations embodied in critical reviews and certain other noncommercial uses permitted by copyright law. For permission requests, write to the author.

For my husband.
Because you believe in me like August believes in Emery.

Chapter One

SLOANE

It really was unfortunate that her twin's soul had survived. Not that there was any way Sloane could've predicted that Emery's mate could save her.

Mate.

The word made her lip curl in a snarl. Why any witch would want to be tethered to a vampire for all of eternity was beyond her. Especially August Nicholson. When she'd lived at the castle, he was the epitome of a spoiled rotten prince with his head lodged in his perfectly rounded ass. He'd changed since then; she hadn't missed the love in his eyes when he looked at Emery, or the fear when his father slit her throat. It was something she hadn't considered possible. Mates were a bond of magic, not meant to be a proclamation of love, and the very thought that the two should go hand in hand made her stomach sour.

Not that it would matter in the long run. She'd rectify the issue just as she had everything else. How hard could it be to break a mate bond? All she needed was a mate to test it, and if she had her choice, she knew who she would pick.

Sloane rounded the table at the center of the sterile room, her eyes lingering on the naked flesh of the handsome wolf stretched end to end. It turned out he was a better asset than she could have predicted. His wolf was more alpha than beta, and his rage was intoxicating. Although it would have been better if she'd been able to procure a true pack alpha, she couldn't be greedy. Not yet. She'd save that drive for the battles yet to be won.

The wolf eyed her with suspicion. He'd been harder to break than the others. Finding out what motivated him had proven difficult, but once she'd learned he'd been the wolf protecting Emery all those months in New Orleans, she knew exactly where to strike.

She trailed the tips of her fingers, blackened over time with the use of her dark magic, along the bulging muscles in his arm, down to where the silver cuffs wrapped around his wrist. His dark brown eyes sent daggers in her direction, but he didn't speak. Sloane dragged her eyes along the scars on his thighs where she'd taught him a lesson about speaking out of turn.

"Are you going to do as you're told today?"

A low growl reverberated against the plain steel walls.

That would be a no. His loss, really. Sloane didn't particularly enjoy torturing him; she'd rather save it for those who deserved her wrath. But if he wasn't willing to join her cause, she'd do what it took to get what she needed.

"Suit yourself." She shrugged and reached below the metal table to flip a switch.

The table groaned and began to tilt, taking the wolf

from horizontal to vertical. When it clicked into place, Sloane pulled the glass syringe from her coat pocket and stepped forward, close enough that she could smell the dirt and sweat of her prisoner.

He snarled and snapped his elongated fangs in her direction. It really was a shame he was loyal to her sister—he would no doubt make a fine lover.

In one swift motion, she stabbed the needle into his jugular vein and pressed down on the plunger. The opalescent purple potion entered his blood, and Sloane opened her free hand, calling her magic to her palm. Darkness flooded the space between them, and the tendrils of her magic wrapped around him. Eyes narrowed, Sloane urged the spell to travel from his neck to his heart. The racing beat of his blood pounded in her mind, and she tasted fear and loathing as her magic maneuvered its way to the organ that would, in moments, send her will to his brain and turn him from loyal wolf to feral animal.

She knew the moment it overwhelmed his system, his brown eyes dilating to pure obsidian. Fur erupted from his skin, and his fingers lengthened into claws. It didn't matter that he fought against her—magic as dark as hers trumped free will every time.

Sloane leaned forward and ran her tongue over the ridges of his abdomen to where his heart beat in his chest.

"How about now? Are you ready to do as you're told?" she asked again.

He snarled at her once more, but this time it wasn't out of hatred. This time, it was because he would do anything to sate the monster inside him. His wolf was hers to control. It sought to claim anything and everything in its path in its quest to find its mate. All Sloane had to do was promise she would bring him back.

"Sebastian is waiting for you. But I need my army first. I'll give him back to you if you give me what I want."

"Mate." He howled and thrashed against the restraints. "Dorian."

Sloane raised a brow. That was a new name. Usually, his wolf called for Sebastian. Her research had revealed that Sebastian had been a hybrid, wolf and witch, who'd died. Sloane used that to her advantage. She couldn't bring back his mate any more than she could bring back her own mother—without the body and fresh blood it was impossible—, but his wolf didn't know that.

Occasionally, he would call for Emery and her baby, in which case she'd weave an illusion of her torturing them to get him to comply.

But Dorian was a new thread to pull.

"Who is Dorian?"

"Fae. Mate. Fated," his wolf growled. "Dorian," he growled again, and this time the metal of the restraints groaned in protest.

Sloane stepped back, and a trickle of fear slid down her spine. If he broke free, she wasn't in a good position to stop him from tearing her apart. She turned away from him and smoothed the front of her coat as she inhaled a steadying breath. "Turn the humans, and I'll find Dorian."

A low growl was all she got in response.

Exiting the room, she nodded at Wren on the other side of the two-way mirror, signaling for her to open the door that would allow the first five drugged humans to enter. The moment they did, the wolf would be released to do his job. And then it would be rinse and repeat until morning, when the full moon receded below the horizon.

"Who the hell is Dorian?" she asked.

Wren shrugged. It still struck Sloane as concerning that Wren chose to side with her over her sister. They'd been best friends, but it was only because Wren was tasked with babysitting Emery. Wren felt overlooked—as the daughter of Vishna's sister, she believed that she should have been in line to rule. The best she could hope for was a seat in the inner circle. Apparently, she'd always been fascinated with the darker side of magic, and now that the coven was destroyed, Wren had every intention of becoming Sloane's second-in-command. And she was good at it. More ruthless than half the elders who'd come before her.

Jessi, who had stood silently behind Wren until that moment, spoke up. "He's August's right hand."

Sloane's eyes widened. "August has a fucking fae on his side, and you didn't think this was imperative information?"

If Jessi had been a pain in the ass when they were Culling women, she was even more so now. But Sloane couldn't deny she'd been useful. Jessi brought with her extensive knowledge of the castle and the vampires who lived there, far more than Sloane would have been able to find out herself. Then again, Sloane hadn't been willing to spread her legs for the king.

Jessi tossed her blonde hair over her shoulder. "I didn't know he was a fae. What the hell is a fae anyways?"

"Never mind. Wren, find me everything you can on the fae and why the hell August has one as his second."

Screams erupted from the other side of the glass as their prisoner went to work, ripping open the chests of the humans and slicing through their hearts. Only half of them would survive the change, and, among those, only half would survive the spell that would instill bloodlust and prolong their lives. But those who did would be loyal only to her. They would become an unstoppable force to be reckoned with.

"The dead are piling up, Mistress. Where would you like us to dispose of them?"

She'd been careful thus far not to let Emery and August know what she was up to, but seeing as she'd almost amassed the army she needed to destroy them, it was time to start the next phase of her plan.

"Leave them somewhere they will be found. It's high time we let my sister and her mate know we are coming for them."

Chapter Two

EMERY

A name.

What they were doing—the deliberations and decisions of these advisors—would echo forever in supernatural history. They were the advisors to the soon-to-be reigning vampire king of the Americas, in a time of war no less, and the crotchety old bastards were hung up on a damn name.

"All we're saying is Vanya is a strong name for a princess." Constantine, the oldest of August's inherited council and the biggest thorn in her side, argued.

It shouldn't surprise Emery; they were pro-vampire and against anything remotely related to the witches. It was a running theme with them.

"We are not naming our daughter after a queen famous for her high witch body count and playful murder sprees." Emery's darkness swirled in her chest as it had been doing more often, thriving on any anger and chaos that surrounded her. The black magic that mixed with her golden light scared the shit out of her as it continued to grow more prudent in its attempts to slither its way to the forefront. But Emery had seen what it could do. She'd made witches bleed and felt the sinister intent woven in its tendrils. It might be a part of her, but she didn't want to touch it and risk becoming like Sloane. Especially while pregnant.

Emery gritted her teeth and tamped down the untapped magic. As much as the vampire advisors pissed her off, they didn't deserve her darkness. At least not yet. Though some days they tread a fine line. Most days she couldn't figure out how August's father ran a kingdom with these idiots advising him. Well, that wasn't true. She suspected they weren't advising him at all. Lewyn ran the kingdom as he saw fit, a dictator if she'd ever seen one. His advisors were just there for show and the notoriety of being in the room where decisions were made. Even if they didn't actually contribute anything of worth.

Emery glanced over to where her mate sat beside her, his hands steepled in front of his mouth to hide his smirk.

He was enjoying this.

Jackass.

The darkness that begged for release sent her images of Emery tying August to his ornate throne and punishing him for wasting her time. In particular, it wanted her to suck his cock and bring him to the edge of insanity before letting him finally come inside her where his seed belonged.

Fuck, she needed to get laid.

The two of them had been so damn busy running the kingdom in the wake of the attacks during the hunt that they'd barely seen one another except to sleep.

She also needed to figure out what she was going to do

about the dark magic woven through her soul like a tightly knit sweater. The images were its newest attempts to goad her into tapping into its menacing intentions.

August slipped his hand onto her thigh, likely because he sensed the shift in her mood through their mate bond. He'd become more overprotective of her since the attack on the castle and the merging of himself. She'd assumed getting August back would mean she'd get her reasonable mate back. Her assessment had been wrong. Merging August and Augustine only enhanced both sides of his personalities. So much so that she was still learning who she should expect on any given day.

Scratch that. Any given moment.

Most of the time she didn't mind, though she preferred August in the streets and Augustine in the sheets. When his personality reversed and she got Augustine in the council room is when she was really thrown for a loop.

She'd finally convinced August to compromise about her role in the ongoing war. She wouldn't overexert herself with magic until she was no longer pregnant with his child, and he would try to stop being an overbearing ass. The arrangement was an easy one on Emery's part—if August hadn't made her promise she wouldn't touch her dark magic until after their daughter was born, the images of the witches with their blood being pulled from their souls haunted her dreams and were enough to deter her. Their cries echoed in her ears, and she'd felt the power she could wield. She didn't want to be defined by that.

What August didn't realize was that just because she wasn't training her magic or looking for her sister with the sentinels didn't mean she wasn't busy from sunup to sundown trying to put out the fires of their people. Of which there were many.

Which is what she expected to be discussing at this meeting. Not names for their daughter. They should have been discussing the fact that Sloane had gone mostly silent for almost three months. She still had Ansel, and the only sign of her was the continued kidnappings of wolves, vampires, and humans. None of whom they'd been able to track.

Or they could be discussing the fact that earlier that morning the Pine Shore pack found a pile of what looked to be bodies on their lands, steeped in Sloane's purple death magic. But that wasn't a topic of discussion. Neither was the fact that the nobles wanted nothing to do with the witches and that was becoming more and more of a problem. Sure, they pretended and played nice in the castle, but if they had it their way, they'd kick their potential mates to the curb without a second glance. The tension grew every day.

Another old vampire shuffled the papers in front of him and lifted his hand to gather her attention. "But Vanya also—"

Emery slammed her hand down on the war room table, sending papers and dust flying. "No."

Her abdomen tightened with the rise of her temper, and she had to hide her wince.

Damn Braxton Hicks.

August squeezed her thigh, and she could feel his apprehension through their bond. Emery responded by sending him a push of reassurance that she was okay.

Each of the advisors visibly jerked back at the sight of her, and she didn't need to see the soft amber light radiating through the dimly lit circular chamber to know her eyes were glowing. Likely they were also seeing the rings of darkness that lined her irises pulse and grow black.

Emery inhaled a breath, steadying the dark surge in her chest.

Her eyes were a constant of who she was. Their glowing quality gave her authority, but also served as a reminder to the advisors that she wasn't like them. It didn't matter that she sat in the place of their queen. It didn't matter that she carried their heir or that she'd proven herself to be on their side. She was still a witch, and while they respected her to a certain degree, they also feared her. She wore the visage of their enemy and harbored the same magic in her veins.

Well, almost.

Thankfully, her magic was more light than dark.

Mostly.

Hopefully.

She couldn't deny the weight of the doubt in her mind—was she a danger to the people around her?

The warmth of her light magic swirled in her chest, taking the place of the dark at the same time the bond she shared with August radiated a mix of amusement and annoyance. Emery didn't need to look at him to know he was biting the inside of his cheek to hide the lopsided grin she loved so much. She could practically feel it down their mate bond.

You're loving this.

Watching my mate chew my advisors a new asshole? Absolutely. August teased down the bond that tied their souls together and allowed them to communicate in one another's heads. It was his preferred method of communicating with her, mostly because there was no denying the feelings in their words when mixed with their emotion-sharing mate bond. It was his August side shining through. She'd never tell him, but his August side was a bit of a sap.

This meeting is a sham and you know it, Emery argued. Anger surged in her chest, and she struggled to keep the darker tendrils of magic firmly coiled within her. *We shouldn't be arguing about a damn name when there is plenty we could be doing to settle the tensions in our own court. They are trying to ice the witches out, keep them in the fields, and only deal with them as necessary.*

We are doing everything we can, August placated, but she could sense the lie in his words.

Are we? They are using this meeting to discuss a name so we don't have to address the elephant in the room. The fact is, they would rather we didn't find a way to connect mates with one another. They'd rather continue in a world where we are enemies. They don't see us as a force to be reckoned with, August. They see me as another enemy to their kingdom, just one that they can tolerate for now. But how long will that last?

It felt like she was fighting a battle on two fronts. The only thing uniting both sides was the rage that came with the great loss during the hunt, combined with the fact that Emery had nearly died. Though many would argue she should have stayed dead. Some even suggested it.

The only reason she remained alive was because August threatened to kill anyone who tried to take her from him.

Sometimes she really wished he would go back to being Augustine and not the diplomatic August in front of her.

Maybe then they'd be getting somewhere instead of arguing over a name.

You're right. I wouldn't let them kill you. And I'll keep in mind you like my ragey side better.

She felt the smirk he was no doubt wearing.

Damn it. Emery dropped her head to the table and exhaled a heavy breath. She hadn't realized she'd sent her thoughts down the bond—a mistake that often occurred when she let her emotions get the better of her. It became impossible to filter her thoughts from the bond.

August sent a blast of soothing emotions toward her, but she shrugged him off. They only confirmed he wasn't going to rage, even though he absolutely should.

"What does Your Majesty think?" one of the advisors asked.

Emery turned her gaze to her mate, and raised a brow. This was his chance.

"Regarding my daughter's name?" August shrugged at the vampire like he hadn't just been talking Emery off a ledge and gave her a wink. "Happy wife, happy life."

Emery rolled her eyes at his copout, even though she loved the way that word rolled off his tongue and made her insides turn to mush. *Wife.* She fidgeted with the heirloom ring on her third finger. It seemed so trivial when she and August shared so much more than just a commitment spoken out loud. They were mates tethered by the fates. But if he wanted to remind everyone that she was his wife, she wasn't going to stop him. Especially because she knew how much the advisors hated it.

Now if she could just get him to give her a little more leeway in taking a stand for her people and calling out his own instead of making her a glorified piece of arm candy. Maybe she could use his motto against him.

You best remember that.

August parted his lips and made a show of running his tongue over his elongated fang. *That's one.*

Hello, Augustine.

Flutters erupted in her core and thoughts of war flitted to the edges. Emery clenched her thighs. Damn hormones, taking her from one end of the spectrum to the other with just two words. Despite the frustration she held against him, she loved this game he played. She was glad it wasn't something lost when August and Augustine became one.

Eye rolls annoyed the shit out of her fiancé. But eye rolls also meant punishment, and punishment meant alone time with her mate. Alone time with little to no clothing, and, if she was lucky, a light spanking. Emery sent a silent prayer to the stars that he followed through on his promise. At least the problem of getting laid would be solved.

"But she's not your wife, Your Majesty."

Emery whipped her gaze to the advisor who spoke out against her mate, her brows meeting her forehead.

A low growl bubbled from his throat as August narrowed his eyes at the offending advisor. She thought his name was Roland. It didn't really matter, though, because he was running the risk of being dead.

"I suggest you choose your words very carefully. She is my intended, my fiancée, my mate, and your future queen." August placed his hands on the table and stood, sending his chair tumbling behind him. "In fact, let's make it official. Call whoever needs to be called. Let's get this over with so everyone can see that this is not changing, ever. My mate wants me to take action and I want you to see that she is our future, as is our daughter."

All of his advisors spoke up at once in protest.

"But Your Majesty—"

"You can't just—"

Emery reached out and placed a hand on his arm, sending love and calming down their bond, even though she was ready to fight at his side for this. They'd come so far together, and she couldn't wait to stand with him. She loved the way he claimed her. But unfortunately, as much as she hated to admit it, their marriage was about more than them. *August, we can't. As much as I want to marry you this very second, our people need this. Those who see us as their future need to be a part of our union so they can be a part of building our kingdom.*

August turned, his twisted blue eyes locked on her. *And I need you.*

The evidence of his need swirled through their bond. Love. Lust. Desire. Dedication. Desperation. He pulled her against him, crashing his lips to hers.

This. Fucking. Vampire.

A shiver wracked her body as he sucked her bottom lip between his fangs. It didn't matter how many times he kissed her, she couldn't get enough of it. Of him. August swallowed the involuntary moan that escaped her, and the hand that kept her pulled tight against him fisted the fabric of her dress.

Remembering that they were standing in front of a room full of vampire advisors, Emery tried to pull away, but August tugged her tighter against him. He didn't seem to mind the gasps and heated stares coming from his advisors. He bit down, piercing two small holes with his fangs, and sucked her blood between his lips.

Mine.

Emery tugged back until he released. "Forever. And despite your barbaric possessive tendencies, I will be your queen. But let's plan a coronation when we are no longer at war." She spoke out loud against his lips in an effort to reassure the vampires who were now cowering in their seats that he wasn't completely insane.

Not that they'd ever give her the same consideration.

His eyes swirled with indecision and desire. *You know I love when you call yourself my queen.* He'd grown so much since he'd embraced every facet of himself, but at his core he was still just a man.

"Get out." August growled and Emery looked away from him, shaking her head.

"Your Majesty—"

"If you are not out of here in five seconds, I will rip your eyes from your sockets and shove them in your ears. I also suggest you talk amongst yourselves and figure out a plan to include the witches on your council moving forward."

"But—"

"Now," August roared.

Emery pressed her lips together to stifle the smile at his orders to include her people, while her thighs chafed trying to hide how much his barbaric possession turned her on.

Chairs shifted and his advisors moved in a blur of motion until only Emery and August were left in the room.

Maybe this meeting was worth it after all.

Chapter Three

AUGUST

"Was that necessary?" she asked as the last advisor shuffled out of the room, pulling the door closed behind him.

"Completely." He softly growled against her lips, teasing them with his own.

"You can't just end a meeting because your cock wants to rise to the occasion whenever someone points out I'm not your wife."

August scoffed and didn't bother to point out that her thighs were clenching, and he could smell the arousal pooling between her legs. It was about more than that and she knew it. He wouldn't even try to argue that she wanted this just as much as he did. Somehow in the last five minutes, she'd become the diplomatic one, leaving him to take desperate measures to ensure he got what they both wanted.

He knew at heart Emery wanted his people to love her. Nobles included. But he didn't give a shit what they thought most of the time. They would fall in line or wouldn't—either way, as soon as he was officially crowned, those advisors would be replaced with people he trusted. Until then, they had to play the game with his father's leftovers and tread lightly when implementing changes to the old guard, even if they were pompous, bigoted assholes with their heads stuck in the past who demanded he take them into consideration every waking moment of every day.

Usually he didn't mind—listening to irritating advisors was part of the job. But the time away from his mate had started to weigh on him. The kingdom demanded his attention all day every day, which left little time for the two of them.

If he had to go investigate the bodies left by Emery's traitorous sister, he was going to do it after a proper send off from his mate.

August slid his hands down the curves of her hips, his thumbs caressing her tight rounded belly. "Yet, Emery. You're not my wife yet. And I can and will ensure that they know who the fuck you are every time someone questions your legitimacy at my side."

"August—"

"Little witch, don't fight this," he sighed. "We've both been so damn busy. You with Lily and Bronwyn trying to keep the witches happy while researching how to recreate Celeste's damn spell, and me trying to keep all the moving pieces in order and find Sloane's whereabouts while keeping the peace between the factions not only in our kingdom, but around the world. Let me have you. Soon it won't be just us."

August dropped to his knees, and his hands drifted

over her belly as he peppered it with kisses. "Ignore what I'm about to do to your mother, *gealiach bhig*."

Little moon.

If Emery was the stars in his sky, his daughter was the one who brought light to his dark nights. He already loved her more than life itself, but he'd be remiss if he didn't consider how much their lives were going to change when she entered the world. It both thrilled and scared the ever-loving shit out of him.

"August, I am the size of a damn whale. We aren't doing this. At least not here." She may have feigned disinterest but the way she rolled her hips forward told a different story.

"I thought you liked it when I embraced my savage nature."

He ran his hands over the swell of her belly and down the curve of her hips. August loved her pregnant body. The way it adapted to bring new life into the world made him want to worship every inch of her. He wanted to be sure she knew every change was perfect and beautiful. He hated that she didn't see herself the way he did.

August leaned back on his heels and drew his gaze up her body. "You are the most beautiful thing I've ever seen, little witch, giving my daughter life and ensuring the future of our people. I hope you know as soon as this war is finished, I plan to keep you swollen with my children for the foreseeable future. There will never be a time I don't want to fuck you. Your body was made for me, and I plan to remind you of that every chance I get. Now slide up onto the table so I can ravage your body where I plan my battles so that every time I look at these maps I'm reminded what I'm fighting for."

Her mouth dropped open, and August beamed with pride that he could still manage to shock her. Emery inched back toward the table, but he didn't need the movement to know she was all in. He felt the heat and desire in their bond. It flooded him like a torrential rain, and he struggled to keep himself from losing control.

August's cock strained against his jeans, and he inhaled what was meant to be a steadying breath but the sweet smell of Emery's arousal and pheromones filled his senses. He was far from steady. In a matter of seconds, his intentions shifted from loving fiancé to desperate addict. He'd wanted to woo her, to give her something to think about when she was alone waiting for him to return, but that was no longer an option.

"Bloody hell, Emery, do you know how fucking intoxicating you are?" He lifted the hem of her dress and dragged his tongue up her thigh to where her soaked panties clung to her slick folds.

A shiver tore through her, and Emery sucked in a breath. "August," she panted, and her need was a palpable entity in the air around them.

He trailed his fingers along her thighs, dipping beneath the hem of her dress to the scrap of lace that separated them. "I'm torn between the need to cancel everything and memorize every inch of your body and taking you hard and fast right here until my cum is dripping down your legs, reminding everyone who you belong to."

"Now. I need you now." She pulled up her dress until it bunched around the top of her belly and propped herself up on her elbows so she could see him. "And later."

A wicked smile tipped his lips. Fuck, that perfect logic of hers.

She looked so damn exquisite, carrying his child and smiling at him like he was the center of her universe. He didn't deserve her, but he was a selfish being and would covet everything she offered.

"Relax, mate, let me enjoy that sweet pussy I love so much." He hooked his fingers on the lace of her panties and tore them from her skin, shoving the scraps in his pocket. She'd ream him for it later, but he'd already ordered more to make up for the number he'd ruined.

August flattened his tongue and swiped up her sex from bottom to top, his fangs scraping her clit. Emery's hands slammed onto the wood table at her sides, and she let out every bit of air from her lungs.

His fingers danced along her soaked slit. She was already fucking ready for him. He stood, unfastening the button of his pants and freed his cock with his free hand. Pre-cum dripped from the head, and he was so close to coming that if he wasn't careful, he'd lose control.

That's what she did to him. From the moment she entered his life she'd driven him to the edge of insanity. And he wouldn't have it any other way. But he had to hold himself back. Frustrating as it was, he didn't want to hurt her or their daughter with the filthy images of all the ways he wanted to fuck her coursing through his mind.

August gripped his shaft and stepped forward, swiping the tip of his cock through her slick folds while pledging a silent promise to his mate. The moment his daughter was free and Emery was recovered, he would give his mate a night filled with every fantasy either of them had ever had.

"Please, Augustine," Emery moaned, raising her hips in an attempt to gain the friction she wanted. He loved when she begged. Even more when she used his full name. The way she accepted every facet of him.

"Please what, little witch?"

"Take me. Claim me."

Four simple words. A request he'd never deny her.

August pistoned his hips forward, sheathing himself completely in one fluid stroke. "Bloody hell," he moaned. "You were made for me. You're perfect. So damn tight."

"Until I push a watermelon through it," she sassed, but it was curtailed by a moan as he slid his cock out nearly to the tip and thrusted in again.

"Even then." He bent his knees, changing his angle so he hit the deepest parts of her.

The most delicious moan fell from Emery's lips, and he nearly came then and there. He didn't hesitate, continuing to move in and out, stoking the fire in her. Emery captivated his soul. She held it in her chest, and he would give everything for her. He loved to watch her orgasms build, the way a sheen of sweat coated her body, and how her eyes rolled back every time her clit hit the base of his shaft. Her channel tightened, clamping hungrily on his cock, and her fingers wrapped around his forearms, seeking leverage in an attempt to both meet his thrusts with enthusiasm and stave off her impending pleasure.

Emery's moans grew louder, her thighs quivering under his palms as his balls tightened, and he recognized his own orgasm cresting. Their bond flared with need. To claim. To own. There was nothing but this moment, this place, the two of them together. He would taste her on his lips and fill her with his seed.

August lifted her right leg over his head and rolled her onto her side, his hips never slowing.

The moment he shifted her, Emery cried out, "Holy hell. I'm gonna come."

Her words spurred him on, and August leaned down, trailing his tongue along her shoulder until he reached her ear. He sucked her lobe between his lips and growled.

"Come with me, little witch."

August rocked his hips, picking up his pace until Emery was crying his name. She tightened around him, her orgasm clenching his cock like a vise and sending him over the edge. As his release took him, he sank his fangs into her shoulder, and their bond radiated with power the moment her blood passed his lips. August could feel every bit of love they shared, plus a hint of the darkness that bonded them.

She was his source of life. His end and beginning.

He licked the wound at her neck, sending a shiver through her.

August's legs shook as he slid himself from Emery and quickly grabbed a towel from the bar cart. When he returned, she looked up at him, her eyes wide and glassed over, and August couldn't help the smug smirk that tugged at his lips. He was the reason for that look.

Emery rolled onto her back and closed her legs to him. "Leave it. I thought you wanted them to know I was yours."

Bloody hell, she was perfect.

His cock twitched, coming back to life, and he had to stop himself from taking her again. Instead, he leaned forward and pressed his lips to hers, stealing a kiss that was chaste in comparison to the way he'd just fucked her. He savored her taste on his lips, and dread spread through him when he realized he'd be walking away from her for the first time since he'd lost her.

As if reading the turmoil in his thoughts, Emery asked, "Do you have to go?"

"You know I do." As much as he wished he didn't. He'd much rather spend the evening wrapping his arms around his mate, but all comms had been rendered useless by Sloane's magic. Since the dump site was in the remote wilderness of the Pine Shore pack lands, his connection to Emery was the only way to relay information back instantly and call for any backup that might be needed. This was also the first time they'd found any remnants of Sloane's movements. Prior to this, there had been kidnappings and speculation, but nothing concrete.

This was yet another reason why he wanted to go. He couldn't sit by and allow Sloane to continue to take from them and pose a threat to his kingdom and his family.

"Take me with you." Emery sat up and snaked her arms around his neck. "I could help you assess the magic and then we could find a tree and go for round two. I seem to remember you have a penchant for fucking me against them."

He did. And more than anything he wanted to agree to her demand. The image of her in Scotland pressed up against the bark under the light of the moon was in his top five favorite memories. But this wasn't about his penchant for trees, and they both knew it.

August shook his head. "Please, Em. I don't want to argue."

The rings around her eyes thickened, the visible sign her darkness was growing. What had started with his darkness leaving a permanent mark in her eyes when he gave her a part of his soul to save her had become an outward sign of her own darkness growing. It taunted him every day, and he was helpless to fix it. Emery might not bring it up, but he saw it every time she grew angry. He tried to fight it in his own way, doing his best to keep her happy, but this wasn't something he was going to budge on, darkness be damned.

It wasn't the first time and it wouldn't be the last time she pressed him. Emery wanted so badly to be out of the castle tracking Sloane, and if he was honest, he wanted her at his side. But the thought of anything happening to her made his chest tighten and his bloodlust spiral out of control.

"I don't want to argue either. I just want to help." She let out a frustrated sigh, and with it the high they rode from their love-making shattered. "I need to do more than sit in this castle and play queen."

He'd suggested she take up knitting, but that got him a shot of magic to the chest, and he wasn't about to go through that again.

"But queen is what you'll be." He knew his argument would fall on deaf ears. "You need to be here, for our people and our daughter."

"For now."

August turned away, unable to make himself agree with her. He stepped out from between her legs and ran his hand through his hair.

"August," It didn't matter that he wasn't looking at her, he could feel the daggers down their bond. "I can't stay locked up here forever."

His heart raced in his chest as he worked through all

the ways he could indeed lock her up forever. For instance, he could tie her to his bed.

"I can't lose you," he whispered. Not again. Not ever.

Emery didn't understand. Couldn't understand. She was the air he breathed. The only thing that kept him going. The memory of her falling to the ground... the way her blood seeped from her lifeless body... it would forever haunt his nightmares. If she was gone, he'd tear the damn world apart to bring her back. He'd already split his soul.

"You won't lose me." She scoffed like he was being unreasonable. "I'm literally an immortal witch with three concentrations of magic. I know you are trying to protect me, but we are at war. This is my sister. I can't just sit back and relaaaaaa—"

Emery's hands flew to her stomach and inhaled a sharp breath. "Fuck."

August was at her side a split second later, his panic mingling with the pain in their bond as he took her in his arms. "Emery, what's wrong? Are you okay?"

"I'm fine. It's just fucking Braxton Hicks," she hissed.

"Come." He slid his arm around her and picked her up bridal-style before darting down the hall to their temporary bedroom. She tensed in his arms but allowed him to help her. When he reached the bedside, he slid her down his body until her feet touched the floor. "You need to lay down. Preferably on your left side."

Emery scoffed and shoved his hands away. "I'm fine. It's already passed."

"They say real contractions can be mistaken for Braxton Hicks. I'm going to call Dr. K and have her come check on you."

"I'm fine, August." She huffed but narrowed her eyes. "But who exactly is they?"

"Doctors. Experts. Whoever wrote those damn books Malcolm gave me."

Her jaw dropped, but he didn't miss the hint of amusement in her gaze. "You're reading baby books?"

Of course, he was. "Our daughter is part human, I figured it was best to be prepared."

Emery's eyes softened, the dark rings around her irises thinning as they welled with tears. "That is quite possibly the sweetest thing I've ever heard."

August reached up and tucked a piece of pink hair behind her ear. He trailed his thumb over her cheek, catching a stray tear. "Don't cry, princess."

"I hate these fucking pregnancy hormones." She crossed her arms over her chest and stuck out her bottom lip.

"Don't tell anyone about the books. I've got a reputation to uphold."

She smiled at that. "Your secret's safe with me."

He pressed a soft kiss to her temple and tugged her against his chest. "I won't apologize for wanting to keep you safe, little witch. But I will try to be better about letting you be involved with the war. And I'd like for you to train after our daughter is born."

She tipped her head back. "You mean that?"

He nodded.

"Thank you for asking for witches to be added to the advisors," she whispered.

"Melding our worlds is not going to be easy, but it's the right thing to do." Even if it wasn't, he'd do anything to see the smile she was giving him right then. "Now, I need to go, before I decide round two is far more important than hiking in the woods. Plus, Draven will be waiting."

"I'd wager your entire fortune he's doing the exact same thing with Flora right now."

"Fighting or fucking?"

She gave him a pointed look and shook her head. "Promise me you'll come back to me."

"Always." He leaned down and nipped her lip before delving his tongue in her mouth for a searing kiss.

When he broke away from her, breathless and wanting more, he forced himself to turn on his heel and head for the door, knowing that if he didn't leave at that moment, he wouldn't leave at all. He was nearly to the gardens where he was set to meet Draven when the whisper of his mate echoed in his mind, and her love flooded his chest.

I love you.
Forever.

Chapter Four

EMERY

The heat was oppressive. It rendered the shower she'd just taken useless the second she stepped outside. The witches didn't seem to mind, though. Maybe it was the fact that many of them had lived in the humidity of New Orleans—this heat was nothing next to that. It was also possible that though they'd conformed to her request to keep the nudity to a minimum, the witches had found creative ways to still wear next to nothing.

Not that the vampires at the castle minded. From the moment the witches moved their camp from Scotland to the clearing outside Lily's cottage, many of the vampires who had sought sanctuary in the castle were intrigued.

And Emery couldn't blame them. She remembered her first few weeks in New Orleans. Even if the majority of the witches had been complete assholes to her, they had a mystical way about them that begged for people to stare. They moved with a subtle elegance that was somehow rough around the edges. Their sexual prowess and offhandedness drew people in, but, in this case, it was their hidden kindness spurred by their desire to find their mates that kept the vampires a consistent presence in the tent city.

The royal vampires, on the other hand, were still a bunch of crotchety bastards. Their distrust—and often dislike—of witches was very poorly disguised. But Emery tried not to hold that against them. Then again, after the meeting she'd just had, maybe she should. She needed to do something to get the royals to see beyond the trivial bullshit and take an interest in the real issues concerning the kingdom.

Emery stepped away from the castle doors and muttered the incantation to open a portal that would take her to the clearing that housed the witches.

As soon as she stepped through, she heard her name.

"Emery!" Haven yelled, running up the path to greet her. "Is Thea with you?"

The sweet little witch had become instant friends with the youngest royal, and it was unusual to see one without the other.

"Not today, but I bet if you ask your mom you can come with me back to the castle and see her."

"Really? I'll go ask!" She gave Emery a big hug and then bounced away toward the first row of tents.

Emery smiled and rubbed her belly. She couldn't wait to meet her daughter. To see the way she'd grow in this community and forge her own path. If she was anything like Thea and Haven, though, they were going to have their hands full.

Rows of deceptively small tents lined her path, and she made small talk with the witches she passed. Most of it was good-natured, but a few joked about how they were happy none of them had turned out to be mates with the noble vampires in the castle.

Emery's heart ached for them. They wanted to find their other halves more than anything, but were now realizing that maybe finding their mates wouldn't be all sunshine and sexy time. Especially if they were paired with a vampire who hated them for what they were. She knew the feeling all too well. The image of August standing over Chelsea's body, claiming he could never love her because she was a witch, was one that still haunted her dreams. She knew they would never end up there again, but it was a constant reminder of where their people had been and how far they had to go.

When she reached the end of the rows of tents, Emery's gaze fell on the large open arena they'd set up for training. A pang of jealousy zapped through her as she watched a group of young elemental witches learn to hone their elements. Emery stepped up to the fence, her belly hitting the wood and reminding her why she couldn't be out there.

There wasn't anything she wouldn't do for her daughter, but she couldn't deny being pregnant made her feel useless. The last few weeks, using her magic in any sort of training capacity had wiped her out, rendering her useless for the rest of the day. She longed for the days in Scotland when she trained with Dorian and Ansel all afternoon, wielding her wind and fire like they were an extension of her limbs while intermittently stunning them with offensive balls of light magic.

Soon, she reminded herself. She only needed to pop out this kid and she'd be back out there.

From across the arena, the door to Lily's cottage flew open and Bronwyn flew out, her eyes locking on Emery. "Thank goodness you're here. I need your help."

Emery gave one last longing look at the witches' training and turned to where Bronwyn now stood beside her. "Lead the way."

Her chest tightened as she stepped through the entrance to Lily's cottage. It was warm and homey and reminded her of Scotland. To think she'd give anything to spend even just one day back in the Highlands was absurd, but even with all the turmoil, life had been easier. Their little family had been whole, and Emery saw far more of her mate than she did now, even if it was the darker side of him.

Bronwyn extended her arm, beckoning Emery over to the small kitchen island.

"Let me preface this by saying I know this is a long shot, but I'm at a loss when it comes to anything that logically makes sense so I've got nothing left but to trust the stars."

"That doesn't sound like you." Bronwyn was a scholar. It's what afforded her a seat within the inner circle, and why she'd become Lily's right-hand woman.

"I know, but at this point I will try anything to figure out how to find my mate. The mates of all witches." More than a hint of desperation filled her voice, and it gutted Emery when Bronwyn's head dropped to her chest and she let out a deep sigh. "I've just...I'm tired of living this life alone. I see what you have with August, what Lily has with Malcolm, and it's beautiful. I feel like the stars are punishing us for something. Maybe because we created vampires in the first place. I don't know, but it's as if forcing us to be fluid in our sexuality wasn't enough—they're taunting us with the notion of happiness and deliberately making it impossible for us to obtain it. I just... the light at the end of the tunnel seems so dim most days, just when we thought we were so close."

Emery rounded the island and pulled Bronwyn into a hug. The small witch immediately wrapped her arms around her and let out a choked sob.

All they wanted was their mates.

It was what fueled everything they did since the attack at the hunt. They were prepared to fight against Sloane to preserve the future Emery and August promised them. The same way she wanted a better world for her daughter, the witches wanted a world where they could safely start families of their own. Even if it was with the vampires.

The problem was mates weren't finding one another and they couldn't explain why. Even at the castle, where the largest numbers of vampires and witches congregated, only one other pair had managed to bond, and it was mostly by accident. The same as it had been for August and Emery and Lily and Malcolm—they just happened to be in the same room. This didn't bode well for their attempts to do away with the Culling.

They had no idea when or how they would be able to stop the Culling marks from appearing on the wrists of the human women spelled to be the potential wives of the royal vampires. Emery, Bronwyn, and Lily had spent the last three months trying to figure out how to recreate the spell that created the Culling. Their only lead was in a passage they'd managed to decipher from one of Celeste's old texts (provided by Octavian), which stated that mates were supposed to wear each other's mark to make it easier to find one another. Almost like the mark the human women wore when the vampire prince started his Culling.

Still, it didn't make sense, because none of the mated pairs so far wore any sort of marking. The only answer they'd come up with was that as long as the spell that bound royal vampires to the Culling was in place, mates wouldn't be able to find each other except by accident.

It wasn't perfect but it was the only hypothesis they had.

Emery ran her hand up and down Bronwyn's back, trying to soothe the ache she knew all too well. The feeling of knowing the person who would complete your soul was out there but just out of reach. "What do you need me to do?"

She may have found her person, but she wouldn't rest until every witch and vampire also found theirs.

Bronwyn tugged away and wiped a single tear from her cheek. "I've finished translating the last of the components for the spell. The ingredients themselves are ancient and the bane of my damn existence. They don't exist in any of my texts or at least any I could possibly get my hands on. I need you to read some tea leaves, pull some cards, find a crystal ball, or hell, make an offering to the stars, and ask them to tell you how the hell we're supposed to pull this off because I've got nothing. And I can't fail. Not for me, but especially not for them."

Her heart sank and the look of agony on Bronwyn's face sliced it open all over again. Emery had seen firsthand what the spells cast by Celeste had done to the witches. She joked about their hypersexuality, but the trauma dug itself deeper than that. Sex was casual, but what tore them apart was the cries of witches behind closed doors after another month of negative pregnancy tests. Every witch prayed from a young age that somewhere in their lineage was a drop of royal blood that would allow them to conceive. As they aged, they turned to casual dating that left them feeling only temporarily sated—they unknowingly longed for the connection to their mate and didn't understand why they didn't feel whole.

Witches and vampires deserved to find what Emery had with August. Unfortunately, her star-touched magic didn't work the way Bronwyn was hoping. She couldn't snap a finger and have a vision. Her visions happened to her, not the other way around. And, more often than not, they happened at inopportune moments, were filled with a variety of possible outcomes of inconsequential events, and left her feeling drained for hours. It was few and far between that Emery saw something worth sharing.

"I wish I knew how being star-touched worked so I could give you a magical answer, but this is all new to me too. I don't know the first thing about tea leaves or tarot. Agatha was the only star-touched witch I've ever met, and she didn't exactly teach me anything. But I'll keep an eye out for anything in my visions."

Bronwyn pressed her lips together and nodded, blinking back the tears that had started to form again in her eyes.

Fuck.

Emery just wanted to help. She threw her hands up and smiled. "What the hell, let's give it a try. Grab the cards and start a pot of water. At this point we have nothing to lose. It's not like I can go out and train, and maybe something will spark a vision. The stars can't leave us hanging if we're trying, right?"

They could, and they likely would. They both knew that. But Bronwyn needed hope, and if that's the only thing Emery could give her, she would.

"Thank you." Bronwyn grabbed the cards and started the water.

When Emery stood, her stomach tightened and an intense, sudden pain knocked her back a step. She inhaled a sharp breath and gripped the island with one hand, wrapping her other hand around her expansive belly.

"Are you okay?"

"It's just these Braxton Hicks contractions. I don't understand why women need practice contractions to preface the real deal. Like it's already going to suck pushing a watermelon out a ten-centimeter hole, do we really need to practice first?"

Bronwyn chuckled. "Remember this when you decide to have another one."

"Nope. All I'm saying is it's a good thing I already know this baby is going to be damn adorable, because otherwise I'm not sure I could deal with this. And I can't even entertain having any more at this point." Emery stood and waddled over to where Lily kept a tin full of various types of tea.

"Grab the raspberry tea. It's supposed to help with preparing your body for labor. Maybe it will make the real contractions come faster."

"I'll try just about anything." Emery gathered two cups and saucers and deposited a pinch of loose-leaf raspberry tea in each of the cups.

The two of them chatted about nothing in particular as they drank their tea and pulled cards from the tarot deck, trying to decipher what they meant. None of them sparked a vision, nor did they give any sort of clarity as to what the future would bring.

Bronwyn's brow furrowed. "I think the Hanged Man means sacrifice, or maybe it's release." She sighed. "This is the one area of witch education I didn't put much stock into."

Emery chuckled. "You mean you didn't plan to have a long-lost cousin dropped in the coven and find out when her magic was unbound that she was star-touched and needed someone to teach her how to harness her rare and flighty magic?"

"Psh. That's an understatement."

"What about these?" Emery pulled two cards and placed them side by side.

"The Fool and the High Priestess? It solidly means Malcolm and Lily are going to be the next ones to pop out a kid."

Emery snorted. "He is our jester, isn't he?"

"Yesterday he got Haven and Thea to help him put googly eyes on all the herb bottles in the apothecary tent. The three of them sat outside and giggled every time someone walked in there and screamed in surprise."

Emery shook her head laughing. Malcolm was the one who kept them smiling on the hard days with his ridiculous gifts and pranks. She remembered when she first met him and thought he was the dark and broody type. It turned out he was just heartbroken over Sloane and worried about his brother. With Lily at his side, she'd seen him transform into not only an excellent advisor, but the life coach they didn't know they needed, with a side of mischievous devil. He was going to be an amazing dad someday.

Bronwyn turned to Emery and smiled. "Thank you for this."

"For what?"

"I needed to get out of my head for a little bit, and this was the perfect break."

Emery reached out and gave her hand a squeeze. "Glad I could help."

They finished their tea and after one look at the leaves, gave up trying to decipher what the little flakes meant. They looked like a dick, a cat, and a raspberry. Nothing enlightening happening there.

The sun started to set as Bronwyn cleared the island. "Shall we head up to the castle for the weekly staff meeting?"

Emery smiled. She looked forward to these meetings. Even if they typically ended with more questions than actual progress, she cherished the time with their family and friends as they tried to build their kingdom from the ashes left behind by their ancestors. It wasn't easy, but it was a weekly reminder that they were all in this and were stronger together.

"I'll meet you up there, I need to take Haven to Thea. I told her she could hitch a portal up to the castle with me."

Bronwyn nodded and cleaned up their mess while Emery headed out to find Haven. She found her playing with the other young witches.

"You ready?"

"Yup!" The way she popped the p made Emery laugh.

The two of them walked through the witches' village and, once they got to the outskirts, Emery stopped and readied herself to open the portal.

Haven tugged at her hand, and when Emery looked

down to see what was the matter, gone was the bouncy excited girl from moments before.

"What's wrong, Haven? Is everything okay?"

"Yes…no. I don't know." Her brows furrowed, and she chewed her bottom lip like she was trying to figure out the meaning of life. "Can I ask you something?"

"Of course."

"How did you know your magic was dark?"

Emery's mouth fell, and she opened and closed it trying to figure out what the little witch was trying to get at. It was the last question she expected.

She turned to face Haven and took her hands in her own. "Is there a reason you are asking?"

"I don't have access to my magic yet. I can't make it glow in my palms or anything, but I can hear the dead. I can feel their emotions. My mom said Sloane is a nasty dark witch with necromancy that defies the earth."

Emery held back a wince. She could totally picture Eva saying that to her clique of friends, all of whom loved to sit around the apothecary and gossip. They were always speculating and rarely took notice of the young ears listening.

"I just…what if I have nasty dark magic?"

Emery gently squeezed Haven's hands and tucked a stray strand of her wild black curls behind her ear. "Well, let me tell you there is nothing nasty about dark magic. It can be a little scary, but it isn't nasty."

"I don't want to be dark like Sloane."

"What if you are dark like me?"

"You aren't scary."

From the mouths of babes.

There were so many moments she had treated her

darkness as the nasty stepchild of her magic. She wasn't lying when she told Haven it could be scary. It was downright terrifying. Whereas she controlled the majority of her magic, the darkness liked to remind her it could control her. It sent her dreams and snippets of its power, and Emery was helpless to do anything about it. She didn't want to scare Haven, especially if this tiny witch had even an ounce of darkness in her, but Emery couldn't deny the notion she could hear the dead was worrisome.

"Can you tell me about what the dead tell you?"

"They are angry at Sloane. They don't want her to control them. She takes their freedom and forces them to do her bidding. They say that's not what necromancy is."

Emery didn't know enough about the other concentrations of dark magic to say one way or the other. As it was, she struggled to find any information on the blood magic coursing through her own veins.

"I can't tell you if they are right or wrong, or why you are hearing and feeling them. But if you do have dark magic in you, I want you to know that you are not bad or nasty, Haven. You are perfect just the way you are, and I'll help you through every step."

"Promise?" Her little voice held so much hope.

"I promise."

"Can we go see Thea now?"

"Of course." Emery called her magic to her hands. "Oh, but Haven?"

"Yeah?"

"Let's maybe not tell everyone about you hearing the dead. While dark magic isn't a bad thing, it isn't something people understand yet, so let's keep it between us."

"Okay." Haven said, smiling.

Emery portaled them to the castle so Haven could play with her best friend, but she couldn't stop the uneasy feeling in her chest. The little witch had given her a lot to think about, primarily how she needed to come to terms with her own magic so she could say everything she'd said without feeling like a complete imposter.

Chapter Five

EMERY

She was two steps outside Thea's suite, heading for the meeting with everyone, when her stomach tightened and pain shot through the base of her spine.

Emery stopped and pressed her hand against the stone wall, her other hand caressing her rounded belly. "Holy hell, little urchin, do you think you could wait until I'm not walking?"

"You feeling okay?" Flora pressed a gentle hand to Emery's back.

"If by okay you mean my entire abdomen tensing like a stretched rubber band then snapping back and wrapping around my spine, then yeah, I'm feeling fine."

Flora snorted, and when Emery glanced up at her, she wore the same post-sex glow Emery did hours before. It was a good thing August didn't actually take her up on that wager.

A smirk tipped at her lips. "You said goodbye to Draven?"

Heat filled Flora's cheeks, and Emery smiled. It didn't matter how much Flora had grown into a truly incredible woman and even more amazing Luna to the Moon Ridge Pack, the shy castle girl still shone through from time to time.

"August and Lily arrived in Moon Ridge, and she portaled me back to the castle before they left for Washington."

Emery saw the trepidation in Flora's gaze. It was always there whenever Draven was forced to leave her side. And she did mean forced. The two had been inseparable from the time they'd mated. She understood, though. The look on Flora's face mirrored the anxiety in Emery's chest. At least she had the tie to August through their bond that would tell her if anything was wrong.

Emery lifted her hand toward where their friends were waiting in the royal parlor at the end of the hallway. "Shall we?"

Flora looped her arm around Emery's, and the two of them made their way down the dimly lit passage. It wasn't long ago they'd walked down these same halls as very different women. There was no way they could have known they would both be mated to two of the most powerful men in America's supernatural community. Most days she still didn't believe it. But one thing remained the same—there wasn't anyone Emery would rather have at her side when shit hit the fan. Especially now that Flora was a bona fide badass hybrid.

Flora pushed open the heavy door and, though they were late to the meeting, no one seemed to notice. They were all too busy catching up with one another. It didn't matter that they almost all resided at the castle full time; it seemed that in the wake of the attack at the hunt, they didn't get to see each other except at these weekly meetings.

Bronwyn sat on the sofa, already poring over an old text with a temporarily lucid Octavian chiming in as they tried to navigate what came next for the witches.

Malcolm and Dorian leaned against the wall near the bar cart in the corner, whispering. Emery would bet money they were plotting how they were going to get August back in their prank war. The brothers had gone out of their way to try and keep Dorian's mind occupied so he didn't go crazy with the need to find Ansel. No one had realized just how deep a bond the two of them had formed prior to Sloane taking their beloved wolf.

Thinking about it broke her damn heart. This life wasn't fair, and none of them had asked for it, but as she looked around the room, she knew they were the best options for the job. Even if it seemed they were perpetually heartbroken in one way or another.

Graves and Braxton, the newest members of their group, sat on the wingback chairs opposite Bronwyn, carrying on with their own conversation. The Grecian vampire king and August's general had become an integral part of their group, helping with diplomacy overseas and keeping the sentinels ready at a moment's notice, respectively.

Emery's eyes were searching the room for the missing two members of their council when one of them called her out.

"How nice of you ladies to join us."

Emery and Flora turned around to find Callum leaning

against the damask-papered wall by the door they'd just come through, a smug grin on his face.

"Where's Lily?" he asked, surprised to see she wasn't with the group. "I thought she was just dropping the boys off?"

Malcolm scoffed and replied. "She decided to go with August and Draven to ensure the magic returned to the earth as it should."

Emery kept her face blank, but annoyance flared within her. If anything, she should have been the one with them.

"I take it you both sent your mates off?" To anyone else, Callum's question would have been polite conversation, but Emery didn't miss the lilt of his innuendo.

Emery's lips tilted up at one side in amusement. "A lady doesn't kiss and tell."

Callum tsked and cocked a brow, a playful taunt if she'd ever seen one. "That's not what your advisors told me when I arrived."

Emery pressed her lips together and shook her head. "You can sit through the meeting with them next week." It never surprised her that Callum knew everything about everyone. She'd stopped wondering how the hell he did it. It was just one of his many talents. It was annoying as fuck, but she couldn't deny it had been helpful more than once.

"Not a chance in hell, lass. I've got my own table of crotchety bastards I've got to deal with when I get back to Scotland."

Emery's face fell. "Is your father still not running the kingdom?"

Callum's mask of indifference fell off for a split second, and Emery saw the hint of sadness in his eyes before he pulled his disguise back into place. "He's too preoccupied with feeders and scotch to notice anything. As if that didn't make him unfit to lead already, his proclivity to murder any witch in sight makes him a hazard to us all."

Which basically meant Callum would be taking over the Scottish kingdom for the foreseeable future. Not in title, but in every way that mattered. It was probably for the best. Lochlan was only a smidge better than his brother had been—at least he hadn't teamed up with Sloane and then slit Emery's throat. Not that he wouldn't currently love the opportunity. Lochlan held Emery personally responsible for his brother's death, even though it was August who'd committed the act. In his words, 'If she hadn't shown up with her witchy vagina, none of this would have happened.'

It should have stung more than it did. Especially because he wasn't wrong. But Emery liked to think change was on the horizon. The Scottish kingdom wasn't happy, and unhappy people eventually realize they deserve better.

She just gave the timeline a swift kick in the ass with her presence.

Callum shook his head and pressed off the wall, walking toward the center of the room. "Shall we get this meeting started?"

Flora followed him, but Emery hesitated, her eyes narrowed on Callum's back. Something niggled in the back of her mind, leaving her feeling off kilter, though she couldn't quite put her finger on what it was. It didn't feel like a vision coming on, but that didn't mean it couldn't be a new facet of her magic she'd yet to experience.

Emery tested her bond with August to ensure the uneasy feeling wasn't coming from him, and found it still hummed strongly between them. Their daughter rolled in her stomach as if she knew Emery was feeling for her father, and the thought of their sweet child wiped away the unease.

Malcolm moved to the edge of the couch beside Bronwyn, while Dorian joined Flora cross-legged on the floor. Emery lowered herself onto the vacant oversized sofa chair and looked up to where Callum paced.

Graves nodded in her direction, his boyish smile directly clashing with the dark obsidian of his gaze. "Did your advisors provide any insight on how we can mitigate The Culling moving forward?"

Emery snorted. "No, they were more interested in naming my daughter after a murderous vampire."

"Vanya?"

"That's the one."

"She was misunderstood," Octavian chimed in, still in one of his more lucid states. "She made a mean spiced mead, though."

Leave it to Octavian to not only know about the vampire in question, but to have interacted with her enough to know her hobbies.

Malcolm cut in, waving his hands in disbelief. "Hold up, if you consider Vancy or Vaggy or whatever over Malcolmina, I officially resign as favorite uncle."

Emery chuckled. "Misunderstood or not, your title is safe, Malcolm."

"So, you're considering it?"

"Not a chance in hell." Emery smiled, but it only lasted a moment before she turned back to Graves. "The advisors don't feel any need to stop the Culling, so it's low on their priority list. They would rather keep the status quo. Unfortunately for them, that's not happening."

"It seems that's the general consensus around the world right now," Graves responded grimly.

After August and Emery shared their union with the world, most kingdoms agreed that they would be willing to forgo Cullings, at least in public. In private, there were many monarchs and courts that would rather ignore the fact they had mates. The hatred between witches and vampires ran deep, and those private declarations were starting to melt over into public opinion with noble vampires around the world.

Still, most kingdoms were running into the same problems they were. In the modern world, the feud between the factions didn't translate beyond the royals. Most vampires wanted to be free to mingle with the witches and had been doing so behind the backs of their monarchs.

"We've got a spell we think might reverse it as long as Lily's blood is strong enough to trick the magic into believing she's Celeste. Which might work since she's her granddaughter," Bronwyn added hopefully, though even Emery could hear the 'but' coming a mile away. "The problem is we need to gather some pretty rare ingredients, one of which I am pretty sure doesn't exist anymore."

Octavian waved his hand in front of her face, his off-handed way of gesturing to see the list. She offered it to him, and he nodded as he looked it over.

"Hmmm, yes." He stroked his chin with his thumb and forefinger before offering the list back to Bronwyn. "The only one you will have trouble finding is *brigh an dorchadais*. It doesn't exist."

"Yes, it does," Dorian whispered so low that Emery almost didn't hear him.

But it was clear every vampire in the room did, because all their heads whipped toward him at the same time.

"Where?" Octavian asked with childlike fascination. "I've only ever heard of it from Celeste and that was many centuries ago."

"It translates into 'essence of darkness'. It's ancient unseelie dark magic that was never supposed to exist in this realm." Dorian looked toward the dark window on the far wall, his eyes glassy. "It's the core of what runs through your blood, Emery, and your sister's. Any born dark witch really. It's what fuels your dark magic. After so many years, it would only be found in trace amounts. But in mine..." his voice trailed off, and he pressed his lips together for a beat before continuing. "I can give you what you need."

Emery's mouth fell open, and she searched Dorian's eyes for any dishonesty, but found none.

Dorian had shared his secret with August after the hunt, and he'd given the go-ahead for them to share it with their council of friends. They all treated him like he was still Dorian, their beloved friend and sentinel. He still wore the glamor that hid his true nature, and he never spoke about his past or how he came to be in August's court. He'd proven himself more than once to be their ally, and that was enough for them. But he had never talked about his fae nature so openly before.

Emery's darkness stirred in her chest, like it was a living being who knew it had been referenced. It rolled and beckoned her to reach out to Dorian and see if what he said was true. She'd never felt dark magic from him. Hell, she'd never felt much of anything from him. She did notice he wasn't feeding like he used to and assumed it had been to keep up pretenses. It just went to show there was so much she didn't know about the fae in front of her.

Every pair of eyes was zeroed in on him, hanging on his every word, waiting to see if he was going to share more. When he didn't continue, it was Emery who finally broke the silence.

"I...why do I have fae darkness in my blood? Why do you?"

Dorian stood and walked toward the window, his back to them as he spoke as if he couldn't bear to face them. "We...I..."

"Dorian, you don't have to explain it to us if you aren't ready," Malcolm offered.

The hell he didn't. Emery had dark fae magic in her blood, and she damn well deserved to know how that came to be.

Are you alright, little witch? August's voice called down the bond.

I'm fine. She fired down the bond. *Did Dorian happen to mention I had fae magic in my blood when you discussed his fae identity?*

He alluded to the fact the witches lived and died by the stars because of the fae, but I didn't press him. I figured he would tell us about his past when he was ready.

Well, he's about to.

And why does that have our bond flaring with anger like a firework on the Fourth of July?

I'll be fine.

Are you sure?

Yes.

We are just heading out into the woods. I'll let you know what we find.

Emery remained silent, her eyes pinned on Dorian's back, but sent love down the bond.

"No, it's fine. It's time I told you more about who I am." He scrubbed his face with his palm and pressed his lips together in a tight line as he exhaled. "All witches have some element of fae in their blood. It is the fae who gifted the original witches their magic."

"Plural? I thought Celeste was the only one."

"No, she was the only one to come here from the Feywilde and survive long enough for anyone to remember. She was a member of the last remaining human kingdom in the Feywilde, but when she and her sister came here, their memories were erased. They were tasked with keeping magic alive and balanced in this realm."

"You've been keeping this from us?" Malcolm spat accusatively, and Emery felt every bit of his anger mirrored in herself.

Dorian closed his eyes and lowered his head. "It's not my story to tell."

"You're fae, Dorian, if it's not your story then whose is it?"

"I'm not...There is a code of laws that we live by, and that means keeping the Feywilde secret from this world. Especially from the supernatural world. The fae already have enough problems." He growled the last part, and Emery almost pressed him, but the way his shoulders tensed told her she'd be pushing too far. She needed him to want to tell her, because at the moment he was their best chance at breaking the Culling spell. And just maybe he'd be able to teach her more about her magic than the ancient witch texts that held nothing of use.

Dorian turned and met her gaze. "My loyalty is to you,

Your Majesty, and your mate, and I will do whatever it takes to protect your family. Your kingdom. I have given you no reason not to trust me. Please understand, there are kingdoms and fae both in the Feywilde and in this realm that also need my protection. My silence is their safety."

Emery swallowed the questions burning in the back of her throat. She understood what it meant to put a kingdom first. It was one of the harder lessons to learn as August's mate, but just like Dorian, she'd do anything to keep them safe and provide a place for her daughter.

She heaved herself from the sofa and waddled across the room, placing a hand on Dorian's shoulder. "I understand, Dorian. I can't pretend I'm happy being left in the dark, but if you will promise to keep us informed as needed about the fae, I am okay with that for now."

His glistening eyes searched hers, and he nodded. "I will."

Usually, Dorian was the epitome of strength. The only time she'd seen him break was when Sloane took Ansel, and even then, that had been unbridled rage, not the deep sadness that she saw in his gaze now. She wanted to pull him into her arms. To promise him they'd figure this out together as a family—because that's what he was to her. Family.

She squeezed his shoulder and gave him a forced smile. "So, how do we get what we need from your blood?"

Dorian's lips quirked up at the corners, and his stoic facade slid back into place. When he spoke, his tone was once again all business. "That's the tricky part. Celeste would have been able to bring it with her from the Feywilde in powder form. It doesn't thrive here except in the bodies of the witches it inhabits. As blood, the second it hits the air of this realm, it loses its potency, and I fear you won't be able to complete the spell without draining all the blood from my body."

"And that means?" Graves asked.

"We have to go to the Feywilde to compose the spell, or kill Dorian." Braxton chimed in, reading between the lines of what Dorian was saying.

"We're not killing Dorian," Emery assured him.

"I appreciate that, Your Majesty." Dorian said dryly. "But there may be another option. To find out, I would need to go alone. It might be possible, but unsafe. I need more information"

"Go," Emery said. "Do what you need to."

Dorian nodded and when Emery smiled, his lips tipped up slightly. "I'll be back as soon as I can," he said, then vanished from the room the same way he did the night of the hunt.

"Did anyone else see that coming?" Malcolm asked, scrubbing his jaw with his hand.

"There is never a dull moment with this group, I swear on the stars," Bronwyn breathed, followed by what sounded like a muttered string of curses. "We need to gather the rest of the ingredients so that we're ready when Dorian arrives."

"Okay. Shall we…?" The room swayed, the telltale sign of an impending vision. "Fuck." Emery muttered and lowered herself to the ground. She knew she'd be safer lying down while pregnant if the stars decided to send her a lengthy vision. She'd learned the hard way that the baby made her top heavy.

"I don't think August would appreciate it if we—"

She didn't get to hear the rest of what she was sure was

a snarky comment by Flora before she was sucked into the vision.

Emery glanced around her, trying to figure out what she was seeing. She was alone in a dark, damp cell. The dungeons. A shiver tore through her, fear gripping her spine. For a moment, she thought she was remembering something that had happened to her—after all, she had spent time in this very dungeon. But as the vision grew clearer, she realized: she wasn't herself. For the first time, she was seeing a vision through someone else's eyes... and she wasn't in control.

Together, Emery and the person in her vision winced as they rolled over, facing the bars of the tiny cell, every part of their body aching.

"Are you ready for another round?" The female voice was distorted, almost as if whoever's mind she was in was stuck underwater. But that wasn't right. They were lying on the floor in a puddle of nothing but their own despair.

Another round of what?

Emery tried to force the person to sit up, but they didn't move.

"You are my secret weapon. Just wait until they see what you've done."

The person she inhabited groaned, the sound low, rumbling, and masculine.

The world began to shift around her and Emery knew it meant she was going to be pulled from the vision. She tried to hold on, hoping to see anything that might give her more context, but the stars didn't care about her interpretation of the vision. They just gave without any thought to practicality.

Emery blinked her eyes and brought her hand to cover the light from above that blinded her.

She hated visions like that. They didn't add or subtract

from the need to know. They only served to confuse her more.

Flora was there at her side, handing her a piece of chocolate. "What did you see?"

"Nothing useful."

Bronwyn opened her mouth, and Emery pinned her with a glare. She could already hear her friend reminding her that the stars would never give her anything useless, even if the vision didn't make sense right then. Emery wasn't sure she agreed with that philosophy—it seemed to her that the stars could be fallible, just like any other sentient being, but she also knew Bronwyn couldn't see things that way. Her friend needed to hold on to the hope that it would all become clear someday.

As much as she'd hated her after everything that happened with Vishna, Bronwyn had become the older sister Emery never wanted, but loved having. She wasn't as wrapped up in their family as Lily was and always gave an unfiltered opinion, even when Emery didn't want to hear it.

Callum appeared above her and offered her his hand. The second she leaned forward and placed hers in his, she felt a small pop low in her abdomen. As he helped her up, she felt a gush between her legs.

Her eyes widened and panic gripped her spine as she let go of Callum's hand and slid back down to the floor.

"Emery, are you okay?" Flora asked, her brows knitted in concern.

"Just peachy. But I think we need to get August back here, asap."

"Why's that?"

"My waters just broke."

Chapter Six

AUGUST

The cool Pacific wind whipped through the trees, adding to the bite of rain pelting their skin. Washington was living up to its reputation of having the shittiest weather of all the pack territories.

August walked beside Lily as they followed Draven, Kade, Mateo, and the alpha from the Pine Shore pack through the dense forest on the outermost edges of their lands. He tipped his head back and inhaled the wet air. Emery would have loved this. He could picture her walking beside him, testing her elemental magic, parting the rain and meeting the wind with a dance of her own.

An involuntary sigh fell from his lips. He knew he was holding on too tight, but he couldn't stop himself. Even now, he wanted to race back to her and ensure she was okay. Emotionally. Physically. Mentally. He needed her to be okay so he could pretend that the image of her lying there lifeless before him didn't haunt him every waking moment of every day. Each night, while Emery slept soundly beside him, he replayed that night on repeat, analyzing every way he could have protected her. Every way he had failed.

Heavy was the head that wore the crown, and he felt the weight now more than ever. Between his worry for Emery and their daughter and the turmoil of the kingdom, August was at his breaking point. Not that he'd let anyone see his struggles. That wasn't the Nicholson way. He didn't want to be like his father and turn to anger and rage, but he didn't want to be weak either.

In the past, when the world around him got to be too much, he turned to his men. He'd find Rex and their team and get lost in whatever battle they were up against. Only this time, there wasn't a battlefield. There wasn't a strategic plan to perfect. Sloane became an invisible enemy after the hunt, and his kingdom was walking a tightrope above shark-infested waters as they adapted to their mate-filled future. And it seemed there was always something ready to knock them down.

He wanted to protect Emery from the weight of it all. She should have been focusing solely on enjoying the last weeks of her pregnancy and the joys of being his queen. But instead, she was in a meeting, being forced to face truths that he was confident would leave her questioning her magic. She already carried so much guilt over the dead and for her sister's role in the war; she didn't need one more thing to weigh her down.

August shook his head. There was no doubt Emery could handle it. She was the strongest damn person he'd ever met. She had to be, to stand at his side. But that didn't mean it was what she deserved. She'd been strong her entire life.

Fucking Dorian. He couldn't wait until he returned

from Washington? The fae hadn't peeped a word about his heritage beyond the drunken night the two of them had shared after the hunt. It was a cathartic purge of shitty emotions between friends. In some ways, Dorian knew him better than his own blood, mostly because they shared a sentinel's mind in a way Malcolm and Callum never would. But the asshole knew better than to stress out Emery. Especially while August was gone.

Bloody hell. He wasn't sure when he became such a bloody fucking romantic—probably around the time he melded himself into one sappy asshole—but he would do anything to give Emery and his daughter the world. He'd paint the sky with stars if it made them smile, and he'd kill anyone who threatened them.

Which is why he was trudging through the wilderness, looking for bodies steeped in magic. So she didn't have to.

"How much farther is it?" Mateo, Draven's lead enforcer, asked, shaking out his left leg. "My balls are beginning to chafe."

"You're the tracker, asshole, you tell us." Draven's second-in-command, Kade, snapped.

The two of them reminded him of Ansel and Dorian. He'd worked with them previously when they were hunting down the Mistress— before they knew it was Sloane. They were thick as thieves, finishing each other's thoughts, them against the world, but there was an underlying tension that spoke of something more.

Richard, the Pine Shore alpha, lifted his arm and pointed in front of them. "It's not much farther, but this is as far as I'll take you. The magic barrier is just beyond those trees. You won't be able to miss the purple shimmer that coats the ground. That's where you'll find it."

"The grave?" August asked, wanting to clarify once more what they were walking into.

"If you can even call it that."

August winced, and Draven, Mateo, and Kade grew quiet.

"I can feel it," Lily said quietly. She had been silent most of the hike. She closed her eyes and looked toward the sky, the drops of rain that fell through the trees splashing against her face. "The magic is chaotic and filthy. It's jagged, and the earth doesn't know what to do with it."

August opened his mouth and inhaled deeply, trying to sense Lily's magic the same way he did Emery's. Whereas Emery's magic gave him hints of the same sweet smell as her essence, what flooded his senses now was bitter and thick. "I can taste it."

"Me too," Draven confirmed.

"She's growing stronger. Adapting her magic in a way I've never experienced." Lily lowered her head and opened her eyes. They were filled with a mix of wonder and horror. "Whatever this is, it's darker than before."

"What does that mean?" Mateo asked.

August was glad Lily had opted to come with them. Usually, the witches sent Bronwyn out with the sentinels to search any questionable findings. Not that there had been many. The kidnappings were always the same, with only traces of low-level magic or none at all. But this was the first real sign of Sloane's magic since she'd destroyed the castle, and Lily was the most well-versed in stronger types of magic, having lived in the time of the original witches.

"I'm not sure." Lily took a step forward, leading the way toward where the alpha had indicated.

"Thank you, Richard," Draven whispered and offered the alpha his hand.

"May the Goddess be with you," the alpha replied.

A low growl rumbled in Draven's chest, and August bit back a laugh. He'd heard the part the Goddess of the Moon played in Flora becoming a hybrid, and wasn't surprised his cousin held some resentment.

The trees grew more sparse as they continued forward, until they opened up into a clearing small enough to just barely be considered one at all.

Magic was the first thing to catch his eye. His stomach clenched. That purple shimmer had haunted the depths of his mind since the first time he'd seen it months before on the cragged edge of the land where Sloane's zombies had slayed so many of his kind. Now it clung to the earth, desperately trying to find its way back to a vessel.

Their small group all paused on the edge of the space, and August's gaze followed the trails of purple to a dark mound, shaded by the darkness of the surrounding trees. His mouth fell open, and he imagined the others wore similar expressions. On auto-pilot, he took a step forward, only to be stopped by Lily's outstretched arm. Bile rose in his throat and though he wanted to look away, he couldn't. Doing so would be disrespectful to the lives lost.

It was a bloody massacre.

Literally.

He'd killed plenty throughout his life, but he'd never seen carnage like this. The bodies in that pile, if they could even be called that, were mutilated. Some beyond recognition.

"What happened to them?" Mateo whispered mostly to himself.

August looked beside him to where Lily stood, her face frozen in a blank stare as if she hadn't heard the wolf's question.

"Lily?" He brushed her hand with his, and she instantly tensed.

"Fan out. But don't touch anyth—"

"No." The panic in Draven's voice instantly had August on edge, and everyone's gaze snapped to where he stood with his nose raised into the faint breeze that managed to funnel its way into the clearing. "Fuck. No." His eyes widened, and he shook his head before starting to manically walk the perimeter of the magic. "It can't be."

August inhaled deeply, trying to ascertain what it was Draven was losing his mind over, but all he managed to scent was wet earth and decay.

"Kade!" Draven barked, "Get me a branch, something, anything that I can use to move the bodies without touching them."

Bodies was a generous description. It was more like a jumble of... parts. At first, he had assumed that all the bodies were human, but now that he looked closer, he saw fangs hidden behind the lips of some disembodied heads, and some of the limbs sported claws for fingers. Others looked as if they were frozen between vampiric and wolf shifts. Limbs were strewn in haphazard piles among torsos and heads. Every inch of the bodies glimmered in magic, and if it were any other situation, he might appreciate the beauty of its glow against the dark forest. But it wasn't and he didn't.

"Draven, you can't touch them," Lily pleaded. "We don't know what this is or if the magic is set to trip other spells when touched."

"I have to make sure he's not here," he growled.

August had never seen Draven so much as snap at anyone, let alone one of the women. He was quiet and calculated. He rarely let his guard down, and he never let himself lose control.

"Who?" Lily's eyes darted over the pile, searching for whoever Draven thought was there.

"Ansel."

Bloody hell.

August's chest constricted, and the same desperation he saw etched on each of the wolf's faces clawed at his heart. He focused on keeping his side of the bond closed off so Emery wouldn't ask what was wrong. He couldn't bring himself to admit to her that the guard dog she loved with all her damn heart might be in the pile before him.

He swallowed past the lump in his throat. "You think he's in there?"

"I don't know. I smell him. He's everywhere. He's on the bodies. In them. Whatever game Sloane is playing, she knew leaving them here, on pack lands with his scent mixed in, would catch my attention." Draven shook his head as if it would clear the scent from his palate. He lowered his head and rested his palm on the back of his neck as he exhaled. When he spoke, his voice shook. "He's my pack, August. I was supposed to protect him, but instead I let her take him."

August rounded the magic perimeter and gripped his cousin's shoulder, knowing exactly how he felt. They weren't close by any means, but they were family, and from what he knew, Draven was one of the most honorable men and leaders he'd ever met.

"We're going to find him. This isn't your fault," August

assured him, knowing that no matter what he said, Draven would always harbor the guilt of losing one of his men. And Ansel was so much more than just another enforcer.

It was the same way August felt about Rex and the rest of his team. Their loss broke him.

"Isn't it?" Draven whispered.

"No. It's Sloane's fault. You wear the crown, but she wears the blame."

Draven raised his head, his eyes rimmed with silver and narrowed on August. "Did all your fancy years at the castle teach you that?"

"Surprisingly, no. Your asshole brother is the one who has to remind me of that daily so that I don't take my anger out on my people or, god forbid, Emery." It was just another way he was learning he couldn't do it alone.

Callum was the bane of his damn existence, but he kept August in line. He forced him to channel his rage in ways that wouldn't hurt those around him or force him into a bloodlust he couldn't come back from. As arrogant as his cousin was, Callum understood what it meant to lead.

Kade returned with a branch long enough to reach the center of the bodies without crossing the thick line of magic. With Draven's help, the two of them carefully poked and prodded, moving the torsos, limbs, and heads, while Mateo and August's eyes darted over the pile looking for any sign of their brown-eyed wolf.

When they reached the bottom, Draven let out the breath August was sure he was holding the entire time. "I don't see him." His voice hovered somewhere between relief and defeat. "I don't know why his scent clings to the bodies, but he's not here."

Losing Ansel weighed on all of them. They may have

not gotten along when they'd first met, but that man had protected what was his while Augustine dislodged his head from his own ass. He owed the wolf the lives of his mate and daughter. Not only that, though. Ansel was family. Pack. Whatever their little band of misfits could be called.

"I know why," Mateo whispered, and when they all turned to look at him, his face was pale. He ran a hand through his hair and pointed to a chest that had a jagged scar running down its sternum. "Look right there, at that torso. Does that scar look familiar?"

"No," Draven scoffed. "Ansel wouldn't dare."

Mateo sighed and scrubbed his face. "Facts are facts, hermano."

"He wouldn't dare what?" August asked, not seeing the connection.

Draven lips pulled into a tight line, his eyes never leaving the dead. "That line down the center of that torso over there...Flora wears the same scar. It's faint, but it's where I sliced her chest open and cut her heart with my claws under the light of the full moon so she would be... like me."

"Are you implying that Ansel is creating wolves?"

"Not just wolves, he's creating an army," Lily stated matter-of-factly. "Or rather, Sloane is creating an army with Ansel's help."

August turned around to see her kneeling, her hands raised over the shimmering purple magic. She wasn't calling it to become a vessel for the magic, but instead tested her own magic against it, allowing it to ebb and flow like two currents meeting in open water.

"What do you mean?"

"This magic contains the same remnants of death that I picked up on the bodies at the castle after the gala. It's been enhanced, strengthened, and then given a touch of life. It's not strictly wolf, but it's not hybrid magic I'm sensing either. Each body has a different signature."

"She's Dr. Frankenstein, is that what you're saying?" Mateo huffed a laugh, but looking at the bodies with this new information, August thought he might not be far off.

"I don't know," Lily answered. "But this is dangerous magic. It's dark. Darker than anything I've ever felt. It goes against everything witches have stood for as long as we've walked this earth. It's why we banished dark magic."

August opened his mouth to ask if it was the same type of dark magic Emery had, but panic shot down the bond, landing in his gut. With a groan, he doubled over.

Emery? he cried out down the bond. *Are you okay? What's wrong?*

Um. I'm fine, mostly, but you should probably wrap up whatever you're doing and portal back.

Why, what happened?

Don't freak out.

We're at war, Em, you can't start with that.

My waters broke.

The baby is coming now?

*If you could get your ass back here, yes. I...*her voice shook as it trailed off. *I can't do this without you.*

You'll always have me. I'm on my way.

August ran his fingers through his hair and turned around to where Lily and the wolves stared at him with raised brows. "I'm going to be a dad tonight."

Chapter Seven

AUGUST

August tore through the portal. Every moment away from Emery felt like an eternity. She needed him. He could feel her stress through their bond, and it spurred him faster.

He'd demanded Lily portal them directly into the birthing suite, but she refused. Apparently, she had a thing about portaling indoors.

August couldn't give a rat's ass about the reason. All that mattered was getting to Emery.

Two steps out of the glittering ring of magic, and he fell to his knees, pain ripping through the bond he shared with Emery. His guts felt like they were being torn from their home, wrapped around his spine, and used to string him up in the rafters of the castle.

"Bloody fucking hell," he gritted, nearly biting through his lip as he fought against the agonizing throb gripping his abdomen.

"Fuck, August. Are you okay?" Draven dropped to his knee beside August and rested a hand on his shoulder.

"Emery...pain..."

Words were impossible to formulate until the tightening ceased. When it did, sweat clung to his brow, and he finally felt like he could breathe again.

Princess, you are a damn saint for enduring whatever the hell that was, but I need you to close the bond if you want me to make it to you.

Sorry it slipped, she panted. *Contractions are a fucking bitch.*

Bloody fucking hell. Childbirth was no joke. If that was what she was feeling every three to five minutes to bring their child into the world, then he owed her so much more than everything he'd ever given her.

When he'd caught his breath, Draven helped him up. The two of them ran toward the castle. Draven fell behind as August moved with the speed of a vampire on crack, taking the stairs five at a time until he skidded to a halt outside the state-of-the-art suite he'd had created for this moment.

A crowd of family and friends congregated outside the door. They all looked up at him, smiling. Malcolm was the giddiest of them all. He was holding up his phone, playing *Under Pressure* by David Bowie and Queen on full blast beside the door.

He was sure Emery was *loving* that.

The only one not brimming with excitement was Callum. His face was pale and his hair tousled like he'd been running his fingers through it non-stop. August almost stopped to ask if he was okay, but when a scream slithered down his spine from behind the heavy birthing suite door, everything ceased to exist beyond Emery.

August burst into the room to find his beautiful mate lying on the bed, her feet up in stirrups, and the doctor standing between them getting a full view of the pussy that was meant only for him. He swallowed back the growl that threatened in his throat. She may have been one of the best vampire obstetricians in his kingdom, but his instincts didn't allow for much leeway when it came to Emery.

"Now's not the time to go feral on her, August. She's bringing your child into the world," Flora growled.

Emery whipped her head toward him, her face screwed up in pain as she tried to breathe her way through another contraction. Flora was at her side, wiping the sweat from her brow and allowing his mate to turn her fingers purple with her death grip.

"You're here," Emery sighed at him through tears. Her hair was slicked back away from her face, and he could tell she was gritting her teeth. August had never seen someone so beautiful.

"I'll always be here." He crossed the room in three long strides and pushed a stray pink lock of hair from her forehead behind her ear. Gods, she was incredible. August leaned in and pressed a kiss to her forehead before twisting to look up at Flora on the opposite side of the bed. "Did you not offer to bite her? Why is she being left in so much pain?"

"Oh, I offered and so did Malcolm, and Callum. I never thought I'd see that man beg, but Callum was practically on his knees. We all told her it would take the edge off the pain and help her body relax and push out the baby, but she's being a stubborn princess and wouldn't let anyone near her throat that wasn't you."

Good girl. He purred down their bond and pride shone in his eyes. As much as he wished she would have let them take the edge off, he was thrilled she only wanted him.

Emery gave him a weak smile.

August pressed a soft kiss to her lips before dragging the tip of his tongue down to his favorite spot on her neck. "As much as it makes me hard to know you only want my fangs in your neck, you should have done what was best for you, little witch," he murmured.

Emery squirmed, trying to pull away so she could see him and likely rip him a new asshole, but he didn't give her the chance before he plunged his fangs into her flesh.

Emery let out a groan and dug the nails of her free hand into his biceps, clinging to him as if her life depended on it. Her essence flooded his system, and he pushed every ounce of calm and pain relief that he could through his venom.

"And on that note, I'm going to go," Flora said softly.

"Don't you dare," Emery cried, clenching Flora's hand tighter.

"Really?"

"You're my best friend, Flora. Plus, I want you to know what you're getting yourself into when Draven inevitably knocks you up."

Flora scoffed. "If you think I'm letting him near me after this, you're sorely mistaken."

August chuckled against Emery's neck. Those two were worse than he and Emery were, always sneaking off to some small alcove or room only to return later with tousled hair and lazy grins plastered on their faces. He gave it a year before Draven had an heir.

August licked the wounds he'd created and gave the

doctor a pointed look. "How far along is she?"

"I suspect she's been in labor for the majority of the day, she's almost at ten centimeters. I've never seen someone progress so quickly. Usually, humans carrying vampire children endure long labors, but hers has been uncharacteristically quick. It could be a witch trait."

"It is," Emery answered as the song outside the door changed to *Push It* by Salt-N-Pepa. Her eyes narrowed, and she muttered under her breath. "I'm going to kill that fucking vampire."

August and Flora chuckled. He didn't want to be around when Emery decided to retaliate against his brother.

"Okay, Emery, next contraction, I want you to push," the doctor directed.

August placed a soft kiss on her lips. "You can do this."

Emery's lips pressed into a thin line, and he could feel her apprehension, but she nodded.

With Flora holding one of her legs and August holding the other, Emery's next contraction came. She pushed as hard as she could. His eyes widened as he saw his daughter's head emerge, complete with a tiny tuft of blonde hair. Tears welled in his eyes but when the contraction stopped, the baby's head slid back in.

He turned and smiled at Emery, "She's right there, Em. I can see her."

"You can?" Her voice quivered. She was exhausted, but he didn't miss the hint of wonder and excitement.

A single tear fell down his cheek as he nodded. "You can do this, princess. You are the strongest person I've ever met."

Emery nodded, just as *I Wanna Be Sedated* by The

Ramones started playing outside the door. As much as he wanted to kill Malcolm, it was exactly what Emery needed to psych herself up. To remember she wasn't alone and she had an entire room of people waiting to love on her and their daughter the moment they welcomed her into the world.

The next contraction came, and Emery pushed as hard as she could. Her face turned bright red, and she cried like a warrior leading her men into battle.

She was bloody fucking incredible.

"Come on, little witch," he whispered.

With that big push, the head was out.

Emery shook her head, panting and desperation shining in her eyes. "I can't do this."

August pushed her hair from her forehead and kissed her tears away. "You can. One more. One more big push, and she'll be here."

With the next contraction, Emery gripped his hand with white-knuckle force. As she pushed and screamed, their daughter entered the world.

Blood, mucus, and silence clung to the tiny babe.

August held his breath as the doctor rubbed the baby with a towel. It wasn't until his daughter finally began to scream that he expelled air from his lungs and choked on a sob.

She was beautiful.

The doctor handed her to August, and just like his father had done when he was born, and his father before that, he tore the umbilical cord with his fangs.

She was so tiny in his arms. His sweet little moon, hung between the stars of fate and destined to be the brightest thing in his sky. Through teary eyes, he searched hers, one blue and one amber. Ten fingers and ten toes, and the cutest little button nose. His heart felt as though it was freefalling from his chest.

August blinked through his tears and took her to Emery, bending down to kiss his mate. Together they held their daughter in their arms.

"You created the most perfect little girl," he whispered.

"We did."

"I love you, Emery."

"I love you too," she sobbed.

"She's incredible." Flora chimed in before backing away and giving them some privacy. She opened the door a crack, presumably to tell the rest of their friends and family of their daughter's arrival.

The moment Flora opened the door, the sound of a ukulele filled the room as *Somewhere Over the Rainbow* by Israel Kamakawiwo'ole filled the space.

August didn't need over the rainbows. Not anymore. Every dream he'd dared to dream was cuddled in his arms. He watched as Emery cooed at their daughter, whispering a lifetime of promises to love and protect her.

"Evangeline Colette Finlay Nicholson," he whispered, testing a combination of the names they'd been considering.

Emery looked up at him with love and adoration. "It's perfect."

"For a perfect little girl."

Emery shook her head and swallowed hard before succumbing to a sob. "I miss him."

It should have been a moment of pure joy for their little family, but there was never a chance for that. Not when there was a tangible hole that would never be filled gaping in their chests. They'd said their goodbyes to Miles, but August feared they would always long for the little boy who was taken too soon.

August smiled, putting on a brave face. "He's here too. He'll live on in her. We'll make sure of it."

Evangeline's face scrunched up, and she started to fuss. August's eyes darted over her small form searching for the cause of her discomfort. "What's wrong with her?"

Emery chuckled. "I think she's hungry."

"For what?"

"I have no idea." It was the first of what would likely be an infinite number of questions they faced raising a hybrid daughter.

Royal vampire babies didn't need milk from their mothers. In fact, most of the human mothers didn't even produce milk after birth. Instead, the babies survived on blood from their fathers. The royal blood helped fortify them and protect them as they grew until they developed fangs and could eat on their own. Usually, their bloodlust set in around puberty, which was nature's version of a sick joke considering the last thing anyone wanted to deal with was a hormonal teenager with an unbridled need to feed.

"If I may," the doctor chimed in from where she cleaned Emery up. "Based on the research I've done comparing vampire and witch pregnancies, I believe that the child will need both blood and milk."

Emery's brows raised. "Both?"

"Emery, you've already shown the signs that your body is preparing to lactate. Your daughter will need to feed from you, but will also need to supplement with blood from His Majesty. We'll have to see how she adjusts." The doctor flipped the sheet down over Emery's legs and set the bed back to normal. "Latch her onto your breast and see if that satisfies her. If not, then try giving her some of your blood, Your Majesty. Also, you'll want to give Emery more of your venom, to help speed up the healing process."

"Thank you so much, Kileen," Emery offered as she brought Evangeline to her breast. She latched on and began to suck beautifully.

"Congratulations, Your Majesties."

August nodded, and Kileen turned and exited the room. When she did, Callum popped his head in.

"She's okay? Both of them?" His eyes were wide and panic edged his voice.

Flora would have told him so, but August understood his cousin's need to make sure. He'd lost his own wife and child in childbirth, and Emery held a special place in the mysterious vampire's heart.

"They're perfect. Would you like to meet her?"

"I …" He shook his head and a half-hearted smile tugged at his lips. "Enjoy your time as a family. I just needed to see for myself."

"Get your ass in here, Callum," Emery hollered. "In fact, tell the whole damn lot of them to get in here. You are our family, all of you. We know you'll make sure our daughter will always know just how loved she is."

Callum's half smile tugged upward until a dimple appeared on his cheek—August could count the number of times he had seen it on the fingers of one hand.

"But tell that asshole that if he plays one more song about labor, I'm going to strangle him."

August tipped his head back and laughed. There may have been a war raging around them, but in that moment, as their loved ones filed in to meet the newest member of their family, he somehow knew they were all going to be okay. What they had was stronger than anything Sloane could throw at them.

Chapter Eight

EMERY

Exhaustion was no longer a state of mind. It was the entirety of her being. Between fielding requests from the witches and feeding Lina every three to four hours and tracking down August to make sure he provided blood for her, Emery was running on fumes. Not to mention the vampires were using this opportunity of her absence at their meetings to push their agenda of delaying the abolishment of the Culling.

"Please close your eyes, Evangeline." She stared into the two colors of her daughter's eyes, love and contempt dancing in her voice as she pleaded. "You will feel so much better after you've napped."

Translation: *I need you to sleep because I want to take a nap before there is another fire to put out.*

Lina smiled up at her and fluttered her eyelashes, while a desperate sob threatened to choke Emery. She was lucky she was damn cute. It also helped that her mother loved her with every ounce of her being. From the moment she entered the world, Emery's heart beat for her daughter. Everything she did was so that those ten little fingers and toes could someday walk in a world that was better than what Emery had faced.

That didn't mean it was easy.

Emery swayed around the makeshift nursery, sending up a silent prayer to the stars for sleep. Sunlight poured in through the gaps in the shades, highlighting the weathered walls. It wasn't much, considering these had once been servants' quarters, but the royal wing of the castle had been destroyed during the attack, and even though they had magic to help the restorations along, it was still taking time. She didn't mind, though. The nursery was homey, with a small lounge chair and a crib that went unused most nights because August wanted their daughter close while they slept. The room was used most often during the day, when their council crammed into the small space, insistent on holding meetings here so they could all get their time with the newest royal.

Lina smacked her lips and made the cutest little grunting sounds. Emery let out a sigh and lowered herself onto the lounge chair. It was hard for her to stay frustrated when just the tiniest sounds from her daughter softened her heart.

"You look like you are ready to keel over, lass." Callum leaned against the doorframe, looking immaculate, as usual.

Emery glanced down at her clothes: a wrinkled sweater that she was pretty positive had spit on its sleeve, and leggings that she was sure she'd had on since the day before. Possibly the day before that. They all seemed to blend together.

"I'm fine, I just need her to sleep so I can maybe catch a nap before I've got to head out to see the witches and help

Bronwyn gather the last of the ingredients for when Dorian returns." She closed her eyes and rocked Lina. "What are you doing here?"

"I wanted to see the wee lass before I head back to Scotland, but now I'm more concerned for her mother. You can't keep up like this, Emery. Has your mate seen you?"

Emery scoffed and glared at Callum. "He sees me every night when we both roll into bed, too exhausted to do much more than send every ounce of love we have down our bond before both of us are dead to the world… until we have to feed Lina."

It wasn't Callum's fault, but he'd poked the bear. She was exhausted and when she was tired, much like when she was hungry, she couldn't be held accountable for her actions.

"Here, give me the bairn." Callum stretched out his arms.

"But aren't you leaving for Scotland to investigate another gift left by my sister?"

Callum tsked and shook his head. "Scotland can wait."

Emery placed Lina in his arms and watched as Callum began to shift his weight, whispering to her daughter in the tongue of their ancestors.

He looked up at Emery and nodded at the small sofa across the room. "I know you won't leave her, even though you should go shower and take some time for yourself. You and August are doing way too much when you should be enjoying this sweet bundle of joy. At the very least, lay down and close your eyes, lass. I've got her."

Callum looked down at Lina like she was the center of the universe. Not in the same way her father did, but in the way of a man who longed for a family of his own.

Emery opened her mouth to argue that as much as they'd like to do that, the kingdom wouldn't fix itself on its own, but opted to take the help instead.

She was no good if she was tired.

Emery shimmied down until her head hit the pillow on the edge of the chaise, her eyes already growing heavy. "Five minutes. That's all I need."

Darkness consumed her. Anger. Rage.

Her eyes shifted to find the thing that drove her to such volatile emotions but found nothing. The castle was empty.

Emery stalked the halls, searching for her enemy with one goal in mind.

Kill.

There was no other option. No other way.

She traversed the path to the throne room. The same path she walked every day, only this time she knew the end was near. Their future was in her grasp. All she had to do was restore the balance.

The silence was eerie, but she tried not to focus on it. She could do this. She would be what Lina and August needed. She would be the vanquisher of evil.

Emery called on her darkness, and it flooded her system like a welcomed drug. It would never betray her when she needed it most.

She gripped the ornate gold handle and pushed her way into the throne room.

Two steps was all she took before pain seared her chest. She looked down, a gurgle forming in her throat as she saw the sword protruding from her chest, the Nicholson chest etched into the hilt.

A gasp filled the room. All the air left her lungs. Emery glanced up to see August standing at his throne, Lina in his arms, his hand still outstretched from where it held the sword only moments ago.

She opened her mouth to scream but nothing came out. How could he hurt her like this? Why would he take her away from their daughter?

"August. Why?"

"You chose wrong."

Whispers filled the air around her as she fluttered her eyes open. The lamp was set to its lowest setting and the windows of the nursery were open, revealing the stars. Emery bolted up and blinked, adjusting to the light.

Her heart pounded in her chest, and her eyes darted around the room, looking for reassurance that the danger of her dream had passed. That it wasn't a vision coming to life.

She settled when her eyes landed on Lina sleeping in Cosmina's arms while Malcolm and Thea played on the floor.

"Sleeping beauty awakes," Malcolm whispered.

Emery raised her hands above her head and arched her back, stretching out her muscles, sore from sleeping on the sofa. She shook her head, trying her best to shake the grip her dream still had on her mind. "How long have I been asleep?"

"A few hours, I think," Cosmina answered softly. "I came in and took over from Callum just a bit ago."

"Shit." Emery stood, straightened out her sweater and re-tied her hair up as best she could. Callum wasn't wrong when he said she could really use a shower. She could also use another three hours of sleep, preferably uninterrupted by dreams of betrayal and dying.

She didn't know what that was about, but her dreams had started taking on vision-like qualities, and it was impossible to keep up.

"Don't worry, Em. I had Callum tell the witches you were resting, and they aren't expecting you until tomorrow morning to plan for the celebration."

She'd completely forgotten about the celebration the witches insisted upon to welcome Lina into the coven. There had to be an unwritten rule somewhere about the supernatural community and their love of parties for every occasion. If it wasn't a garden party, it was a hunt or a gala.

This particular celebration was apparently held for every royal witch and, according to Bronwyn, her daughter would be no different. Emery tried to protest, pointing out there were far more important things than a party for them to be worrying about, but Lily backed Bronwyn up and insisted the witches needed this.

Morale was low. Lower than low. They needed a win. So much so that even the refugee vampires in the castle were excited about the celebration. The uppity nobles not so much. And what they didn't know was the ritual was a glorified orgy. She would love to see the look on their faces when they walked into the ballroom and saw every naked inch of the witches in their castle. Unfortunately for the witches, Emery was not going to allow an orgy in the presence of her daughter, so they were having to find some workarounds to accommodate the giving of orgasms to the stars in thanks. The sexuality of the witches never ceased to amaze her. It was a miracle they'd managed to get them to keep their clothes on as long as they had.

Thea reached up from where she sat with Malcolm, patted Emery's leg, and signed, *"I drew some art for Lina's nursery. Can I show it to you?"*

"Of course, sweet girl. I would love to see it," Emery signed back.

Thea ran off to gather the drawings she'd made, and Emery turned to Cosmina and Malcolm. "Have you heard anything from August?"

He'd taken off that morning with Draven and Graves to check out another one of Sloane's dumping grounds near Ambersey. It had been found by another one of the packs in upstate New York. It was the fifth grave site discovered that week alone.

"You're the one with the mind connection or whatever that soul bond is."

"I don't want to bother him while he's at the grave site." If it could even be called that. Her stomach turned every time she considered what Sloane was doing, and how all signs pointed toward Ansel being involved. Every site smelled of him, and she knew it was beginning to affect Draven that Sloane would use his pack mate to wage war on them.

Her heart hurt for her wolf too. Ansel was as much her best friend as Flora. He was supposed to be there holding her baby, playing jokes on Emery when she was tired, and bickering with Dorian. She didn't want to believe it when August told her Ansel was being used to create an army of wolves for her sister. And yet, the signs were all there.

Emery shook her head, unwilling to think about it any

further before adding, "He gets snappy with me when he's out there."

"You're right—my brother is a moody asshole," Malcolm said with a sly smile.

Cosmina shot him a look that only a mother could perfect before softening her features and speaking to Emery. "He's already back, dear. I think he's in a meeting with the advisors."

At least he hadn't forced her to attend this one. Still, it hurt that he hadn't come to check on her or even sent her a message down their bond. The two of them had been on separate pages since Lina was born, not purposely, but life didn't stop just because they had a newborn. He tried to keep up with feedings as much as he could, but more often than not, she'd end up using one of the blood bags he'd provided for Lina as supplement. He was busy being king, and taking on more so she didn't have to. Which she appreciated.

Mostly.

As much as she'd fought him to do more while she was pregnant, after Lina was born, she'd realized she hadn't anticipated how hard being a mother to a newborn would be. Especially because she refused to allow anyone else to step in. Which, the more she thought about it, may have been to her own detriment, but she needed this. The connection with her daughter helped her to heal and remember what they were fighting for. It helped keep the darkness locked deep in her chest. Still, she couldn't deny she also needed her mate.

"Has anyone heard from Dorian?" she asked, changing the subject.

"No." Malcolm shook his head. "It's been over two

weeks and I'm starting to get worried. It's not like him to just disappear like that. He always checks in."

It was out of character, but she had to trust that wherever Dorian was, he was doing everything in his power to help them move forward with ending the Culling once and for all.

Lina stirred in Cosmina's arms, rooting toward her grandmother.

"I think she's hungry."

"She's always hungry." Emery smiled and took Lina from Cosmina. Sitting on the lounge, she covered herself with the blanket and brought her daughter to her breast.

At that moment, Thea bounced back into the room with a stack of papers and a smile. *"I got them! Also, I'm supposed to tell you Dorian arrived, is going to shower, and then will meet you in the garden."*

Malcolm jumped up and stormed from the room, presumably to go find Dorian and either beat the shit out of him for worrying us all or hug him because he missed their bromance.

Emery stared at the door, torn between the need to also rush to the fae's side, and staying to feed her daughter.

"Finish feeding her and I'll keep an eye on her while you go to the meeting," Cosmina offered with a smile. "Also, if you would be open to pumping, I could help you more with Lina. I never had to do what you are doing, but I know being a queen takes everything you have and will rip your soul in two if you aren't at the top of your game. I have watched you handle everything with grace and honor these past two weeks, but you need to take care of yourself, Emery."

A single tear rolled down her face as she nodded and

dropped her chin to her chest, every single one of Cosmina's words echoing in her heart. "I just want to be a good mother and queen."

"And you are, but you are also as stubborn as my son." She paused, and Emery looked up at Cosmina. The love and devotion in her eyes forced another tear to fall. Emery had a lot of people come into her life that cared about her, but she'd never felt a mother's love. Not like this. It was all-encompassing; she only recognized it because it was the way she felt for Lina.

"Let us in, sweet girl. You aren't alone."

Emery nodded and smiled. "Thank you."

"Now wipe away those tears. Those boys are going to need your smarts to figure out what comes next. I may have raised them to be independent, but gods know they need your voice of reason."

Emery chuckled and wiped her eyes. She wished it was all as simple as Cosmina made it sound, but she couldn't help the bit of dread that hadn't left her stomach since waking up. All she could do was hope Dorian had good news for them.

Chapter Nine

AUGUST

He couldn't keep his thoughts straight. Not when they were sitting in the same spot where he'd first tasted Emery. It seemed like so long ago that she'd been his newest Culling woman; definitely not eight months.

The edge of the stone fountain dug into his thighs, and he tightened his fists. August missed her. The taste of her. The feel of her skin against his. He missed talking with her about nothing and everything. Not that they got to do that much before Lina arrived, but now any time together was generally spent passed out in bed trying to get as much sleep as possible before one of them had to get up to feed their daughter or put out a fire that only the king could handle. Between discovering more mutilated bodies left behind by Sloane and the gentle suggestions from his nobles to eradicate mates and fix the kingdom with the snap of his fingers, the fires were a constant blaze. Any spare time he somehow found was being spent resurrecting the royal wing of the castle so he could get Emery and Lina out of the old, worn-out quarters and into rooms that fit their stations.

They were supposed to be enjoying their time in mated bliss. Emery should be too sore from taking his cock to think about anything else. They were supposed to be welcoming their daughter and learning how to be a family. Everything his family wasn't. And yet there he was, falling into the same routine as his father where he wasn't present except to force-feed his blood down his child's throat.

He felt her before she stepped into the garden and knew the moment she spotted him. She didn't bother to hide the heat that flooded their bond as she recognized the spot where he sat.

August straightened his spine and allowed his eyes to wander to where Emery crossed the grassy courtyard. She was beautiful. The moonlight danced between her blonde and pink waves, and her curves swayed with every step, beckoning his dick to take notice. He wanted nothing more than to tangle his fingers in her hair and crush his lips against hers. If there weren't a half dozen other people expected in the garden in minutes, he'd already have her underneath him, reminding her of the first time he tasted her delicious heat.

Instead, he was forcing himself to think of anything else to get his half-erect cock under control.

He extended his hand to his mate, and when she reached him and placed her hand in his, August pulled her into his lap and nuzzled his nose into his favorite spot on her neck. *I've missed you, little witch.*

I missed you too. How were the advisors?

Riveting and imaginative as always.

Emery looked up, like she was about to roll her eyes, but thought better of it. *Do you know what Dorian found?*

His lips quirked up ever so slightly, knowing she was

trying to be good for him. Gods, he wanted nothing more than to reward her for her thoughtfulness. Instead, he gave the round of her ass a squeeze and replied, *No, I was only informed of his return after my meeting and came straight here. How's my little moon?*

She's with your mother, cute as can be, and refusing to nap as usual.

Flora and Draven entered the garden, followed by Lily and Malcolm. He assumed Callum was already in Scotland and Graves had headed back to Greece to gauge the climate of the eastern European kingdoms.

The three highest-ranking supernatural couples sat on the fountain and silently waited for Dorian to arrive. They fidgeted nervously, but none of them spoke, not wanting to break the hope that came with Dorian's return. His success would be a step forward for not only their kingdom but vampires and witches everywhere.

August knew there was nothing more important to the survival of their people than the ability to find their true mates. He couldn't fathom his life without Emery; it would be empty and lackluster. He couldn't even imagine what it would feel like not being able to find his other half, after knowing the love they shared. He knew the other two couples felt the same way. If Dorian succeeded and they were able to end the Culling, it would be a win their people needed.

At least most of them.

August tried not to think about the coming battles with the nobles. They were growing more restless and vocal in their opinion that the Culling shouldn't be banished. Not all of them wanted mates. They wanted to keep the status quo and have nothing to do with the witches. They even had plans to avoid meeting witches, on the off chance they inadvertently found their mates.

It was something he'd been trying to shield Emery from since Lina was born. Every time he thought it was the right time to tell her, he backed down. He told himself it was because she already had enough on her plate; it would only upset her more and he could figure out a way to stop it. But the truth was, he wasn't entirely sure he wanted to take away the right of his people to disagree with him, and he feared that's what Emery would push for.

They didn't have to wait long before the doors from the castle swung open, and Dorian strolled out. His hair was wet as though he'd freshly showered, but his eyes were sunken in, one of them sporting a black-and-blue shiner, and his cheeks looked almost hollow.

"Thank you for joining me. I didn't want to involve any of the others until I'd had the chance to speak to you all as the leaders of the supernatural community."

"What the hell happened to you?" Emery was out of August's lap and across the garden quicker than should have been possible. She cupped Dorian's cheek with her hand, and smoothed over the skin with her thumb.

A low growl burst from August's chest, which earned him a scathing over-the-shoulder look from his mate.

Dorian gave a half-hearted smile and pulled her hand from his cheek. "Thank you for your kindness, Your Majesty, but I think I'd like to keep my head attached to my body, and His Majesty doesn't look very forgiving."

He wasn't wrong. It didn't matter that Dorian was his second, or a man he trusted with his army and his kingdom. When it came to his mate, any man touching her made him ragey. Emery would scold him later, but he wouldn't apologize for coveting what was his.

Emery sighed and stepped back from Dorian, murmuring down their bond something about him being an overgrown barbarian. "What happened to you?"

"I need to feed, that's all."

Emery pulled up the sleeve of her shirt and thrust her wrist in Dorian's direction.

August growled again. He stormed across the space between them and stepped between Emery and Dorian. His lip curled in a snarl, and he narrowed his gaze on his obstinate mate. *Only me, little witch.*

Emery met his stare and for a split second he thought she might argue, but instead she dropped her hand in defeat. *Then get him a fucking feeder.*

He turned around and wrapped his arm around Emery, pulling her to his chest. Before she could orient herself, August sunk his fangs into her neck, claiming what was his.

Emery's sweet essence calmed his mate bond and sated his needs.

He could practically feel her rolling her eyes before a soft moan fell from her lips. "If you're done being a barbarian, I'd like to hear what he has to say."

Mine.

Even through her annoyance, Emery's love radiated through their bond. *Always, you overgrown bat.*

August pulled himself from her neck and licked the wounds. When he looked up, Malcolm and Draven were shaking their heads and Lily and Flora were trying not to laugh.

Dorian nodded at him, understanding in his eyes. "I

appreciate your offer, Your Majesty, but I don't need your blood. I'm not a vampire, remember?"

"Then what do you need?"

"Magic, specifically death. That's why feeding as a vampire worked to keep me hidden for so long. Only I generally chose to feed from other vampires and then compel them to forget. The death in their blood keeps my magic sated."

How had August never noticed that? Come to think of it, he'd never seen Dorian feed on any of the missions they went on together. He never pulled bags from the fridges nor did he visit the feeders. "Is that a fae thing?"

"Yes and no." Dorian's face gave away nothing. As always, he was locked up tight when it came to his heritage. A fact that was becoming increasingly more frustrating as the fae became more involved in their world.

Malcolm stepped forward and offered Dorian his wrist.

Dorian nodded in thanks. "I'll just take enough to get by."

"Take what you need."

Dorian wrapped his lips around Malcolm's wrist and took a handful of pulls. When he finally let Malcolm's wrist drop, blood pooled at the corner of his lips, which he promptly wiped away. When he looked up, his features had filled out almost completely.

"Why don't we go inside, and you can tell us everything that happened."

"It's safer if we meet outside."

"Why?"

"Because there's no way to be sure I'm the only fae in the castle, but out here I can sense life and death, which allows me to ensure we are safe to talk."

"Are you going to elaborate on that?" The hurt and annoyance in Malcolm's jab made Dorian's jaw tighten.

They'd all gotten close the last few months. August would go so far as to say that Dorian had become their missing middle brother, who both kept them in line and egged them on.

"It's time you told us about the fae, Dorian," August said gently, not wanting to sound like the King, but also ensuring Dorian knew if he needed to, he'd pull rank. "If we're being monitored, then we need to know how to protect ourselves."

"You aren't in any danger. I would never allow them to harm you. They are lesser fae, and likely are only there to grow in the magic of this realm. My worry is they don't know who I am, and I'd like to keep it that way."

"And who are you?" Emery voiced the question they were all wondering.

Dorian's gaze fell to his feet. "Who I was doesn't matter here. I am your second-in-command, August, and my loyalty belongs to you. But they don't know what I was before. The sins I am trying to atone for. What matters is I'm not a danger to them or to you."

"That's not exactly an answer," Lily pressed, eyes narrowed.

"As I told you before, there are things I can't tell you. This is one of them."

Emery's spine straightened, her jaw tight and anger radiated down their bond. "What can you tell us?"

Dorian sighed and ran a hand through his hair. August could taste his nervousness and defeat in the air. "I can tell you that my people aren't going to help us. The price for allowing us to visit to secure my blood for the spell was too high. The only option is for me to give you my blood."

"No," Emery shouted at the same time August growled, "That's not an option."

"What was the price?" Flora asked, her voice small compared to Emery and August's outburst.

"It doesn't matter."

"We'll be the judge of that." August offered, but he already knew if Dorian thought it was too high, there was no way in hell he was going to agree to whatever it was. Dorian may have his secrets, but he was the best damn second August had ever had. And that was saying something, considering he'd had Rex at his side for centuries where he'd only had Dorian for a few months.

Dorian understood the art of war and politics. He could see ten steps ahead. Not only that, but he had the heart and mind of a leader. He knew how to take calculated risks but also when it was time to retreat.

Dorian shifted his gaze to Emery before softening his eyes. "They wanted you, Your Majesty. More specifically, they want a favor from you to be collected at an unspecified time. I can't let you get involved."

"That doesn't seem so bad."

"He's right, Emery," Malcolm agreed, before August could add his two cents. "We can't agree to something so open-ended. Not only because it opens you up to being taken advantage of, but because we are a kingdom at war. They could side with Sloane and use you against us."

Dorian shook his head. "I don't believe they would do that. Nico doesn't want Sloane to succeed in upsetting the balance of the supernatural world. The fae rely on the magic of this realm to tether their world, and Sloane's upsetting that. But they are unwilling to get involved unless it becomes a matter of protecting the realms. In the same way, I am reluctant to allow you to get involved with their politics. It's better if the realms remain separate. History has proven that."

Emery untangled herself from August's grasp and, though he wanted to hold her back, he let her take her stand. "Firstly, it's not your call to be made if I choose to get involved with the fae. Second, we are not allowing you to sacrifice yourself so others can find their mates. We'll find another way."

"I've already started the process of collecting the encapsulated vials th—."

"Well, unstart it," Emery growled.

Dorian looked around the circle, likely hoping to garner favor with the other members of their council, but found none. They may be the leaders of the greater North American Supernatural world, but they were also his friends and none of them wanted to lose him.

Draven, usually the silent pillar of the three monarch pairs, broke his quiet observance and asked the question that none of them dared to approach. "What do you expect me to tell Ansel when he returns?"

Dorian swallowed hard, and despite his trying to hide his emotions, August could see the deep connection to the wolf in his eyes. "You'll tell him I was doing my duty to this kingdom."

"It is also your duty to stay alive and be my second-in-command. But beyond that, you are a part of this family, Dorian. We have proven that blood doesn't dictate who we love, and we are not willing to let you sacrifice yourself. We will find another way."

"Okay," Dorian sighed reluctantly.

Emery threw her hands up and began to pace the length of half the fountain. "So, we're back to square one."

"Maybe." Lily tilted her head as if she was working through something. A small smile tipped her lips. "You said Emery's blood has the same dark essence as yours, correct?"

Dorian nodded, "In trace amounts, yes. It's a factor of her dark magic."

"Does that mean her sister does, too?"

"In theory, yes, but she's not entirely alive any longer. When she killed herself and was brought back, it changed who she was, including her magic." Dorian paused. "I see where you're going with this, but I'm not sure it carries enough life in it any longer as Emery's does. Because of that, I don't know if it will work as a spell component."

"But in theory it might?" Malcolm asked, hopefully.

"Correct."

"So, all we need to do is drain Sloane of her blood and hope there's enough," Flora concluded, bringing the thought full circle.

Dorian shook his head. "While I want nothing more than to end that wicked woman's life, even if we did, I'm not sure her blood holds enough essence, nor if it will be enough to complete the spell."

In one failed swoop they'd had hope and lost it again.

"So, square one." August hated the defeat that hung in the air. He didn't want to say it wasn't fair and risk sounding like a petulant child, but that's exactly what it felt like. No matter how hard they tried, no matter how much of themselves they gave to the cause, they were always one step behind and a dollar short. Sloane continued to kidnap and further her sinister plot, while their people grew frustrated.

His gaze slid to Emery beside him, who appeared to be lost in thought, but he knew her better. She was spiraling. The dark rims of her eyes pulsated, growing larger with every passing moment. He reached out down their bond with calming and love.

I don't need you to placate me. I need you to rage with me. You promised to be my darkness, August. You don't want me to touch mine, but I am at a point where I can't keep ignoring its call. We need to do something. Anything. We can't lose anyone else. I refuse to lose Dorian too.

The desperation in her voice paired with the silver tears that rimmed her eyes gutted him.

We can't rage without a target, princess. I want to unleash hell on our enemies. I want to raise cities and taste the blood of anyone who would seek to harm our people, our family, but I'm being tossed about in this storm right alongside you. Rest assured, once we find solid footing, I will bring you the head of our enemy. But my sweet Emery, I'm not willing to risk the darkness against your soul.

I am.

What about Lina?

What about her? She'll see her mother as a woman with the strength to do what is necessary.

And when you lose yourself to the darkness?

I won't.

But I will. I'll follow you anywhere, and while you may be confident you can make your way back from the clutches of the dark, I'm not. I won't. I need you to bring me back.

August, I just…we can't simply do nothing.

He hated that she was right. They'd been playing

defense for too long, and it was time they considered taking the fight to Sloane.

"Sorry to interrupt, Your Majesties, but an urgent letter arrived and I was ordered to deliver it to you at once."

August took the thick parchment from the steward and ran his fingers over the purple wax seal. He popped it free, and Emery peeked over his shoulder to read the elegantly typed words as he spoke them out loud.

> *Your Majesties—*
> *You are cordially invited to Talamh Heil at the castle of the Mistress. The ley lines will open, and the magic of our earth will bless those worthy of its claim.*
>
> *Come celebrate the gifts bestowed upon us with our new brethren.*
>
> *The Mistress.*

Scrawled below, in blood-red ink, was a note to Emery.

> *I look forward to seeing you, sister. Don't forget my niece needs to commune with the earth.*

"What does that mean?"

"Talamh Heil, or Heil is the celebration of our magic," Lily explained, slightly worrying her lip as she spoke. "It is the pilgrimage that witches make to the nearest ley lines each year to commune with the earth and ask it to continue to bless us with magic and prosperity."

Emery furrowed her brow. "Why would I need to bring Lina?"

"It's tradition, and those who don't commune every year, grow weak."

"I've never communed before and I'm one of the strongest witches in our coven. And you lived at the castle for all those years, it's not like you were gallivanting to a celebration with the witches as a traitor."

Their bond hummed with fear and frustration, some of it his, most of it Emery's. There was no way they were going to put Lina in danger. He'd sooner bind his daughter's magic than allow her anywhere near Sloane.

Bloody hell.

August's throat bobbed as he swallowed hard. If he bound his daughter's magic, he'd be no better than the witches who bound Emery. Why the hell would he ever think that?

"Your magic was bound," Lily explained, "the earth didn't recognize you as a magic-wielder. If you don't allow Evangeline to commune, she'll grow weak in her magic."

"But it doesn't have to be where Sloane is, right?"

"Correct. We have ley lines here at the castle. It's how I was able to continue to commune each year. It will be nice to do so with a community of witches this year and with your daughter." Lily reassured Emery and he felt his mate relax slightly. "My fear isn't for Lina though, it's for the witches that choose to follow Sloane and join her celebration."

"Why?" Flora asked.

"Heil is a celebration of life and the magic the earth provides. It is led by the strength of our ancestors through royal bloodlines. Sloane has the blood of royalty, but she doesn't represent life. I fear what will happen when she taps into the ley lines and calls forth the magic to bless the witches present."

Nothing could be simple. Not one single thing.

Emery's lips twisted into a smirk and her eyes darkened. "That's why we're going to bring the fight to her. She's inviting us to her castle. She wants us to attend. It's two months away. Let's give her a party she won't forget and end this before she can tap into the ley lines."

Her darkness called to him. It gripped him at his core, beckoning him to answer her call for bloodshed. He should be focused on a million other things and all the ways this could go wrong, considering Sloane had whipped their asses at the hunt. But at that moment, all August could focus on was the way Emery wore her darkness like a little black dress, hugging every curve of her soul, and all he wanted to do was wage war with her divine radiance at his side.

Chapter Ten

EMERY

THE ROOM DRIPPED WITH A FRESH ELEGANCE THAT SHOULDN'T be possible when the world was slowly falling apart around them. It had been turned from a stuffy vampire ballroom into a fairytale dream. The once closed off castle had been restored after the hunt and transformed with skylights that allowed the evening sunset to paint the walls in oranges and pinks while still protecting the turned vampires inside from the sun's rays. The walls were draped with elegant purple fabric strung across green walls of vines with beautiful white blooms that called to her elemental magic.

Even though it was a largely unnecessary spectacle, Emery couldn't deny that everyone's hearts seemed to be lighter. There were smiles on the faces of her people when they usually held deep, worried frowns. Even the nobles seemed to forget themselves in favor of the gathering. They still kept their distance from the witches, but she noticed a few twitchy smiles shine through during the short amount of time they attended. Their departure didn't go unnoticed, but for once, no one cared. The night was about celebrating their future, and Lina was the bright spot of their kingdom, thawing hearts and bringing mortal enemies together. Even if she was sleeping through the entire event.

Not that Emery was complaining. She'd pumped at Cosmina's request and ensured there was enough of August's blood on hand to last them a year if necessary, so that she could enjoy the night with her mate.

It was the first time they'd spent any real amount of time together since Dorian's return. Each day they were in each other's minds, but somehow it still felt like they were passing ships destined never to share a port of call.

August traced his fingers down her exposed spine before wrapping his arm around her and tugging her against his side. Heat pooled in her belly at the same time irritation bubbled in her chest.

Don't tease me, Augustine.

He brushed his lips against her shoulder, and spun her so she was pressed against his chest. His long fingers intertwined with hers and he swayed her to the classical melody echoing throughout the ballroom. *You should know I don't tease, little witch. I promise.*

Until he was inevitably called away.

Emery almost said as much, but instead tipped her head back and smiled at him, forcing herself to enjoy the moment. The world tilted when August twirled her and only steadied again once she was pressed against him.

I've dreamed of feeling you against me.

"Then why haven't you done something about it?" she asked.

August frowned.

Fuck, she was ruining this perfect moment. They were dancing, closer than they'd been in what felt like ages, and all she wanted to do was unleash the anger and darkness that had been building slowly since Dorian's return to him. Any woman would be elated to be on his arm, especially dressed in his royal best. He may not have been coronated, but August already embodied the title. The crown was just a formality.

"I'm sorry," she whispered, "I'm just...I shouldn't take out my issues on you."

"That's what I'm here for, Emery," he whispered against her hair before spinning her away from him and pulling her back against him. "You and me. We've never had it easy, but we can't start shutting each other out again."

Emery sighed and lowered her head to his chest, the steady beat of his heart grounding her. "I feel like I'm being pulled in a million directions, and none of them feel right. I need—"

"Your Majesty," a sentinel interrupted her, pulling August's attention from her. "There's been an issue at the camps, we have—"

August held his hand up, stopping the sentinel from continuing. "Generals Braxton and Dorian are on duty tonight. I suggest you find them."

"Right." The sentinel looked at him with as much confusion as Emery. August never said no. He didn't let others step up where he could be involved. It had been the topic of one too many arguments between them. He didn't want to be his father, he wanted to be involved and present and she admired the hell out of him for it. It was one of the many reasons she loved him.

But she loved this side of him too. The side that was steeped in selfish darkness and put her first.

August's eyes raked over her surprised expression, and

he pinned a wicked smile in her direction. "Would you like to get out of here?"

Emery rolled her eyes. "We can't leave our daughter's celebration."

"She's asleep, I don't think she'll miss us. I've already got my mother and Flora on duty to ensure she's fed and taken care of until morning." He leaned in and his hand slid down her back until he was cupping her bottom. He pinched the round of her ass. "You know what happens to little witches who roll their eyes."

A shiver tore down her spine and her nipples pebbled against his chest. "We're alone till morning?"

"I would tell you more, but that would ruin the surprise." His breath tickled the shell of her ear, his thick voice sending heat to pool in her belly.

She hated surprises, but when he spoke with a tone that dripped of sex and promises, she could get on board with being left in the dark. Emery looked up at him and smirked. "Then lead the way."

He took her hand in his and led her through the throngs of scantily clad witches and intrigued vampires. It was probably better that they leave now anyway, considering she didn't trust the witches to keep their pants on much longer. She only hoped they listened to her plea and kept the orgy limited to their camp in the woods.

Emery spotted Malcolm and Lily on the edges of the crowd talking with a group of witches. Malcolm lifted his hand and wiggled his fingers goodbye, a knowing smile plastered on his face. That was never a good sign. If Malcolm was in on this, she could literally be walking into anything.

Where exactly are we going?

Again with trying to ruin my surprises. She could hear the amusement dripping from his words.

"I hate surprises."

"I know."

He guided her through the empty halls of the castle toward the wing along the back wall that had been destroyed during the hunt.

"Close your eyes." August's voice had changed from seductive to downright excited. He practically bounced in front of her.

Emery hesitated and searched his icy blue eyes for any indication of what she was walking into, but he gave away nothing. Upon closing her eyes, she was swept off her feet. She wrapped her arms around August's neck and pressed her nose into his chest. His fresh pine scent enveloped her, and she relaxed into him. She'd never admit it to him, but this was her favorite way to travel.

The distance was too short for her liking, and she let out a small sigh when he set her down.

"Don't look yet."

He stepped away from her, and she heard a click of metal followed by silence.

"Okay, take two steps straight forward and then open your eyes."

Emery followed his instructions, and when she opened her eyes, her jaw dropped.

She took two more steps into the room, her eyes darting in every direction in an attempt to capture every detail. The suite was everything she'd ever imagined for herself and her mate. It dripped with modern elegance and a hint of royalty.

It was dark yet airy, with the last of the evening sun

casting shadows from the open floor-to-ceiling glass doors that led to an expansive balcony.

All the walls in the suite, except for one, were a soft white, which contrasted with the dark wood of the bookshelves and deep emerald sofas that made up the perfect little reading nook. The exception was the wall behind the bed, which featured an intricate herringbone pattern and was painted a dark navy blue that reminded her of Augustine's eyes.

From the vaulted ceiling, a beautiful brass chandelier in the shape of a branch hung with teardrop crystals scattered between the soft lights as leaves. Underneath it was a massive bed with dark satin sheets and white pillows that contrasted with the gorgeous dark gray leather headboard. Her first thought was it was smart, considering the amount of blood that was shared between her and August in bed.

Sitting in the middle of the bed was a small stuffed dragon. Emery let out a small gasp. "Is that Copper?"

She rushed across the room and clutched the small toy to her chest. The simple little dragon had been a source of comfort for her all her life. He'd been her friend when she had none and kept her company on the lonely nights when Ada would send her to bed without dinner. She hadn't seen him since before the gala. Before everything went to shit.

"I found him after you left for New Orleans." August stepped behind her and wrapped his arms around her. His head dropped, his lips finding purchase on his favorite spot on her neck. He peppered a dozen kisses over the spot. "I'll admit at the time he was the only thing about you I liked, but as I fell in love with you again, he became my comfort while you were in Scotland, and I was stuck here with my father. I figured it was time I returned him and gave him a new home."

Emery turned around and faced August, tears in her eyes. "This suite...it's mine?"

"Ours. I wanted us to have something, somewhere in the castle that belonged to only you and me. A sacred space for our family. There's also a sitting room and a nursery adjacent so that we can have our babies near while they are young, a luxury bath with walk-in closets, and a studio for us to create music together."

"Together?" Emery forced the words past her shock. He did this for her.

"My mother told me how much you loved to play, and music was a central part of my life before all this." He gestured to the thin crown that circled his head. "With the music room destroyed, I wanted us to have a place to release some of the worries of our days. Outside the bedroom, of course. Because I fully plan on tying you to that headboard and taking out every bit of tension on that sweet ass of yours."

Emery smiled and shook her head, her tears falling freely. "When did you have time to do all this?"

"Any moment I could spare that I wasn't with you or Lina was spent here overseeing the construction. I had hoped to have it ready before Lina's arrival, but seeing as she came a few weeks early, I wasn't able to get it done." August cupped her cheeks with his hands, his eyes searching hers. "Do you like it?"

"Like it?" Emery choked on a laugh and went up on tiptoe to press a kiss on his lips. "August, it's perfect. It's everything I could have asked for and more. But, if I'm honest, I would have taken a wooden shack in the woods if it meant I got to spend more time with you."

August smiled and it was the kind of smile that made his dimples pop beneath his stubble. The kind of smile that made her fall in love with him. She'd do anything to keep that smile on his face.

"We've definitely skipped that step, haven't we? We should be living in mated bliss, with me not letting you leave this room except to tend to our daughter. Even then, the selfish man in me would have the wet nurse tend to her so that I may keep you at my whim for days on end, never letting your pussy know a moment without lavish attention."

Emery inhaled sharply, her heart beating wild in her chest, and she clenched her thighs together. She wanted that. Every bit of that. It wasn't that she'd trade their life for another, but there was a part of her that was desperate to connect with her mate.

"As it turns out, though, war waits for no one, and regrettably I've been shirking my duties to my mate." August tucked a stray strand of pink hair behind her ear and trailed his hand down her neck, along her shoulder. "I'd like to make it up to you."

Emery tipped her head back and looked at him. Her darkness came alive in her chest, very much on board with the way things were going and fueling her forward. She reached up and trailed her hands over his broad chest, shoving his suit coat from his shoulders. "And how would you propose you do that?"

"First, I'm going to strip you down and take my time tasting every inch of your delicate skin until you're a bundle of nerves anticipating my next move." August took a step forward, forcing her back so the back of her knees hit the bed. "Then, and only then, will I slip between your legs and give you the first of many orgasms." He lowered his head and sucked her lower lip between his fangs and tugged back, scraping along her lip. "I seem to remember quite a few eye rolls that have gone unpunished, but seeing as I'm feeling rather benevolent, I think I'll give you a choice. Would you rather keep in the spirit of the night and have an orgasm for every eye roll from the only man you should be worshiping, or would you prefer a spanking at my hand for each?"

Emery clenched her thighs together. She'd never been so confused and turned on at the same time. It was a trick question. It had to be. The simple answer would be to take the orgasms, but nothing was ever simple with Augustine.

"What's the count up to now?" She whispered.

"Nine."

Holy shit. Nine orgasms. She'd had at most three or four with August at any given time. Nine seemed impossible. But if the sly grin stretched across his face told her anything, August would deliver every single one of them with nothing but the purest joy in his heart.

"Spankings."

"Such a shame," he tsked, but the way his eyes darkened made her question if she'd chosen correctly. "I thought for sure you'd go for the pleasure."

Her voice quivered in time with the butterflies in her belly. "Won't it be?"

"What?"

"Pleasurable?"

August took a step back, raking his gaze over her from head to toe, until she could almost read every lust-filled thought behind his eyes. "There's such a fine line between pleasure and pain."

Emery sucked in a breath. His words slithered down her spine and radiated like lightning through her, finding ground in her clit. She shifted under his gaze, wanting both sides of the coin he was offering.

"Yes, please," she breathed.

"Then, the only question I have for you is…bedroom or studio?"

Chapter Eleven

EMERY

If she thought the bedroom was gorgeous, the studio was breathtaking.

The vaulted ceiling and majority of the walls of the turret room boasted large offset acoustic panels. Along the top were rectangular windows that filtered in the last bit of daylight and made the space feel larger than it was.

Vines traveled the length of the far wall, reaching up toward the ceiling. They were beautiful, dotted with small yellow flowers with black centers. Emery reached out and caressed them with her magic. The fact that August considered adding in elements that would bring her comfort warmed her heart.

But what nearly brought her to her knees sat in the middle of the room. Sleek and black, with brass accents, the Steinway baby grand was the focal point of the studio. When she'd learned the attack on the castle had destroyed the music room, there were tears. Heartbroken didn't even begin to describe how she'd felt. The room held so many memories—teaching Thea, losing herself in the music, finding refuge when the trials of the Culling became too much—she couldn't fathom it being gone. Even more, she'd mourned the fact she'd never be able to make memories there with her daughter.

Now she had a place to do so.

August stepped up behind her, his chest flush with her back and fingers teasing her hips. "Do you like it?"

"I love it."

He kissed her neck and dragged his tongue over her skin. "I love you."

Emery lolled her head to the side, giving August more room to explore. She whimpered as he set his fangs on the column of her neck and bit down. He trailed his fingertips down the flesh of her arm, the slow trickle mimicking his venom as it worked its way through her veins.

Heat flooded her core, and if she wasn't already turned on, she'd bet money August just used his venom to heighten her pleasure and make her forget everything other than him.

He was succeeding.

She clenched her thighs and shifted her hips back, searching for any amount of friction to soothe the ache between her legs.

August backed his hips away and healed the wounds at her neck. "Uh-uh, little witch. Punishment before pleasure."

Emery let out a soft whine and called her magic to her palm before sending a small zap in his direction.

August growled when it made contact, and Emery felt the rumble from his chest radiate through her and land straight on her clit. She arched her back, the need for release growing every minute he didn't touch her.

"That's ten."

He intertwined his fingers in hers and stepped out from behind her, guiding her toward the back of the piano.

A wicked smile tipped his lips. "Would you be a doll, and extend some vines for me from the wall?"

Emery cocked a brow, surprised by his request, but if it would get him to touch her, she'd do just about anything. Within seconds, she'd grown four strong vines from the plant that climbed the wall and willed them toward August.

"Perfection." He placed a soft kiss to her lips before picking up one of the vines and feeding it under the piano. She leaned into his lips and tried to suck them between her teeth to keep him there. August chuckled and pressed his hand to the center of her shoulders, his fingers searing her skin with desire. He gently pressed her chest against the rounded butt of the piano. "Stay there."

Emery listened to his steps as he rounded the side and pulled a small round eyelet from beneath the piano. He slid the vine she'd created through it before tenderly wrapping it around her wrist. Then he repeated the same process on the other side until her arms were spread wide on the lid of the piano.

"Do you know how incredible you look in this dress, draped over this magnificent instrument with your cunt dripping your intoxicating arousal?"

She'd picked this dress specifically with him in mind. The thin straps left her throat and shoulders exposed and the deep cut back allowed her to feel his fingers splayed at the base of her spine as he guided her on the dancefloor. Heat filled her cheeks. She'd never felt more adored than under his stare, but hearing it did things to her that were downright sinful.

He ran his hand down her spine and over the curve of her ass. "It's a shame I'm going to ruin this."

She wasn't sure if he meant the dress or her ass, but she found herself wanting to beg for either. Maybe both. "Yes, please."

The rip of the fabric reverberated off the walls, and Emery winced. She really liked this dress.

I'll buy you a new one.

August draped the fabric forward around her, leaving her standing in nothing but the dainty lace thong she'd chosen because it wouldn't leave panty lines. Not that they would last long now. Her mate had a penchant for stealing her panties.

Or destroying them.

Sure enough, seconds later she was standing naked, tied to the piano with her own vines, and all but begging for the sting of his hand.

August ran his fingers over the round of her ass, warming her skin, dipping them between her cheeks and teasing her already-soaking slit just enough to make her shiver, but not enough to give her arousal any sort of relief.

"Ten strokes," he said gruffly, and she could have sworn there was a slight quiver in his voice. "Five on each cheek."

Emery curled her hands around the vines that held her and craned her head up to stare at the opposite wall. He'd never given her spankings like this. He'd slapped her ass more than once when he was fucking her from behind, but this felt like more. This was dark. It was a punishment and yet, even though she was nervous as hell, it was something she had no doubt she would crave.

"Relax and breathe, little witch, you aren't going to

enjoy this. I've dreamed of punishing you this way, but our sweet daughter's presence in your womb stopped me from taking my release out on your delectable ass. It won't be pleasant, but I promise it's all for you."

For her? How the hell would smacking the shit out of her ass be for her?

She had barely exhaled the breath she'd been holding when August let his hand fly, applying four rapid smacks, alternating cheeks, with more force than she'd anticipated.

Each slap echoed through the room, and even though heat bloomed from her ass cheeks, it wasn't entirely from the pain. She sucked her lip between her bottom teeth and bit down, stifling the moan that caught in her throat. The bond between them vibrated, and she found herself unable to settle when he paused and ran his hand over her sensitive flesh.

The pain mixed with the tender way he soothed her left her head spinning. Emery tried to back up into his palm but August placed a hand on her spine to stop her. A small whine built in her chest but she bit it back.

"Remember what I said about this room being soundproof?"

She nodded her head, unable to form words.

"Don't hold back. I want to hear you take my punishment. I want to feel the release in your soul. Every moan. Every shriek. It's mine to find pleasure in. If you don't give me everything you have, we'll start over and you can count every stroke."

She nodded again. His words confused her. Was this for her or for him?

Three more smacks in rapid succession, each one harder than the last. Emery cried out, her grip tightening on the vines. She couldn't stop herself from raising on to her toes and bowing her back. Her skin wore a sheen of sweat and her core was coiled so damn tight that she knew the second he touched her dripping pussy it would be over. But he didn't touch her, save for his soft breath as he peppered a kiss to her reddened behind.

Emery let out a whimper. She should feel humiliated, but she didn't. Her body quaked with need and her mind threatened to float away. She didn't know if it was the venom or the vines, but being at August's mercy, vulnerable and unable to move, snapped something in her mind. With each smack she let herself fall deeper into her mate. What started as a punishment to deter her no longer held that weight. Instead, it sparked something deeper. A freedom she hadn't known she'd needed.

But Augustine had known. This connection between pleasure and pain fed the darkest and most depraved parts of her soul, just like it did him. While she was strong and independent, this simple act of submission acted as a release for all the pent-up frustration that plagued her day in and day out, and her mate was the only one who could deliver them from her.

"Gods, you're perfect." August whispered, rubbing his hand again over her heated skin. "Three more, my queen. You're doing so well taking everything I have to give. Maybe this time you'll remember to keep those eyes of yours from rolling to the back of your head."

They both knew it had nothing to do with the eye rolls, but if it was how she got this all-encompassing release, this deep connection with him, then she'd be acting out a hell of a lot more.

The last three smacks were the hardest of all, and

Emery tipped her head back, her mate's name both a plea and a prayer falling from her lips, though she didn't know if she was hoping he'd stop or continue. Her mind floated from her body and every thought beyond that moment grew hazy.

There was only him. Only them.

After the last strike, Emery fell slack on the piano, a panting mess.

August crouched behind her and rubbed her flaming ass. Her legs trembled with each of his loving strokes. She widened her stance as his hands neared her aching pussy and subtly shifted her hips in his direction.

"How are you, Emery?"

"I need to come."

"Soon." She could hear the smile in his voice.

Emery let out a small moan and shifted her hips lazily. "Now, please."

August leaned forward and bit into the flesh he'd just heated, his fangs adding just enough pressure to sting but not break the skin.

Emery yelped and twisted her wrist as far as she could, sending a sucker punch of magic in his direction. Given the fact all she heard was his throaty laugh and not a gasp of pain, she knew she'd missed. She couldn't hit the broad side of a barn at the moment, even if she tried.

August stood and trailed kisses up her spine until he reached the shell of her ear. "I'm going to untie your hands and put you exactly where I want you. If you behave, I'll give you as many orgasms as you want until you beg me to stop."

"And if I don't behave?" she teased, wanting more of his punishments.

August cocked a brow. "It sure would be a shame if I had to go deal with whatever bullshit issues my advisors have drummed up."

"You wouldn't," she glowered, but the mischievous look in his near-midnight eyes told her he absolutely would. He'd take her all the way to the edge and walk away, then corner her when she least expected it and extract the orgasm that already sat just beyond reach.

"Do you understand me?"

"Yes, sir." The honorific rolled off her tongue laced with sass, but she didn't miss the way August's eyes widened, and he shifted his slacks beneath the piano.

"Good girl."

August untied her and lifted her onto the piano so that the edge of the lid dug into the sensitive flesh of her ass and her feet rested over the edge across the keys. He lifted one arm, draped it across her abdomen, and restrained it with the vine from the opposite side of the piano before repeating the same on the opposite arm. When he was finished, August admired his work with a glint in his eyes. He leaned down and cupped her breasts, which were now pushed up and on full display for him.

"I love what pregnancy has done to these," he murmured to himself.

Before Emery could answer with a snarky remark, his heated blue gaze captured her attention, holding her captive with sheer love and desperation. She squirmed against his ties, needing more of him touching her, but he released her and moved between her legs. With quick precision, he tied each of her legs to hooks in the key blocks at opposite ends of the piano, leaving her spread wide for him.

If she thought his gaze was heated moments before, it was downright scorching as he trailed it over her exposed flesh.

"You are so fucking beautiful, Emery," he hissed, trailing his fingers along her inner thighs. "Do you have any idea what seeing you like this does to me?"

"No." Her voice was barely more than a raspy whisper. "Tell me."

She wanted his words just as much as she wanted his touch. She would memorize them. Etch them onto their shared soul. But in true August fashion, he couldn't give her what she wanted. He had to give her more.

"I'll show you."

Chapter Twelve

EMERY

It might have been the sound of the piano bench being dragged across the aged wood floors that sent shivers up her spine. Or it could have been the fact that when August sat, he leaned forward so his mouth was inches away from her pussy. There was also the distinct possibility it was the fact Emery was still somewhere between heaven and earth and desperate to come, so every movement felt like pins and needles.

"Please, August," she begged.

His fingers spread over the keys and his right hand began to play. At first, she didn't recognize the melody, but she didn't need to know the tune to be mesmerized by August's playing. He played as brilliantly and beautifully as he had all those months ago when she'd met him at his bar in Chicago. She missed this side of him, the one few got to see. August poured his soul into every note he played. It was as if he didn't know any other way.

She was lost in the music when she felt his lips against her thigh. Emery instantly recognized the classic notes of the intro to *Layla* by Eric Clapton. She wondered if August knew the origins of the song, the tale of forbidden love between Layla and Manjun. It could have been the beginning of their love story.

August took his time, drawing out the heartfelt notes of the first verse. Just before the chorus, his lips brushed against her inner thigh again, and Emery jumped against her restraints. He peppered teasing kisses until he reached her center. Her entire body stilled with anticipation as his breath danced over her arousal.

Then, with his mouth pressed against her pussy, he sang the chorus to her, replacing Layla's sultry name with her own. His hands moved lazily over the keys without a single slip in the melody as his tongue danced along her in time.

Emery groaned, relishing the vibrations of the piano beneath her as it added another layer of sensation. She arched her back as much as she could and pushed up her hips to force his lips to her clit until she knew one more touch, just one more, would make her explode. And just then, August pulled away.

"Fuck. Please, August. Make me come," she whined.

With his lips hovering over her clit, he worked through an interlude and changed songs to another she immediately recognized. The ominous notes of *Ain't No Sunshine* by Bill Withers echoed, hitting Emery in the depths of her chest. Leave it to August to pick two songs that were melancholy and soulful to convey his love for her while he teased her beyond comprehension.

You are my sunshine, little witch. August leaned back just enough to flash her a seductive grin before he buried his face between her legs. He curved his tongue between her folds and moaned in time with the music.

The moment he flicked his tongue upward and grazed her clit, Emery lost all control. It was like lightning had struck through the windows above and lit her on fire from the inside out. Her muscles contracted, forcing stars to burst behind her eyes.

August backed off her clit, but continued his long languid strokes as he continued to play, and she rode the endless waves of her orgasm.

When she finally relaxed against the piano, a panting, shaking mess, she opened her eyes and saw the blooms on the vines around the room had doubled. A smile tugged at Emery's lips. The earth magic inside her, controlled by her heart's desire, found an outlet in her pleasure.

August slowed his fingers between verses, and when she lifted her head to look down at him, he smiled at her lazily. "That's one. Shall I keep going?"

Emery's lips twisted into a smirk, and she challenged him. "You promised me as many as I wanted."

"Always, princess," August replied in a husky voice that was filled with promise.

He pressed a soft kiss to her clit before attacking it with lips and fangs in time with the staccato bridge of the song. Emery screamed through three more back-to-back orgasms, after which she could no longer focus on the music or the room around her. There was only August. Only her mate and the bond that tethered them mind, body, and soul.

He didn't relent, and she lost count of how many times she'd risen and fallen over the edge of the waves on the choppy sea of pleasure. At some point, August had stopped playing, his talented fingers now orchestrating a different tune against the deepest parts of her.

Tears welled in Emery's eyes, and she pleaded. "No more. Please, I'm done."

He relaxed his movements and lifted his head, his lips soaked with her arousal. "One more, but for this one I want you stretched around my cock, milking every last ounce of my seed into your womb."

"I swear to the gods, Augustine, if you get me pregnant again…"

"I make no promises, little witch." The bastard winked at her and disappeared from the spot between her legs.

Moving too fast for her to track, he undid her restraints and was back sitting on the bench. He gently lifted her up and pulled her down to straddle his already exposed cock. It wept between her legs, and even though she slumped forward against him to catch her breath, she couldn't stop herself from rocking her hips forward and sliding her clit against his length.

"Fuck, Emery," August growled against her neck. "If you keep doing that, I'm not going to last long."

"Then I suggest you fuck me."

August lifted his arms and tugged his shirt off, exposing his chiseled chest. Then he carefully lifted Emery so his cock was notched at her entrance.

"Use me, Emery," he ordered. "Take your pleasure."

He had no idea what a gift he was giving her. He'd already pushed her body to the brink of pleasure, but there was still a part of her that had yet to be sated. The darkness swirled in her chest, and she was sure that when he looked at her, August would find her eyes blown black with a mix of desire and magic.

Emery hooked her arms around his neck and tangled

her fingers in his short blond hair, then slammed herself down on him, her pussy greedily swallowing his cock.

August's fingers dug into her hips, and he released a sound that was somewhere between a growl and a moan. Emery crashed her mouth against his, sucking his pleasure into her and claiming it for herself.

Her grip in his hair tightened, and she used the leverage to rotate on his shaft, lifting and rocking her clit against him every time she slammed down. She picked up her pace, riding him with reckless abandon.

"Fuck, look at you, little witch." August leaned back, his gaze dropping between them. "Fucking my cock like it was made for you."

Emery's magic rose inside her, the darkness in his blood calling to hers in a raw, carnal way. She untangled her hands from his hair and with her hands on his face, kissed him fiercely while working her pussy up and down his length, searching for the spot that would send her over the edge. When she found it, all coherent thoughts left.

"I'm going to come."

August's gaze locked on hers, his pupils dilated. "Take me with you."

Emery smiled and tipped her head back, slamming herself down two more times before her body exploded around him. Light filled the room, and it took her a moment to realize it came from her hands.

She fucked him, and he fucked her right back. When she lifted her hips, he met her with a thrust of his own. This moment would be etched on her heart forever, this perfect union where the only thing that mattered was memorizing the feel of their love.

Wrapped in her magic, August followed her, pushing

his hips up with wicked-hard thrusts until he was shaking. With one final thrust, he leaned forward and plunged his fangs into her shoulder as he emptied himself in her womb.

It wasn't until they slowed to catch their breaths that either of them took notice of the room around them. Her magic hung in the air almost like an electric current, its beautiful golden color swirling in waves around strands of inky-black dark magic. Emery tipped her head back and closed her eyes, feeling the connection to every inch of her magic.

Child of light and dark. Embrace your destiny.

Emery's eyes widened. "Was that you?"

August's brows furrowed? "Was what me?"

The voice had been a broken whisper, and she didn't think it had been in her head. Not like when August spoke in her mind. This voice was ominous and spoke as if it were delivering an omen instead of encouragement.

She shook her head, not wanting to ruin the moment. "Nothing. Thank you for this." She pressed a kiss to his lips. "For everything."

"The pleasure was all mine." He reached up and cupped her face, tracing his thumb across her bottom lip. "I promise to find more time for us. For this."

"Me too." Emery nodded, but her thoughts were still on the voice, its words echoing in her head.

August stretched his arms around her. He began to play the chords to the song that made her fall in love with him all those months ago, and her lingering thoughts of the voice fell away.

When a Man Loves a Woman.

Their song.

Emery snuggled into his chest and allowed her mate to serenade her as he slowly rocked his still-hard cock within her.

It was the perfect night. She only hoped it could stay that way for longer than a few moments.

Chapter Thirteen

AUGUST

August scrawled his elegant signature on the last of the decrees to go out to the kingdoms and packs across the world. It amazed him that even in a modern day and age, where every king and alpha was kept up to date and knew their every move, he was forced to handwrite a letter of alliance for it to be recognized as binding. Almost finished, he gently caressed his edge of the bond with his mind, only to find Emery had closed herself off from him.

It wasn't unusual for her to do so when she was busy, but he couldn't deny it stung a little whenever he noticed it.

Things with Emery had been hot and cold since the night of the celebration. Hot in the sense that they'd made it a point to spend every night together tangled in each other's arms, only pausing to tend to their daughter and sleep when exhaustion finally took hold. Their night in the studio had been the opportunity they needed to reacquaint their bodies with one another, and neither of them was ready to go back to the complacency they'd fallen into before.

It was the dark steel-like hardness of the cold that worried him. August couldn't quite figure out where it was coming from, but there were moments where Emery seemed lost, a million miles away from the castle. Not in the way her visions took hold, but like she was holding back from him and everyone around her. Every time he questioned her about it, she found a way to distract him, either with duties to their kingdom or by conveniently losing her clothing.

His office door creaked open, but he didn't look up. It was likely his steward, Colin, bringing him something else to sign. It seemed the paperwork was never-ending. What amazed him was he never saw his father do any actual work.

"Your Majesty, I think you better come down to the ballroom."

He stopped writing and closed his eyes, his jaw tense with annoyance. "What happened?" he ground out.

"Um. It's Her Majesty."

August dropped his pen and shot up from the table. "Is she okay?"

"Oh, um, she's fine." Colin rubbed the back of his neck and shifted nervously. "It's Aberforth you should be worried about."

Bloody hell. The mouthy vampire was the most outspoken of the nobles. He was constantly pontificating against mates and the introduction of hybrids into the kingdom, and unfortunately, he wasn't without followers. As time went on without progress toward ending the Culling magic or defeating Sloane, it got harder and harder to keep the narrative focused on anything else. Two sides were emerging, and he worried that they were closer than ever to fighting within their own walls. If they weren't already there.

August tore from his office down to the ballroom. From outside the doors, he heard the whispers.

There were those who clearly sided with Emery.

"Finally, someone is doing something about the noble problem."

"Maybe if she kills him, they'll see we aren't going anywhere."

Mixed in were those who resisted any change.

"What's she going to do to him?"

"Why are her eyes black?"

"Is *this* how she intends to rule?"

Fuck. He wasn't just dealing with Emery; he was dealing with her darkness.

August slipped silently into the ballroom, his gaze tracing over the crowd of witches and vampires on the far end of the room. Starting from the back, they noticed his presence and parted so he could reach his mate.

Emery had Aberforth wrapped in thorny vines, pressed up against the wall of the ballroom, his toes lifted several inches off the floor. Blood pooled beneath him, and his eyes were wide. They doubled in size when he saw August.

"Your Majesty, she's lost her damn mind," the noble vampire snarled. He may appear to only be a few years older than August and Emery, but Aberforth was a centuries-old bigot who would have licked his father's ass if he thought it would gain him favor.

"I highly doubt that, Aberforth," August mused, feigning disinterest in what he had to say. He turned to Emery, and quickly raked his eyes over her to ensure she was safe. "I thought we agreed to keep the kink in the bedroom, my queen."

Her lips twisted into a sardonic smile, and she tilted her head playfully, her darkened eyes narrowing. "If you'd like to bring him there, I'll gladly allow him to watch as I ride your cock, mate. Maybe then he'll understand the joys of having a witch for a mate."

A low growl rumbled from his chest, overpowering the choked laugh that threatened. His mate was gone. In front of him was a woman on a mission to prove her point; and while he'd usually stand at her side, this was a delicate situation. One that wouldn't only affect their kingdom, but the war at hand. Other monarchs were scared to put their faith in change, and if it looked like he and Emery were forcing the hands of their people, it wouldn't end well in their attempt to garner allies.

He stepped forward and extended his hand to rest on Emery's lower back. He sent waves of calm down their bond, even though she still had him blocked from her. "Although I think it would be an eye-opening experience, I'd rather not have to kill him because he's seen what's mine."

Emery stepped away from his touch and scoffed. "He's already on his way to becoming a dead man. At least then he'll know what he's missing as he leaves this world."

"What's his offense?"

"Aberforth thought it would be good to lay his hands on a witch because she was, and I quote, 'A filthy hussy, who should be wiped from the earth because she can't keep her legs closed and wants to trap an upstanding vampire into believing they were meant to be together.'"

A soft voice spoke and August turned to see a slight

woman curled up on the ground. "I promise Your Majesty. I didn't. I... wasn't trying to... he...my skin vibrated and something pulled me in his direction. I just wanted to talk to him." The witch peeked over the arms she wrapped around herself as protection, and he didn't miss the ring of bruises blooming on her bicep. Her eyes were wide and her lip quivered.

Fuck.

They're mates. You see why I couldn't just let him go.

Bloody fucking fuck.

August shook his head. *You can't kill him either, little witch. What happens to her if he dies? Doesn't she deserve her mate?*

He's a fucking prick, August. You can't expect me to allow her to be alone with him. He's never going to accept her. He's never going to accept our daughter as our future heir.

What would you have me do?

Emery pressed her lips together, inky black swirling in her amber eyes. He was asking his mate, but he saw the fight in her gaze as she tried to formulate an answer that was both diplomatic and fed her need to make an example out of the idiot dressed in her thorns.

August turned back to Aberforth. "What do you feel when you look at her?"

"It doesn't matter what I feel," Aberforth spat, blood pooling at his lip. "It's wrong. It's because they cursed us when they created us. I didn't ask to feel this way. None of us did. And you keep trying to put a band-aid on the problem by making promises you can't keep. You keep telling us we are going to come around and see them the way you do, Your Majesty, but we aren't. We don't. And we are no closer to a new supernatural world today than we were months ago. The Mistress is in the wind, and we are being forced to become something we never wanted to be."

"Mates are fated by the stars. It's the future." Emery spoke with the decree of a queen, but what she failed to understand was that if they forced people, then they were no better than the dictator before them.

Aberforth huffed a laugh and shook his head. "It's not my future, witch. I am not of the stars. I'm created from blood and magic, and nothing more. My children will be those I have sired, not half-blood filth."

August growled. "I will not have you tarnishing hybrids. My daughter is the future of this kingdom. You would do well to remember that and show her the respect she deserves."

"She may be your heir, but she doesn't have to be my future. I will not live where I am forced to recognize her as my queen."

"What would you have me do, Aberforth?" August asked him the same question he had of his mate. He knew neither of them would back down, but neither of them had an answer either.

"Find a way to sever the mate bonds."

The crowd around them was a mix of gasps and cheers.

"You would have me deny my people the right to their mates?" Emery growled.

August hid the wince at the line Emery had drawn in the sand. She'd said 'my people.' Not our people. Not the kingdom. My people. It was the first time he'd ever heard her slip and define herself as wholly witch. But it was the wrong move. She hadn't yet perfected the political game. It was one of finesse and strategy, not heart and emotions.

"Even if it were possible," Emery continued, "vampires were literally created to be bonded mates. Protectors of witches."

"I didn't give my consent to be bonded to *your* people." Aberforth threw the dagger Emery had unsheathed with her words. "I want nothing to do with you. With the witches," he nodded to the witch still cowering on the floor, curling his lip in disgust. "I want nothing to do with *her*. Take *your* people, and get the hell out of *our* kingdom."

The entire room was silent except for the tiny gasp from the rejected witch, followed by soft sobs.

"Get him out of my sight," Emery hissed. "I want him locked up in a dungeon where he can't hurt any other witches."

Gods help me. He offered up the prayer to any deity who would listen, because his mate was likely going to kill him.

"He's right," August whispered.

Emery whipped her dagger-like gaze toward him. "What?" she shrieked.

"I love you, little witch. I want to spend every gods-damned day with you for the rest of eternity, but who am I to decide what is best for everyone else?"

He'd for sure be sleeping on the couch that night. Hell, she might kick him out of their entire damn suite.

But it needed to be said. Not because he needed to save face with his people and avoid looking weak, but also because it was true. They couldn't lead with an iron fist, and that meant hearing the worries of their people.

"You're the gods-damned king, August. That's who you are to decide."

"I am the king, but I am not my father. If it had turned

out that Callum and Sloane were mates, what would you tell him?"

Emery didn't take more than a second to consider her answer. "That she could be different."

It was a knee-jerk answer and he knew it. She wouldn't force Callum, someone she loved and respected, to be mated to a murderer.

His gaze narrowed and his heart ached for his mate. "Can she? She's killed so many."

"So have you."

August took a step toward her and took her hands in his. He searched her eyes and down their bond pleaded for her to understand. "But I wanted to do better. To be better. She doesn't. Aberforth doesn't."

"Hey, wait, don't lump me in with—"

"I suggest you shut your mouth if you want to remain able to use it," August snarled.

He turned back to Emery. "Your grandmother created us to protect you in a time when witches were hunted and needed protection. That is no longer the case. And while some of us are ready to find our mates, that won't be the case for all. They deserve the option to walk away."

"And what about their mates? What happens to them?" Her voice didn't waver, but their bond revealed the desperation in her words.

He ran his thumb over her fingers, praying the connection reminded her this wasn't his fight, but his people's, and he couldn't ignore them. "They figure it out. They continue to live as they did before."

"You can't ignore the bond," Emery spat, the darkness in her eyes swelling with her emotions. *You know that.*

August chewed on that thought. She wasn't wrong, but

he couldn't force his people to give in. He didn't have the choice, but he loved Emery before he knew she was his mate. Everything about her called to him, and he willingly gave into the call. But there was a time when he wished for the same thing. The dissolution of the bond that tied him to her. He couldn't say for sure that all mates would love each other. But it wasn't his place to force them into something they didn't want. If they figured it out on their own later, that was on them. It wasn't for anyone else to decide.

He chewed the inside of his cheek, and spoke the words that felt like a physical dagger to his chest. "Maybe we need to consider looking into a way to terminate bonds for those who don't wish to be bonded."

"Seriously?" Emery yanked her hands from his, and her eyes lost every ounce of amber.

"Emery, I'm not saying—"

"I know exactly what you're saying. You're giving the vampires an out and condemning witches to a life unfulfilled."

"We don't know that it will be unfulfilled if the bonds don't exist."

Emery glared at August. To anyone else it would seem as though they were silently waiting for the other to back down, but the reality was their bond hummed as though it were a tuning fork struck too hard. The vibrations echoing anger and dissent rocked him, but it was the underlying distrust that gave him pause.

They'd come so far. Over and over, they found their way back to one another. This wasn't supposed to break them. So why did it feel like they were once again a million miles apart?

"Do with him what you want, but you better make sure

I don't see him again," Emery spat. She fell to her knees and pulled the sobbing witch into her arms. "Let's go, Sage. I've got you."

She helped the young witch up and, without looking back, exited the ballroom. One by one, the witches present followed her, leaving him standing alone with his people.

He watched her walk away, helpless to do anything. There was no winning in this situation. It was either disappoint his mate or his kingdom.

The moment Emery disappeared, Aberforth fell to the floor and the vines that held him loosened. He lifted himself and grumbled. "That wicked—"

"I suggest you think very carefully about how you speak about my mate," August growled.

Aberforth froze and averted his gaze. "I'm sorry, Your Majesty. Thank you for standing up for me."

August fought the urge to spit on the man in a pile at his feet. "I didn't do it for you. You are a piece of shit who lays his hands on women and in no world do you deserve to breathe based on that fact alone. But I do believe it's not my place to force anyone into accepting their mate, despite it being the best thing that ever happened to me."

"Thank you anyway," Aberforth muttered.

"I suggest you make yourself scarce. In fact, you should consider leaving the castle."

Aberforth jerked back, his eyes wide with confusion. "But, Your Majesty, I'm one of your trusted advisors. You can't just kick me out."

"I can. But I'm not going to. The facts are, my mate doesn't trust you, and I'm inclined to side with her. While I am not going to build my kingdom on a tyrannical rule, I have been transparent that I am trying to build a kingdom that is inclusive. My daughter is the best parts of my mate and myself. She will one day rule as my heir, and if you can't learn to be okay with that, then there isn't a place here for you."

Aberforth kept a stone face, his eyes narrowed. It was the look of a man who had lost, but was not out of the game and that worried August more than if he'd taken a swing at him in front of his entire court.

August then added. "There's also the fact that my mate might very well castrate you if she sees you again."

"I'll take my leave, then." He bent at the waist in a low bow, likely the last sign of respect he'd ever show August, and stormed from the ballroom.

August glanced at the remaining vampires. "If anyone else feels like Aberforth, I suggest you think long and hard about whether or not this is the kingdom for you. As we have said before, there will be no repercussions if you go, but we will not tolerate the blatant harm of any members of our kingdom whether they be vampire, witch, or wolf."

The room remained quiet.

When he was sure there was nothing left to say, August turned and left them to gossip amongst themselves. He was sure the entirety of the castle would know what happened by dinner if they didn't already.

Malcolm fell into step beside him. "You are an idiot, you know that?"

Well, that didn't take long.

August stopped in the hallway and ran his fingers through his hair "I assume you've heard?"

"Oh, I got an earful." Malcolm looked both ways, before nodding to one of the many sitting rooms behind them. Once they were both inside, he asked, "You're really going to ask the witches to find a way to dissolve mate bonds?"

August shrugged and shook his head. "We can't even figure out how to undo the mark of the Culling, what makes you think that they'll be able to find a way to undo the bonds completely?"

"But if they can?" Malcolm pressed. And August knew what he wanted him to say. He wanted him to say that everything he'd said had been for show, but he couldn't.

August grimaced. "Then yes, I will support it."

Malcolm threw up his hands and cursed under his breath before retreating to the bar in the corner of the room. August thanked the gods his father thought to have whiskey stocked in any and every sitting room for occasions such as this. "You and I both know that's not the right answer."

August followed him and waited for Malcolm to offer him a glass. When he didn't, August poured his own. He sipped the decades-old liquid, savoring the burn. "I can't force them to choose their mate. It may be the best thing that ever happened to us, but I can't pretend that bigotry won't still exist after all is said and done. I'd rather dissolve her bond than force Sage to live a life tethered to an asshole like Aberforth."

"I can understand that, but until then you are condemning her to live a life with an unbearable ache in her chest."

"Better an ache and alive than the alternative." He finished the contents of his glass and poured himself another before crossing the room and sitting in one of the uncomfortable high-back chairs.

Malcolm followed, but didn't sit. He stood in front of

August, looking down on him with the weight of not only his decisions but his kingdom. "Could you live without Emery?"

"Bloody hell, Malcolm. You know I couldn't, but you didn't see the disgust in his eyes." August wished there was another way, but how could he condemn a woman to live with a mate who hated her? "What if it were Lina? What if her future mate is a psychopath or a purist? The stars aren't kind. They will fuck us every which way if it serves a greater purpose. I...I would do anything for my daughter to know the love I have with her mother. If that means giving her the option to walk away so she may find love outside of her mate, I would do anything to save her."

Malcolm shook his head. "This is a fucking mess."

"You're telling me." August ran a hand through his hair and tugged the ends. "I'm worried about Emery."

He reached down their bond, knowing before he did that he'd hit the expansive wall she'd erected between them. The look on her face when he'd told her he'd support his people's decision if they could destroy the bonds haunted him. There wasn't a world in which he'd ever want to fight with Emery, but he was trying to look at this from a logical standpoint, while she was lost in emotion.

"I'm worried about your balls. She was fucking pissed when she reached the witches' camp. She barely got the story out before she was cursing your name, and I knew that was my cue to find you."

"She's too stressed as it is and this isn't helping. Not to mention, I think her dark magic is growing restless."

"Her eyes?"

August nodded, letting out a weighted sigh. "You noticed too?"

"Yeah. Yesterday she got frustrated when Dorian suggested again that we let him sacrifice himself, and I saw a flicker of darkness. Has she said anything to you?"

"No." He shook his head. "She's taking on so much between Lina, the witches, and ensuring she's a present member of our court."

"What about a girls' night?"

August cocked a brow. "A what?"

"You know, like the bachelorette parties that came into the club sometimes."

"You want me to send my future wife out with the girls for a bachelorette party where they will do… what? Take shots of tequila and dance with strange men? You do realize we're in the middle of a war?"

It was official. Malcolm had been hanging out with Lily and the witches too much. He was trading in his assholish nature for the sexually charged prowess of his mate's people.

"No. Gods, you need to stop strategizing for five minutes and watch more movies. I'm saying let's send the women to Scotland for a night with games, booze, and music, and give them a night off from all," he waved his hands around, gesturing at the castle, "this."

August weighed his suggestion. It wasn't a terrible idea, and Scotland's wards were as fortified—if not more so—as those around the castle. Not to mention there was no way he was getting on Emery's good side anytime soon. It might be a good way to get her to let off some steam.

"Fine, but you need to get Emery on board."

"Not a problem. We both know I'm her favorite Nicholson," he said with a wink.

August rolled his eyes and stood. "Thank you."

Malcolm pulled him into a half hug. "I still think dissolving bonds is a terrible idea, but I understand why you are fighting for your people. I'll always stand beside you."

They left the sitting room, and August headed back to his office while Malcolm left to find Emery. As much as he felt the need to pull her into his arms and make her understand where he was coming from, he knew it wasn't the time. He needed to finish the alliance requests; and, if he was honest, he wanted to give Emery time to cool down.

Hopefully that would help him protect the integrity of his balls.

Chapter Fourteen

AUGUST

Somehow Malcolm pulled it off. Emery and the other women were off having a girls' night with at-home spa kits and more popcorn than he thought was necessary, and likely talking an epic ton of shit about him. Not that he was in any place to question it. He was happy each of the women was taking a step back and relaxing, especially Emery. They each did so much for each of their respective kingdoms and the future of the supernatural world. They deserved the break.

Emery hadn't exactly thawed toward him after the Aberforth incident earlier that week, but he was hoping some girl time might help her along being able to talk about it without the conversation ending with her throwing whatever she could grab at his dick. He knew he was right in his decision to back his people in giving them a choice, even if it made him public enemy number one with Emery.

August stared down at his daughter and hummed his favorite jazz tune. Lina's eyes fluttered and her lashes swept over her cheeks as she finally drifted off to sleep.

Emery had been worried about leaving her, but he was a parent, too—he could handle some time alone with his daughter.

He hadn't anticipated how much he would enjoy it. He'd cleared his schedule and the two of them lounged around, doing tummy time and watching educational kids' shows that would undoubtedly expand her month-old brain and make her a bona fide genius by the time she was five.

He shook his head and smiled. This is what they were fighting for. Moments like this. The uneventful evenings with his hybrid daughter. Her future and the future of all mates and their children.

With silent steps, he slid out of the room and gently shut the door before heading to the bar cart in the corner of the common room. He was exhausted, but after his first successful night alone with Lina, he more than deserved a celebratory whiskey.

The clink of ice hitting the glass tumbler was interrupted when the door to the suite flew open, and Braxton appeared heaving and covered in blood.

August dropped the glass as his eyes took stock of any injuries Brax may have.

His general shook his head, "It's not mine." And then he muttered the words August hoped he'd never hear in his castle again. "We're under attack."

Time stood still, and August's chest constricted. In every previous war, he'd had nothing on the line but his own life and the respect of his father; this time, it was different. This time there was the sleeping child in the next room and the woman he loved half a world away to consider.

"Why didn't I hear anything?" He tipped his ear and expanded his senses. All he heard was an almost eerie silence. It normally would have struck him as odd, but he was so wrapped up in Lina that he hadn't realized he couldn't hear the beautiful chaos that usually flooded the castle after dark.

"The alarms wouldn't sound. And now that you mention it," Braxton paused and his gaze narrowed. "I can't hear it up here either."

"You weren't meant to," Dorian interjected, crossing the room from where he'd appeared by the window. His shirt was ripped across the front, and he wore a splattering of blood across his face. "I think you're the target. Well, one of them."

"Sloane?" August snarled, but he already knew the answer. There was only one person who would dare attack his castle. That didn't mean he didn't hope it was someone else. Someone they had a fighting chance of defeating.

Dorian nodded.

Bloody hell.

"How and where did they penetrate the wards?" August asked, his brain sliding into battle strategy.

"We're not sure how they got past them, but they entered through the front gates and stormed the entrance. Our sentinels were no match for her beasts." Braxton's voice didn't waver, but August didn't miss the fear in his general's eyes. This man had seen war; to see him shaken spoke volumes. "They keep saying 'Surrender, King of Vampires.'"

"Beasts?"

Dorian answered, "Monsters. Half-wolf, half-human, but not in the way Draven and his people are. They aren't like anything I've ever seen before. They are dead, but alive, and wholly magic."

Fuck. So, this was the army she was creating. A collection of monster hybrids that they knew nothing about.

"Has anyone gathered the sentinels? Braxton said the alarms won't sound."

Dorian shook his head. "I've tried to gather the witches and the sentinels that aren't on duty, but they are trapped in their respective camps. They're sitting ducks and the men on duty at the castle are no match for... whatever they are."

"Trapped?"

"I mean, they can't get out. I can get in because my fae magic isn't hindered by whatever darkness she's cast, but I can't portal like Emery. I can't get them out. And even if I could, I'm not sure the magic would be able to penetrate whatever barrier Sloane's created, because I'm sure the witches are trying."

"Bloody hell. How the fuck did this happen?"

Neither of his men answered. It was as much rhetorical as it was a valid question. Rage filled his blood. He ground his teeth together as he quickly processed the situation.

His castle was under siege, and they had no army, no magic, nothing to fight Sloane with. They were sitting ducks waiting to be slaughtered. History wasn't supposed to repeat itself. Not when they had done everything to prevent it. There were complicated wards in place and the depths of sentinels patrolling should have been more than enough to stop a second attack on the castle, but with the ease Sloane's forces had strolled into the castle unannounced, you would have thought they'd forgotten to lock the door and been caught with their pants around their ankles.

August ran a hand through his hair, gripping the length at the back of his neck. "What's happening now?"

"I sent Brax up here to get you and told the castle sentinels to retreat and get as many people to the rendezvous points as possible, and I'd be there as soon as I could. Malcolm is ensuring your mother and Thea get there as well."

"Can you get them out?"

Dorian shook his head. "Not by myself. I need a powerful witch who can hold open a portal."

Emery, we need you and the girls back at the castle.

Seconds passed like hours as he waited for her response, but nothing came. August sucked in a breath, and reached out down the bond. It caught in his throat when he felt nothing. No soft edges, no lingering breath of fresh air—even when she blocked him, he could always feel her there, breathing and living on the other end. After what felt like the longest seconds of his life, he detected a faint edge that told him it was possible she was alive somewhere in the world, but she wasn't at the end of his bond.

He leaned forward and placed his hands on his knees as all the air left his lungs. Every ounce of rage he'd felt moments ago at the thought of the castle being breached shifted to bone-chilling fear. Images of Emery lying on the ground in a puddle of her own blood filtered through his mind. No matter how much he tried to breathe, he couldn't get enough air to fill his lungs. He searched the bond over and over, trying to breach it, but came up with nothing but cold emptiness.

"I can't reach her," he choked out. "It's like she's shut the bond, but it's wide fucking open and I can't get to her."

Dorian's eyes widened and August didn't like the trepidation he saw in their depths. "Where is she?"

"She's at the cottage with Lily, Flora, and Bronwyn. Girls' night. We didn't announce it for their safety." He spoke between panicked breaths.

Dorian knelt before him and pressed his hand to his chest. "I'll find her. But I need you to shelve this panic attack for when we have the time."

August looked up, expecting Dorian's hard glare. If it were anyone else, that's exactly what he would find. But his second understood what it was like to lose the one you loved. It was a battle Dorian fought every day. So, it shouldn't have come as a surprise that he saw nothing but loyalty and devotion settle in Dorian's gaze. It was enough to calm August's momentary slip and reignite the fire in his blood.

"Find her," he growled.

"I'll give my last breath if that's what it takes. I'll find her and we'll get our people to safety, but I need you to—"

"Take Lina with you," August ordered. "I won't be able to put the kingdom first unless I know that she's safe."

"Perfect, I'll grab your mother too and take them to—"

"No." August held up his hand. "Don't tell me or Braxton. It's better if we don't know, especially if I truly am the target."

Dorian narrowed his gaze, and August sensed the hesitation when he agreed.

"Go." He turned to his general, the calm of war settling in his bones now that he knew his daughter would be safe and Dorian was going to Emery. "Braxton, you're with me."

Dorian nodded. "Don't do anything stupid, Your Majesty."

A wicked smile tipped his lips, and he allowed the darkest parts of him—the parts that Emery had begged him to allow free—to wash over his mind, body, and soul. His fangs elongated and when he glanced at Dorian, he spoke a solemn vow. "I'm going to end this."

Chapter Fifteen

EMERY

How the hell did she let Malcolm and Lily talk her into this? As much as she loved being back in Scotland and hanging out with all the women in her life, this seemed over the top. Not that Emery had anything to compare it to. The Culling women were far too prim and proper for this, and growing up she'd only had Wren as a friend. She was older than Emery and though they were close, they weren't braid-each-other's-hair-and-swap-sex-stories close.

Which probably should have been the first red flag that Wren would turn on Emery and side with her evil twin sister.

Still, Emery couldn't deny it was nice to just hang out with the girls and try to forget about how August had publicly defended his advisor's desire to end mate bonds and her sister was still nowhere to be found.

"I can't confirm or deny if the rumors are true." Flora's cheeks flushed a bright pink, and Emery couldn't tell how much of it was from the wine versus embarrassment. "I will say it's the best sex I've ever had."

Emery did her best to stifle her grin. That absolutely

had to be the alcohol talking, because there was no way her sweet best friend would ever divulge information about her sex life if she were sober.

Bronwyn threw a pillow across the coffee table, narrowly missing the giant bowl of popcorn and barrel of licorice, hitting Flora in the face where she sat with Lily on the opposite couch. "You can't say that and not tell us about it!"

Flora shrugged, not bothering to hide her ear-to-ear grin. "Bag yourself a wolf, and you can find out what knots are all about."

"I still can't believe Callum sent you to Moon Ridge and you came back a hybrid and mated to Draven," Emery mused. She wasn't quite buzzed, but she was definitely more relaxed than she had been in what felt like forever.

It was a nice change of pace, and Bronwyn, Lily, and Flora were under just as much stress as she was. They understood what it meant to put everything before themselves and lead in the name of what they believed in. Because their kingdoms deserved better.

Emery had to admit that perhaps Malcolm had the right idea sending the women off for a night filled with movies, facemasks, and too much wine. She'd never tell him that, though. Especially since she knew he was doing it for August.

She sighed internally. Even though they were fighting, he'd done everything he could to support her after their initial argument. And after every subsequent argument. He wanted to make sure she knew that just because he was fighting for the rights of his people, he still valued her as his mate. He didn't want to dissolve their bond.

Emery understood his argument, but she couldn't

imagine living a life without him. She lived with magic in her veins, with the ability to see the possibilities of dozens of futures. It made sense to her that the stars would give them mates. They balanced each other. It was a version of supernatural yin and yang. But the vampires didn't live by the stars, they didn't feel the magic in their blood. She wasn't sure she could ever make them understand the gravity of their bonds.

"You and me both," Flora snickered and sipped her drink. "Imagine my surprise when Draven dropped the mate bomb on me, followed by his knot."

"Did you ever want to walk away?" Emery asked, knowing she was skirting the line of breaking the rule that they would not talk about kingdom business. "I mean, after you found out he was your mate."

"Actually, yes." Flora's eyes softened, and Emery scooted to the edge of her seat, intrigued to hear her answer. "I'm not a wolf, and I wasn't a hybrid yet, so I didn't understand the depths of a wolf's mate. The way the connection is carved into their soul. It didn't help that Draven had also agreed to marry another woman and then dropped this bomb on me once we were in Reika's realm with killer shadow wolves and no way out."

Emery chuckled. "But you came around, right?"

Hope dripped from her voice. She needed something, anything to help explain to August why mates were so important.

Flora raised a brow and smiled. "I see what you're doing here, Em, and we agreed no castle talk."

"I know." Emery sighed. "I'm just feeling a bit helpless and it's not easy fighting with August."

"I can't imagine it would be." Flora picked up a piece of

popcorn and plopped it in her mouth. "But I will say that I'm pretty sure I loved Draven before he told me. And it's possible that made all the difference as to why I was okay with it."

Emery chewed on that piece of information and everything August had said. He had asked her what she would think if Sloane ended up being Callum's mate. Her response had been… flawed, she could admit that to herself. The truth was, it was impossible for her to understand a bond without love. They were supposed to go hand in hand, but maybe they didn't. Maybe one needed to precede the other for it to be successful. But if that were the case, then it didn't make sense for the stars to create the bond.

Fuck, her head hurt just from thinking about it.

"Okay, but like, is it always swollen or just when you fuck him?" Bronwyn giggled, changing the subject, and held up her fist, opening and closing it, mimicking how she figured a knot functioned. "I'm asking purely for scientific reasons, of course."

"Oh yeah, I'm sure it's scientific," Lily scoffed, but her smile betrayed her mock disgust. "Just as I'm sure it was scientific when you asked me last week if I could make Malcolm hard by sending horny emotions through the mate bond."

Bronwyn's mouth dropped open, and she clutched her chest as if there were pearls there. "It was a genuine scientific curiosity. If I'm to find my mate someday, I'll have a leg up on how all that works."

"You will find your mate, Bron," Flora reassured. They still didn't have a definitive way to gather the dark essence from Dorian's blood, but they weren't giving up.

"We are definitely not going down that road right now." Bronwyn stood up and rounded the sofa over to the kitchen island where there was a spread of snacks Callum had made for them. The damn vampire might as well have been a five-star chef with his skills in the kitchen. Bronwyn popped a chocolate-covered raspberry in her mouth and then bent over and pulled out two bottles of liquor. "No castle talk! Stars know we all need the break. Soooooooooo, how about we turn off whatever this 'music' is and I'll make us some shots."

Emery looked at Flora, and they both nodded and jumped up from their seats at the same time. She liked drunk Bronwyn.

Lily pinched the bridge of her nose but did a terrible job of hiding the way her lips tipped up at the corners. "I'm pretty sure that's not what August had in mind when he asked us to have a girls' night."

"No, he'd want us to have a knitting circle and trade recipes," Emery muttered sarcastically as she searched for shot glasses, opening cupboard after cupboard until she found what she was looking for. "I have been covered in nothing but spit up and breastmilk for the last month, so I, for one, am going to take advantage of this tiny taste of freedom."

"Here, here!" Bronwyn shouted and lifted the bottles over her head.

"Is that what I think it is?" Emery eyed the slim bottle with a purple and gold label in Bronwyn's left hand.

Bronwyn wiggled her eyebrows at Emery and nodded. "A certain prince who shall not be named may have smuggled me a bottle of the top-shelf whiskey from behind the bar at August's club."

Emery tipped her head back and laughed. "Oooh he is not going to like that."

She remembered the first night they met, when she ran up a hefty tab drinking the stuff. Well, she didn't actually remember it. She'd gotten more drunk than was safe to with the two vampire princes who sought to change her life forever. At the time, it seemed like the worst night of her life, but now looking back, it was the stars at play. There weren't many memories after the first few shots, but tucked away was a hazy picture that involved that bottle and her mate singing to her after she begged him to dance.

Lily rolled her eyes, and Emery was sure she was sending Malcolm a slew of irritating feelings down their bond. It was probably a good thing they didn't have a soul bond and couldn't communicate like her and August because he might not like what she had to say. Still, she couldn't deny how perfect they were for each other. Total opposites, yet somehow, they completed each other in the way only mates could. Lily pushed Malcolm to see himself as more than just the useless spare he'd always been told he was, and he encouraged her to put herself out there and give life outside of isolation a chance. The way they complemented each other made Emery believe that occasionally the stars got something right.

How was it that August and the noble vampires couldn't see that?

"Do we have anything other than whiskey?" Flora asked.

"Do we?" Bronwyn crouched down and pulled out two more bottles and a mixer. "I came prepared. Contrary to popular belief, I had a life before the inner circle. You are looking at Miss Sweet Concoction, New Orleans' premiere mixologist at The Alchemist Club."

Emery choked on a laugh picturing Bronwyn slinging drinks in a seedy bar on Bourbon Street. "You are just full of surprises. And to think when I met you, I thought you were just a stuffy scholar."

With a shrug and a glint in her eye, Bronwyn started pouring. "I became what I needed to, just like we all did."

Lily sauntered over to the kitchen island and stood next to Flora. "I just want to go on the record saying this is a terrible idea."

"Noted." Bronwyn winked.

Lily let out a slow sigh, the last of her resolve leaving with it. "Alright. What are we drinking?"

Emery and Flora cheered and the three of them slid onto barstools and watched Bronwyn expertly spin bottles while she regaled them with stories about her late nights in New Orleans. Emery countered with stories of her own from her time at her uncle's bar, while Flora and Lily chimed in with stories of aristocrats gone wild at various galas.

For a moment, they were just four women enjoying each other's company.

Flora changed up the music, and after another two rounds, she jumped on the island with Bronwyn and the two of them began an epic sing-off to the only song that mattered in bars across America, Journey's *Don't Stop Believin'*.

Halfway through the song, a wave of nausea rolled through Emery. At first, she shrugged it off, assuming the mixing of wine and liquor was catching up with her. It wouldn't be the first time she'd made that mistake. She got up and poured herself a tall glass of water, but the feeling didn't go away. It morphed from something deep in her core to a shiver up her spine that left the hairs on the back of her neck standing on end.

Emery mouthed the words to the song, but her focus was no longer on her friends. Her gaze darted around the cottage. Nothing seemed to be out of place and none of the other women seemed bothered. The doors were locked and the wards would have alerted them long before anyone made it to the door. Still, she couldn't shake the disturbance in the air.

The song came to an end, and just as she was about to ask Lily and Bronwyn if they felt anything off, the front door swung open and a wave of heavy magic slammed into them.

"I wish you guys would have waited for me. It seems my invitation to girls' night got lost in the mail."

Time stood still. And Emery hesitated. She fucking hesitated.

She'd dreamed of this moment. Planned exactly what she would do. She could have blamed the alcohol, but deep down Emery knew the real reason she didn't immediately dismember her own flesh and blood.

Sloane, on the other hand, couldn't care less.

By the time Emery gained her bearings and called her magic to her hands, it was too late.

Sloane threw down what looked like a crystal ball and purple magic exploded like smoke throughout the room. When it settled, a wicked smile tipped her lips, and Emery was frozen along with everyone around them.

Her sister's voice dripped with sarcasm. "You should

really see the look on all your faces. I'd almost think you were shocked to see me. I told you I was coming."

The note?

Emery scrambled to remember every word her sister said, but there was no indication of this. Nothing that could have prepared her. And now she was once again helpless to her sister's magic.

Panic threatened to rise in the back of her throat, but Emery swallowed it down along with the darkness in her chest. It sent her images of growing vines and tightening them around Sloane's throat until she stopped breathing, followed by calling all the blood from her body and burning away every ounce of the tainted substance. But even if she did want to follow through, there was nothing she could do so long as Sloane held control of her.

Sloane sauntered away from the door and stopped in front of Emery. "Don't worry, sister, I'm not going to slit your throat this time. I was surprised to see you survived, but leave it to your mate to figure out a way to keep you breathing. That's when I realized it's so much more fun to surprise you and steal your blood when I'm running low."

The sadistic bitch.

Emery studied every move Sloane made. Rage and sadness fought for dominance in her chest. She shouldn't care, but her sister looked terrible. The amber eyes that should have matched her own were more black than gold and sunken in against ashen skin. Her blonde hair had lost its luster, and she was impossibly thin. The darkness was consuming her one strand of inky magic at a time.

Maybe she had been right not to touch the stuff, even if the edges of it tempted her more often than not.

Sloane lifted her hand and inspected the sharpened

stiletto nail on her blackened index finger. "I promise not to leave you for dead this time, but I suggest you find a first aid kit. Or maybe Flora can heal you. Your mate is going to be…busy for a while."

Panic gripped Emery's spine, and she instinctively reached for the bond tethering her to August. A knot formed in the back of her throat as she desperately tried with everything she had to reach him, but Emery couldn't feel her mate. It was like the bond was stretched out—an endless highway in an emotionless desert.

She reached for his soul and relief flooded her to find that he was still alive, but she couldn't communicate with him. Whatever the hell magic Sloane was using to bind her kept her from August.

Sloane dug her nail into Emery's wrist and sliced through the skin. Her blood dripped down her fingertips to where Sloane set a glass vial. Once she'd collected the blood she'd come for, she winked at Emery and smiled. "Thank you for your contribution, sister."

Emery screamed in her mind for her sister to stop, but it was useless.

Sloane's gaze drifted over the women as she tucked the vial with Emery's blood in the pocket of her coat. "Don't worry, your mates are safe with me."

With that ominous statement lingering between them, she turned on her heel and calmly strutted out the door.

Hell broke loose the second the door latched and the spell broke. Emery fell to her knees, her blood dripping onto the floor. Flora's lips pulled back in a snarl, and she raced after Sloane. Pulling the knob with enough force that the door should have flown off the hinges, her tiny frame strained. She slammed her fists against the wood and tried again, but it still didn't budge.

Emery's vision vibrated in time with the ringing in her ears. Her gaze shifted to where Bronwyn and Lily were calling their magic to their palms and mouthing the incantations that should have opened a portal.

Nothing happened.

Emery called her own magic to her palms but nothing came. She called to the elements, but none responded. The wind stayed calm and the earth ignored her heart. Even the darkness in her was restricted to her chest, begging her to let it consume her and find a way out.

A cold sweat trickled down Emery's spine, and each of the women's faces reflected the fear bubbling within her. They were the most powerful females in the supernatural world and they'd been reduced to four walls and no way out.

And Sloane was on her way to their mates. To Lina.

Emery tipped her head back and sent up a prayer to the stars, begging them to protect her kingdom. Her family. Her mate.

Then she opened her eyes and welcomed the darkness into her soul.

Chapter Sixteen

AUGUST

Chaos was too simple a word to describe what he found when he reached the bottom floor of the castle.

There wasn't a single surface that wasn't covered in blood splatters. Bodies littered the floor, some still twitching, while limbs were scattered around. It wasn't until they'd reached the hallway outside the grand foyer that August got his first glimpse at the monsters that invaded his castle and massacred his people.

The term monsters wasn't enough—they were vicious killing machines.

Human legs, clothed in cargo pants, gave way to broad exposed torsos and chests covered in thin fur. Some gray and some brown with a few speckled in between. The fur continued over their backs in a single line down their spines. Some of them had tails that poked through their pants, while others didn't.

Their faces were chiseled, with sharp cheekbones that then scrunched almost as if a snout never grew where it should have. Their noses upturned like a wolf's, but their fangs were all vampire.

One of the monsters scanned the hallway, looking in their direction. August quickly snagged Braxton's shirt and tugged him into an alcove before the beast saw them. If he'd once thought he was prepared to reconcile a new kind of wolf-vampire hybrid, he'd been wrong. He lost all ability to think when he saw its eyes. An eerie glowing amber stared back at him, with black specks that floated in its irises.

Witch.

These had to be what Sloane was trying to make. What Ansel helped her create. And he'd bet money it's what Sloane was using Emery's blood for.

It didn't matter that his sentinels had guns, as their shots ricocheted off some kind of magic shield that surrounded them. And though their swords made contact, they didn't pierce the Kevlar-like skin of the beasts. It was like they were hitting them with gods-damned pool noodles.

The monsters, on the other hand, had no problem slitting the throats of anyone they came across and tearing their hearts out for good measure. They were faster than his men, who were no match for their enhanced genetics.

His kingdom had been prepared for a lot, but nothing could have prepared them for this. None of the alarms had sounded and all of their forces were trapped outside the castle. He'd fought many witches in his long lifetime, but vampire speed had always been their advantage. His men could move undetected and take out the most powerful of witches with the snap of a neck. But Sloane was more powerful than they'd ever imagined. Her magic had been a force to be reckoned with at the hunt, but they had adapted after that. They'd fortified their wards. She shouldn't have been able to touch them.

But she did. Once again, she'd hit them where it hurt. And he'd failed to protect his people.

They waited until the monsters moved into the foyer, and then August and Braxton slipped from the alcove and rounded the last corner before reaching the grand staircase. August nearly ran into Draven's wolf outside the royals' ballroom entrance, blood matted in his onyx fur. August had no idea when he got back from Moon Ridge, but he was happy to have him at his side.

When Draven looked up and saw August, he immediately shifted. "Have you contacted the women?"

August glanced both ways and saw the shadows of two beasts closing in on them. He pushed Draven and Braxton into the royal suite and slammed the door behind them. "No. I can't reach Emery."

A growl erupted from Draven's chest, and he punched the wall beside him, cracking the stone.

"Dorian is going to them. He's going to get them to safety."

"Good." He nodded, but his eyes were distant, likely working a million miles a minute to compartmentalize everything. It was the same thing August did. "They need to get far away from here. Hell, we need to get out of here."

August let out a low growl. "I'm not surrendering my home to her, Draven. This is my kingdom. My people. She doesn't get to take them from me. From us."

"Wake up, August." Draven gestured around them, his eyes wide. "She's already taken it. There are defected wolves rounding up members of your court and corralling them so Sloane's witches can then bind them in shackles.

There are hybrid monstrosities taking out sentinels by the dozen without any reinforcements. We aren't going to survive this unless we regroup. We are fighting with one arm tied behind our backs and a fatal wound to the gut."

"Defected wolves? When did that happen?"

"Ambersey. Fernando decided Sloane was the better option for him to gain power."

Fucking hell. They couldn't catch a break. He couldn't charge in and save the day. There was no saving his home from the clutches of dark magic. There was only lessening the blow; saving those they could and getting the hell out.

He hated that Draven was right.

How did they get here? He'd been having a beautiful night with his daughter while his kingdom fought to stay alive.

Because that's how she wanted it.

Fucking Sloane. When he got his hands on her, he would enjoy slowly ripping her apart.

"What do you want to do?" Braxton asked, ready to follow whatever orders he gave.

August quickly calculated all the potential scenarios and weapons they had at their disposal. "Okay. We need to get as many people out as we can, and we need to figure out how to get the army and witches out from under Sloane's control. Dorian can bypass Sloane's magic, but he needs a witch powerful enough to hold open a portal for an army."

"Lily and Emery," Draven said, following his thinking.

"Exactly," August nodded. "But we need to give Dorian time to get them. We'll use that time to get everyone out."

"Okay. There are ten monsters in the ballroom. They've got a couple handful of noble hostages situated in the far west corner. We've got a dozen sentinels trying to breach their hold, but they're tiring fast. Kade and Mateo are at the witches' village stopping any monsters heading that way."

August nodded, mentally picturing what his cousin was telling him. "If you can distract the monsters, Braxton should be able to get them out through the feeders' quarters on that side."

Brax nodded. "Absolutely."

Draven narrowed his gaze on August. "What are you going to do?"

A wicked smile tipped his lips. "I'm going to poke the fucking bear."

"Sounds reckless."

"It is." But if he pulled it off, it would be the thing that gave them the time they needed. "Sloane wants me, so I'm going to go right where she expects me."

"Emery will never forgive you if you fuck up. Hell, she'll never forgive me if I let you, and I've seen what she can do. I like my blood in my body, thanks."

"It's me she wants, not any of you. I can sell water to a whale, if given the time. Just hurry your ass up and get them out, then meet me in the throne room."

Draven looked like he wanted to disagree, but the plan was solid. If August could distract Sloane, it would give them enough time to get as many people out as possible. They might even be able to get the army and the village evacuated before he needed backup.

"I want to go on record saying I hate this fucking plan," Draven said, extending his hand. "Good luck."

August shook it, and pulled him in for a half hug. "You too."

They took off in opposite directions, Draven and

Braxton toward the ballroom and August toward the throne room.

He reached the ornate gold-painted doors and came face to face with two of Sloane's abominations. These two were larger than the ones he'd seen when they'd descended the stairs, and they wore sashes across their furred chests, signifying what, he didn't know.

When they saw him, they snarled in unison. "Surrender, King of Vampires."

Fat fucking chance.

August didn't hesitate. He launched himself at the first one, tearing into its neck as he wrapped his hands around its jaw and tore its head from its body. "I'd really rather not," he grunted.

The second monster lunged for August, and narrowly missed him with his clawed grip.

August leapt out of the way and used the monster's forward momentum to his advantage. Moving as fast as he could, he circled behind him and thrust his hand through the monster's back, ripping out his heart.

The monster fell, and August could have sworn he heard the faint whisper of "Mistress" before he hit the ground.

August heaved a breath and dropped the heart beside its former host. He wiped the thick black blood onto the drapery that lined the doors before pushing his way into the throne room.

It was empty, as he'd expected. If she were taking the castle, Sloane wouldn't want to destroy the place where she would hold court. He knew the mind of a power-hungry tyrant. His father had set the perfect example his entire life.

THE UNITED

Each step toward his throne was an anthem. A silent proclamation to no one but himself that no matter what happened that night, this kingdom would survive. He swore an oath that it would live to see another day under his rule.

When he reached his throne, he lowered himself, back straight and chin held strong. The steady beating of his heart rang in his ears as he waited.

It wasn't long before the doors opened, and the Mistress herself stood before him, five monsters surrounding her.

Sloane aimed for this to be her sanctum.

Too bad he wasn't giving it up.

Chapter Seventeen

EMERY

They wanted answers. Emery wanted revenge.

Bronwyn, Lily, and Flora tested every window and door. They tried every spell they could think of and made every attempt to call anyone who could possibly save them.

Nothing worked and no one answered.

Which was exactly how *she* wanted it.

Emery sank into the plush cushions of the couch and called her magic to her palms. It didn't appear, but ice flooded her veins instantly, instead of its usual warmth. She closed her eyes as her blood hummed, the affinity of her darkness exciting beneath her skin. Her other concentrations fought for a seat at the table, her fire licked beneath her skin and gusts of wind blew, throwing up her hair around her. She reveled in it, allowing it to consume her. For the first time in a long, long time she felt the desire to be wicked—no longer a calling, but a welcome force within her.

She called her magic again, fighting against the wall of her sister's magic. Her light was too weak to break through, but her darkness held untapped strength. Emery closed her eyes and focused all her attention on obliterating the wall in front of her. When she opened her eyes, she wasn't surprised to find her magic in her hands, inky orbs with only the barest flecks of gold. Her eyes darted around the cottage, calculating faster than her mind could match all the ways she could continue bypassing her sister's magic. The wards on the cottage were strong, but they weren't impenetrable. The question was, could she escape before her friends noticed the shift in her?

They wouldn't approve, but Emery was tired of playing by their rules. They all wanted the same thing: to end Sloane. This was the way to get it done.

Somewhere in the back of her mind, the thought of killing her sister brought a pang of sadness, but Emery pushed it away. She couldn't think about that now. Not when the kingdom was in danger. When her mate and her daughter's lives could hang in the balance.

She thought back to the last words she'd spoken to him before she'd gone to Scotland. *You can't have it both ways, August. You can't want me and want to end the bonds that tie our people. Get your head out of your ass and embrace the fate of the stars.*

Her heart threatened to shatter, but her darkness wove its way around it and kept the pieces whole, whispering promises that together they'd ensure their mate lived.

They had to.

Suddenly there was a soft pop and the magic in the air rippled around where Dorian appeared.

"There's been an attack on the castle. I need you and Lily to help me get the army and the witches out and—" He stopped mid-sentence, and Emery saw recognition dawn on his face. He shook his head. "You tapped into it. Fuck, Emery, I would tell you this is not the time and that there are so many things you need to know before you give in, but unfortunately this is exactly the time, and we don't have the luxury of preparing you."

Emery cocked a brow, amused he'd finally lost the honorifics when shit hit the fan. She lifted herself from the couch, ignoring his observation. "Is Lina safe?"

"Yes," he nodded, "She's with Cosmina, Thea, and Malcolm at the rendezvous point."

Fuck.

She choked back the emotions that threatened to catch in her throat. That meant August had already called for a retreat. The fear was instantly replaced by the rage that filled her heart at the thought of losing their home. She struggled to keep herself from freeing the turbulence in her soul. It might not hurt Dorian, but she had no doubt it would bring the other three women to their knees.

"Take me to him."

Dorian looked around the room, ignoring her order. "Where are the others?"

"They're upstairs. I'm sure they'll be along shortly." She narrowed her gaze on him, searching for any sign he lied to her. "Dorian, I need you to be straight with me. How bad is it?"

"With you and Lily, we should be able to get everyone out."

Emery's lips twisted into a grimace, and she clenched her fists at her sides. That wasn't exactly an answer, but it told her everything she needed to know.

Lily, Flora, and Bronwyn clamored down the stairs, talking loudly about what they would try next. Their eyes widened when they saw Dorian standing there, but they gasped when they saw Emery. Bronwyn winced and retreated, surely remembering the other times she'd seen Emery lose control. It ended with blood spouting from her eyes, ears, and nose.

Lily padded down and stopped in front of Dorian. She spoke to him, but her eyes kept glancing over to Emery. "How did you get in here? You shouldn't have come, now you'll be stuck too."

"Sloane's magic can't stop my ability to sieve. But I can only take a few people at a time. There was an attack on the castle. The sentinel army and the witches are each trapped in the same sort of one-way vacuum you are. I can get us in, but we need to figure out a way to portal out to be able to get the people in the castle away from Sloane."

Emery shook her head, growing impatient. She was growing more agitated with every second her mate was in the hands of Sloane. Their kingdom was in danger—they needed to *act*, not plan. "I need you to take me to the castle."

"His Majesty will kill me if I take you there."

"And I'll kill you if you don't," she growled.

Dorian narrowed his gaze, his eyes dilating to inky depths that she was sure matched her own. "With all due respect, Your Majesty, you can't kill me, and I am just following orders."

"So now we're back to Your Majesty. I'm not a precious flower, Dorian. You've seen what I can do. Let me fight for our kingdom."

He let out a weighted sigh and his magic crept over her body, leaving painful tingles over her flesh. She gasped and stepped back, as it caught her off guard. It called to her own darkness, but Dorian's held an intensity she didn't think hers could ever match. It was steeped in an ancient strength she couldn't comprehend. It didn't seek to maim, it sought to kill and right then, it was threatening her.

Flora slowly creeped up to Emery's side, careful not to touch her. "Emery, there are—"

Emery snarled at her best friend, cutting her off before returning her fiery gaze back to Dorian. "I will go the second I am free from here, and leaving me makes me a sitting duck ripe for the picking should Sloane return. You know I'm right, so I suggest you just do as I say."

He hesitated, but finally nodded and pulled back his magic. "Fine. But first we get our people to safety."

"Can you get me into my cottage?" Lily asked.

"I should be able to, yes. Why?"

"The wards in my house aren't the same as the castle. They are older and were set by my grandmother. They are linked to one of her safehouses. There is a chance that we will be able to portal from there. Sloane is using dark magic, but she is still young in her practice. The issue is, we would have to move from inside the house."

Dorian mulled over her words, and Emery almost snapped her fingers in front of his face to hurry along his thinking.

Finally, Dorian answered. "It's risky, but worth a try."

Well, thank the gods for that.

"How do we get the army out?" Bronwyn asked, keeping a healthy distance between her and Emery.

Good. At least one of them was thinking clearly. She wouldn't hurt Bronwyn again, but the witch was the only one who had felt her darkness and knew what she was capable of. Emery wanted everyone to look at her with that kind of unwavering skepticism. She wanted them to know she wasn't a helpless queen, which they seemed to have forgotten.

"I'm not sure, but we will figure it out on the way. Right now, we need to get those at the castle rendezvous points out. The castle isn't vacuumed in yet, we can still get in and out. We need to do so before Sloane knows we're there."

"Okay, let's do this," Emery said, her darkness sending her creative ways to dismember every person in the room, not giving a shit that they were her friends. "Every moment we're standing here, more people are likely dying at Sloane's hand. and I, for one, am not going to let that bitch win."

She didn't miss the wince Dorian tried to hide, but she didn't care to look further into what set him off.

"Have you seen Draven?" Flora whispered, anxiety evident in her voice. It was a worry that came from knowing they were likely walking into a bloodbath and that their mates wouldn't back down from the fight.

"He's at the castle. Mateo and Kade are with him."

Flora nodded.

"Okay, first we'll go to the castle and get those who are hiding, then we'll get the witches," Lily confirmed.

Emery nodded her head as if she was going to go along with the plan, though she knew damn well she wasn't going to follow it.

"Place your hands on my shoulders or arms," Dorian said and they all moved to comply. When they were all in position, a wistful smile tipped his lips. "You might want to hold your breath."

It was the only warning he gave before the world

turned upside down, and it felt as though she'd been thrown in the deep end of a lake. Her vision vortexed around her as if circling a drain. When her feet finally touched down on soft earth, she swallowed down the bile that threatened at the back of her throat.

Bronwyn wasn't as successful. She vomited up the contents of her stomach into the grass.

"Drinks were a terrible idea," Flora commented.

"There was no way we could have known Emery's bitch of a sister would show up," Bronwyn grumbled.

But they should have. Emery should have. They had grown complacent in Sloane's disappearance, and she used it against them.

Trying to shake off her anger at her own foolishness, Emery oriented herself. The soft neigh of horses echoed against the towering stone of the backside of the castle. It felt different than it had when she'd left for Scotland. The air hummed with magic, both light and dark. The dark called to her, beckoned her to come play in its depths, and Emery couldn't help the slight grin that tipped her lips. For the first time, she felt her sister's magic caress her own. Now that she'd opened herself to every facet of her magic, she could feel Sloane's nearness. Like they were two sides of the same coin.

Dorian crossed the space between them and the castle and pushed away the vines that hid the secret passageway she'd escaped through months before. Life had been so damn different then.

He rapped his knuckles on the stone and the door immediately opened from the inside. Braxton stood in the passageway with a few dozen vampire nobles.

"Aren't you a sight for sore eyes," Braxton rasped, blood trickling from his lip.

Dorian frowned. "Is this everyone?"

"All that I could find before we had to get out. She's taken over the bottom floor and has her monsters combing the rest of the castle."

Emery's heart sank at the same time her blood boiled. This was it. In a castle full of people, this was all that he could find. And they weren't even the people most deserving of the rescue. They were the nobles who thought like Aberforth. They didn't want mates or think Emery deserved to be at August's side. They wanted to disown her daughter because of what she was. Yet here they were, begging for Lily and Emery to save them. To portal them away from the big, bad, scary witch. The witch they should have been fighting against all along instead of being a thorn in her side.

Kill them. The darkness in her soul whispered, but fast on its heels came a reminder from August's soul, struggling to keep her focused on where her rage should be aimed.

Damn him.

Because even in the darkness, she knew he was right. Even if they'd been fighting her every step of the way, they didn't deserve to die because of it. She was many things, but a monster like her sister wasn't one of them. She was better than them.

"Which rendezvous point are we taking them to?" Lily asked.

"Five," Dorian confirmed. "It's the most secluded."

Lily nodded and muttered under her breath, opening the portal. When she did, Cosmina came into view with

Lina in her arms and Thea at her side. Malcolm strode toward them, his obsidian eyes wide and filled with fire. It wasn't until he crossed the barrier and had eyes on Lily that he visibly relaxed. He strode over to her and pressed a kiss to her hair.

"Alright, let's go, everyone in," Braxton urged, taking a head count as they rushed toward the glowing teal circle of the portal.

Emery's eyes locked with Cosmina, and she nodded at her. The queen returned her nod, a silent understanding of why Emery couldn't come right then. It was a promise between queens, one in which Cosmina vowed to take care of her daughter while Emery put the kingdom first. It didn't matter how badly Emery wanted to run and take her daughter in her arms; there was a battle to be fought and won.

Cosmina's gaze held more than mere understanding—it held a plea, one that, months ago, Emery wouldn't have understood. It was the silent cry of a mother asking for her son to be brought home to her.

A grim smile pulled at her lips, and she pressed her fist to her heart in a silent pledge to her mother-in-law. Then she turned to duck into the passageway, using the commotion to slip away from the others.

She only made it two steps before her head began to spin.

Fuck. Not now. She cursed mentally.

She stumbled back against the wall and pressed her hands into the cool stone as the telltale signs of a vision gripped the base of her skull and thrust her into the realm of possibilities dictated by the stars.

The throne room vibrated with magic, hers and Sloane's

mingled into a heady mix of light and dark. Mostly the latter. The wall dripped with blood too dark to belong to a witch or a vampire.

Sloane stood in the middle of the raised dais, a wicked smile stretched across her face.

Emery sucked in a gasp when she noticed the form at her feet. His hands were bound behind his back, and his face was lowered subserviently, though she could see it was by the force of her sister's magic. Sloane lowered herself onto the throne and crossed her legs, kicking August onto his side.

He let out a strangled groan, and Emery took a step toward him.

"Uh-uh, sister. He's mine now." Sloane threw her hands up and halted Emery's movement. *"Surrender, and I'll spare his life. Keep him as a pet. Fight me, and he'll become one of my army before I deliver you his head."*

"You won't win."

"Oh dear, sweet, summer child, I already have. This," she lifted her hands and gestured toward the castle, *"is mine now. This kingdom, and soon the greater Americas, will bow to me. Magic will be superior, and mates will serve no purpose."*

Tendrils of inky black magic that held only a faint shimmer of pure purple light rose from her hands and floated toward Emery. They wrapped their way around her, pinning her arms to her sides. Emery's magic fought to free her, but it was like trying to empty a pool with a dixie cup. For every little bit she managed to free, Sloane's magic pushed back. Her sister had far more practice channeling her darkness.

The magic wrapped around her throat, and Emery let loose a strangled breath.

"Please. I'll do anything." August protested. *"Don't hurt her."*

"Anything?" Sloane mused.

Emery opened her mouth to object, to tell August that Dorian and the others were on the way. That they weren't alone. That he didn't need to protect her. They had a plan. A plan that would work. They just needed to buy them a little more time.

Her vision started to fray, and Emery wasn't sure if she could remain conscious. She tried to hold on as long as she could. To hear what August would say next. What Sloane wanted from him...but it was no use.

Emery was torn from her vision and slumped back against the stone wall, her breath ragged.

August. Please, hold on. Don't do anything stupid. We're coming. She sent the plea down the bond, praying he'd receive it.

Dorian cupped her face and forced her to meet his gaze. "What did you see?"

"He needs us," she gasped, the urge to run to him consuming her every thought. She had to change her vision—do something, make a different choice, ask a different question—anything to change what she'd seen.

"Go." Dorian nodded down the dark passageway. "I'll get the witches out and meet you there."

Emery nodded and took off toward the throne room, praying to whatever gods would listen that she could do enough to change the future.

Chapter Eighteen

AUGUST

Emery.

Her voice sounded in his head. A plea laced with an edge of insanity.

Bloody fucking hell. He could feel her desperation and darkness caressing his soul down their bond, fueling his fight.

What the hell was Dorian thinking bringing her to the castle? She was supposed to be with Lina, far away from this shit show.

As much as he wanted to answer her and focus on ensuring she was safe, he couldn't. He could only hope her darkness would be enough to protect her.

August spit out the blood pooling in his mouth and squared up to take on the next monster. Two down, three to go.

Whatever the hell these things were, they were not like what guarded the throne room. Those he'd fought and easily killed. These particular monsters—the ones Sloane kept at her side—were stronger, faster, and able to match his every move. Their punches were packed with magic, sparking against his skin with every strike.

From the moment they'd entered the room, he'd never stood a chance against her. First, he'd tried speaking to her civilly, but her answer had been to use her magic to catapult him from his throne. The second he got up, she'd ordered the first of her guards to fight him. One by one, he'd defeated them, but he was one man, and his body couldn't last forever against them.

"You're no match for them, August." Her voice dripped with disdain, and when he spared a look in her direction, she was examining the tips of her black-stained fingers. She buffed her nails on her cloak as if he was boring her. "Give yourself to me and all this ends."

August reached up and wiped the blood from his lip with the back of his hand, glaring daggers in her direction. "In what world do you think I'd ever give myself to you?"

"That's simple. One in which Emery is no longer an option," she replied flippantly. Her gaze connected with the monster in front of him, and she nodded.

The monster growled and returned his focus to August. He lunged forward, and though August was prepared for his claws, Sloane's words forced him to hesitate, and he wasn't fast enough. The monster's swipe connected with him, shredding past his shirt and ripping into his abdomen.

August hissed and stumbled back. He brought his hand to his stomach, inspecting the wound. He winced when he brought his hand away, blood dripping from his fingers. It wasn't deep enough to be deadly, but it wouldn't heal quickly. Pushing the pain to the back of his mind, he narrowed his gaze on the monster.

It brought its hand up to its mouth and licked the blood from its claw before letting out a low snarl. The distraction was just enough for August to take it by surprise. He dashed forward and leapt toward it. Finding a grip on its neck, he swung his weight around and perched himself on the monster's back. Before it could reach up and grab him, August tore into its neck with his fangs and ripped its head from its body.

Three down.

The remaining two monsters stood against the far wall, waiting for Sloane's orders. She opened her mouth to speak, but closed it when the door to the throne room burst open and Emery rushed inside, wide-eyed and panting.

She was stunning. Her hair tugged back in a loose braid, she still wore the leggings he'd seen her in before she'd left for girls' night, but she'd ditched the oversized sweater so only a camisole remained. Her arms were encased in magic tendrils of gold and black, and her eyes were inky and unforgiving.

If he wasn't so damn angry she was there in the first place, August might be turned on by the sight of her.

Emery's gaze locked on him, and her eyes trailed down his body, taking stock of his injuries.

Are you okay?

August nodded.

"I wondered if you'd find your way out of Scotland, Emery."

Emery whipped her eyes to where her sister sat on the throne. "No thanks to you. I didn't take you for a coward, locking up the strongest of your enemies so you could attack untested."

"Hmm. Seems like I'm a better strategist than you, sister," Sloane mused in the nonchalant tone that was beginning to drive August crazy. "I suppose you want me to give up and leave the castle."

"We both know that would be asking too much of you," Emery hissed.

"Let's cut through it, shall we? You won't kill me, so what are you doing here? Why aren't you hiding with the others?"

Emery didn't respond, and her hesitation said everything. He knew his mate could feel the anger radiating down their bond, but even in her darkness, she still held hope for her sister. It was the light that couldn't be doused. It was the piece of his soul that kept her from embracing the darkness completely. The part of her that he loved. The one who wanted to see the goodness in everyone. August's stomach twisted as he watched her eyes fill with panic and confusion. Emery hadn't learned to reconcile the two sides of herself. He'd never given her the chance, and now she warred on two fronts.

Fuck, he'd been so wrong.

He shouldn't have forbidden her from learning her dark magic. He should have encouraged her. She'd been the only one to pull him back from the dark. He should have seen the light in her all along and trusted it was strong enough to tether her to him. To their daughter. Emery wasn't him. She wasn't bound by her darkness, she was rooted in it, but she was also made in the light. But she didn't see it. She saw how he could be both, but she didn't see that she was the same.

"I don't want you dead, Sloane." Emery's eyes locked on her sister and didn't waver as she spoke. "But that doesn't mean I won't kill you."

She opened her palms at her side and allowed her magic to pool into large balls of golden light.

"That's where we differ, Emery." Sloane ran her fingers down the gold-plated armrest of his throne. "I'd love for you to be dead, but I need your blood for just a bit longer. I also think I'd like for you to witness my rise to power. I want you to watch as I take everything from you."

Emery shook her head. "Why?"

"Because I can. Because the grass may not always be greener, but you, dear sister, were made for life in the sun and I was destined for the shadows. This is my chance to win, my chance to take what should have rightfully been mine all along but would have been given to you because I am not what *they* deemed as worthy. Darkness isn't a curse, it's a fucking gift, and I'm going to show the world just what I can do with it."

"It doesn't have to be like this," Emery whispered. It wasn't a plea, but a statement and for the first time since she arrived, he saw the gold in her eyes emerge.

"You do your darkness a disservice," Sloane spat.

Emery opened her mouth to argue, but Sloane's hand whipped up and streams of purple magic jetted from her palm. The other hand waved toward August and when he tried to run, he was frozen just as he was the night of the hunt.

His eyes darted to Emery, whose tendrils had freed themselves and now tangled with the purple magic of her sister. Wind whipped around Emery, seemingly strengthening behind her, pushing her forward and aiding her in her battle.

With every step forward, her magic held steady, but August could feel it draining her from the inside out. He tried to feed her everything he had down the bond. Encouragement. Love. Darkness. Anything he thought might help, but even though Emery remained determined to reach Sloane and protect their kingdom, she wasn't going to make it.

Please, little witch. Stop.

Emery ignored him.

He glanced around the room, searching for something, anything he could do, but there was nothing. He was helpless against Sloane's magic.

The monsters stood as frozen as he was, but blood dripped from their eyes and nose. It was the only physical sign of Emery's magic manifesting in the room. August shifted his gaze back to Sloane, and noticed Emery's magic hadn't affected her at all.

It wasn't until Emery was halfway to the dais that a single drop of blood fell from Sloane's nose.

That was it.

Emery's magic had produced one single drop, when he'd seen Sloane easily pull blood from a field full of witches.

A wicked smile tipped Sloane's lips. The knowing look of a woman who reveled in the knowledge that she had the upper hand. She flicked her wrist, and dusty purple smoke sprawled across the floor. Emery's eyes widened but she didn't pay it any mind. Sweat trickled from her brow, and she continued to force her magic at her sister, despite the way it drained her.

Emery! August shouted down the bond.

She visibly shook off his plea, a shiver tearing through her as the smoke wrapped around her ankles. He needed her to look at him. To hear him. He needed her to survive for the both of them, for their daughter. For their kingdom.

Fuck. He fought against the magic that held him, knowing it was no use. This wasn't supposed to be their defining moment. There was so much life they hadn't gotten to yet. So much he hadn't gotten to say to her. She was his happily ever after.

"Would you like to see what comes next, sister?" Sloane taunted Emery.

His mate didn't reply nor did she flinch when the smoke started to form shapes around her. Soon they became the clear depiction of everyone they loved. His mother. Thea. Dorian. Bronwyn. Malcolm. Lily. Lina.

They stood in a line, and stared at Emery with sorrow in their eyes. Instead of lifeless smoke beings, they appeared real. Lina cooed like she had at him not hours ago, and his mother's gentle smile was a perfect replication. Behind each of them a monster appeared, made of smoke but appearing as real as their friends and family.

Without warning, the first monster stepped forward and slit the throat of his mother clear through her neck until her severed head fell back.

August screamed in silence while Emery remained stoic, her magic still fierce and connected to Sloane's, even though it was slowly draining her.

It wasn't real, he told himself, but it didn't erase the image of his mother crumbling to the floor or the blood that spilled from her body.

One by one, the monsters decapitated their loved ones. One by one, they fell to the floor.

Emery winced when Thea fell, she wavered when Malcolm cried out for her to stop this. And a single blood-filled tear fell when Lily cast her eyes up toward the stars and cursed Emery's name.

August felt Emery break when the monster held their daughter in its arms. Their bond began to shake in time with Emery's heartbeat, and August could sense the sobs that threatened to consume her.

It's not real, Emery. That's not Lina. She's safe with Dorian. He got her far away from here. I need you to stop this. I need you to go to her.

I can't. Emery shook her head, and he could tell there was more she wasn't telling him. Whatever was driving her to be there was so great that she wouldn't give up.

You need to, little witch. Our daughter needs you. Please, August pleaded and he was sure there would be tears of his own streaming down his face if he wasn't frozen.

Smoke Lina wailed and the second the knife slit her throat Emery fell to her knees, her magic connection lost. The cries of a broken mother echoed throughout the room.

"Just as I suspected." Sloane stepped down from his throne and crossed the room, standing above where Emery shook on the floor. "They make you weak. You'll never be able to stand where I do because you allow yourself to be connected to the light. I tried to let others in once. I tried to form the bonds that would have kept me in the good graces of the stars, but they abandoned me. The witches bound me. The vampires hated me. And that's when I learned, the dark will always snuff out the light."

Sloane kicked Emery to her side, but his mate didn't

stay down. She lifted herself to her knees and crawled across the floor to where their daughter lay. With gentle hands, she scooped up the tiny illusion and lay her in her lap before bending over and pressing a kiss to her tiny face. Sobs wracked her body and it didn't matter how many times August screamed down the bond that it wasn't real, Emery didn't hear him, lost in the illusion.

"She'll never be your daughter. Lina was meant for greater things than you or your *mate* could provide her." Slone sneered at the word mate as if it tasted like shit in her mouth.

Emery looked up, her murderous glare pinned on her sister. "You know nothing of great things."

Sloane cocked a brow. "We'll see."

With another flick of her wrist, all the smoky illusions disappeared. All except for Lina.

Emery clutched their sweet little girl to her chest, when she should have protected herself. The rage-filled glare she pinned on her sister did nothing to protect her when Sloane's purple tendrils formed from what was once their friends and family and wrapped around Emery. They forced Lina from her arms, and Emery cried out as she was lifted from the floor. She struggled to open her palms and deploy magic of her own but the wisps died the moment they challenged Sloane's.

August pressed against the magic that held him, the sensation reminding him too much of the hunt—the last time he was so powerless. The last time Emery died. Inside his mind, he screamed at Sloane to release him. To let Emery go.

Emery's back arched, forced by the magic that held her. The dark purple tendrils wrapped around her torso until they reached her neck and forced her head to tip back, her lips parted on a gasp.

Pain seared their bond, and August was helpless to do anything. Emery's eyes sunk into their sockets and her cheeks hollowed.

Stay with me, little witch.

I love you, she whispered. *Remember that.*

No. Don't you give up. Fight her. Fight harder.

Our bond will always be my greatest joy.

No.

His eyes stayed locked on her contorted body, his mind screaming, desperate and panicked.

He couldn't lose her. Not again.

August peeled his gaze from his mate and looked to her twin, willing the evil bitch to look at him.

When her gaze fell on him, she tipped her head to the side and a sardonic grin stretched across her face. "Something to say, Your Majesty?"

She snapped her fingers, and his voice returned to him.

"Stop! You're killing her," he begged, his voice rasped as if every scream he'd wanted to yell while held captive by her magic had fallen from him.

"Don't you worry your pretty little head, August," Sloane cooed. She fucking *cooed* like this was a damn game. "I'm not going to kill her. I only need her breathing enough to carry the light."

"Please," he pleaded. "I'll do anything."

"Anything." The words rolled off her lips like a cat who finally caught the mouse. "You'll be mine?"

No! Emery screamed in his head. *You weren't supposed to do this. I came. I fought her so you wouldn't. This was supposed to change. Please don't do this.*

He had no idea what she meant, but he didn't care. Emery had to survive. If this was the only way, then so be it.

"Take me instead of her," he offered.

Time stood still as he waited. Sloane sucked her bottom lip between her teeth, clearly mulling over his request. It was a smart move. If he was at her side, she could rule the kingdom without contest. It would all belong to her.

August's eyes drifted to Emery. *Look at me.*

Tears welled in Emery's eyes, but she wouldn't allow them to connect with him. Her gaze remained locked on her sister.

Damn it, Emery, look at me. Please, he pleaded.

Emery blinked back the silver in her eyes, and when she opened them, her swirling depths finally met him.

Listen to me. No matter what happens, I'll never be hers. No matter what I say, you know what's inside me. My heart belongs to you, little witch. You carry my soul. Please forgive me.

"Done."

Emery cried out in his head as warning bells echoed. He expected a fight. A counter-argument. Anything. Sloane had agreed far too easily for someone so sure of her power. But he'd examine what that meant later. All that mattered right then was getting Emery safely out of the castle.

August held his head high and extended his arm to Sloane. "Make a vow that you won't hurt her. That so long as I am your prisoner, no harm will come to her or my daughter."

Sloane sauntered toward him and stretched out her arm. Placing her forearm in his hand, she wrapped her fingers around his arm. "I swear to let my sister go and no harm or plans thereof will come to her or my niece so long as you are my king, and you reciprocate the vow."

August repeated the vow. Sloane's magic immediately flared to life, wrapping tendrils around his wrist. They didn't lick at his skin as Lily's had when she'd made her vow to protect his Culling women; instead, they felt like tiny pinpricks demanding his compliance.

The moment the magic sank into their skin, binding the vow, Sloane flicked her free hand up and threw Emery against the back wall.

Emery crashed into the stone, and he heard the air leave her lungs before she slid to the floor with a loud thud. August growled at Sloane, but it was cut short by the magic that flared in his wrist, sensing his intentions to harm. It traveled from his wrist to his chest and August doubled over when it reached his core. He clutched at the tattered fabric of his shirt as if it would somehow remove the agonizing burn deep in his abdomen.

"Oops. I guess my magic slipped." Sloane shrugged innocently.

Like hell it had.

What the fuck had he gotten himself into if he couldn't even think murderous thoughts about Sloane?

He held his breath and fought against his own pain until Emery lifted her head. Her gaze darted between Sloane and him, contempt flaring for both of them for very different reasons.

Go.

No. We said forever.

The warning magic subsided within him as a pop of magic echoed through the chamber, and Dorian appeared by the door. His eyes searched the room, finding Emery first before darting towards him. His lips pressed together and his eyes narrowed.

August nodded, knowing his second would understand.

"No!" Emery shrieked. *Don't do this, August. You don't have to do this. She'll kill you to hurt me.*

As long as you and Lina are safe.

Dorian vanished and reappeared by Emery. He quickly knelt and scooped her up against his chest.

Emery's black-rimmed amber eyes seared themselves onto his heart. He knew they were what he would picture to get him through this. Their bond was flooded with love and desperation.

I love you, little witch.

Don't do this. I will never forgive you, August. Be my darkness. Be mine. Don't do this.

August wanted to shut his eyes. He'd give anything to turn away from the hurt he was causing her, but he wouldn't do that to her. She deserved his full attention, even when his own heart was breaking right alongside hers.

Dorian gave him one last nod before vanishing with Emery in his arms.

The second they were gone, Sloane flicked her wrist, and August doubled over at the loss of his connection to Emery. The bond was disconnected; she was no longer in his head, even if she'd always be in his heart.

He had done the right thing.

His heartbeat rang in his ears, his eyes trained on the spot where she'd just been, but all he could do was repeat that mantra over and over.

He had done the right thing.

She was safe.

"Who was that?" Sloane barked.

"Dorian," August whispered.

"The elusive fae."

"So it would seem."

Sloane stepped in front of him and leaned down, gripping his face between her thumb and forefinger. "Tell me everything you know about him."

August smirked. He hated her, and if she thought for one second he was going to help her, she was dead wrong. He might be hers to control, for now, but he didn't have to make it any easier on her. Especially now that Emery was safe.

"That wasn't part of the deal," he said with a half smirk.

Sloane's face twisted in anger, but only for a moment before a sly smile tugged at her lips. "If that's the game you want to play, so be it."

August opened his mouth to speak, to tell her that this was no game she could play and win, but never got the chance before his world went black.

Chapter Nineteen

EMERY

"No!"

It wasn't supposed to happen like that. Fighting Sloane, taking the brunt of her magic, was supposed to protect him. She'd gotten there before Sloane had him at her feet, he wasn't supposed to give himself to her. Sloane wasn't supposed to win.

Emery beat her fists against Dorian's chest as hard as she could, which admittedly wasn't very hard. Whatever the hell magic Sloane had wrapped her in had drained her very will to live. Her muscles quivered weakly. It took everything she had just to keep her head upright.

"Take me back, Dorian." The world spun like a whirlpool around her, and she wasn't sure if it was from sieving with him or the sudden slice to her soul when the connection between her and August was severed. He was once again gone from her orbit, and she was left without her sun.

She reached for her darkness, hoping it would dampen

the ache in her soul, but when she grasped the dark tendrils in her chest, they were a fraction of what they had been before. It was as if they'd been drained of their power.

Dorian set her down on a patch of soft moss. Bile threatened the back of her throat, but Emery swallowed it down. "Take me back, Dorian. We can't leave him."

He looked at her with a pained expression before scrubbing his face with his hand. "I can't do that, Your Majesty."

"I swear to the gods, Dorian." Emery tried to stand up, but her legs gave out immediately. "If you don't take me back to save him, I'm going to—"

"You'll what, Emery?" Dorian snapped, and Emery was taken back by his tone. "You have no idea what she did to you. Sloane is stronger than you. Her darkness is necrotic, it steals life from anything and everything around it. Maybe if you knew how to hone your blood, you could do the same, but so long as she can suck the damn life from your soul, you aren't going anywhere near her. August was smart to make sure you were safe. He's already mostly dead as a vampire. She can't suck life from someone who isn't alive, and she needs him alive to get to you. You are our greatest weapon at the moment, and your daughter needs you to stay that way. Your kingdom needs you to stay that way. Stars above, I need you to stay that way. I suggest you fucking remember that."

Emery's mouth fell open. Dorian had never spoken to her that way. He was always professional and logical with her. The man in front of her was wide-eyed and seconds away from frothing at the mouth.

He inhaled a steadying breath, working to find his composure. "I'm sorry if that was harsh. I just— we're not exactly in the clear yet, and I need you to be ready to lead your people the moment I figure out how the fuck I'm going to swing this."

What the hell was he talking about? Swing what?

For the first time since Dorian pulled her from the throne room, Emery took a moment to look around. The soft moss she sat on stretched all around her, damp beneath the canopy of looming pines despite the light peeking through. They were absolutely not at any of the rendezvous points she knew of. Wherever they were definitely wasn't in the same time zone as the castle, considering it had been nearly midnight five minutes prior.

"Where are we? Where is everyone?" she asked hesitantly as she reached out to the land around her. The magic was different there, stronger and somehow more potent, yet muted at the same time. Like a misty rain. Not quite there but still saturating the air.

"We're in Scandinavia, more specifically Sweden. While we were getting the witches out through Lily's cottage, more than a few of the monsters made it through the portal."

Emery sucked in a breath. "Lina?"

"Is safe. I sieved her, Thea, Cosmina, and as many of the children as I could to another location, and Lily and Malcolm were able to defeat the beasts with the help of the witches and vampires. That's why it took me so long to get back to you."

Her heart calmed ever so slightly. At least they were safe. They'd gotten them out of Sloane's clutches and somewhere they could regroup.

"You got the army too, then?"

Dorian shook his head, his lips pressed into a grim line

"No, Sloane still has them at the castle. We only have those we were able to get out of the castle and cottage."

Fuck. Not only did Sloane have their army, she had the one man who they'd listen to. August wouldn't flip sides, but Sloane had proven she was ruthless. If she had August, she had their army.

Emery tried to stand up again and this time when she did, Dorian offered her his hand. "So why did you bring me here then and not to those who escaped?"

He tugged her up, and she brushed off the dirt from her leggings. Not that it mattered. She was covered in dirt and grime from her battle with Sloane.

Dorian took a step back, looking distracted, his eyes continuously darting around the clearing. "Because I want this to be where we go next, but I need you to be ready for that."

"Where?"

"Turn around."

Emery managed not to wince as she twisted her body around. Behind them, in the middle of the trees that lined the clearing, was a large stone archway with a rickety iron gate across it. Aside from looking completely out of place, it looked old and weathered. No trees touched it, and it didn't seem to lead anywhere.

"That's the entrance to a fae realm. A piece of the Feywilde created and stashed away in this realm by gods and fae to give those stranded here a place to come and rejuvenate their magic. It's where I visited when I was gone, to ask them if they'd allow me to bring you there to extract my blood so we could complete the spell to break the Culling."

"They wanted me to agree to an unspecified favor." She

stared at the archway, trying to figure out how it was an entrance. It didn't glow or hum with magic like the doorways Lily had spelled in the past. It just stood there, inconspicuous iron and stone, almost like the entrance to a building that had once been erected but was long gone now. "Correct. And trust me, you don't want to promise something like that to the fae. You can't trust them."

Emery turned back around and sized Dorian up. "But I trust you."

Dorian's jaw tightened. "I'm not them."

"What are we doing here then if we can't trust them?" Emery was growing more agitated by the moment. She wanted to get to her daughter and reassure their people they were safe, but first she needed a plan, and if that's what Dorian was getting at, he needed to get to it quickly.

"Sloane has proven she can find us and get through our wards. If we set up at one of the rendezvous points, it's only a matter of time before she finds us again. She will never stop hunting you. Even if you go to her, she'll wait for you to lead her back to Lina because your daughter is another way to further her agenda and take everything from you. We need somewhere we can go where she can't follow us because it doesn't exist here."

Emery followed his train of thought and hated that he was correct. Everything he'd said made sense. Sloane wasn't just vying for power. She'd played her hand and proven that more than ruling, she wanted to destroy Emery, and that meant taking everything that she held dear. She'd already stolen Ansel, her protector, and now her mate. It only made sense that she'd go after Lina next. And there was no way in hell she was stealing her daughter.

"You want us to flee to this pocket realm."

"Exactly."

"Is it safe?"

Dorian shrugged. "In theory."

"I'm not going to put my people, let alone my daughter, in danger."

Her hair prickled on the back of her neck and the magic in the air pulsed as if from one moment to the next it had been supercharged. Emery searched the tree line in front of her, but before she could turn around, she heard a voice that dripped with magic and malice.

"Danger, like beauty, is in the eye of the beholder, don't you think, Dorianthian?"

Emery whipped her gaze back to the archway but before she got a look at the owner of the thick gravelly voice, Dorian stepped in front of her.

"Nico," Dorian growled, bending his knees like he was ready to defend her.

The air pulsated around them, and Emery's eyes widened when she realized this magic felt different. It was coming from Dorian. His magic was dark, darker than hers and Sloane's. It made what she'd felt from him before look like child's play. It wasn't rooted in the world around them; it seemed to come from a well within him. Like he was the end and the beginning of its limits.

What the fuck? He'd been holding out on them all this time. Emery's eyes narrowed on Dorian's back, and if she had anything left in her own magic stores, she likely would have thrown it at him. He could have helped take down Sloane. They didn't have to leave August behind.

She knelt down and dug her hands into the moss around

her, feeling for the magic of the earth. She may not have her own, but the world could give her what she needed. Maybe not darkness, but her regular magic could pack a punch.

"Emery," Dorian gritted, "I can feel you pulling your magic. If you're thinking about using it on either of us, I suggest you think again. Now is not the time. I will explain everything to you, I promise."

"You said I shouldn't trust the fae," she sneered.

"He's not wrong." The mystery man chuckled. "Especially him."

Emery tested the magic she'd pulled toward her. Sloane had done a fucking number on her, and the last thing she needed right now was to appear weak. She stood and stepped around Dorian's broad form.

In front of the archway stood the most beautiful man she'd ever seen. And that was saying something, considering she was constantly surrounded by royal vampires who somehow all looked like they belonged on the cover of every edition of the world's hottest men.

She didn't need to see the soft points of his ears to know he was otherworldly.

Even from where she stood a few yards away, she had to tip her head slightly to meet his mossy gaze. He was pale, but his features were dark and chiseled, which made him seem more god-like than sickly. His obsidian hair hung to his shoulders, accented by the shimmering black horns that jutted out about an inch behind his temples and curled backwards. His dark-gray, short-sleeved Henley did him every favor, defining his lean muscles down to his low-slung jeans. His arms were crossed over his chest, his hands fisted, but Emery could just make out several dark tendrils that seemed to stain the skin on the backs of his hands, much like Sloane's.

"Like what you see, human?" Nico cocked a brow.

"Not particularly. I'm not into douches with pointy ears." It wasn't a total lie, but he didn't need to know she found him attractive. "What did you mean, especially Dorian?"

As much as she wanted to lay into Dorian for all the apparent secrets he'd been keeping, she trusted him more than the man in front of her. Ultimately, he hadn't given her a reason not to, but she still wanted to get to the bottom of everything he'd been keeping from her.

"A story for another time." Nico mused, his eyes lingering on Dorian before falling back on her. "I suppose you're Emery. The witch who will *change everything.*"

She didn't miss the sarcasm in his statement, nor did she like that he knew who she was when she knew nothing about him.

Fucking Dorian.

Emery flexed her fingers, rolling the minute amounts of magic she'd been able to pull between the tips. "That's me. I'm glad Dorian speaks highly of me. And you, I gather, are Nico. Unfortunately, you are nothing but a name at this point, but I hear you—or maybe it's your king—wants something from me."

He stepped forward, crossing the space between them in three large steps. He extended his hand, and Emery sucked in a sharp breath. His fingers were black as night as if they were dipped in darkness. From each finger, inky black swirls twisted like smokey veins up his hands and onto his forearms.

Emery wanted to look at Dorian and see if it was safe,

but it would be a sign of weakness, and that was the last thing she wanted Nico to see.

She doused her magic and carefully placed her hand in his. "I assure you, I don't bow to anyone, and what I want from you is a simple spell."

Nico brought it to his lips and pressed a soft kiss to her skin. Immediately her magic flared to life and shot from her chest to her hand, zapping Nico.

His eyes widened as he snatched his hand back and rubbed the affected flesh. "Interesting." A half smile tipped his lips. "You are stronger than I imagined. You've been holding out on us, Dorian."

"I don't owe you anything. If anything, you owe me," Dorian ground out, his eyes never leaving Nico.

Emery wanted to ask questions, to understand what the hell was passing between them, but it wasn't something she could just blurt out.

This was the political game August always talked about. Emery hated it and would much rather have all the cards on the table, but this wasn't her world, and without her mate, she had to learn now more than ever to play by its rules.

"Is that what you think?" Nico scoffed. "I don't owe you a damn thing after what happened at the peaks."

Dorian took a step forward, his fists clenched at his sides, ready to swing, but halted as if he'd thought better of it. "I lost everything to help you. Then when I had finally rebuilt it all, when I was happy, I lost that too, because I trusted you."

Emery turned to Nico, studying his features as he spoke. "I have more than atoned for my sins, brother. I am not going to apologize again."

Brother? Emery's eyes darted between Dorian and Nico. They couldn't have been more different, but if they were related, that would make so much sense. She could understand hating your sibling for what they'd done. If Nico was anything like Sloane, she'd gladly stand beside Dorian and take this new fae down a notch.

"He's not my blood, Emery. I suggest you stop broadcasting your feelings so loudly. Fae can sense thoughts and emotions, and Nico won't hesitate to use them against you." Dorian's eyes never strayed from Nico's. "We need access to Enchanth."

Fucking fae. Emery built up the walls in her mind like she would in her bond with August and hoped it did the trick.

Nico's lips tipped up into a sly smile. "I already told you what my price was."

"It's not just us anymore. We need refuge from Emery's twin."

"Interesting." Nico's smile widened as he looked at Emery with a glint in his eyes that hadn't been there before. "The twins of light and dark. It finally happened."

Dorian nodded.

Emery's eyes pinballed between the two of them, her hackles raised. "What does that mean?"

"The plot thickens. You've been keeping secrets from all of us, haven't you, Dorian?" Nico walked toward Emery and when he was almost to her, flicked his wrist and produced a black rose from thin air. "You and your sister were foretold when Celeste was sent to this realm. Her ancestors were chosen by the gods to be the keepers of balance, ensuring there was magic in both worlds. But even within each realm there must be balance. When

Celeste's twin perished, the land promised that when the twins of light and dark returned, their war would determine the future of the realms."

Nico offered the rose to Emery, but given everything the two of them had said, she didn't trust Nico's gift. Instead of taking it, she turned to face Dorian, hardening her features so he wouldn't see the cuts each of his lies had dealt. "You didn't think this was important to tell us?"

"We can't get involved," Dorian explained, the slight plea in his voice telling. She imagined it was why he hadn't stepped in and destroyed Sloane himself. "I didn't want to give you hope. I have done everything I can to help you and your kingdom. As I told August, my allegiance is to you."

"But you were sent here by Nico."

Dorian remained silent, so she posed her question to the only other fae who might give her answers. "Why?"

"There are many reasons I sent him," Nico replied, picking the petals from the flower she'd rejected and letting them fall to the mossy ground surrounding them. "Primarily, it was to see what your mate was like as he prepared to take over for his father. When I established Enchanth, it was to protect those fae who'd been stranded. At the time, I didn't have a need to know much about the kingdoms where my doors lay. But as unrest grew in your realm, I needed to know where your kingdom stood."

"Because?" Emery fished for more information. If he wanted her help, he was going to have to give her more than a bullshit diplomatic answer.

"Are you agreeing to help me?"

Emery cocked a brow. "Are you granting us asylum?"

Nico thought for a moment before nodding his head.

"Temporarily. I won't have Enchanth become a haven for vampires and witches."

"What about hybrids?" Emery narrowed her gaze, ready to do whatever it took to protect her daughter.

Dorian fidgeted beside her, and she imagined he wanted to jump in and negotiate for her, but thankfully he didn't. As much as she wished August was there to mediate this, she was now the highest ranking official of their kingdom, and she needed to be the one to make these decisions.

"What about them?"

"Are they going to be a problem?"

"I prefer them over you."

Emery nodded. She wanted to ask why, but it wasn't the time. "Then, what do you need from me?"

"As I said, a simple spell only a star-touched witch can perform."

Emery mulled over his words. "I won't kill anyone for you."

It was the only stipulation she could think of off the top of her head. A spell she could do…maybe. She hadn't really perfected incantations aside from opening portals, but Nico didn't need to know that.

Nico chuckled. "If that's your only provision, then we shouldn't have any problems."

Emery didn't trust him, but there was something in his eyes that made her want to help him. His magic was dark, like hers and Dorian's, but she could also see he had a heart. One that, if she read between the lines, she could see bled for his people. He wanted to protect them, and even though he didn't have to, he was willing to help hers too.

"Deal." Emery extended her hand to him. A gentleman's agreement.

"Don't shake his hand." Dorian warned, placing his own hand on her shoulder and pulling her back a step.

Nico's eyes flicked to Dorian, and he smiled. "Spoilsport."

Nico turned around and strolled toward the gated arch. He pressed his hand to the stone and muttered a phrase in what sounded like a dialect of Scots Gaelic, but she couldn't be sure. Light flowed from inside the archway, which now emitted a soft pink glow. Nico pushed open the gates, which had transformed from wrought iron to black obsidian, and lifted his hand.

"Welcome to Enchanth."

Chapter Twenty

EMERY

"You should lay down while I get the others," Dorian said as he watched her pace the room Nico had indicated would be hers to share with Lina while they stayed in Enchanth.

She couldn't bear to stay here one moment longer without her daughter. One look at the mountain of pillows on the king-size bed, and her throat swelled with a sob. It was too big to be hers alone. She knew if she tried to lay down as Dorian suggested, there would be nothing to save her from the emptiness in her chest where her mate belonged. At least with Lina there, she would have a connection to him.

In Enchanth, she could no longer feel August. At least in the mortal realm she still felt his living soul, but in the fae pocket realm both bonds were completely severed and her only tie to her mate was the piece of his soul inside her, keeping her alive. She wanted nothing more than to curl up, mourn the loss, and allow her magic to recoup, but she was the acting queen of their kingdom, and queens didn't get to fall apart.

No. The longer she could put off facing the fact he wasn't there, the better. Which meant she needed to get her people to Enchanth.

Emery scoffed and searched the walls for something that could help her orient herself, but while the vampires' castle had been brimming with history and warmth, the onyx crystal walls of Nico's castle were noticeably barren.

"Your Majesty, please," Dorian said with a sigh.

"Oh, so it's Your Majesty again?" Somewhere in the back of her mind she knew Dorian didn't deserve her sass, but she couldn't bring herself to care. He'd lied to them, or at least omitted the truth of who he was and the role he'd played in their lives. It was hard to separate him from all the other people who'd lied to her and used her.

Ada. Wren. Sloane. Even August had used her when they first met.

Dorian huffed a sigh and gestured across from her. "If you want to get out at the entrance to the archway, you need to go this way."

"Maybe if the layout in this castle made any sense or there were any landmarks whatsoever to make one part of it different from the other, I wouldn't get so lost," Emery spat as she strode forward.

"It's because of the ground sprites. They kept taking the few things Nico did put up and stowed them away in their bunkers, so he stopped trying."

Nico had asked that they give him an hour to inform the residents of Enchanth of their arrival so they wouldn't be caught off guard. She'd yet to see the fae that lived there, but she had to admit the underlying current of elements and magic had her curious.

It was unlike anything she'd ever experienced. Magic that was deeply rooted and ancient, yet somehow bounced almost playfully in the air around them. It was nothing like their realm, where magic didn't flow as freely and was tied solely to the land.

"Is Nico the king here?"

Dorian tipped his head back and cackled. "Nico? Hell no. That man wants nothing to do with royalty."

It was the first time since Ansel had been taken that she'd heard a genuine laugh from Dorian. Even with all the pranks he pulled with Malcolm, she always got the sense that he was putting on a show for them. Maybe that should have been a red flag that he was hiding something.

Even though she was still fucking furious with him, she couldn't deny that he looked good. Like a weight had been lifted now that his truths were out in the open.

Well, most of them. She'd be kicking his ass later once she regained the use of her magic. She reached for the small tendrils and found only the frays of her light in her chest. It was as if the darkness had fallen away, which was probably a good thing, otherwise it would be giving her ideas of all the ways to end Dorian for lying to them.

"If you aren't going to rest, at least eat this." Dorian pulled something from his hand and offered it to her. It was a piece of chocolate. "I snagged it from Lily's cottage."

"Thank you." She stared at the peace offering before nodding and taking it. A small groan filtered from her when the sweetness melted on her tongue and her magic purred. "This doesn't mean you're forgiven."

"I know." The light that had momentarily filled him

disappeared, and Emery almost forgave him right then and there.

Almost. She wasn't about to let him off without the full story.

"So," she looped her arm in his and let him lead the way. "If he's not a king, then how did he end up here?"

"That's his story to tell and treads the line of breaking the laws of the feywilde, but as he said before, he created this place for the fae that were stranded in this realm. Either by choice or banishment. It's an in-between where they can survive."

Emery gritted her teeth, annoyed by the fact there was so much he wouldn't tell her. She understood, but it didn't make it any less frustrating. "You both mentioned that. What do you mean by 'survive'?"

"Most fae can't live outside the magic of the Feywilde forever. The magic in your realm isn't as pure since it was gifted from ours. The factions strengthen it, but a fae, especially a lesser one, cannot survive any long period of time without going back."

"Just like I can't use my magic endlessly."

"Exactly."

It fascinated her how fae magic and her own operated so similarly, and yet it felt so different. Purer. Like it was the well from which life around it stemmed, including her own magic. And maybe it was. If Celeste had truly come from the last human city in the Feywilde, then it stood to reason that their origins were here.

Emery tipped her head to the side, a thought hitting her. "You survived in our land without having to come back here, though."

"Not all fae rely solely on the land for survival. As I

told you before, I survive on death as much as the land, which allowed me to exist in your realm for longer periods of time without having to visit."

"Do you look like him? I mean, in your fae form. I assume you don't look like this all the time."

Dorian winced. "Yes. Nico and I are of the same species. If I were to drop my glamour, I would look like him."

Emery nodded and tucked away the various tidbits of information to examine later when she had a moment to breathe. In the last hour, she'd gathered so much knowledge of the fae there was no way to comprehend it all in one sitting.

They walked in silence the rest of the way to the archway, Dorian leading her so she didn't get lost again.

Enchanth was absolutely stunning in the most unearthly way. If the two suns hadn't clued her in that this was an entirely different realm, the dark purple treetops of the forest would have. The castle, which was made from onyx, both reflected and absorbed the rays of the two suns in the sky. It loomed in contrast to the forest surrounding it, instilling a bone-chilling sense of fear. If she'd stumbled upon it on her own, she'd absolutely think twice about approaching.

Emery gasped when they stepped through the archway and back into the mortal realm. It wasn't like traveling through a portal, or even sieving with Dorian. This was akin to strapping on a weighted vest and sledging through mud during a torrential downpour.

Emery shook out her arms and legs, trying to dislodge the tightness in her muscles left behind by the arch.

"You'll get used to it," Dorian assured her. "Time moves slower in the real world than it does for us."

Emery froze. "How much slower?"

"About a third. So, for every three days in Enchanth, it's roughly one here."

Fuck. His words gutted her, flaying her heart open on the mossy ground. She should be worried about how the hell she was going to fight for her kingdom while working against a time shift, but all she could think about was how Lina would grow without August. Three days for every one of his. As long as Sloane was alive, as long as they fought for control of their kingdom, he would miss everything.

But it wasn't just the time that weighed on her. The moment she'd entered the human realm, her bond with August had snapped back to life. He was still cut off from her, but at least for a moment she could feel his life force again.

Emery blinked back the tears that seemed perpetually ready to fall, and swallowed hard. For five minutes, she didn't want to be queen. She didn't want to do the right thing and lead their people into a pocket realm that severed her from her mate. She would, because that's what was asked of her. But at the end of this shitty day, she'd much rather curl up right there and hold on to the other half of her soul.

He was alive, she told herself, and that was enough. It had to be.

"Do you think you can portal, or do you want me to go and bring Lily back?"

Dorian's voice pulled her from her thoughts and she shook her head. "Go. I can't hold it open."

She hated to appear weak, but it was all she could do to keep herself standing. If she'd even attempted to pull more magic into her from the world around her, it might drain her more after the fact, and at the very least she needed to get her people to safety.

With a quiet pop, Dorian disappeared. Seconds later, he returned with Lily, who pulled Emery into her arms.

Emery choked back a sob and dug her hands into her ancestor's shoulders.

Lily didn't bother holding back and sobbed against her. "You're okay. I was so worried when Dorian said you went after August."

"I'm fine. I promise."

Lily pulled back until her eyes met Emery's, searching for what she wasn't saying.

Emery did her best to smile, but she suspected Lily saw through her. "Can you bring Lina to me?"

"Absolutely." Lily smiled and waved her hands, muttering the portal incantation.

Sparks of teal whirled in front of them and opened to the lavender fields of France. Immediately, Cosmina stepped through with Lina in her arms and Thea at her side. Brax, Malcolm, Draven, Flora, Callum, Bronwyn, and Octavian weren't far behind.

The moment they crossed, Emery dashed to them, sweeping her daughter into her arms. She inhaled her scent—August's fresh pine still lingered on her as if he'd handed her to Emery himself. She clutched the sleeping baby to her chest and fell to her knees.

Cosmina dropped beside her and wrapped Emery in her motherly embrace. "Shhh, sweet girl. It's okay. You're okay."

"I couldn't save him." Emery sobbed into her daughter's hair.

Cosmina pressed a kiss to her forehead and whispered, "You're safe. That's what matters."

Emery looked up at Cosmina through tear-filled eyes and saw his mother holding back tears of her own. "He traded his life for mine."

This woman, who gave her mate life, was comforting her when she had every right to hate her. If Emery had never come into his life, he'd be with them now. Sloane likely wouldn't be targeting them like this.

Cosmina reached up and wiped away her tears, a small smile tipped at her lips. "That sounds exactly like something my August would do."

Emery gave a half-hearted laugh that was choked by her tears. "I'm sorry. I'm so fucking sorry."

"There's nothing to apologize for, Emery. This is part of war, and August knows how to handle himself. You'll get him back. I know you will."

How could she be so sure when Emery felt like she was walking a tightrope, ready to fall with the slightest breeze? This was what she wanted, to rule, but she'd always imagined doing so with August at her side and never with the weight of her emotions crushing her beyond measure.

She waffled back and forth between wanting to give up and wanting to destroy the world for her daughter. She was the queen, but also still the Culling girl in way over her head and a mother who had already lost her son.

"How do you do it?" Emery said, her voice barely a whisper.

"What, my dear?"

"How do you remain so stoic when your world is falling apart?" And that's exactly what it felt like. The moment her darkness fell away and the gravity of the situation hit her, Emery felt like she was fighting a losing battle. Without her darkness in the forefront, she felt every stab taken at her chest.

"That is something I won't share with you. Your strength is in your ability to feel. Without it, you lose sight of what you're fighting for." Cosmina then leaned in and whispered, "You are a better queen already than I ever was, Emery, but a long bath at the end of the night helps."

Emery pulled back and spared a timid glance at her future mother-in-law. "You don't hate me?"

"Never. We are blood and that means we stick together, even when times are hard."

Emery nodded, sure that if she opened her mouth more sobs would come out. Having a family was new to her, and it continued to amaze her how deep their bonds ran. Every time she thought she finally understood the depths they would go to for her, they surprised her again.

Bronwyn stepped up to help Lily fortify the portal with her magic, and Malcolm helped Emery to her feet.

He tugged her against him, hugging her and Lina to his chest.

"We'll get him back."

Emery nodded silently as she pulled back and watched the rest of the witches and vampires file through the portal.

"No fucking way. I'm not going into another pocket realm. The last time, I went into one as a human, almost died, and came out a hybrid." Flora's voice echoed through the clearing, and Emery looked to where she stood talking with Dorian and Draven. Her arms were crossed and she looked like she wasn't kidding around.

Draven cocked a brow, and smiled. "You also came out with a mate."

Flora's eyes narrowed on him, and Emery couldn't help but notice the upturn at the corner of her mouth. "Ok, there was one good thing about it. One."

Emery crossed the clearing to join them and nudged her best friend with her shoulder. "I promise you won't get trapped. You might lose a few days, though."

"Great." Flora threw her hands up in the air. "Another time mind-fuck."

"What does she mean by that?" Roland, one of Aberforth's trusty sidekicks, pushed forward until he stood inches from Emery. "I did not sign up for losing time and living with…who are we living with."

"The fae." Emery snapped and called on her darkness. She knew it had answered her call when her eyes began to glow and black tendrils snaked down her arms. "And as of right now, I trust them more than I do you. If you have a problem with staying here, then go back to the castle. Let Sloane strip you of your freedoms, because that's exactly what she'll do. She'll tell you she's going to free you of your mate bond, and allow you to choose your future, but that's only so long as it aligns with her bigger picture. You can go fight for her, but when we win, and so help me, Roland, with the stars as my witness, we will win, I will expect you to grovel at my feet. And maybe, just maybe, I will welcome you back."

That was a lie, and she knew it. Darkness or not, there was no way she was letting anyone return after lifting a finger against their people. It wasn't as if they'd been misinformed. They knew the stakes and still chose not to embrace change.

"What will it be, Roland?"

He looked around him to see if any of his cronies were

going to back him up. When they didn't, he bowed his head slightly. "I'd like to stay."

"So be it. But if you utter one word, or lift one hand against any of our people, I will personally ensure you are unable to return to our home."

Roland swallowed hard before nodding and stepping back into the crowd that surrounded Emery.

She turned back to Flora and forced a smile. "As for you and Draven, you don't have to go. You guys can go back to Moon Ridge."

"We aren't leaving you, Em. And anyway, Moon Ridge isn't safe for us anymore. Sloane sent a few of her monsters there with Fernando and some of his pack. They're rounding up those who won't align with her plans for the future. We're trying to figure out how to get them out."

Shit.

Relief should have flooded her, considering she got to keep Flora and those she loved close, but only anger flared in her chest. Sloane was always one step ahead of them.

"They can come here."

"Nico won't like that," Dorian grumbled.

"Nico can suck a witch's titty. If he wants my help, then this just became the unofficial headquarters for the opposition."

"I think we can come up with a better name than that," Bronwyn scoffed as she joined their little circle.

"All that matters is we are together," Callum added as he joined and wrapped an arm around Emery and Lina, giving her a reassuring squeeze. "There is a lot we need to figure out."

"Well then, let's get started, shall we?"

Chapter Twenty One

AUGUST

Emery's fresh flowery scent filled his senses, and August sank into her presence before he reached out to pull his mate against him.

When his hand met empty sheets, he blinked his eyes open and searched for their bond. Panic gripped his spine when he felt nothing. He searched for her in his mind, coming up with only a faint hint of her soul as the events of the night before filtered through his mind. At least he assumed it was the night before. He had no idea how long he'd been asleep.

August held onto the glow of Emery's amber eyes and the look of desperation on her face as Dorian carried her away. He prayed she was safe—far, far away from the castle with Lina and the rest of their family.

"How nice of you to join us. I was beginning to wonder how long you'd sleep."

That voice.

It was similar to Emery's, but all wrong. It was rough

and void of the lilt that made his heart race. The hair on the back of his neck rose, and he bit back the growl in his throat. She shouldn't be there. This was his sanctuary with Emery.

August shot up, clutching the sheets to his waist as he oriented himself. His gaze darted to the corner where Sloane defiled the space.

"How long was I asleep?" He wiped the sleep from his eyes, using it as a cover to expand his senses.

The castle was silent, or appeared to be. Sloane might have had the same wards up she'd had before when he hadn't heard her monsters arrive. Instinctively, he reached for his bond with Emery, but it was the same as before. He knew she lived, but he couldn't feel her beyond that.

"Twenty-one hours. You should be hungry." Sloane slid up the sleeve of her shirt and extended her wrist in offering.

His fangs lengthened against his will. She was right to assume he was hungry. After expending himself the night before, he needed to feed, but there was no way in hell he was taking anything offered from Sloane.

"I'm fine," he gritted through his fangs.

"Suit yourself. You'll soon realize you have very few choices when it comes to feeding. I'm the least offensive."

So she thought.

"I'll take my chances." August weighed his options for escaping. Even if they were alone in the room, he was certain Sloane would have ensured he was guarded at all times. It's what he would have done. Not that the extra muscle would've mattered. She could subdue him with her magic.

He swung his legs off the bed and entered the

bathroom. He stared longingly at the shower, but didn't trust Sloane not to try something while he was cleaning the blood from the night before off his skin.

Instead, he continued on into the closet, shucked his frayed jeans from his body and tugged on a fresh pair and a long-sleeved Henley.

When he entered the bedroom again, Sloane still sat stoically in the corner, her gaze focused on the night sky out the balcony. "What am I doing here, Sloane?"

It was hard to believe she was once a member of his Culling. She seemed so different back then. Then again, he knew what darkness could do to a person.

"You're mine." Her eyes trailed lazily up his body, leaving him feeling like nothing more than a whore to be claimed. "I thought we made that clear when you traded your life for my sister's." Sloane stood and sauntered toward him, her bony hips a stark contrast to Emery's lush curves.

August stilled, his fists clenched, preventing him from flinching when she rounded him and trailed her blackened fingers across his shoulder.

"It was a bit excessive if you ask me. It's not like I would have killed her. I need her blood to make things live. That's the pesky part about technically dying to get out of your castle the first time. Oh, the irony. Unfortunately, my light magic died with me. Not that I need it. Emery has enough for the both of us."

He chewed the inside of his cheek and tucked away the information she gave so freely before pressing her for more. "If you needed her alive, why take me at all? You don't need me."

"That's where you're wrong." Sloane slipped her hand

in his and tugged him toward the balcony. He hesitated, but allowed her to lead him outside. She turned around and leaned against the railing, giving him a small amount of freedom. A test to see if he'd jump. "Even if I sit on that throne, you are still the face of this kingdom. With you at my side, the vampire army will fall in line. I didn't need the witches, but having your extended army at my beck and call will make the other factions think twice before going against me."

August weighed his options. Not that he had many. He stepped forward and leaned against the railing beside her, his eyes trailing to the back of the castle grounds where his men were trapped in their barracks. "If you think they'll follow me just because I'm at your side, you underestimate their need for freedom. They won't follow me blindly if they think you're in charge. You killed members of their families, and have given them nothing to believe in."

"It won't be blindly when you publicly denounce your mate and declare your allegiance to me. Oh, and let them know you'll be supporting my cause to end mate bonds."

Bloody hell.

That was the nail in the coffin. The one that would get his people—the nobles, anyway—and many other kingdoms around the world to follow her without a second thought. That didn't mean he would follow along like a good little lap dog.

"What's the end game, Sloane?" August growled, biting back the outright denial he wanted to shove in her face. If she thought he would ever publicly denounce Emery, she was delusional.

"Besides the need to ruin everything my sister holds dear? I plan to create the supernatural world I should have been raised in. One where there are no factions, but instead one supreme leader who ensures no one race is too powerful and no one is shunned for what they are. I will lead, and they will follow, and if they don't, they will perish. There is no room for mates or alphas, kings or queens, not even your hidden fae will try to break what I've created. This realm is on the brink of a greatness you can't fathom, and I am going to lead us there."

There was a gleam in her eye that he was sure she meant to keep hidden. A hint of the girl he'd once known, who was hurting because of the injustice she'd faced not only at the hands of his people, but her own as well.

How the hell was it he felt bad for her? He'd never understood Emery's need to see the goodness in her, until that moment. August watched his greatest enemy blink back her vulnerability, and for the first time he considered that maybe they were meant to be on the same team.

"Your sister wants the same thing." Albeit with less darkness and destruction. "A world where we can be wholly ourselves."

"No, Emery wants rainbows and mates, hybrids, and fate predestined by the stars." Dark purple magic formed in her palm, and she rolled the small ball over her fingers. "The stars can go fuck themselves for all I care. I'm making my own future, and everyone else is getting in line."

And just like that, his compassion burst like a balloon that flew too high. He'd heard that tone before, recognized the stubborn pride that couldn't be penetrated by anything short of death.

"You're no better than my father then."

"I'll succeed where he failed," she said, confidently

lobbing her magic into the air and tipping her head back to watch it explode over the tree line behind the castle.

"Then it won't be with me at your side."

Sloane slowly turned to face him, her brow cocked and her lips parted slightly. "Are you saying you won't be mine? Even if it means your end?"

"I'm saying I already belong to someone, and nothing you say or do will change that."

"We'll see." Sloane shrugged and pushed off the railing. "Are you sure you'd rather be a prisoner than a king?"

"I'd rather be true to my heart, my kingdom, and my mate than reign with power that is tainted by lies and a need to perpetuate darkness."

"Isn't that the pot calling the kettle black? Not five months ago you were killing bar patrons for fun while pursuing my men."

"I'm not the same man I was before." Emery and his daughter made sure of that. The vampires who looked to him to lead made sure of that. He'd heard them and wanted to do better. They all deserved better from him.

Sloane scoffed. "You've grown soft."

"And you've lost sight of what truly matters, if you ever knew what that was to begin with."

August didn't need his senses to know he'd stepped too far over the line. Sloane glared at him and he was sure if it were possible, steam would be billowing from her ears.

She slammed her hands together and muttered under her breath. Purple sparks flew around him, and he barely had a chance to look over his shoulder in time to see a portal open. Sloane's eyes narrowed, and her lips twisted into a sardonic grin. "Take a good look at your friend, because what I have in store for you is so much worse."

Sloane slammed her hands forward, pushing him through the portal and into darkness.

August scrambled to his knees and tried to crawl back through, but the portal swirled shut before he could reach Sloane. He blinked his eyes, trying to adjust to the dim room he'd been thrust into. The air was moist and smelled of minerals and decay. The cell was stone on three sides with reinforced steel bars across the front wall.

He was in the dungeons of his own castle. The prisoner she promised he'd be if he disobeyed.

August ran to the bars and shouted, "Is anyone there?"

It was wishful thinking to hope there were any of his own guards remaining.

Instead, a husk shifted in the cell across from him. The body rolled over and faced him, struggling to find its balance. The figure groaned as it crawled to the bars of the cell and gripped the steel with filthy fingers. With one hand, it reached up and pushed its matted hair from its face.

Broken brown eyes met his, and a gasp fell from August's mouth.

It couldn't be. This couldn't be the same wolf that protected his mate and brought joy to their lives.

"Ansel?"

"It's about damn time you showed up, blood sucker."

Chapter Twenty-Two

EMERY

Crying had woken her...again.

Emery rolled from the corner of the bed she'd resolved herself to and padded across the room to the attached sitting room they'd made into a makeshift nursery for Lina.

"Good morning, sweet girl." She yawned. "I assume you're hungry."

She hadn't done anything for the last three days except sleep and feed Lina. The two of them napped and played in their room while Emery's body and magic healed from the attack on the castle.

Still, guilt gnawed at her.

The rest of their kingdom was outside her doors adjusting to life in Enchanth. Emery should be with them. She knew that; but despite Malcolm and Lily having tried multiple times to get her to join them in getting everything settled, she couldn't bring herself to do much more than sleep and care for her daughter. It was like the guillotine that hovered over her had finally fallen, and she'd succumbed to its blade the moment she'd gotten everyone safely to Enchanth.

She'd been going non-stop since the attack at the hunt. Really, since she'd arrived at the castle all those months ago. There were moments of peace, but overall, she'd been thrown into problem after problem, and even though this wasn't the first time the weight of it all caught up with her, this time it crippled her.

August was with Sloane. Ansel was creating terrible monsters. Vampires were more divided than ever. They were forced to retreat to a magic fae realm. The list went on and on.

Emery picked up Lina and cuddled the tiny baby to her chest before sitting in the oversized armchair by the window and offering her daughter her breast. She couldn't hide forever, she knew that, but these stolen moments would get her through the hard times ahead.

Lina latched on and her tiny hand wrapped around Emery's finger, melting her heart. She blinked back tears as she studied her daughter's features. Her eyes, one blue and one amber, the way her lips bowed like her daddy's, and the tiny, almost invisible freckles that came from Emery. She was the best parts of each of them, along with her brother. This sweet little girl was Emery's entire world and didn't even know it. She was the connection Emery needed to August so long as she couldn't feel his soul.

A soft knock sounded at the door, and Emery looked up to see a frail old woman in the doorway of the sitting room. She was dressed in a simple shift, her shoulders hunched over like time had made her bones weary, and her face and hands filled with the deep wrinkles of experience. She clutched a tray with two cups, a teapot, and an array of cheeses and fruits.

"You must be Emery," she smiled in a way that only the

elderly can. Like they're a sheep in wolf's clothing, sizing you up while they feign innocence.

Emery's grip tightened on Lina, and she grabbed the muslin blanket from the back of the chair to cover herself. "And you are?"

"Trine. Dorian sent me to check on you and bring you a cup of tea." She lifted the tray. "And don't fuss with the cover dear, what you are doing is completely natural and to be celebrated."

Emery's eyes narrowed and she set the muslin back down. Lina hated it when she used a cover. "He could have sent Malcolm or Lily."

"That's true, but they don't know the first thing about the sight. I do."

"So, you're a peace offering?" Emery wasn't surprised; Dorian had made himself scarce while she hid herself away. Likely because she hadn't hidden the fact she was still pissed off at him for keeping so much from them.

"Of sorts." Trine shrugged. "It's also purely selfish. I haven't met another star-touched witch in many, many moons."

"You're a witch?"

"Of sorts," Trine said again. Emery was starting to think that vague answers were a fae trait. "The fae don't have witches, we have crones, or what you would call star-touched. I can't wield any other magicks, but I can read the leaves and pull cards with great accuracy, and I've been known to mediate visions and dabble in other sights. I believe I can help you to hone your sight. To search for what you need." Trine took a step forward, and her eyes darted to the empty chair across from Emery. "Are you quite finished with your inquisition? My old bones aren't meant for standing."

Emery gestured for Trine to join her, and the woman set the tray down on the table between them.

"You're a fae crone. Does that mean you knew my ancestor?"

"Celeste?" Trine scooped the loose tea leaves from the ramekin into each cup and poured the piping hot water over the top. "She was a member of the coven in my hometown."

"The last human city in the Feywilde."

Trine looked up over the bridge of her nose and grinned. "I see Dorian has been filling you in."

"Reluctantly," Emery grumbled.

"Have a little patience with him. His story is one that has only just begun to have a happy ending." She plucked a grape from the tray and offered it to Emery, who gladly took it. "Now drink your tea, but leave a small amount at the bottom."

Flavor burst on her tongue, and she couldn't stop the small moan that fell from her lips. Malcolm and Lily had been holding out on her. While the bread and soup they'd been serving her was delicious, it had nothing on the tea's incredible flavor and the freshness of the fruit.

"The food here is the best part," Trine said with a wink.

There was something about the old crone that called to Emery and settled her soul. She reminded her of Agatha, mixed with a little bit of the wild glint in Octavian's eyes. There was an innate pull to trust her, and though Emery was hesitant to put her stock in anything Enchanth had to offer, something about Trine felt right.

"How did you end up here?" Emery sipped the hot tea.

It reminded her of her mornings in New Orleans at the cafe with Ansel. "Dorian said this was where stranded fae lived."

"As I said, I'm a crone. We are the seers of the fae and trusted advisors to the highest courts. I foretold a future that the king didn't have any interest in coming true, so he banished me."

Emery shook her head, and dropped her chin to her chest to stare at Lina, who was no longer eating. "Banishing you doesn't make it any less true."

"Exactly. But as you know, vision and readings are open to interpretation. It's in finding the common thread that links them together that you find their truths."

Emery considered the visions and dreams she'd been having over the past few months and shuddered.

Lina.

And August.

Her family was the common thread.

She focused on the little girl in her arms, cooing and smiling without a care in the world.

In every vision since Lina had been born, either her daughter or her mate were at Emery's side. In life, in death, it didn't matter if anyone else was there, it was always them.

But what the hell did that mean?

"I can see you starting to connect the dots."

"Yes and no. I'm still confused as to what it all means."

"I wish I could say I had a manual to give you, but each seer is different. What means prosperous for me may mean drought for you. But with time, you will learn to interpret your gift. Until then, I will help you learn to focus."

"And what exactly does that entail?"

"Hand me the babe." Trine stretched out her hands and wiggled her fingers, a full, wrinkled smile tugging at her lips. "I could use some snuggles, and you need to concentrate."

Emery's grip tightened on Lina, and she hesitated. She studied Trine's eyes, the kindness and fire in their depths. There wasn't deception, and just as she'd felt before, there was already an innate trust in the woman. She stood and handed Lina to her, and the baby smiled and cooed, reaching for the silver pendant at the crone's throat.

"Alright, take the cup in your hands."

Emery followed her instruction, the aroma of lemon and sage lingering above the cup.

"Now close your eyes. Picture yourself, or whoever it is you want to read for. Maybe it's your kingdom. The leaves or the cards will always be clearer when it's self-introspection, but it's not impossible to read for others; it's just not as straightforward."

Emery shut her eyes and pictured herself staring into a mirror. There was very little of the woman she was before. The scar on her brow from when she fell off her bike when she was six was still there, but it was overshadowed by who she'd become. There was hidden strength in her eyes, lined by the onyx rings that tethered her to her mate, and bonds of sisterhood in the magic that plaited her arms in gold and black. She ignored the tiny wisps of fear she held for the dark magic in her soul. It didn't define her. She couldn't let it, not when it could lead her down the same path as Sloane. No, the woman before her stood in the light. Gone was the girl who didn't have family, who searched for meaning in the world around her. Emery had found everything and more, and the determination to protect it shone in every facet of her being.

"Now swirl the cup in your hands three times clockwise, and flip it over on the saucer."

She did as she was instructed and waited for the remaining liquid to drain from the cup, leaving the leaves.

"What do you know about reading?" Trine asked as she made faces at Lina.

"Not much more than what the basic book from the coven's library could teach me. Leaves on the rim designate the present, the sides are events not far distant, and the bottom tells the distant future. The nearer the symbols are to the handle, the closer to fulfillment they are."

"Correct, but the leaves need intention, guidance, if you will. When you flip the cup, continue to focus your thoughts and imbue the cup with your magic."

"Won't that affect the leaves?" Her brow raised in skepticism. She'd never heard of any witch using magic directly to read the leaves. Then again, she didn't know any star-touched witches.

"The stars will guide them."

Emery nodded and called forth her magic, her hands glowing around the cup as she flipped it over.

The leaves were plastered to all sides of the cup, and Emery stared for so long, her confusion could have been misconstrued as understanding.

"What do you see?"

"An ax in the present." That one she remembered from the book, it meant there were problems to overcome. Vague but not totally inaccurate. "Along with something that could either be a dagger or a knife."

"Help from friends or a disaster met through fighting and hatred."

Emery winced. "Neither are too far-fetched from our current situation."

"No, but don't take the leaves at face value. Allow them to resonate with you throughout the day. Sometimes you'll find it takes a bit for the leaves to reveal their true meaning. Emery nodded and continued to interpret the leaves. The sides of the cup held a cross, an hourglass, and what almost looked to her like a masted ship: trouble, delay or death, imminent danger, and a successful journey. The odds for her immediate future weren't looking good.

"Not what you wanted to see?"

Emery shook her head and looked to the bottom of the cup. A hammer, wavy lines, and mountains.

"What do these mean?" She offered the cup to Trine.

"The hammer means challenges to overcome and the wavy lines mean a difficult journey. It's the mountains that are concerning, they could mean a powerful friend or a powerful enemy."

"I could use a powerful friend. We've got plenty of enemies."

"Ah, yes. That you do. Although I think you will be surprised that not all your enemies will remain that way."

Emery cocked a brow. "I take it you've seen something."

"Nothing for certain," Trine mused, while smiling down at Lina. "All I will say is you will need to decide if forcing your ideals is worth the price."

"You speak of the vampires. Of our mate bonds."

"Take it from someone who witnessed the rise and fall

of the greatest fae dynasties, coexisting is far superior to the wars of brothers."

The words were a slap in the face, even if that's not what Trine intended. This wasn't just about coexisting with those who didn't want mates. It was also about those who would be forced to live life unfulfilled. She didn't know that there was a happy middle ground; a place where they could coexist in peace. It broke her heart to consider that there might not be a happy ending for some while others would know all the benefits of having their souls complete.

A soft knock rapped at the bedroom door, pulling Emery from her thoughts. Before she could get up and get there, Dorian poked his head into the sitting room.

"Does no one wait for the door to be answered before entering?"

"At least they aren't sieving in. That's when things get really interesting." Trine wiggled her bushy brows, well past the ominous words she'd shared and clearly picturing Dorian naked.

"Gross. He's in love with one of my best friends, even if neither of them will admit it."

Dorian opened his mouth to protest, but Trine was faster. "Oh, I know. I've seen what becomes of Dorian and Ansel."

This caught Dorian's attention, but the old crone got to her feet, handed Lina to Emery and was out the door before he could ask what the hell she'd meant.

"She's a sly one, isn't she?" Emery chuckled.

"You have no idea."

An awkward silence fell between them, and Emery sought to fill it. "Did Bronwyn finish up with the components?"

Bronwyn had been working on getting everything together to break the spell of the Culling marks now that they would be able to obtain the essence from Dorian's blood. Emery had no doubt Bronwyn, ever the scholar, was creaming her pants. Not only at the prospect of getting a hold of his rare blood, but also because this was her opportunity to learn anything and everything from the fae.

He nodded and slouched into the seat Trine had vacated. "How are you feeling?"

"Less like I've physically been hit by a train, more like I've been emotionally dragged behind it."

"I'm sorry."

"Dorian, I—"

He held up his hands. "Let me finish. I'm going to be out of commission for a bit after they filter my blood, and I wanted to make sure we got to talk." Dorian inhaled a steadying breath and lifted his gaze to meet hers. "I know over the last few days I've probably lost every ounce of trust I've ever gained from you, but I have never been more honest than when I tell you that you are my queen, as August is my king. You've given me a family when I had none. You trusted me and I failed you, but it's because I couldn't tell you everything. Not because I didn't want to, but so much is riding on timing, and my silence was as much for your protection as it was for the fae."

"Dorian, it's not that I don't trust you, but there is another fucking prophecy about me and you didn't think that was pertinent information for me to know? Not only that, but I found all of this out after you left my mate behind. You took me from him, Dorian. You and I both know she's not going to let him stay unscathed, and that man has already fought for us enough. For our kingdom."

Emery set Lina, who had fallen asleep for her morning power nap, in her crib and quietly padded out of the room.

She waited for Dorian to follow her and shut the door softly before heading to the balcony. Dorian followed again, leaning his back against the railing while she fisted her hands and rested her elbows next to him. Her gaze drifted out, taking in the beauty of Enchanth. The heat of its two suns warmed her skin while the fresh morning dew called to her elemental magic.

Emery reached out to her magic and called it to her palms. It came easily enough, but still without the magnitude she'd wielded before she'd faced off with Sloane.

"It will return. You just need some rest." Dorian stepped forward.

When she pinned a glare in his direction, his head dropped with a heavy sigh. "It's not a prophecy so much as a promise of the realms. The fae didn't always live in this Feywilde. There was once another land, but it was overtaken."

"The fall of great fae dynasties." Emery whispered Trine's words, more to herself than Dorian. The fae were cryptic fuckers, and she was beginning to think none of them would every speak plainly.

"Trine doesn't know when to keep her mouth shut."

"If it makes you feel any better, she offers the same half-explanations Octavian does."

"It doesn't surprise me. You will too as the sight grows. Say too much, you change the future." Dorian shifted his weight and tipped his head back in the morning sun. "Anyway, when the dynasty fell, those who survived fled that realm and took over this new one. They learned it coincided with another."

"Mine?"

"Correct. For a time, all was right, but then your world began to suffer. The more the fae drew magic from their realm, the more it drew from the mortal realm as well. Your realm's magic. The mortal realm drained faster than the Feywilde because no supernatural beings resided within it to replenish it. Celeste and Runa were the answers. They infused subtle threads of magic into the mortal realm and vowed to sustain it with their lineage."

"Runa?"

Dorian nodded. "Her twin."

Emery let out a noise that was somewhere between a scoff and a chuckle. "Why does it always have to be twins?"

"Balance would be my guess," Dorian said with a slight shrug of his shoulders. "I'm not supposed to get involved. None of the fae are. That was why they sent Celeste and Runa. If we were to interfere in the realm that tethers us, it could start a war none of us want, mostly because the humans would not win. We've watched from afar to ensure the future of our home, but it's not ours to protect. That rightfully belongs to the witches. Or it did. Over time, the factions were born, and though it wasn't our intended plan, it strengthened the realm. Still, I will tell you that I don't think Runa died. At least not until recently. If she did, your realm wouldn't have been stable all these years, even with the additions."

"I don't know that I would call our realm stable."

"Until you, it has been."

"Me?" Emery turned and studied Dorian's profile as he

looked out over the forest. The worried lines at his eyes and the way he pinched his brow made it seem as though he'd seen far too much in his days. "What the hell do I have to do with this?"

"Everything." Dorian pressed his lips together and when he spoke again, he didn't say more on the subject. He was keeping secrets again, or omitting the truth, which was basically the same thing. "I think Runa's been helping Sloane. Or she did. It's the only thing that makes sense."

Emery rolled her eyes, but didn't press him. Dorian had proven he would tell her what she needed to know in time. Even if it annoyed the shit out of her. "Celeste said as much."

"When did you speak to her?" Dorian asked.

Emery stood upright and turned around. Leaning her back against the railing, she crossed her arms across her chest. "I only told August about it, but when I died, I went to a realm with Celeste. Or maybe it was purgatory. She told me that someone had been feeding Sloane dark magic for some time. It would stand to reason that Runa could've been the witch doing so."

Dorian chewed his lower lip and closed his eyes. When he opened them, silver lined the rims. "If that's the case, they are royally screwed."

Emery didn't miss his slip of the tongue or the fear and worry etched in his features. It was easy to forget that Dorian had as much stake in the game as she did. They had both lost the people they loved to her bitch of a sister with no promise of their return.

Emery reached out and placed her hand on Dorian's. "We'll get him back...both of them."

"I wasn't even—"

"You've got the same look on your face that I feel in my soul."

A forced smile tipped his lips, and he gave her hand a squeeze. "At least we know where they are now."

"Yeah." Emery nodded halfheartedly. They might know where they were, but that didn't mean they were safe. Not when they were under Sloane's control. It didn't matter how much Emery wanted to believe her sister could somehow be saved; after the events of the night before, on top of everything else, she just didn't see how it was possible.

Sloane would have left her nothing more than a breathing husk if given the chance. If August hadn't offered himself up, Emery would probably be a soulless blood bag by now.

"Emery, I'm sorry we had to leave him behind, but I can't apologize for getting you out of there. I wasn't lying when I said we need you alive."

"I know. I just…I can't feel him anymore, Dorian." She choked on a sob, and before she could wipe away the tears on her cheeks, Dorian pulled her against him. "I don't know how to do this without him. They're all going to look to me to lead, and I'm still trying to figure out how to be all the things to everyone."

"You don't have to be everything, Emery. You just have to lead from your heart. You, more than anyone I know, always put the needs of your people first. You rule with compassion and yet somehow you also know when it's time to be a raging bitch."

"Hey!" She pulled away and smacked his chest.

A laugh rumbled in his chest. "It's a compliment. Every

good queen needs a dark side. And I think it's time you learned to hone yours."

"I can't. I don't want to end up like her."

Dorian cocked a brow. "You think darkness is what made Sloane the way she is?"

Emery chewed her lip and exhaled. "No. Yes. I don't know. But what I do know is that every time I touch my dark magic, I lose a piece of the light. It threatens to consume me. And that's without giving into the blood magic. Death and necromancy took my sister from me; I won't let it take me from my family."

"Emery, you are the strongest witch I have ever met. The darkness is a part of you that you can't deny."

"I'm just not ready." Emery dropped her chin to her chest for a moment, before lifting her gaze to meet Dorian's. "But when I am, will you help me?"

Dorian hesitated, but then nodded with a smile.

"No more lies, Dorian."

"I can promise you I won't lie, but I can't tell you everything. I will do my best to keep you in the loop now that you know about Enchanth."

"Deal."

Dorian cocked a brow. "No more deals with the fae."

"Are you going to elaborate on that?"

"The fae like to make deals, and they will take everything you say out of context. If you're forced to shake on anything, make damn sure you know what you're agreeing to."

"Do you have any idea what Nico wants from me?"

Dorian pressed his lips together like he was unsure how much to tell her, and when he spoke, he chose his words carefully. "Nico has an agenda. I'm not entirely sure where you fit into it, but I promise I'll make sure you are not a pawn in his game."

"What happened between you two? He called you his brother."

"Once upon a time, we were closer than that, but that is a story for another day." Dorian opened the balcony door and gestured for her to enter. "Ready to go give your witches their mates?"

"Nothing would make me happier."

Chapter Twenty Three

EMERY

Draining Dorian of his blood and filtering out only the dark essence they needed turned out to be a tedious and boring process. It reminded her of donating plasma, but instead of tubes and centrifuges, Dorian lay in a pool of water collected from the mountains that connected Enchanth's pocket realm to the Feywilde.

His wrists were slit and the water's properties would separate the essence from his blood, allowing it to sink to the bottom where Bronwyn collected it and infused it directly into the seeds that would then ferment with the rest of the ingredients. His blood was then filtered from the water and fed through a tube back into Dorian's arm. If all went as planned, the final spell component should be ready in two weeks.

Emery stood at the edge of the pool, her hair plastered to her forehead from the humidity in the greenhouse-esque space, and her lower lip nearly chewed raw. The small fae, who looked like a relative of Albert Einstein had he had a snout nose, assured her that Dorian would be fine after he was healed and his body had been given a chance to replenish itself. Overall, the process seemed a bit barbaric, forcing him to lay in a pool of his own blood, but she was assured it was how it had always been done. Still, she didn't like seeing him lying there looking like a murder victim, with black and crimson flowing from his wrists.

The only upside was that during the process, Dorian would be too weak to keep up his glamour, so Emery was given the chance to study his fae form. He mostly looked the same, just more ethereal. His skin shimmered, and the tips of his fingers were blackened like Nico's. She assumed if his eyes were open, they would be a vibrant obsidian as well. Also, like Nico, he had two horns that curled from just behind his temple, but one of them was incomplete, as though it had been sheared off at some point.

Seeing him this way only left Emery with more questions, but she would have to save them for another time.

She glanced around the room. Bronwyn was deep in a book that looked older than time itself, while Malcolm and Lily were huddled in the corner behind her whispering to themselves. Leaning against the windowed wall that comprised the back of the small room stood Nico with his eyes glued on Dorian. Emery took a moment to study the fae, dissecting the intensity of his gaze.

It was clear they meant something to one another, but when Nico poked fun at Dorian like an older brother would, Dorian showed nothing but contempt for the mysterious fae. Emery couldn't help but wonder what the story was between them. She was sure Dorian would tell her in due time, but she had a hunch everything was tied together—that whatever it was Nico had in store for her was somehow tied to his connection with Dorian.

Nico's eyes shifted, locking with hers. As always, there was an intensity in his gaze, as if he was trying to figure her out, which left Emery to wonder just how much Dorian had reported back to his once-king and brother. Nico pushed off the wall and came to stand next to her. Arms crossed, his gaze returned to Dorian. "He's giving up a lot for your people."

"Our people. He's as much a part of my kingdom as anyone else." The fact that Dorian was keeping secrets from her didn't change her loyalty to him or his to their kingdom. It hurt her personally, but he'd never given them a reason not to trust his motives, so she would continue to stand behind him. Especially if Nico thought he could shake their friendship with doubt.

Nico was the one who made her apprehensive.

"At least he thinks so," Nico quipped.

Emery pulled her eyes from Dorian and narrowed them on Nico. "It doesn't matter what you think. As long as Dorian knows he belongs with us."

A sarcastic chuckle filled the space between them, which only served to irritate Emery more. "He's earned your loyalty, and dare I say he deserves it after everything I put him through, but if you ask me, he's giving up too much."

Her dark magic, only just replenished, sent her a weak vision of exactly how it would love to wrap itself around his neck until his eyes bulged from their sockets. "It's a good thing I didn't ask you."

"Did he even tell you why he has the essence in his blood? Why you do?" Nico dug his fingers into the wound opened by Dorian, rubbing in the fact that he was likely in on the secret.

Emery pressed her lips together and remained silent while shoving down the need to do exactly as her magic suggested.

"I didn't think so."

"And I suppose you aren't going to tell me either?"

Nico scoffed and jerked his head back as if offended. "That's the difference between Dorian and me. I have no problem spilling my secrets if it's going to further my own agenda."

"Which is?"

Nico looked around the room, his eyes lingering on each person as if he were sizing them up. He shook his head before offering Emery his elbow. "Walk with me."

Emery's eyes fell to his elbow, just above where the wisps of black that stained his skin stopped.

"It won't harm you. In fact, you may find it isn't so different from your magic."

She quirked a brow and slipped her hand through his arm, allowing him to lead her away from the safety of her friends.

"My sister has the same marks on her fingertips."

"I know." He didn't say anything more, and Emery wasn't about to ask. He would likely give her a roundabout fae answer, which would only leave her more frustrated.

Patience might have been a virtue, but the fae made it one that was fucking impossible to comply with.

Nico led her away from the greenhouse and into the expansive gardens behind the castle. She did her best to ignore the pang in her heart when she thought of the gardens back home, and her night spent with August so many months ago. Instinctively, she reached out to caress their non-existent bond, knowing she would find nothing. His absence was like the night of a new moon, hauntingly dark. It didn't matter that she had stars to keep her company in the form of her friends and her sweet Lina, because even though they were beautiful, they didn't fill her sky like her mate did.

She hated herself for not telling him more often just how important he was to her. She showed him through their bond and with her body, but lately her words had fallen short. Now he was a realm away, imprisoned by a sister who would do anything to hurt Emery, and she couldn't tell him, remind him, that he was the strongest part of her. August was her other half in every sense.

Without him, she felt lost.

"Where did you go?" Nico asked, and she realized he'd stopped at the edge of a cliff.

"Nowhere." Emery dropped her hand and glanced out toward the sea that expanded from the base of the jagged rocks. The sun had dipped behind the storm clouds rolling in, and the waves swelled and crashed against the shore.

"Are you sure?" Nico pressed, his voice holding a hint of softness she hadn't expected. "I recognize that look."

Emery pulled her eyes from the sea and turned to face the fae. "And what's that?"

Nico released a heavy sigh. "The look of someone who loathes the saying 'Absence makes the heart grow fonder.'"

Emery's eyes widened. It was the absolute last thing she expected him to say. But what was more surprising was the weight behind his words. Like they were as much for him as they were for her. Was it possible that this mysterious fae had a heart behind all those layers of darkness? And if he did, what were the chances he knew the depths of loss like Emery?

"It's true." She shrugged, returning her gaze to the horizon. "But what they don't tell you is that the fondness you feel is just a disguise for a dagger whose penetration is endless, bearing an ache that can never be soothed until your heart is whole again."

Nico didn't respond. No quick-witted retort or vague explanation. When Emery craned her neck and looked up again to check that Nico was still beside her, she knew he'd felt her words. His eyes were lost to the world around him, stormy as the sea before them, and she had no doubt whoever he missed flooded his thoughts.

"Nico."

The fae chewed his lower lip and shook his head. "I need your world protected. And that means the balance needs to remain intact. Although your sister wields a brand of viciousness that once spoke to my soul, it is now a problem I need handled. More than that, I need to know if your blood and the blood of your descendants will be enough to keep the balance intact so we can destroy your sister."

Emery searched his eyes for the answers he wasn't sharing, especially after the whiplash she'd just witnessed, but found his vulnerability gone. "You make it sound as though destroying Sloane now will upset the balance."

"It will."

Shit. Emery's head spun. In everything she'd learned since coming Enchanth about the realms and balance, she'd never considered that there could be ramifications to removing Sloane altogether.

"Is that why I'm here? Why you need me?"

The sky opened up, and a light rain fell to the ground around them. Emery flicked her wrist and shielded them from the water with a steady stream of air.

"Yes and no." Nico started down the path along the cliff's edge. "You are here because you need a place to hide out until you can learn to defeat your sister. Dorian suspected I'd be able to help you, but he wanted to protect you from me."

Emery skipped to catch up, then did her best to match his strides. "Do I need protection?"

"Absolutely, but I am not a threat to you. I can help you learn to harness your dark magic."

She didn't exactly like the idea of spending more time with Nico. It didn't matter that a part of her had felt a kinship to him moments before; at the end of the day, he held an intense darkness that made her skin crawl. "Why can't Dorian help me?"

"Because while he harnesses the same darkness that's in my veins and yours, I control it. He has life because I allow it. Everything in the Feywilde and mortal realms exists because I allow it."

"And why do you?"

"For the same reason you fight for your kingdom's future."

Emery considered her reasons for fighting. It was for her people, yes, but more than that, it was for Lina.

"You have a daughter."

Nico's gait faltered, but he didn't stop walking as he shook his head. "Not yet, but this isn't about me. Right now, it's about getting your magic where it needs to be to succeed."

"And where is that?"

"When we're through, you will be able to harness the darkness your sister wields and strengthen it with your own. Most would believe Sloane's strength is in her necromancy, but even the dead have blood running through their veins—blood tainted with the darkness you hold."

Emery swallowed hard, not liking where this conversation was going. "And that's what you need? Me to hone my darkness?"

"Oh no," Nico chuckled, "that's what *you* need. I need you to work with Trine to hone your sight."

Dorian had basically said the same thing, but Emery still held fast that the last thing she needed was to hone her darkness. The fear that she would lose herself to it still had a grip on her spine, and she wasn't ready to let go.

"Why do you need my sight?" Emery asked.

"Does it matter? We have a deal. Amnesty for your magic."

"I'd like to know what I'm doing."

"That wasn't part of the deal."

"Fine," she huffed, seeing as he was done giving useful information. "What do I need to do?"

"Until your magic is at full strength, you'll train with Trine every morning. She'll teach you to bend your sight to your own desires." Nico stopped walking just outside the entrance to the castle's main hall and turned to face Emery. "When you're ready, you'll learn to hone the darkness."

You will learn.

No ifs, ands or buts.

Her darkness purred in her chest at the promise of being unleashed, and Emery opened her mouth to protest, but Nico had gone inside the castle before she could utter a word. She tipped her head back and flicked away the air that kept the rain from hitting her face, allowing the water to wash over her as she was left wondering if there was a way out of becoming the monster she most feared.

Chapter Twenty Four

AUGUST

Shimmering drool dripped from the snarling monster as he stood between the cells, moments away from sealing his fate.

August shouldn't be praying Ansel would be the chosen one; he shouldn't be wishing that fate upon anyone, but he wasn't sure he could take another minute of Sloane's torture.

Minutes. Hours. Days. He didn't have a bloody fucking clue how long he'd been there. Between the constant darkness of their cells, the fluorescent bulbs of Sloane's makeshift lab, inconsistent sleep, and endless illusions, there was no way he could know for certain how much time had passed.

The dungeon was never meant for torture. The walls were cold stone. They gave off water when it rained and left a dank smell in the air. The place was meant for temporary holding and nothing more. That didn't stop Sloane, though. The lowest level of cells that held August and Ansel were still filthy and not fit for human habitation, but Sloane transformed the upper levels into a sterile maze of horrors.

The beast's gaze flitted between where August sat curled up in a ball against the back of his cell and where Ansel mirrored him across the way. He reached for the door on Ansel's cell, and August breathed a subconscious sigh of relief.

… That was, until a second monster appeared from the opposite end of the hall. August hadn't heard him. Their fucking hearts beat in time like they were one person, an extension of Sloane's madness. The second monster stepped in front of his cell and opened the door.

Damn it.

August slowly rose to his feet, watching Ansel as he did the same. They knew the drill. He'd fought it the first few times they'd come for him, killing more than a few of Sloane's pets, but it only made the torture worse. Sometimes for him, sometimes for Ansel. Sloane wasn't above pitting them against each other. It was easier to comply—to bid his time, and wait and collect information. Though he was beginning to wonder if anything he'd seen was real. He hoped it wasn't, for Ansel's sake.

The monsters marched them up a floor and shoved them into the showers Sloane had magicked into existence. It was the same process every time: strip them down, scrub their skin raw of the filth and blood from previous sessions, and dress them in scratchy cotton sweats.

Every time, the same.

Ansel stripped beside him and the scent of his blood wafted through the air.

August swallowed hard past the knot in the back of his throat.

Bloody fucking hell, he smelled delicious. Nowhere near as mouth-watering as Emery, but she wasn't there, and August craved sustenance. His fangs lengthened with need. Not in the same way he had when the bloodlust took over. This was less drive to murder and more a deep-seated, ravenous urge to rectify the depletion brought on by exhaustion and the rounds of fights against Sloane's monsters.

It took everything in him not to cross the showers, shove Ansel against the wall, and tear into his throat.

But that's exactly what Sloane wanted. Him to lose control. She wanted him desperate and unhinged so he would give in to her whims. And if he was honest, he was almost there. Almost.

He reached for the bond that told him Emery was alive. Somewhere far away, she still breathed and that made every minute of torture worth it. Every painful vision. Every doubt that would creep through his mind. It was worth it as long as he knew she was safe.

August stripped his own clothes and stepped under the frigid water beside Ansel. They didn't speak to each other. They couldn't. Not so long as Sloane was listening. He couldn't tell him how much Dorian loved him, even if he'd never spoken the words out loud. How he would be so proud of Emery for bringing their perfect daughter into the world. He couldn't tell Ansel that even though they were trapped in hell, their friends and family were out there safe and no doubt trying to find a way to get them out.

He wished he could tell him.

Instead, all he could do was offer Ansel his silent strength. Ansel did the same.

They both stood there, demoralized, as the monsters scrubbed their skin until they almost bled. Then, once they were clothed, they were shuffled one after the other to their final destination.

The second August entered the lab, a shiver ran down his spine and bile rose in his throat. Like a death row inmate walking to his execution, August was led to his chair and strapped in. Ansel followed the same protocol, strapped to his table on the opposite side of a windowed wall.

Their eyes locked, both of them wearing the same grim expression. There was nothing to smile about. Not a single thing that could change their fate. The days they were brought there together were always the worst. All they could do was pray it didn't break them.

Sloane's heels clicked down the stone hallway, announcing her arrival. August's gut twisted with nerves. What would she show him today? How much more could Ansel bear before he broke? As it was, August wasn't sure he would ever be the same.

"Good evening, gentlemen." Sloane's voice echoed on against the tile, grating against his ears. "I appreciate your dedication to our cause."

Mocking them was her favorite way to rile them up. The bitch took sick pleasure in finding the open wounds and pouring salt on them before sticking a hot poker through their flayed flesh.

Sloane rounded his chair and stood in front of him. She leaned over and pressed her hands to his knees, digging her nails into his thighs.

"Are you ready to be mine?" Sloane whispered, the same as she did every time she brought him there.

August chewed the inside of his cheek, using his fangs to cut a deep gash in an attempt to ignore the beating pulse in her neck. It didn't matter that she reeked of death, and he had no doubt her blood was toxic. He was fucking starving.

In his peripheral vision, August watched Wren appear in Ansel's room, syringe in hand.

Bloody hell. It was an army day. If it had only been a blood day, they would both survive unscathed.

Draven had guessed Ansel was being used to make wolves, but nothing could have prepared August for the gravity of what he'd been enduring all these months. The blood. The cracking of sternums. Before all this, Ansel was the kindest, sweetest of them all. August had once thought that if people could represent emotion, Ansel would've represented joy. But not anymore. When August looked at the wolf, now he saw nothing but agony.

Sloane's hand snaked out, pinched his chin between her thumb and forefinger and yanked to bring his attention back to her. Then, she asked again, "Are you ready to be mine?"

"Your enemy? Yes. Your executioner? Absolutely. You're going to need to be a bit more specific."

Her free hand whizzed through the air and connected with his cheek, drawing blood where her nails struck him. A small drop poured down his face, and his tongue darted out involuntarily to meet it.

"Your loyalty to my sister makes you weak," Sloane sneered.

August didn't reply. He knew better. As it was, he

shouldn't have taunted her, but he couldn't help himself. The rage this woman solicited in him was beyond anything he had ever felt before. But ultimately, he was at her whim. She could make his life miserable, or Ansel's.

Sloane's lips curled into a wicked grin. One that made the hair on the back of his neck stand on end… never a good thing. She stood up and sauntered off, swaying her bony hips in a way she seemed to think was sexy.

August stifled the urge to gag, knowing he'd just made things worse if he did.

He was pulled from his thoughts when Ansel's head lolled to the side. His eyes connected with August as Wren stuck him with the needle that would trigger his wolf.

Stay strong. This is not your fault. August tried to will the thoughts through the space between them.

His eyes dilated, and in seconds his friend was gone, replaced by the wolf that only wanted one thing.

His mate.

Or who he thought his mate was.

August knew about Sebastian, but that's not who Ansel cried for. It was Dorian. The fae who had stolen his heart. He didn't know much about wolf mates, but Ansel's wolf seemed to have claimed Dorian in lieu of their lost mate. It was a beautiful thing to witness.

August tried to hold on to the image of Ansel and Dorian one day uniting. He tried not to think about the present as, one group at a time, the humans were brought into Ansel's room. He didn't look away. With each person he turned, Sloane promised Ansel she'd find Dorian. She even whispered to the beast that August was the one hiding him from her.

Thankfully, Ansel's wolf knew better. He knew August.

Knew Emery. They wouldn't do that to him. Their bonds were thicker than Sloane's promises. But that didn't quell his wolf's desperation.

Sloane had broken the animal in him. Played on his agony.

Ansel's body heaved as he ripped into the last human's sternum and sliced their heart.

Twenty more people lost their lives.

Always twenty. Four groups of five. They watched each other die as they tried to pry themselves from the room to escape their fate. Sometimes they attacked Ansel, but no human was a match for his wolf.

August watched every death. Every slice of their hearts. It was not only his way of mourning them, but his solidarity with the man who was forced to feel every bit of their transformation. He heard the tears Ansel cried each night. The calls for his sired wolves. The mourning of their deaths when Sloane imbued her magic and killed their souls, claiming them as her own.

He never imagined it was the same for wolves and vampires. The only other turned wolf he'd ever met was Flora, and he doubted she and Draven understood the intricacies of the process. The mate bond would forever trump the bond of sire and progeny, but as far as he could tell, despite the fact that Ansel wasn't an alpha, he still felt a pull to those his wolf had created.

"You could stop this."

August froze.

It was her voice. An impossibility. And yet, even though he knew it wasn't real, the soft velvet tone made his cock twitch and his heart swell.

She wasn't supposed to be there.

Not yet.

She wasn't supposed to show up until after Ansel had finished. Then it was his turn. His turn to ache as the love of his gods-damned life broke every vow they'd ever made to each other.

He'd watch because he was a masochistic fuck, and he lived for any piece of Emery he could hold on to. Even if it was the image of her fucking every single one of his guards. His friends. His family.

Sloane was a sadistic bitch.

August didn't turn his head to look behind him. Not yet. He kept his eyes trained on Ansel's shoulders as they quaked. His body was coated in the blood of his progeny.

"You could put him out of his misery, August. All you have to do is be hers."

August shook his head and pried his gaze from his friend. Craning his neck, he pinned a glare on the visage of his mate standing in the corner.

Dressed in virginal white, the strappy sundress hugged her every curve. He ached to feel her plump lips on his and have her blood slide down his throat as he sank his fangs into his favorite spot on her neck.

She was perfect. He knew it was an illusion, but it was hard to ignore the uncanny resemblance and the way he yearned for her. His body physically needed Emery to survive.

But the woman before him didn't house his soul, and as long as he reminded himself of that, he would survive. It didn't matter that he wanted to take her into his arms and forgive her for what she was about to do. Because she wasn't real. But that didn't mean he didn't want to.

Bloody hell, he was going crazy. Stuck between hypotheticals, illusions, and what he knew was real.

Emery's illusion crossed the room and trailed her hand down his cheek.

August closed his eyes as his traitorous body leaned into her touch, and he only just managed to suppress the moan in his throat.

Her thumb traced across his lower lip. "August, Ansel needs you to be hers. Save him. Please."

"He's done. It's over." August said tightly. He would fight against the urge to give in. He could do this. For her; for them.

"Is it?"

He shot his eyes open and looked past the illusion of Emery to see the door in Ansel's cell open again. Five more humans were herded inside, three of them looking too young to be considered adults.

Ansel lifted his head and released a low whine in his chest. "I can't." He shook his head. "Please. They are children. Please."

His gaze darted to August, pupils dilating against the deep brown irises of the man trapped by his wolf. "Don't. You don't have to do this," August whispered.

"I need him. She'll give him to me. He's all I have left." Ansel warred with himself, and August knew he wasn't hearing a word he said.

"You have me, Ansel. No matter what, you have me," August cried out, pleading for Ansel to snap out of it. No matter what, he was going to get them out of there. He had to.

Emery stepped in front of him. "Save him, August. Please."

His heart couldn't decide if it wanted to break or rage.

She sounded so real. The lilt of her voice. The intensity of her plea. She was begging him. It wasn't her, but his mind struggled to remember that. He never wanted to hear her beg unless it was for his cock. For her pleasure. This was worse than watching her fuck Callum.

"Stop," August roared, his chest heaving.

Ansel froze, and the sobs of the teenagers were the only thing that echoed off the sterile walls.

"What do you want from me?" August whispered.

"Break your bond. Be my consort. Make your kingdom mine in every sense of the word," Sloane's voice boomed from the speaker in the ceiling.

Sloane didn't want him. She'd never wanted him. Or Malcolm, for that matter. Power was the only thing she sought. But this wasn't about power alone. She wanted to steal what was rightfully Emery's. She wanted to take everything that made Emery who she was and leave his mate a husk of the woman she could be. He was just a means to an end. The minute he was no longer useful, she would toss him aside to rot in a dungeon.

Sweat dripped off his forehead. "Making me yours isn't going to change that you aren't my people's queen. They may not like Emery, but she didn't kill their families."

"Then they will die. Kill enough of them, and they'll change their tune."

"I can't just break my bond. Even if I wanted to, I'm not a witch. Give me something tangible. Anything to take this burden from Ansel."

"All right then, August," Sloane purred.

August's blood ran cold with dread. She sounded too

pleased with herself; too sure. Whatever was coming, it wouldn't be good.

The door to his room burst open and Jessi stumbled in. She righted herself quickly and patted down her dress.

"Sire her," Sloane said gleefully.

August's heart sank.

Bloody fucking hell.

He couldn't catch a break.

Sloane couldn't yet tie herself to him for eternity, so instead she punished him with the one woman who tormented Emery at every turn. The woman who slept with his father to get ahead.

Jessi sauntered across the room and draped herself across his lap while illusion-Emery situated herself behind him.

He wondered if Jessi knew she was there. Not that it mattered. He was already in hell either way.

"I missed you." Jessi trailed her hands down his chest and to the buckle of his pants.

August let out a growl, and she jumped back, almost falling to the floor.

Jessi sat up and jutted her lip out in a pout. "It's too bad you didn't miss me too. We could have been so good together. We still could be."

"If I won't be Sloane's, what makes you think you stand a chance?" August ground out.

"I don't need to be your mate or your queen. I just need your sire bite. I might not be a royal vampire, but I'll be of royal lines. That's enough to pave my way in this new world. Plus, I'm useful to our Mistress."

For now, August thought.

His gaze drifted to Ansel, who stood with his eyes

locked on August. His eyes were feral, and his chest heaved but there was no doubt he was still the man who fought for what was right. The man who protected his mate and daughter when August couldn't.

For him, he could do this.

Emery reached over his shoulder and pushed Jessi's head to the side. She brushed away her blonde curls, exposing the fleshiest part of Jessi's neck. The heat of her breath tickled his neck, but her scent was all wrong. His mate didn't smell bitter. She was everything fresh and sweet, which would instantly make his mouth water with need. Right then, all he wanted to do was vomit.

Still, he couldn't deny the shiver that shot down his spine when she spoke in his ear. "Sink your fangs in her. Give her everything you'd give me if you could. Take her essence, feed your hunger, and make her your progeny."

August's mouth dropped open, his fangs vibrating with need. He blinked, and when he opened his eyes, they locked with Ansel's. It didn't matter how badly August didn't want to be tied to Jessi; Ansel's broken gaze solidified his fate.

For Ansel, he could do this.

He repeated the mantra over and over in time with Jessi's pulse.

"I need my hands," he breathed.

A loud click sounded and the shackles at his wrists snapped open. August pulled back on the fingers of both hands and pushed them forward, stretching his wrists.

"I'm looking forward to your intent. I remember the way it felt to writhe on your cock as you fed from me." Jessi squirmed against him. "I still think about it when I touch myself."

August's lips threatened to curl up in disgust, but he pushed away the thought and instead gave her a smug smile. He leaned forward, making her believe he was feeling the same way before he whispered. "If you believe I'd think twice about a whore who slept with my father to garner her place in his kingdom, you're wrong. I haven't thought about you since Emery walked into my life."

Jessi opened her mouth to scoff, but August didn't give her a chance to make a sound. He sank his fangs into her flesh. Though he tried, he couldn't help the moan that broke free.

He was ravenous. Each pull was deep, and even though it wasn't from the source his body craved, it fulfilled his need for sustenance.

When he'd taken enough to make him feel more like himself, he pushed his venom forward — his intent a murderous vision of exactly how he wished he could kill Jessi.

Her muscles tensed and a high-pitched shriek filled the room. Jessi tried to scoot away from him, but it was no use. August was stronger, faster, and more monstrous than she could ever hope to be. They'd forgotten who he was, but for just this brief moment, he'd remind them.

He continued to pump his venom into her system, basking in her screams and the way her body quaked in fear. Her heart began to slow, and August knew he'd have to kill her soon. It needed to be deliberate, with as much intent as his venom. He couldn't risk what Sloane would do to Ansel if he accidentally killed her.

At least he'd enjoy every second of ending her life.

Moments before she would have gone limp in his arms, August pulled his fangs from her neck. He placed his hands on either side of her head and with one quick jerk, snapped her neck.

Jessi fell to his lap in a heap of limbs, and he rolled her off of him onto the floor.

"She'll likely need my venom for the next few days to ensure the turn takes."

Sloane stepped through the door and crooned. "Good boy."

"Fuck you," August growled.

She flicked her fingers, and his arms snapped back to the rests on the chair with the shackles clicking into place. "That's the idea, August. You're the one with morals."

He ignored her and searched for Ansel. At some point while he was lost in his feed, Ansel had been removed from the room.

"Don't worry. He's safe for now. You just need to keep being useful."

August opened his mouth to tell her exactly what he thought when the pinch of a needle in his neck stopped him. His words were a garbled mess and the last things he saw before the world went black were Emery's pink locks and her wicked smile.

Chapter Twenty Five

EMERY

"Five, four, three, two..." Emery held her breath, waiting to see if her vision came true.

Roland, the crotchety advisor who liked to remind August that Emery wasn't actually his wife yet, stood with his lips pressed together and his arms crossed while Bronwyn and Jada, one of the younger witches, played with a small sprite that jumped from flower to flower as Jada created them. She flipped and twirled, and Bronwyn encouraged them to keep going faster and faster, leaping around the common room.

Emery's eyes were on Roland, so she didn't miss the way the corner of his lips twitched upward.

"One." The sprite flipped before Jada could create another flower, falling from the air and landing with a plop in Roland's coffee mug.

The sprite laughed, unaware of the tension between witches and vampires.

Jada sucked in a gasp and ran to help the sprite, but

Bronwyn snatched her hand and tugged the witch behind her, putting herself between Jada and Roland.

His eyes narrowed, and Emery's gaze darted between Roland and Bronwyn. She'd seen this end two ways. Both endings would result in a smile on Bronwyn's face; the question was, would Roland be laughing with the two witches or soaked from head to toe in his coffee?

Emery let out her breath slowly as Roland tipped his head back and laughed. "Bravo!"

Bronwyn's brows quirked upward, confusion plastered on her face, while Roland clapped. He looked down into the cup on the table and offered a finger to the sprite to help her out.

"That was fantastic. It has been a long time since someone reminded me of better days."

Emery had seen the change in Roland slowly the more she focused her training on seeing visions of the people around her. He wasn't happy about being trapped in Enchanth with the witches, but his anger had slowly begun to thaw as he was forced to get to know them beyond the walls of their home. He didn't stay locked in his room as much, choosing to eat in the common areas, and he even went out of his way to talk with some of the children. She wouldn't have believed it possible if she hadn't witnessed it with her own eyes.

The sprite tilted her head, her squeaky voice lilted through the air. "Better days?"

He scooped her out of the coffee, and the sprite fluttered her small wings in Roland's hand. "The way you jumped from flower to flower reminded me of my brother and I many, many years ago. We would jump from stone to stone crossing the river until, inevitably, one of us fell in."

Roland looked up, his eyes far away as if he was seeing the river in vivid color. "Those were the best days of my life. Carefree summers with my brother."

"What happened to him?" Jada whispered, peeking out from behind Bronwyn.

Roland pressed his lips together and looked away. "He died not long after I was turned."

"I'm sorry," the tiny sprite said, placing her hand on his and giving it a gentle squeeze.

"Thank you." Roland shook his head and lowered his hand for the sprite to hop off onto the table. His eyes softened as he looked over to Bronwyn and Jada. "You know, if you were to set this up as a race, I bet you could get a lot of vampires to take bets on a winner. Vampires are notorious gamblers."

"Are they?" Bronwyn asked, intrigued. It surprised Emery too. She had no idea.

"Absolutely. We've got centuries of money and nothing to spend it on."

A mischievous smile pulled at Jada's lips. "Are you proposing an alliance with us?" She turned to the pixie on the table. "That is, if you are up for the challenge, Cora."

"Oh, I am in." She bounced excitedly from foot to foot. "But don't tell Nico. Nothing fun ever happens around here, and he's sort of a spoilsport."

Emery snorted. Nico was one hundred percent a spoilsport, but she had a feeling he had reason to be. He kept Enchanth running smoothly and hidden from the realms it hid between. It was no different than the weight she bore—or August's, Lily's, Draven's, or Callum's. They were the last defense for their kingdoms.

"Are you enjoying watching the ice between them

thaw?" Trine slid into the plush chair beside Emery, a knowing smile on her face.

"I've been watching this play out in my mind for the last three hours. This is the first time I've successfully narrowed it down to two outcomes and witnessed it take place in real time."

Each morning over the past two weeks had been spent pulling cards and drinking tea while playing with Lina. The tiniest royal was the center of attention in Enchanth. She had every fae, vampire, and witch under her spell. It was incredible to see them all crowd around her as she practiced rolling from her back to her tummy and back again. Their afternoons were spent in the gardens where Emery sat with Trine while Cosmina and Thea watched Lina, and Callum would stop by to feed Lina royal blood.

It broke her heart when they used the last bag of August's blood. So much so that she almost launched a stealth mission to get into their castle and retrieve the stores they had tucked away. The idea was immediately shut down, and Callum and Malcolm volunteered to step in since they were the only ones with royal Nicholson blood.

"You're becoming more attuned to your sight," Trine mused, catching Emery off guard. The old crone rarely gave compliments.

When they began, Trine taught her to clear her mind first, before searching out the fates that she wished to see. It was easiest when she was holding a memento that belonged to the person or persons she wanted to divine, but a few times she'd been able to conjure a vision based on a strong memory alone. The best part was learning to keep herself sitting up during her visions, for which she was grateful.

"How come none of this was in the coven's books?" Emery remembered studying them for hours. She had also pored over Lily and Callum's books when she'd been confined to the cottage. The information about sight-touched witches had been sporadic at best, but there had been nothing about control. All the texts made it sound like there was no rhyme or reason to it. Visions were sent by the stars and interpretations were haphazard at most.

Not that Emery thought the stars knew what the hell they were doing. The fates were fickle bitches on a good day and downright evil the rest of the time. They may have given her August and Lina, but they also took Miles, and she wasn't sure she could ever forgive them for that.

"Celeste hadn't grown into her full magic when she was still in the Feywilde. By the time she had, there was no one in your realm to teach her the full extent of her sight. I want to believe she eventually learned to hone it, but seeing as she wasn't exactly forthcoming about a lot of things, it doesn't surprise me that there were no texts on the vast abilities that come with this type of magic."

Emery sipped her tea and watched Bronwyn and Roland hatch what was sure to be an elaborate scheme. "What else can it do?"

"The sight is tangled with time and fate. It's the wind from the past that propels the wings of the future. It's free will and predestined. It's yesterday and tomorrow. The sight allows us to view time as more than linear."

"How so?"

Trine smiled, but her usual curiosity when it came to

Emery's questions was somehow not as light as before. "Have you ever had a vision of the past?"

"I've had nightmares, but I wouldn't call them visions of the past. I've definitely replayed my worst moments." The most recent one was the look on August's face when Dorian carried her from the throne room. She'd failed him. Failed their bond. She'd left him there.

"Are they, though? Everyone dreams, but not everyone has the sight. You, my dear, have a gift that allows you to walk the timeline. Why shouldn't you be able to focus on it like you would the future? To alter it."

Emery stopped watching Roland and shifted her gaze to Trine, her brow raised. "Change the past?"

If she could change the past...the possibilities were endless. She could go back and stop Vishna from taking Miles. She could stop Sloane from falling into her darkness. She could stop Celeste from ever thinking it was a good idea to hide witch mates from their vampire counterparts. The supernatural world would be entirely different. Possibly better.

Then again, she wouldn't be who she is now. Neither would August. They would still be mates if fate was to be believed, but the things that made her who she was wouldn't exist. It was possible she would have discovered her darkness years prior and would have ended up exactly like Sloane. Was that really a better option?

She couldn't say for sure, but her instincts told her absolutely not.

"No, no, nothing like that. The past can't be changed. But perspective can be altered. Just like we find the threads of the future to determine which is the most probable to happen, we can find the past and change the perspective."

Emery tilted her head and her brow furrowed. She was trying to connect the pieces of what Trine wasn't saying, but didn't quite understand what it was she was getting at.

"Think of the sight like weaving a basket. The past has already been completed. It's the basis of what will frame what we see in the future. Though we can't change the pattern that has been woven, we can change the way we look at it. How we see it. Are we looking in the basket or gazing upon the outside? We can change the way someone remembers things."

"We can alter people's minds?"

"In a sense."

Unease swirled in her stomach. In theory, it was amazing to think her magic had the ability to do such a thing, but in reality, it was terrifying and didn't sit well with Emery. It was one thing to change the past and alter the entirety of the space-time continuum, but to alter someone's mind—to take from them whatever made them who they are—felt wrong. Like stealing a piece of them.

Emery considered the nightmares that plagued her. Would she want them gone? Five minutes before, she would have gladly given up the memory of August's face when Dorian carried her away. The love and loss that were etched in his features. The fear for himself and the hope for her that echoed down their bond. She wanted to forget it in the moment, but the second that possibility became a reality, she clung to it with claws extended, ready to fight off anyone who would dare take it from her.

That memory was part of what drove her to figure out how to save him. It forced her to push forward when all she wanted to do was give up. As much as it cut her to her core to remember it every night, she didn't want that memory changed in any way.

Emery chewed her lip and shook her head, firm in her stance. "I don't think I'm comfortable with that. Whether it's joy or pain, it's a part of who a person is, and that's not for me to take."

"But is it your job to change the future then? Every time you look to the sight to tell what is to come, you are taking the free will of those around you to live as fate intended. You can change fate by knowing what happens."

Emery reached up and rubbed her temples. The ethics of this conversation made her brain hurt. Comprehending the nuances of fate and time, and the magic…It was all too much. There was right and wrong, but Trine made it sound like they lived in a gray in-between. "But it doesn't change fate, or the future. It just solidifies it. Free will changes it, but ultimately what is meant to happen will happen, right?"

"Hmm," Trine mused, looking out the window where the sun peeked through the trees. "From what we can see, yes, but we don't know for certain. The gods of fate haven't deemed us worthy to understand the nuances of their gift."

"I wish they would just give us a damn manual," Emery muttered, to which Trine laughed.

"Would you like to give it a try? See for yourself?"

"I don't think I am comfortable changing someone's past."

Trine winced, but quickly furrowed her brow to try and cover it up. Emery noticed, though, and it gave her pause. Why did she want her to look into the past so badly?

Emery pressed her hands to the arms of the chair, ready

to end the conversation, but before she could, Trine shot her hand out and placed it on top of hers.

"What if it was your own past? You don't need to alter anything, just look. Get a feel for the magic."

Emery tightened her jaw, the magic in her chest urging her toward the suggestion. The past was supposed to remain where it was. It was made up of memories that were both cherished and learned from. Good and bad, it was what made a person. But if she was only to see her own, then it would be just fine. As much as there were things she would love to change, the ramifications were enough to stop her.

She sank back down into the chair. "Okay, what do I have to do?"

Trine smiled and gave an excited wiggle as she scooted forward to the edge of her chair. "Fantastic. Just close your eyes and call your magic."

Emery inhaled and did as she was told. Her light magic hummed just beneath the surface of her skin while her darkness stirred in her chest.

"Now, focus on a moment and allow yourself to fall deep into the recesses of your mind."

She decided to pick a happy moment; one that she wouldn't be tempted to change once she was already there. A moment with August.

"Own the moment." Trine's voice faded to a whisper as she replayed the moment she first saw August in her mind. "Find the—"

The common room faded away, and Emery opened her eyes to see the crowded bar around her. August's bar. It was the night she'd seen him sing. The night Malcolm found her and forced her to sit with them. Only she wasn't standing in the crowd watching him, nor was she tucked into the booth negotiating with the brothers.

Instead, she was standing at the bar between them, although Malcolm might as well have been invisible with the way she was looking at August. Her hips were turned so she was facing him, one hand holding a shot glass filled with an amber liquid while the other was pressed to his chest.

His chin was tucked so he could look at her, and even though his eyes were narrowed, she could see the twitch in his lips while he tried to keep from smiling. Why didn't she remember this? It must have been later in the night when she was blacked out because she definitely would have remembered the way his hand slid down her side and gripped her hip.

"Dance with me." Her voice held a bit of a slur, but she was enthusiastic.

Emery knew August didn't stand a chance. Not when she was drunk and had come up with what she was sure she thought was a brilliant plan.

"That's not a good idea," August growled.

Sweet summer child that she was, Past-Emery threw back the shot of whiskey and tugged his hand from her waist, leading him to the dance floor. "This is my favorite song, and my last night of freedom. You owe me this."

"I don't owe you a damn thing," he scoffed, but allowed her to manhandle him toward the crowd.

August pulled her against him as her favorite song continued on. His hand found the center of her back, and he kept her close as the slow and sultry blues melody echoed around them. He leaned down and whispered in her ear. "Is this what you wanted, Emery? To tease me with this perfect body of yours? Make me regret asking you to join my Culling?"

Emery lifted her hand to her ear and gasped. Though she was watching from across the bar, it was as if she was the version of herself in his arms. She could hear him, feel his hot breath on the shell of her ear, the warmth making her entire body shiver.

"I just wanted to dance, anything else is just an added perk," she heard herself answer as she swayed against him. Her body fit perfectly against his, as if even then the fates were already trying to show them they were meant for one another.

August guided her away from him, spinning her out, and she took the moment to throw the hand he wasn't holding up in the air and swing her hips in a suggestive manner. It was clear the alcohol in her system had given her the confidence to do exactly as he'd suggested.

Emery laughed as she watched herself act like a complete fool, but what she wasn't expecting was the heat and possessiveness in August's gaze.

He pulled her in until she slammed against his chest, and she was forced to tangle her hands around his neck to stop herself from falling. August wrapped his arm around her waist, pinning her against him. He stepped with his leg between hers, so her pussy met his thigh and swung his hips so she was helpless to do anything but follow.

"Who the hell are you?" he growled.

"Your worst nightmare," Emery giggled.

At that time, she had no idea what he meant, but it was obvious even then he felt it. The pull. The need to be close to her. Emery had felt it too, but unlike him, she'd been focused on the fact that he was her enemy. There hadn't been any room for attraction.

Butterflies erupted in her stomach as she continued to watch. She wished she'd remembered this moment that following morning. It would have changed everything.

And nothing.

The slam of a door jerked her attention from where she and August danced, tangled in one another. She searched the room and saw nothing, but the edges of the space seemed hazy, like they did in a vision, and somehow, she knew she was being pulled back.

She closed her eyes, committing to memory the night she'd forgotten.

When she opened her eyes again, the sun of the common room blinded her.

"Did you like what you saw?" Trine asked almost timidly.

"I did. I wouldn't change it, though." Not for the world.

"There may come a day where you don't have a choice."

Emery cocked a brow. *What the hell does that mean?* Before she could ask, the old crone was up and across the room, far faster than should have been possible.

She didn't like the implication of Trine's words. They sounded too much like a premonition, and she'd had enough of those to last a lifetime.

Dorian entered the common room, flanked by Malcolm and Lily. Emery's eyes widened as she took in his fae form. It was much more intimidating now that he wasn't lying in a pool having his blood drained from his wrists.

He smiled at Emery as he crossed the room, though his steps faltered a little when he saw her frown.

She quickly shook the thoughts of her conversation with Trine and returned his smile. "Come join us. I'm happy to see you up and about."

"I'm happy to be out of a damn bed." Dorian stopped behind the sofa opposite her. "We're actually here to come get you to join us."

"And where are we going?"

"Through the archway. The components are ready. It's time to break the Culling spell."

Nervous butterflies erupted in her belly. This seemed like such a monumental step for their kingdom and witches and vampires everywhere. The Culling spell kept them from finding their mates; with it gone, maybe the two factions would find more peace.

She shuddered to think what Aberforth would make of it. Thank goodness she wouldn't have to hear it anytime soon since he hadn't returned to the castle. But that didn't mean that there wouldn't be those who opposed their push for uniting mates.

Emery stood and a smile stretched across her lips. "Let's do this."

Chapter Twenty Six

EMERY

The air was sucked from her lungs, leaving her gasping.

It had been weeks since she'd entered the mortal realm, and even though her heart ached for her mate every single one of those days, she wasn't prepared for the onslaught of their bond snapping back into place.

Her tie to August wasn't just emotional. It was visceral and all-consuming. Reuniting with that part of her soul left her wanting to claw out her own heart to soothe the aching organ.

But it wasn't just their bond she missed. She missed the man too. In everything she did, she remembered the little things that made their relationship special. The heat in his eyes when she walked into the room, the way he slapped her ass when she got out of the shower, the errant touches and the subtle glances stolen between them that meant nothing and everything in a single moment. It might not have always been sunshine and roses, but he was the constant in her days.

Emery blinked back the tears as she reached out and caressed his side of the bond. She imagined it was what people felt like when they lost a limb. The phantom pains that lingered just out of reach. There was no cure except to accept that, for the time being, there was no way to cure the loss.

And yet somehow, she felt closer to him than ever, as if due to having been so completely cut off from him all these weeks the phantom pains brought a comfort that didn't make sense to her.

Malcolm stepped up beside her and rubbed a hand between her shoulder blades. "Are you okay?"

Emery looked up at him with misted eyes, the crescent moon in the sky behind him taunting her. The moon controlled the tides, tethered to the earth as its mate. Her moon was absent from her sky. She chewed her lip, unable to answer his question with words for fear she'd lose it. Instead, she nodded her head and pressed forward to where Dorian stood with Lily and Bronwyn, surrounded by every witch, vampire, and wolf who came with them to Enchanth, as well as those who had joined them since.

They should have stayed behind; as it was, being in the mortal realm with no protection against Sloane made them sitting ducks, but she couldn't bear to take this moment away from them. This spell was the beginning of something new for their people. It was a small win, but a win they needed when everything else seemed a bit hopeless.

And August wasn't there.

She pushed the thought from her head and crossed the clearing. Lina's sweet laugh caught her ear, and she glanced to where Cosmina stood holding her daughter. Emery instantly abandoned her need to be beside Lily and

Bronwyn as they completed the spell in favor of holding her daughter close.

The air around them was charged with magic and the nervousness of everyone as they congregated around Malcolm and Lily. Emery forced her lips to remain smiling even though she couldn't help the jealousy flaring in her chest.

It should have been her and August at the center of the circle. It was their mateship that had brought the factions together. It was their story that inspired so many. They should have been the couple to break it. Not that she wasn't thrilled it was Malcolm and Lily. If anyone deserved a happily ever after it was those two, but logic didn't lessen the sting.

She watched as the two of them stood facing one another, hands entwined. Lily tipped her head back and Malcolm leaned forward to press his forehead to hers. His lips moved, and Emery was sure he was whispering words of love and encouragement to his mate. Each movement of his lips was a hot poker to her heart.

Emery pulled Lina close and breathed in her perfect baby scent before pressing a kiss to her soft blonde hair. At least she had her daughter. The best parts of August and Miles, she reminded herself. She wasn't alone. For her, Emery could remain strong.

Malcolm's phone chirped, and he pulled it from his back pocket. He'd become the unofficial liaison for those who stayed behind in the mortal realm. He also stepped in when Flora and Draven needed to visit various packs. They were losing packs to Sloane's cause every day, and she knew they were torn about how to handle it.

"Callum needs a portal. He's at Octavian's villa."

Lily murmured the spell, and the telltale sparks of her teal magic swirled to open one.

Callum stepped through, his dark hair longer and more disheveled than usual. A middle-aged woman followed him through the portal.

Emery's brow furrowed as she studied the woman. It wasn't like Callum to bring women around. He was holding out for his mate, which begged the question: who the hell was she? Her features weren't perfect, her nose a little crooked at the bridge, which ruled out vampire. But there was no doubt she was otherworldly. She carried herself with her shoulders pinned back, gliding with an elegance that Emery had only ever witnessed in the inner circle. Her dark gaze was meant to intimidate, though the hint of a smile at her lips was welcoming.

Lily and Malcolm stepped forward, stopping her from moving any further into their ranks without an introduction.

"There is no need to posture. This is Nina, she's the leader of a faction of hybrid wolves and witches that have been living in hiding for centuries."

Emery's mouth dropped along with everyone else's. She tugged Lina tighter, all the thoughts of what this meant for her daughter filtering through her mind.

She wasn't alone. There were more out there. An entire community. She may be the first vampire-witch hybrid, at least as far as they knew, but she wasn't alone. Draven wasn't alone. There was an entire faction living under the noses of the supernatural world, thriving.

Her movement caught Nina's eye, and she fixed her gaze on Lina. "So, what Callum said is true. Your daughter is the first royal vampire-witch hybrid."

Emery nodded and stepped forward. "She is."

She didn't offer the newcomer any more information. Something about her didn't sit right. She had to be safe for Callum to bring her because he wouldn't risk Lina's life, but something about the glint in her eye when she looked at her daughter left Emery with a pit in her stomach.

Bronwyn piped up from the opposite side of the circle, her hands laced in front of her stoically as if she were still a member of the inner circle. "I hate to break up the exciting introduction, but it's almost midnight in this realm. We need to move on with the spell if we are going to utilize the light of the moon to amplify the components."

Callum nodded and led Nina away from the center of the circle to the side opposite Emery. His eyes locked on hers and though he wore his political smile, his eyes were wistful. Not because of Nina's presence. No. This was about the spell. It was what they'd been fighting for. Him. Her and August. Lily and Malcolm. The connection they shared, that was what he wanted for himself.

Emery watched as Bronwyn situated Lily and Malcolm in the center of the clearing. She asked them to face each other and hold hands.

Once again, Emery was lost in the way the mates looked into one another's eyes. It was as though the lyrics of their hearts were written in their gaze. These two healed the scars left behind by past loves and a life of isolation. Their mate bond was the happily ever after they both deserved; breaking the spell only made it more real.

Time seemed to slow, and Emery felt the world melt away from them. Tears rimmed her eyes and she hugged Lina tighter. She didn't just miss August. She craved him in the deepest parts of her soul.

Bronwyn knelt beside them and flipped open the grimoire she'd been working from. She took a long strand of white cloth and dipped it into the dark components. When she lifted the cloth, it was stained black with flecks of silver speckled across it like a starry sky. She held the cloth up toward the moon and murmured the spell Celeste had used to bind the Culling. Once she'd finished, she wrapped the cloth around Lily and Malcolm's hands while repeating the inverse of the spell.

Balance was key, always.

She wrapped the cloth up Malcolm's arm, across his shoulders and down his other arm, binding it in their fingers. Then she repeated the process on Lily, winding it up her small frame, across and back down before tying the ends in an intricate knot.

Bronwyn tipped her head back, and with her eyes closed, chanted the words of their ancestors.

Ceangail na rudan nach bu chòir a bhriseadh a-riamh. Seula ar crideheachan air ar n-anamaibh.

Bind together what should have never been broken. Seal our hearts upon our souls.

With each chant, more voices joined in. First the witches. Then the vampires. Even the wolves in attendance called upon the magic of the earth to hear their plea.

The tears she'd held back fell with reckless abandon as Emery echoed the cry of her heart. She'd found her mate, but this was the beginning of something new for everyone. For witches and vampires around the world. This was their moment.

A silver glow grew from the cloth that bound Malcolm and Lily. Their hair whipped around them as the earth heard their cries and answered with its might. The trees swayed, echoing their call, and the ground trembled beneath them. With each reiteration of the chant, the cloth grew brighter, almost blinding.

As they finished the tenth and final chant, a sudden and powerful light exploded from where Lily and Malcolm stood. A flash of heat filled the clearing.

Emery gasped and gripped Lina to her chest, shielding her from the light as heat seared her left wrist. Her heart beat erratically in her chest, and her lip trembled. It wasn't painful so much as it was shocking. More than anything, it reminded her of when August removed her Culling mark, except she'd felt heartbroken to lose him at that moment. This time, the sensation that vibrated beneath her skin was like coming home.

She silently wondered if Lily felt the same way. She was the only other witch present who had been a member of the Culling. She would know what it had felt like to lose the mark when she lost Kipton. This time, though, she was gaining the love of her mate. The connection that made them whole.

When the light faded, Emery shifted Lina onto her hip and held up her left hand. There, entwined in silver, were the vines of August's Culling, wound around her forearm instead of in a circlet this time. Also different this time were the four flowers blooming from the branches, along with a crown that was etched into her skin, on top of her forearm.

Emery's lip quivered as she studied the mark that she was sure tied her to her mate. Since they'd mated, she'd felt a connection to him, but this was an outward sign of the love they shared. More so than the ring she wore on her third finger, this was the sign of what they were always meant to be.

Whispers started around her and it wasn't long before they erupted into tears and cheers. She looked around and saw that every witch and vampire wore a mark similar to hers. No two were the same, though. Some had flowers while others bore thorns. Where her mark held the crown of their kingdom, every other mark held something that she assumed was particular to their mate.

Emery held her breath and looked down at the wrist of the infant in her arms. There, on her arm, was the mark of her future mate. A tiny woven vine of silver surrounding a dagger with a crown in the hilt.

Her sweet Lina had a mate. She had a future in their world and there was someone out there who would love her with every fiber of their soul.

Bronwyn appeared at her side, tears in her eyes. "They're out there. They exist, Emery. I didn't…I had begun to lose hope."

Everyone had.

"He is the luckiest person in the world."

"Or she."

Emery smiled. "Or she."

Malcolm and Lily were a tangle of limbs, lost in one another, and she didn't blame them. If August were there, she'd—

Did he wear her mark now too?

She didn't have a moment to think about it as Dorian stepped up beside her. "We need to get everyone back to Enchanth. Assuming everyone wears the mark of their mates, it won't be long before Sloane starts looking for us.

And while I am fairly certain we are safe here, I'd rather not chance it."

Emery nodded, but an ache grew in her chest. She wasn't ready to leave. In Enchanth she couldn't feel August. A part of her soul was lost, and she wasn't ready to give up even the slightest connection to him. Not yet.

She handed Lina to Cosmina, who, to Emery's surprise, had a mate mark of her own and wore a smile a mile wide.

"I guess I'm not too old for love," she chuckled.

Emery swallowed the sob in her throat and smiled. "Never. You deserve the world."

She was eternally happy for Cosmina and everyone around her, but every moment she considered her own mate, she wished the floor would open up and swallow her whole. Everyone was basking in hope and Emery wanted to be there with them, but she was missing the most vital part of the celebration. She'd already found her mate, and he wasn't there.

Flora and Draven rounded up the last of the stragglers and headed toward the arch. "Are you coming?"

Emery's gaze fell to their wrists, and she noticed they didn't wear a silver band.

"Your marks," she gasped. "Where are they?"

"No idea," Flora shrugged.

"If I had to make an educated guess, I would say that because Flora is the mate to my wolf and I feel a stronger connection to him, I don't have a witch mate. My alpha wolf trumps the need for a vampire mate." Draven tugged Flora against his side. "But what do I know?"

"Are you okay?" Flora whispered, her knowing gaze falling to where Emery's hand wrapped around her wrist.

"I'll be fine. I just think I'd like to stay a little longer."

Flora opened her mouth, but before she could protest, Callum spoke up. "I'll stay with her. Lily and Malcolm have a tent in the tree line for when they come to this realm to speak with our contacts. We'll keep out of sight."

Flora looked as though she wanted to object, but she nodded silently, and the two of them headed toward the archway.

"Thank you," Emery said softly.

"You're not the only one who needs some space." He ran a hand through his usually immaculate hair and turned away from her.

Callum turned and walked toward the tree line. She frowned and stepped to follow him when Nina blocked her path.

"Your daughter, she needs to be with her own kind."

Emery's nose scrunched, and her brow raised. Who the hell did this woman think she was? It was possible Emery was overreacting with her emotions as high as they were, but she didn't think Nina had any right to question Lina's needs.

"She will be. She'll have me and her father and any other hybrid siblings we give her. Along with the future children of all the mates granted tonight." Emery's gaze fell to Nina's wrist, to the silver swirls that marked her future mate. "Your children will be her kind as well."

Nina pressed her lips together. "I...We have never had anyone stand up for us. We have been shunned by our people for centuries and now there is not only a hybrid alpha but a hybrid heir to the vampire throne. You'll forgive me if it is hard to put the trust of my people into those who have banished us for who we are."

Emery's eyes softened, and she reached out and took

Nina's hand in hers. "I understand your hesitancy, but I vow to protect your people along with my own. You are part of our kingdom now, whether you want to be or not. The future is still being written, but I promise you there is a place for everyone."

"And all the royals feel that way?"

"All the royals that matter." Emery smiled. "The leaders of every faction are on the same page. We are still working on changing the minds of those who are stuck in the past. But what I can assure you is we will not tolerate prejudice against any of the factions, hybrids included."

Nina squeezed Emery's hand and a single tear fell down her cheek. "Thank you."

"Will you be joining us in Enchanth?"

Nina nodded and let go of her hand. "I will be there temporarily until I can coordinate with Callum. Then I will offer the option to those at our compound."

"I hope to meet more of your people."

"Our people."

Emery nodded as hope flared in her chest. This was a huge moment for the future. It was as simple as bringing people together, but also gigantic for their people. It proved they were moving in the right direction.

She ushered Nina to the arch before heading toward the tent Lily and Malcolm had set up on the tree line. She didn't want to think about what they'd done in the tent, but was grateful she and Callum had a place to be that wasn't exposed to the elements.

Emery opened the flap and entered the sitting area. Callum stood by the small bar cart, a staple for any place frequented by vampires. He poured himself a glass of whiskey then looked up at her and lifted the bottle.

Emery nodded and moved to sit on the small sofa. There was no way she'd ever get used to the magic of these tents. They looked tiny on the outside, but inside was like a pocket realm all of its own, nearly triple the size.

Callum tossed back his glass, refilled it and downed it again. It wasn't until he filled it a third time that he rounded the cart and joined her in the sitting area.

"Are you going to tell me what's bothering you?"

Callum handed her the tumbler, his brow cocked. "Are you going to leave it alone if I don't?"

"Probably not."

It wasn't like Callum to sulk. Brood? Yes. Be a secretive asshole? Absolutely. But sulking was new for him. He was usually the one who had already logicked himself ten steps ahead and had a plan he didn't want to share with the class.

Callum let out a deep-rooted sigh and dropped himself onto the plush chair across from her. He set his glass down on the table and rolled up the sleeves of his button-down shirt to his elbows.

Emery's eyes widened, and she let out a small gasp. Both of his forearms were bare. "What does that mean?"

"I have no fucking clue, lass." His brogue was thicker than normal, an outward sign of the turmoil he felt behind his guarded eyes. "This was my fight." His voice trembled, and he picked up his glass and took a long sip. "All I wanted was to find the woman I was supposed to live for. The one who would make me whole. When all this started, when the gods asked me to do their bidding and screw the fates, I jumped at the chance. They told me what I wanted was just out of reach. This was supposed to be my happily ever after."

She'd never heard Callum sound so damn broken. He was the mysterious player in the game. The one who was selfish to a fault if you didn't know him, but once you did, it became clear there was nothing he wouldn't do for those he loved.

"I'm sorry," she breathed.

"I appreciate your sympathy," he huffed, a hint of a manic lilt behind his words, "but I know that's not what you really want to say."

"You're right. I have quite a few questions after those bombs you just dropped, but right now you don't need me to play twenty questions." Emery took a long sip from her own glass to stop herself from saying everything that was on her mind.

She wanted to be angry.

The fucking gods.

Callum was working with the fucking gods. She should kill him. Flora had told her more than enough about Rieka for Emery to know she never wanted to cross paths with the batshit Goddess of the Moon, and here Callum was working with them. Plural. He'd said gods.

He let out a slightly deranged chuckle. "And what do you think I need right now?"

"A friend." *To smack him upside the head and tell him he's being an idiot.*

No. That was the anger talking, because more than smacking him, she wanted to hug him.

Callum dropped his chin to his chest and let out a sigh. "Is that what we are, lass? I bit you the first time I met you, and I've been a manipulative asshole since."

"We're family, Callum." Emery pulled herself from the plush chair, rounded the coffee table and sat on the arm of his chair. She reached over and tugged him against her, wrapping her arm around his shoulder. "And while on more than one occasion I have wanted to slit your damn throat for the bullshit you've put us through, I have been able to see through your facade for a while now."

"I failed," he whimpered and buried his face in her thigh.

"Yourself, maybe. And we are going to drink to that. But for a moment, I want you to consider the gift you gave to every vampire and witch in that clearing just now. Hell, to every vampire and witch in the world. Your dream fueled a revolution. A rebellion. It was the foundation for change in the supernatural world. That is no small feat. You got us all to believe. That was all you, Callum."

He didn't respond. Instead, he untangled himself from her and brought his drink to his lips, downing the rest of it.

"But that doesn't change the fact that you lost something today. And loss is something I'm drinking to tonight." Emery savored the burn as she finished the rest of her whiskey. Then, she stood and gathered the bottle from the cart, tugged the stopper from the neck and set it between them.

Callum frowned, his eyes sizing her up. "Why are you drinking too, lass?"

"Because while everyone else is toasting to their new mate marks, mine is being held prisoner. While hope has been restored for so many, my daughter included, I can't help but feel the loss of what I should have. My soul aches for him and my sister knows it. She will use him against me. She'll make his life a living hell because she knows it will break me. He has fought so hard to become the man he is today, and because of me, he'll be pushed to his breaking point again. It's selfish, and I know it's nowhere near what you are feeling, but misery loves company, so let me commiserate with you."

Callum nodded and picked up the bottle. He didn't bother pouring the contents in the glass. Bringing it to his lips, he took a long pull. When he'd finished, he offered her the bottle. Emery did the same.

"Tomorrow, we can worry about the future."

"To tonight." Emery lifted the bottle and took another pull.

She wasn't sure how many hours had passed, but by the time she finally laid her head down on the sofa, three bottles of whiskey were gone—most of them consumed by Callum but she helped the best she could—and she'd learned that Callum was a fun drunk. He regaled her with great, detailed stories of his youth, his life with Kipton and Lily and the trouble they used to get up to, the highlights of his Culling, and his life since. What he didn't tell her was how he landed where he was. The deal he made with the gods or how he'd been orchestrating everything from the beginning.

That was a story for another day.

Chapter Twenty-Seven

AUGUST

Light filtered across his face, and August rolled over and tugged his pillow over his head.

Pillow.

No, that wasn't right, but it felt so damn good that he didn't dare open his eyes. If Sloane wanted to torture him with luxury sheets and goose down pillows, he might as well let her. It was far better than the visions she forced upon him in her sterile room of horrors.

"August?"

The voice carried from behind him, and his spine stiffened immediately.

He'd spoken too soon. He really should have known better. Sloane was a sadistic bitch. She wouldn't let him off so easily. This was just another one of her tactics. When he opened his eyes, his mate would be standing there, taunting him. Only it wouldn't be her.

This Emery wouldn't speak to his soul. She wouldn't wrap herself around him like he was the sun in her sky.

She would smell of death and decay and slice him with her words and actions until his heart was a bloodied mess in his chest. And even though he would loathe himself for it, he would study every move she made with love in his heart because even though she wasn't his, the bond in his chest would seek out the double-edged sword and cling to her visage even as it tore him apart.

Soft footsteps padded toward him.

"August?" she asked again. "How did I...is it really you? This feels real. Why does this feel real?"

He clenched his jaw and tried to steel his nerves. This was different. Usually, he was aware of the illusions from the get-go, but the last thing he remembered was falling asleep to the sounds of Ansel whimpering across from him. They'd just been put through the ringer, with Ansel making monsters and August being forced to watch Emery fuck every member of his army while Jessi fed from his neck to strengthen her bond with her sire. He'd fought the restraints when she'd sat in his lap and ground herself against the shameful arousal in his pants at the sight of his naked mate. He hated the way Emery's body made his cock come to life. It didn't matter that his mind knew she wasn't real; his body yearned for his mate's.

By the time they'd been returned to their cells, they were both shells of who they'd been when they'd left.

Wait.

August flexed his wrists and felt none of the pain from the torture session. It didn't make sense because even with superior healing, he wasn't drinking blood regularly, which had slowed his healing time to a snail's pace. On most post-session mornings, he'd wake up sore and praying for death. But he hadn't woken up.

This had to be a dream.

No, a nightmare.

That was the only thing that made sense.

When he'd finally reconciled what was happening and trusted himself, August opened his eyes and rolled out of bed.

His gut twisted when he saw they were in their suite. It was the one place that was supposed to be sacred and only theirs. As it was, Sloane had already tainted it with her presence when she'd first taken the castle; he didn't want her to desecrate it further with her illusions.

His back to her, August inhaled a steadying breath and was met with the scent of fresh lavender. Bloody hell. It was so much easier when she smelled like death. His heart constricted and his fangs ached against his gums, his Adam's apple bobbing in his throat. He clenched his eyes shut.

That scent. It was her. How the hell had Sloane managed to recreate it? All of her illusions so far had been steeped in the dark and decrepit death magic that seared its stench on everything it touched.

It's a dream. It's a fucking dream, he reminded himself over and over again.

"We both know this isn't real, Sloane," he spat through clenched teeth. "Take your fucking illusions somewhere else."

He hesitated, waiting for the nasty comeback that always followed when he reminded her he could see through her games. Sloane was like a petulant child and couldn't pass up the opportunity to tear him down.

"August, it's me." Fake Emery's voice quivered and he almost turned around.

Almost.

Bloody fucking hell, he wanted to. His body hummed with need and the underlying hope that it could be her, but he knew it was nothing but a way to break him further. He'd been fooled too many times to trust his body, because there wasn't a world in which any of this was real, despite how badly he wanted to believe it was.

Needing space, August walked toward the bathroom and flipped the shower on. He stepped under the stream, ignoring that he was still wearing a long-sleeve shirt and sweats. It didn't matter. He just needed to feel. He tipped his head back and let the cold bite of the water chill his skin. The sensation reminded him he was alive. He controlled the water, he felt its effects. It might not be real, but it was as close to being in control as he was going to get in this nightmare.

August heard her steps before she spoke, and cursed under his breath.

"August, this is real. I'm real." Her shadow drifted across the tile around him, but he refused to look at her.

"Please," she pleaded, her voice desperate with a hint of anger. "Look at me, damn it."

Despite trying to ignore her, he allowed himself one glance. One moment of weakness.

"Fuck," he whispered, and his cock stirred in his sweats despite the freezing water.

She stood outside the glass door in the little black nightgown he'd given her the night of the witches' celebration after he'd fucked her on the piano. Thin straps attached to half cups struggled to hold the swell of her breasts. He'd picked it specifically for this reason. There was no need to hide one of her best assets from him. He loved the way her nipples tightened beneath the silk, presenting themselves to him like little gifts to be unwrapped.

The waist boasted cutouts on either side, equipped with lace panels that hugged her curves and allowed him the beautiful visual of her creamy skin beneath the dark lace. It flared to the tops of her thighs, just long enough to cover the round of her ass and hide her delicious pussy from him. It was meant to tease him in the best possible way.

His cock now strained against the fabric of his sweats, and he willed it to fucking behave for once. How the fuck was he supposed to resist this when she was wearing the very thing he'd gifted her to drive himself crazy?

"I'm not an illusion. It's really me." Fake Emery took a hesitant step toward him and placed her hand on the shower door handle.

"Fucking stop, Sloane." His voice was feral, snarling her name as a reminder to himself that despite her appearance, this woman was not his mate.

She winced and hesitated.

August pressed one hand against the tile and hung his head, the water dripping down his back. Maybe it was the fact she smelled fucking delicious, or maybe this was simply his breaking point, but he didn't know how the hell he was going to escape his needs. Visions of pressing the woman on the other side of the glass up against the tile and sinking his fangs so fucking deep the wounds might never heal filtered through his mind.

Her sweet scent choked his senses, leaving his head a spinning mess.

He didn't know what black magic Sloane had perfected

to infiltrate his dreams, but this woman was too much for him to resist.

August still wouldn't look at her when she pulled open the glass door, but he let out a low warning growl. It might as well have been a purr for all it did to deter her. He sensed her as she stepped under the freezing waterfall in front of him, trapping herself between him and the wall. Fake Emery tipped her head back, but before their eyes could connect, he closed his.

Their breaths tangled with one another, her lips inches from his. The woman's heady scent wrapped around him, breaking down the last of the walls he'd managed to keep standing. Heat radiated from her, and his cock dripped with arousal, begging to be wrapped up in it.

The rapid beat of her heart taunted him, slamming against his chest and throbbing in his favorite part of her neck. Even though he knew she'd taste of death when he sank his fangs in her flesh, he'd do it just to feel her pressed against him.

It was wrong. This wasn't even bloody fucking real. But his body reacted like it was Emery standing in front of him, making it impossible to discern what the fuck was happening. He needed her like he needed blood. He'd been starving to feel anything for what felt like a lifetime. This connection to his mate would allow him to survive.

This was it.

Sloane had finally figured out how to make Emery real enough so that not even August could refuse her illusions. He'd prided himself on his ability to compartmentalize his mind and somehow remember Sloane was in control of what he saw. Nothing could be trusted.

But this woman in front of him was too perfect. Too

good to be true. His mother used to tell him that the mind will play tricks on you when dreaming. Well, she was bloody fucking right. And because of it, Sloane was finally going to break him.

He ground his teeth, warring against the growing heat in his chest and the violent need that hummed through his body.

If his cock and mate bond wanted her, he'd let them have her, if only for the small bit of reprieve it would bestow on him. But if he was going to allow himself to fall at the hands of the one woman he despised more than anything in the world, he was going to do it on his terms.

August jerked his free hand up, wrapped his fingers around her throat, and slammed her against the tile.

His eyes flew open and his fangs lengthened as he snarled, "Is this what you fucking want? You want to break me? Well, congratu-fucking-lations, you sadistic bitch."

He loathed himself for what happened next, but no longer had any fucks to give beyond the need to nurture the ache in his soul.

I'm going to bloody fucking hell.
This means nothing.
I am nothing.

"Forgive me, little witch," he whispered.

Chapter Twenty Eight

EMERY

He was already forgiven.

She didn't have time to think, to breathe, to protest because August gripped her shoulders and shoved her to the floor. The crack of her knees hitting the floor echoed off the tile surrounding them. She gasped as pain erupted and shot up her spine, nearly causing her to crumble. But before she could, August was there. He shoved his thumb in her mouth and gripped her chin, yanking it up to force her to meet his glare.

It was the first time she was really seeing him. The deep bags beneath his eyes and the stubble on his jaw. He was a far cry from the king she knew he was.

"Is this what you wanted?" His eyes darkened and his lips twisted into a sneer. "To force me to my breaking point?"

Emery thought she'd seen August at his lowest when he was lost in the depths of his bloodlust. She'd heard the stories from Malcolm of his decades lost, and the depression that followed when he finally returned, but the moments she imagined were nothing compared to the shell of a man she saw before her. Even when he'd thought she was his enemy, he didn't look at her with the blatant disregard he did now.

Waking up in what she could only assume was some sort of dream realm had caught her off guard, but upon seeing him, her heart began to soar. She'd believed this was the stars answering her prayers, until he slapped her in the face and walked away after calling her by her sister's name.

Then she saw him—really saw him—standing in the freezing shower, his head hung and his emotions washing off him in waves. He was a shell of the man she knew, broken in ways she couldn't understand. Instinctively, she reached for their bond to show him she wasn't who he thought she was, but it was still barren.

She feared not even their bond could fix the deep cuts inflicted by her sister. The man before her had been stripped of his ability to recognize her as his mate, and she had no way of proving it to him short of forcing herself on him. There was a good chance she'd be dead before she got the chance.

Could she die in this realm?

Emery reached for her magic to see if she could at least defend herself if he did attack her. Her light and dark magicks swirled in her chest, but nothing appeared in her palms.

She had no idea how it was possible for her to even be there, but she wasn't about to waste the opportunity. Which meant she had to convince him without dying and without her magic. No pressure.

Water dripped down her face and with wide eyes she stuttered around his thumb, "August, I—"

"I don't want to hear it. I want you to use that pretty little mouth of yours for the only thing it's good for." He yanked his sweats down, freed his dripping erection, and stepped forward, painting her lips with his arousal. Her involuntary moan was lost around his thumb. "You're going to suck my cock until I'm damn well cured of this insatiable need, and then you're going to get the fuck out of my sight and stay the fuck out of my dreams."

Emery winced when his voice cracked, the only indication he had any feelings behind his hardened facade. He needed this as much as she did to fix the distance between them, lost through spells and realms.

She hated Sloane more with every passing moment. Emery would do whatever it took to prove to him that she wasn't an illusion. Even if it meant allowing her mate to hate-fuck her mouth.

Emery hollowed her lips around his thumb and nodded, a silent promise to take everything he was about to give her. Then she'd return the favor and unleash her darkness on his ass, taking what she needed before she made love to him and reminded him of their sacred bond. Because that's what mates did for one another. They followed each other to the depths of hell and brought them back.

August straightened himself and tangled his free hand in her hair. "If you so much as graze my cock with your teeth, I'll make sure to tear Jessi's throat out the next time she feeds."

Darkness flared in her chest and she was glad she

couldn't tap into it because August would be flat on his ass. What the hell did he mean *the next time she feeds*?

Emery's nostrils flared, and she muttered. "You'd be doing the world a favor if you did."

If he didn't rip her throat out, Emery would. Along with anyone else who touched her mate.

August cocked a brow and hesitated, but only acknowledged her comment with a guttural growl at the same time he pulled his thumb from her mouth and replaced it with his cock, sheathing it until she was gagging on the shaft.

For a handful of painful seconds, he held her there before pulling out just enough that she could breathe around his length. A sardonic smile tipped his lips. "I didn't know illusions had a gag reflex. You should really work on that."

Emery glared up at him, tears leaking down the sides of her face, and her darkness purred in her chest at his menacing display of dominance. She wanted to hate him, but she couldn't. Instead, pleasure rippled through her body at the sight of him, at the way his white shirt clung to his body, revealing the outline of every taut muscle. She shouldn't like the way he was staring at her, like she wasn't anything more than his fucktoy to be used as he saw fit, but the dark, depraved part of her soul wanted to be just that. She wanted to be what he needed.

They'd forced themselves to become picture-perfect mates, dancing around the darkness they both housed without ever letting it consume them. This depravity was just as much a part of them as their love. Emery's magic flared in her chest in agreement.

She inhaled through her nose and tried to pull back and

speak, but August's hands cupped the base of her skull as he thrust his length forward.

"What was that? I can't hear you past my cock at the back of your throat," he taunted her, fucking her face with long languid strokes so that she barely had a moment to breathe and never a chance to recover.

Every thrust was hate-filled, and each one left Emery dripping. Her hands flew to his hips and she dug the blunt ends of her fingers into his exposed flesh.

Fuck, he felt amazing.

He shouldn't have. There was nothing right about this. She'd thought she was sick for enjoying the way he tied her up, but this—she was going to hell for enjoying every minute of the way he was using her.

"You like that? I can smell your arousal. Bloody fucking hell. So fucking sweet, you even smell like her."

A low groan escaped her as he picked up his pace. Her eyes never left his, not even when he cursed her name or moaned her praises when she hollowed her cheeks and sucked him like he had diamonds in his ballsack. Emery's grip on him tightened, holding on for dear life as he fucked her mouth with absolute reckless abandon.

She rocked her hips, searching for the friction that would sate the ache between her legs. The pressure building was nearly unbearable, to the point she was sure all it would take was one or two well-placed strokes across her clit and she'd explode.

August's cock swelled in her mouth, and she knew he was close. Emery pulled him forward and swallowed him the way she knew he liked. He growled and shoved her back, her head hitting the wall of the shower with a loud crack.

"What the fuck, August?" she yelled, reaching up to feel the back of her head. When she brought her hand back around, there was blood on her fingers.

Emery flicked her gaze up at him and snarled. "Are you going to say something?"

"Get the fuck out."

"No."

"I don't want you here anymore." His voice broke at the end as if he was on the verge of losing it.

Emery reached up and grabbed his hand, using him to steady herself as she stood. She was surprised he let her, but his gaze was focused on her wrist. When he looked up again and met her gaze, his deep midnight eyes held nothing but sadness.

"You aren't real." He yanked his hand from hers and backed as far as he could from her in the small space, the water running between them.

"I am." Her voice was somewhere between a plea and a cry, begging for him to hear her. "I am your gods-damned star-fated mate. Feel for me. Trust your instincts. I have seen you think twice. I can't be an illusion. I know things. Like how you love the way I swallow you when you come so that you can feel my throat constrict around your cock."

August didn't breathe, and his only movement was the tic in his jaw. "You aren't real. I swear to the fucking gods this is the only warning I am giving you. Do not fuck with my memory of my mate. I may have not been the prisoner you wanted, but I have done what you asked. I let you use me to control Ansel, despite the fact that I know he may never forgive me. I have taken every lash, every mental mindfuck. I turned Jessi, I let her feed from me to strengthen her sire bond. You've tried to taint my mate's memory every gods-damned day, but you will not ruin the last piece of my soul. You will not. I can't…"

Fucking hell.

Rage bubbled within her and her magic sent her visions of all the ways they were going to kill Sloane, bring her back, and then kill her again.

"I will fucking kill her," Emery vowed.

August's eyes widened when she stepped forward, but he didn't move. The ice-cold water washed over her, washing away some of the rage. This needed to be about him and helping him fight his way back to her. Emery slowly reached up and smeared her bloody fingers across his lips.

Immediately, August grabbed her wrist and sucked her fingers into his mouth. A low groan rumbled in his chest as he sucked her essence off the pads of her fingers.

"It's me," she whispered. "Feel me. Only me."

Emery repeated the words he'd said to her once upon a time and waited for recognition. For any sign that she'd proven herself. She didn't know what she'd do if he still didn't believe her. There was no way of knowing how to even get out of the dream they were in.

She held her breath until August's eyes widened, and he pulled her fingers from his mouth with a soft pop. His shoulders hunched forward, and he sagged against the tile behind him. His eyes softened and his mouth fell open and closed again as if he didn't trust what he was feeling.

"Fuck," he whispered. "Little witch? Is it really you?"

She nodded and stepped toward him, but he held his hands up.

"How? I mean…" He ran his fingers through his soaked hair. "I… you let me…gods, Emery."

Emery slowly lifted her hand and caressed his cheek. "I don't know how. The last thing I remember is falling asleep next to Callum and then I was here."

August growled. "You were sleeping with Callum?"

"In a fucking tent, August. He just found out he doesn't have a mate mark." She held her wrist up and showed him the elaborate design inked into her forearm. "I got him drunk to help him deal. Not that you have any leg to stand on considering you just fucked what you thought was an illusion version of me created by my sister."

"That's what that is?" August looked down at his own wrist and pulled up the sleeve of his shirt to reveal his matching mark. "Bloody hell." He shook his head and pulled her against his chest. "I'm sorry, Emery. Fuck, I just…I don't know what's real anymore. The things she's shown me…" he shuddered.

Emery wrapped her arms around him, digging her fingers into the flesh of his back. She melted into the pounding beat of his heart against her face and it steadied her. "It's okay. I mean, it's not okay, but I am not angry at you. Not for this, not for any of it."

"Why did you let me?" August tangled his fingers in her hair and lowered his nose to his favorite spot on her neck. He breathed her in and let out a sigh that she felt all the way through her.

"You needed it, and if I'm honest I did too."

August pulled back and met her gaze, concern in his eyes. "You want me to treat you that way?"

"No." Emery shrugged. "Not always. But I like a little taste of your darkness now and then. It calls to mine."

"Does this mean what I think it means?" He pointed to the mark on his arm.

Emery's lips curled up and she nodded. "We broke the spell. Mates now wear each other's mark."

"Bloody hell, why didn't you show me this when I first woke up?"

Her brow raised and she gave him a pointed look. "Would you have believed me?"

"No."

"Exactly."

"But Emery, I—"

"Shhh." Emery untangled herself from him and turned off the water. She grabbed a towel for each of them from outside the door and wrapped one around him. "You had your chance to talk, now it's my turn, and as much as I would love to explain everything to you, I'd also like to fuck my mate."

"You'll still have me?"

"Always," she whispered. It was their response, the one that bonded them. The one that reminded them they had been created for one another. "You broke because it was me, because you never stood a chance at resisting me. You are mine and I am yours. But if you don't get on that bed and let me fuck you, then we might have issues."

"I love you, little witch."

"I love you too, my king."

Chapter Twenty Nine

AUGUST

It was real.

She was real.

August groaned and rolled over on the hard, damp stone of his cell. His muscles tensed just like they did every time he awoke in this hell hole, but this time the ache wasn't completely from his imprisonment. This time, the delicious burn in his quads was the result of the long night he'd spent with his mate. It was his own personal reminder of their time together, and one he'd suffer time and time again.

He almost wished he hadn't consumed so much of her life-giving essence, because now that he was fully sated, the pain wouldn't last long.

As much as he wanted to hear every detail about Enchanth and Lina, he'd savored the time with his mate. They chalked up their dream-walking to a gift from the stars when they both needed it most. Nothing else explained it, but they weren't about to complain. After they'd come up with a plan of action against Sloane, he'd spent nearly an hour buried between Emery's legs, atoning for his behavior in the shower, followed by another three hours reminding her she was the center of his gods-damned world.

Emery insisted he didn't need to, but he'd never stop apologizing for how he'd treated her and the things he'd said, and mostly for the fact that he'd fucked her face believing it was an illusion. She reassured him that if she hadn't wanted him to, she would have stopped him, but he wasn't so sure. She didn't know the depths of his hatred for Sloane and her illusions. The things she'd made him watch.

Being with Emery again was like a breath of fresh air, even though it wasn't exactly the same as when they were together in the same place. He missed their bond and the way it took their passion to extraordinary heights, but just being in her presence was enough to heal his mind and steady his soul. It was exactly what he'd needed if he was going to succeed with the plan they'd concocted.

August sat up and glanced across the dungeon to where Ansel still slept. Guilt bubbled in his chest. Not only because he got to spend a night with his mate, but for what he had to do next. The poor wolf had been through enough, but Emery promised him everything was necessary, even if it was going to tear a gaping wound in Ansel's heart. He needed him to react accordingly to really sell their plan.

Purple sparks erupted in his cell, and August lifted his arm to shield his eyes from the light on the other side of the portal as Sloane stepped through.

"Give me your arm," she spat.

"Bloody hell," he muttered.

He glanced at her through squinted eyes. She wasn't dressed in her usual power suit—instead, she was in leggings and an oversized sweater, almost as if she'd just woken up. He hated the way it made her look almost innocent, at least until he met her sunken eyes and furious stare; then it was easy to see her for the monster she'd become.

When August didn't move, Sloane stepped forward and snatched his arm. She peeled back his shirt to reveal his mate's mark. "So, it's true. They figured out how to break the Culling spell and reestablish the mate marks."

August snarled and snatched his hand away. "A lot of fucking good it did me."

Sloane tipped her head. "What is that supposed to mean?"

"I am stuck with this fucking mark for the rest of my life and a mate who thinks getting kidnapped is an invitation to open her fucking legs to any available man." The words tasted bitter on his tongue but he continued giving the best damn performance he could. He channeled the love he had for Emery and what it would feel like to actually lose her. His heart constricted and well-placed tears pricked his eyes. "Oh, and you should probably tighten your wards to include dreams. That fucking bitch can dream walk."

Letting Sloane in on their meeting place was a calculated risk, but they needed to sell the fact that he would turn on Emery. They needed Sloane to trust him if he was going to figure out her plans and find a way out for him and Ansel.

Sloane narrowed her gaze but took the bait. "What the hell are you talking about?"

"Emery came to me in my dreams last night." August gritted his teeth and clenched his hand at his sides. "She told me they'd figured out how to break the Culling spell, and that she'd decided I wasn't worth it. That fucking fae, my second-in-command, convinced her that mates were a construct of ancient magic, and she didn't need me to lead beside her. That a kingdom under her rule would be just as strong, if not stronger. A few weeks apart and she's eating out of the fae's hand. Can you bloody fucking believe that shit?"

The irony wasn't lost on him. It was the same argument he was making for the vampires in his kingdom. When Emery suggested they use it to their advantage, she nearly had to pick his jaw up off the floor.

"He wouldn't do that," Ansel whispered, just loud enough that August could hear, but he was sure Sloane couldn't.

The despair in Ansel's voice was a punch to the gut. He didn't want to do this. Ansel was the only friend he had in that gods-forsaken castle and he was about to destroy that friendship, and possibly Ansel himself.

He whipped his gaze to where Ansel stirred in his cell. "He would and he did. The bastard betrayed us both. He swooped in and stole Emery away and claimed her for himself. Something about wanting to save the fae race. The realms."

"Wait, the wolf's mate is your second?" Sloane's brows rose, skepticism painted on her face. "This just keeps getting better and better."

"Fae don't have mates," August spat like the jilted lover

he was supposed to be, and his stomach churned when he saw Ansel wince. "They are going to create a new kingdom, one where mates don't matter and hybrids are the future, and burn this one down."

"Maybe my sister isn't as weak as I thought."

"She's a conniving bitch." He had never been more grateful that Sloane was a witch and couldn't taste the lie in his words.

"Do you really mean that, I wonder."

"You'd question me? The last time you saw me I let you beat my back and watched as you showed me hours of my mate," he paused, unsticking his tongue from the top of his mouth to correct himself. "Ex-mate, in compromising positions with all of my best friends. All because I didn't want to be yours or give up any information about any of their contingency plans. Is slandering my mate's name not enough to show my change of heart? Is my bleeding heart not enough for you?"

"Prove it."

He'd expected her to want proof, which is why he would give her the one thing she wanted more than anything. "How close are you to breaking mate bonds?"

"Now that the Culling magic is out of the way, we should be able to figure out a way to target the bonds without ending vampires completely."

"Is that a risk?" he asked.

Sloane shrugged. "Potentially. The magic that binds you is the magic that created you. Remember, you were nothing but glorified bodyguards to my ancestors."

Bloody hell, he hadn't even considered the ramifications when he'd stood behind Roland and claimed maybe breaking bonds would be the answer. It could kill their entire species if they weren't careful. He almost bit his tongue as he considered the risk of their plans.

Sometimes the greatest risks bring us our greatest rewards.

The words his mother used to tell Malcolm and him when they were younger echoed in his mind. He was sure this wasn't exactly what she meant at the time, but that didn't make the words any less true. The question was: could he risk the lives of his entire kingdom?

They were already at risk, he argued with himself.

August ran a hand through his hair, playing the part of considerate ruler before returning his gaze to Sloane's. He plastered a solemn expression and nodded, "Break the bonds, and I'll be yours."

"What the fuck are you doing?" Ansel leapt to his feet and gripped the bars of his cell as he roared. "You fucking traitor."

August kept his eyes locked on Sloane. If he looked at Ansel, he knew he'd break.

Sloane raised a brow, disbelief etched in her features. "In more than name?"

"I can't give you that answer." August took a step toward Sloane, his hands raised in surrender. "Not yet. I don't want to be tied to Emery, but I am not ready to give myself to anyone. Not when I have my daughter to think about."

"We'll raise your daughter. With my magic and your army, we'll stop Emery together. We'll end mate bonds and create a world that bows to only our thrones."

"I'll help you, but Emery is mine to end. Make no mistake that our vow still rings true."

"Fine." Sloane stepped forward and extended her hand. "I'll let you have your revenge."

August nodded and placed his hand in hers.

"Perfect." Sloane waved her free hand and opened a portal.

Through the circle, he could see his suite. The one where he'd just spent the night with his mate.

Sloane extended her arm toward the portal, gesturing him forward. "Now, let's get you cleaned up and ready to assemble our army."

August stepped forward, but before he crossed the threshold, he gave Ansel one final look as he stood at his cell door, jaw clenched and eyes filled with rage.

"I'm sorry," he whispered low enough Sloane wouldn't hear him, but Ansel would. And all he could do was hope his friend could someday forgive him for the game he had to play.

Ansel didn't respond before August stepped through the portal, but he didn't miss the agony-filled howl that rumbled from his chest or the way Sloane left the portal open long enough to ensure August would hear it.

He was going to hell for this plan, but he would have his mate by his side if he succeeded. That would have to be enough.

Chapter Thirty

EMERY

One night wasn't enough.

It had been three weeks, and she could hardly remember the way August felt against her or the scent of pine that lingered in his wake. She was on the shitty end of the time continuum. At least for August, only a week had passed. Then again, it was a week spent at *her* side.

Three days after she'd woken from their dream realm and returned to Enchanth, Callum followed. He'd busied himself with running the errands in the mortal realm and checking in with their allies. To everyone else, he was back to his normal self, but Emery saw the hint of sadness in his eyes when no one else was looking. The lingering glances at the marks that foretold of happily ever afters he would never experience. Her heart broke for him.

Callum confirmed that August had denounced Emery as his mate and was moving forward with gaining Sloane's trust. Their plan was set in motion. Still, Emery's resolve cracked a little each day. It didn't matter that they'd planned the whole thing, hearing it still stung. But she knew it was their best chance at beating Sloane.

Now if she could just hold up her end of the bargain and figure out how to meet him again in the dream realm, or at the very least manage to hone her dark and blood magicks...but neither was turning out to be an easy task.

She spent every day working with Trine in the morning to further her sight, looking to the future and reminiscing in the past. Despite how much she hated the idea, Trine insisted it was necessary. She'd spend an hour or two with Lina then drag herself to the training arena to get her ass kicked by Nico and Dorian as they tried to coach her into embracing her dark magic, which she still found difficult. It was one thing to tap into her darkness, but using her blood magic was still a hard stop for her. She didn't want to lose herself, and that's what would happen. The visions her darkness gave her told her as much.

By nightfall, she barely had enough energy left to sing Lina to sleep and throw herself into bed.

"Again," Nico called from the side of the training arena where he sat perched on the perimeter fence.

Flora shot her a sympathetic smile from where she squared up with Draven, Mateo, and Kade at the opposite end of the otherwise empty space. Nico insisted she needed others around her to help her learn to control her darkness and practice where she pulled blood from. Unfortunately for her, word had spread about how she'd nearly drained the witches in Scotland, so her friends were the only ones brave enough to subject themselves to training around her.

Emery's heart raced in her chest and she opened her palms, calling forth her dark magic. It swirled down her arms and into her hands, a gorgeous array of obsidian waves with gold flecks mixed throughout.

Dorian stood across from her, shaking out his hands and stretching his neck, readying himself for another attack. Once his magic had returned, he'd volunteered to be her pin cushion while Nico walked her through each step.

Dorian wiped the sweat from his brow. "You ready to go again?"

"Does it matter if I'm not?" Emery snapped.

She'd been at this for hours and had hardly managed to do more than shoot bursts of dark magic. Calling blood was out of the question—she hadn't managed it once. At least the darkness felt like a piece of her now. She could focus on it and push it into the light magic she'd grown comfortable controlling.

"No, it doesn't matter, actually," Dorian retorted.

Emery pressed her lips together in an effort to hide the way his tone hurt her. He was pissed that she and August had decided to use him in their plan and deceive Ansel. When he found out, he stormed out of the room without a word, and didn't speak to her for days. She'd offered an apology, but they both knew it wasn't a full one—they needed to be convincing if they wanted to trick Sloane, and Ansel's suffering only made it seem more real.

Dorian was only practicing with her because he and Nico were the only two with dark magic and unlike her, they already knew how to absorb it into their bodies.

She'd never get there if she couldn't learn how to wield it consistently.

Nico's eyes darted between them, and he shook his head. "Good. Now concentrate this time."

"I was concentrating."

"No, you were daydreaming," Dorian murmured.

"Fucking fae."

Nico ignored them and continued. "Instead of attacking this time, or trying to pull his blood, I want you to try and feel Dorian's magic. Use your magic to reach out to his. Feel for the darkness that radiates from his magic."

Emery closed her eyes to try and concentrate, but all she could see was August's face. She knew how important this was. She was their secret weapon. If she could learn to hone her darkness and blood magicks, they'd stand a chance against Sloane. But how was she supposed to focus when August was with Sloane? She hadn't been able to contact him, and none of Callum's spies had been able to give them much other than August having been seen publicly at her side commanding his army.

She trusted him. It was her sister she didn't trust. Sloane would do anything and everything to take him from her, and Emery worried she'd find a weak spot and succeed.

"August is fine, Emery. Fucking focus." Gone were the days when he referred to her as Your Majesty and she almost missed them. She didn't like the fae version of her friend standing in front of her.

"Fuck off, Dorian." The problem wasn't only August.

"It's not my fault you are broadcasting your feelings loud enough for every fae in Enchanth to hear. We get it. You're worried about your mate while the rest of us are worried about the survival of our realms and making sure we have a kingdom to return to. For all intents and purposes, *you* are the queen of our kingdom, so I suggest you start fucking acting like it."

Emery swallowed hard past the truth of his words and

embraced the anger building in her chest. "It's not that simple," she told him.

"It is," Dorian sneered.

"And what the hell would you know about it? From what I gather, you're a rejected fae who clung to our kingdom because the one you were a part of pissed you off. How do I know you're even going to stick around for us? Maybe August should be finding a new second." It was a low blow, and a part of her regretted it the moment the words left her mouth.

Her darkness, on the other hand, reveled in it, swirling in her chest and showing her exactly how to take down Dorian. It was the answer she'd been searching for. Her magic showed her the way to grip his and drain it from him.

Emery opened her palms to follow its guidance, but closed them again the moment she saw Dorian's face.

His lips were twisted in a sneer and his brows furrowed, but it was his eyes—the agony and hatred she saw there—that crippled her.

"What would I know? I am a fucking prince without a kingdom, Emery. And do you want to know how I lost it? I trusted someone like you. Someone who was supposed to have my back when it mattered most, but instead betrayed me for love, and I lost everything. My kingdom. My family. Everything. And you are on your way to doing the exact same thing if you aren't careful."

Dorian turned on his heel and stormed off.

Guilt churned in her stomach, and she called after him, but he didn't stop.

Flora and Draven narrowed their gazes and shook their

heads before taking off after him. Mateo and Kade followed too, leaving her alone with Nico.

Fuck. Emery chewed her lip and wished the floor beneath her would swallow her whole. It wasn't her intention to go off on Dorian, he just didn't get it. No one did. She might not be facing this alone, but all the pressure was on her to ensure they could win against Sloane. He wasn't wrong when he said everyone was looking at her to save them.

Nico hopped down from the edge of the arena and walked toward her.

"I told you to go easy on him," he snapped.

Emery scoffed and kicked the dirt at her feet. "You're one to talk. You think I don't know that you're the one he trusted?"

Nico froze a few steps away from her, and Emery looked up at him to see his eyes had darkened. When he spoke, it was barely above a whisper. "Don't make the same mistakes I did."

That was easy for him to say when she had no idea what he'd done. "And how do you suggest I do that?"

"Find and harness your darkness. Hold on to what matters most. Use the blood to your advantage."

Emery threw up her hands and gave him her back, so he couldn't see the tears that pricked her eyes. "You don't think I'm trying."

"No." Nico wrapped a hand around her shoulder and yanked her back to face him. "Dorian is right. You're holding on to what you think you are supposed to. You're living in the light when there are delicious shades of gray rippling around you, waiting for you to play in their wake."

As if to prove a point, he unleashed some of his magic, allowing it to permeate the air around them.

Standing toe-to-toe with him, Emery tipped her head back and met his gaze. "What the hell is that supposed to mean?"

"Dorian said you stood up for a shunned witch at the castle when her mate rejected her. Why did you do that?" Nico stepped to the side and circled her slowly.

His magic caressed hers, begging it to come out and play. Still, Emery kept a tight leash on her own, unwilling to allow it any freedom except when she deemed necessary. She held her chin up high and answered him. "Because it was the right thing to do."

Nico circled back around her, his obsidian eyes narrowed on her face. "And how did you do it?"

Her darkness hummed in her chest as she remembered Aberforth pressed against the wall at her mercy. The fear in his eyes. The crack in his voice. "By stringing her mate up with thorns."

"And how did that feel?"

Her eyes glowed, and she knew they weren't amber any longer. "Fucking amazing."

"Case in point," Nico continued when he saw that Emery wasn't following. "When you let yourself feel the rightness of your actions, you react authentically. Instead of trying to be who you think everyone wants you to be, why don't you try to be the queen you were meant to be?"

But that wasn't right. It wasn't the rightness of her actions that caused her to react authentically. It was opening the door to the darkness just enough that it gripped her spine and forced its actions upon her. She shook her head and muttered, "I can't just string people up in thorns because they disagree with me."

It wasn't right. Her darkness couldn't be allowed to dictate her actions. She would be no better than Sloane then.

Nico stopped behind her and snarled in her ear. "Why not?"

Emery shook her head. "That might be how you do things in the Feywilde, but that was not one of my finer moments as a queen."

"Maybe not. But it was authentic, and that's what it's going to take for you to hone your darkness. It is going to fight you every step of the way if it feels even the slightest bit of hesitation. On the flip side, you need to learn to bend it to your will. Feed it, but control it. Give it an inch but don't let it take a mile. Just as you control your light magic, seize your darkness."

Nico spoke as if it was so easy, even as he stood with his magic surrounding them like it was a Sunday stroll through the park.

Emery took a step forward and turned on him with rage in her gaze. "If it was that easy, don't you think I would have done it already?"

"No, because I think you're scared. You've been told to fear your darkness, and until you embrace it, you're never going to be who you were meant to be."

He wasn't wrong. After Scotland, she was afraid to touch her darkness, except when rage forced her into its clutches. Her darkness recognized her for who she was and guided her as it saw fit. It could have taken things too far, but she'd ignored its impulses, pushing them away to be the queen she thought her kingdom needed.

But that's not what they needed. They needed her to be merciless. They needed her to match their king's ruthless nature and be the darkness when he was the diplomat. They needed her to find balance.

Fucking balance. It was the bane of her existence that taunted her in every aspect of her life. This was to be no different. The problem was she was still afraid of what she could become.

Emery dropped her gaze to the tiny patch of weeds on the otherwise dirt arena. "It showed me how to steal Dorian's magic," she whispered.

"So why didn't you?"

"Because he's mine to protect."

Nico shook his head. "That's where you're wrong. You're not acting like a queen. He's yours to punish."

"Like you did?" Emery hissed.

"That was different. I took from him that which wasn't mine to take. I punished him and forced him into my agenda." Nico looked away, and for the first time she saw a hint of remorse in his god-like features. This man who didn't break was sorry for the things he'd done, even if he'd never speak it out loud. His voice cracked as he whispered. "I took his family from him. I had nothing left to lose and everything to gain. My actions killed his bonded only moments after he'd found them. I sacrificed his for mine, and the difference between you and me, Emery, is I'd do it again. My actions saved an entire realm, but ruined his life forever."

"You didn't ruin his life," Emery offered, having seen just how much joy Dorian held when they weren't at war and he was with Ansel. "You just set him on a different path."

Nico scoffed and waved her off. "I did, but the fates took pity on him, and for that I am forever grateful. Which is why I'm helping you. It's my penance."

"No, you're helping me because you need me to perform a spell."

"One that is going to continue to save the people I swore to protect."

"Which is why I need to learn how to do this." It all clicked into place. Why Nico was pushing her so hard. "To protect mine."

"Now you're getting it."

Just because she understood didn't mean she was ready to blindly give into the darkest parts of her magic. She might be queen, but she was still herself and she didn't want to lose that.

"Even if I learn to hone this magic, how is it going to protect them? Sloane is stronger than me, she's been wielding the darkness and had a witch who taught her everything she knows."

"And you have a fae who knows more than any witch ever could." A truly wicked smile tipped his lips. "You don't need strength to win. You need strategy."

Her heart seized, but she managed a small smile. "You sound like August."

"He's a smart man."

Emery nodded. "He is."

Nico backed away from her, determination returning to his gaze as he reached the spot where Dorian had been standing. "Darkness alone isn't how you are going to defeat Sloane. It's how you are going to keep her distracted while you pair it with your blood magic to cripple her."

"How am I going to do that?" she croaked, feeling the seed of doubt creeping back in.

"Think of it in terms of your light magic. It needs somewhere to go after it is expelled. You feed it back into the earth or harness it yourself to keep your stores from depleting, correct?"

"Right." She'd only just begun to master this aspect of her light magic. Darkness didn't feel the same when she expelled it, though. It was chaos. Which was why she'd nearly collapsed when facing her sister and took ages to recoup after that last run-in with Sloane.

"By learning to pull the darkness to you, you'll be able to harness not only your magic but the magic thrown at you. But paired with your blood magic, there is no reason you can't harness the darkness in Sloane's beasts as well."

Emery chewed her cheek, considering his words. "You're saying I could drain the magic of Sloane's army through their blood and harness it myself."

"Exactly." Nico clapped his hands together and then pointed at her. "Sloane is spread thin, forcing her magic into her beasts to keep them alive. And if what August said was true, they have a bit of your magic in their blood, which should make it easier to call to it."

"Like calls to like." Emery recited the mantra.

"Precisely."

It all made sense, but that didn't mean she wanted to follow this train of thought. Using her dark magic was one thing, but taking their blood, giving into that part of her magic would mean allowing it to consume her. Emery remembered what it felt like in Scotland to drain the witches. She became the darkness, and only August could bring her back. And he wasn't there now.

"Won't all that magic overload me?" she asked, tendrils of anxiety weaving up her spine. "I can barely harness the darkness I have, what makes you think I will be able to control that amount of magic, let alone the darkest of it."

"You won't have to. You'll funnel it to your army."

Emery stared at him with a blank stare on her face. "You lost me."

"Your army is made of witches and vampires." He hesitated, waiting for it to click, but it didn't. Nico rolled his eyes, and she nearly laughed at the sight of the over-the-top asshole fae partaking in such a human mannerism. "You and your sister are inherently dark, you were born with darkness in your veins. But that doesn't mean all witches can't wield dark magic. They can't create it, but they can practice it. In theory, that means they could wield it if it was gifted to them. And through your blood magic, you could give vampires the gift of dark blood."

"That would mean I need to learn to funnel both." It wasn't a terrible idea. And if she could just funnel instead of calling the blood, maybe she would be able to avoid letting go.

"Which is why you are going to get over there and try again."

She still wasn't convinced she could do this, but Nico's ass-backwards logic had worked. Understanding the end goal made it easier to digest, even if she had no idea how to get there.

Once Emery was squared up with him, Nico opened his palms and released his magic into the air. She was nearly knocked off her feet by the sheer power behind it. It moved like smoke, surrounding his palms in billowing waves. It was chaotic, and held the weight of an avalanche in its swirls.

"Now, call your own magic to your palms."

Emery followed his instruction, the familiar warmth of her magic filling her.

"I'm going to push my magic toward you. I want you to pull it to you like you would your light magic."

The onyx wisps never left his hands, but Emery knew the moment his darkness caressed her own because her magic bowed to his.

Traitor.

Nico smiled and urged her on. "It recognizes me as a threat. That goes to show that Sloane isn't one. It never bowed to her."

He was right. Her magic sought to destroy when it came to her sister. It knew from the beginning what she could become.

"Now, pull my essence toward you. Absorb it like you would the light."

Emery coaxed the essence of her magic to tangle with his, and tentatively pulled it toward her. It resisted her demands slightly, but ultimately allowed her to do so.

Holy hell.

The moment his magic entered her body, Emery lurched up, her spine straightening almost like she was floating. The heady essence of Nico's magic flowed in her veins and pooled in her chest. It was darker than anything she'd ever felt, whispering tales of death and destruction in the darkest parts of her mind.

"You are a fucking homicidal maniac," she whispered.

"I never claimed to be anything else," Nico chuckled.

"Now, take what you need to replenish your stores and pool the rest in your hands."

She closed her eyes, visualizing the well inside her and filling it up, but it felt wrong. The magic flowed, his and hers, but the darkness was too much. Her chest ached and bitterness bloomed on her tongue.

No. There was nothing right about the darkness Nico harnessed.

"Good. Now give it back," he instructed.

All too willing to comply, Emery pushed her hands forward and willed the magic at Nico, but nothing happened. Her eyes popped open, wide with fear as the darkness of both their magicks swirled in her hands and clung to her skin.

"Why isn't it working?" Fear etched in her trembling voice. Wind picked up around them, whirling and throwing up the dust of the arena as the first of her elements to come to her aid.

"You are in control. Not your darkness." Nico yelled through the storm. "This is where you tame it, bend it to your will."

Come on, Emery silently battled. *You want me to be a ruthless queen, but I'm not. I won't rule with merciless cruelty. This magic isn't ours to keep. It's not who we are.*

Her darkness sent her images of what they could do with Nico's magic. The fire and destruction they could wield on the castle if they went right now and took back what was theirs.

And then we would have nothing. No kingdom and no trust from those who believe in us and are trapped within those walls. I will be unforgiving to those who cross us, but I will not be without compassion. We cannot do this alone. We are stronger united, and with our help our people can prevail. We are the key. So, get in fucking line.

Her magic swelled and snapped to her will, flowing from her hands toward Nico.

A wide smile tugged at her lips, and Emery huffed an unbelievable laugh as she guided her magic back to his outstretched palms.

"I did it," she breathed. "I fucking did it."

Nico smiled and nodded as the last of his magic returned to him.

"Now you're ready to be the Queen of Light and Dark."

Emery tested the title on her tongue, and her magic swirled happily in her chest. It felt right, like it truly was who she was meant to be, and this was the first step toward her future.

Nico crossed the arena and stood in front of her.

"Thank you," she said.

"You're welcome. You still need a lot of training."

Emery nodded, and for the first time in what felt like forever, she felt hope deep in her soul. There was no way in hell she'd be gifting dark magic to the witches who followed her, even if they could wield it; there was no way she'd subject them to its call. But she could give hers freely and maybe that could be enough.

Chapter Thirty One

SLOANE

Sloane pored over the ancient texts while Wren and Jessi argued in the corner. She wasn't sure what it was about this time, but more than likely Jessi was wrong and Wren couldn't stop without having the last word.

"Can you two take whatever the hell you are squabbling about somewhere else?" she hissed in their direction.

They were two of the most diabolical women she had ever known, and each played an important part in her plan, but some days they were worse than the Culling women she'd grown up with at the castle. Which was saying something, considering Sloane hadn't believed Jessi could get any worse. Becoming a vampire had only amplified the woman's ability to be a conniving bitch. But she was on Sloane's side and that's what mattered. She'd worked wonders in breaking August.

Wren snapped her head toward Sloane and raised a brow. "Did you find anything?"

"Not yet, but I'm close." She ran her fingers over the weathered pages, inked with spells that likely hadn't been uttered for centuries. "These are Runa's grimoires. If, as I suspect, Celeste's were used to break the Culling spell, Runa's would have been directed at breaking bonds."

It really was a shame Sloane had killed her. Hindsight being what it was, she should have anticipated that Runa might have been useful. The problem was that she was going soft in her old age. Hidden away from the witches, her ancestor was the darker half of original witches and the balance, until Sloane took her place. Runa didn't necessarily want to see mates abolished; she just wanted the option to choose. Unlike Sloane, who would do away with the whole race of vampires if she thought she could get away with it. But that was a long way off and likely a fool's goal. Their blood was what kept her army immortal and ultimately, as long as they bowed to her, she could tolerate their continued existence.

She flipped through a few more pages, finding little more than the breakdown of the spells used by Celeste to bond vampires to witches. What she needed was the antithesis and thus far it had eluded her.

"Well, if you don't need me, I'm going to go feed from my favorite sire." Jessi shrugged off her shawl and bounced through the chamber toward the door.

Sloane flicked her wrist and halted Jessi mid-stride. "Has he said anything to you? Anything that would lead you to believe he's playing us?"

Jessi huffed and rolled her eyes, ever the petulant child. "We know he's playing us. There is no way he has forsaken Emery. Those two are gag-worthy in their mate bond."

She'd suspected as much too, but the last few times she'd seen him, Sloane had begun to wonder. When he was working the crowds of vampire nobles that flocked to see if he had truly forsaken his mate, he'd said all the right things to get them to back him. Even his army had fallen in line behind her. Well, him, but he was pushing her agenda so it was the same thing.

"He mentioned wanting to see Ansel," Jessi offered, "but other than that he's been the perfect sire. He even offered to teach me to fight so I could protect myself should I come under attack."

Sloane wanted to scoff that Jessi thought August actually gave a shit about her. It wasn't unusual for a sire to want to protect their fledgling, but the fact that it was Jessi had her questioning his motivations.

Breaking his bond to Emery was the end-goal when it came to using him, but she couldn't deny the part of her that would like someone to confide in at her side. Wren and Jessi were acceptable for now, but having another ruler who understood the pressures and politics it took to be a ruthless monarch wouldn't be terrible.

Fuck. Was she growing as soft as Runa?

She hadn't had anyone at her side since Malcolm, and that was a sham of a relationship if there ever was one. He was all hearts and rainbows when she needed a cutthroat and power-hungry man at her side. Not that she needed a man to define her. Even if she didn't have a mate mark, these feelings were no doubt the work of the bond her magic still yearned for. Which was all the more reason to figure out how to break the damn bonds between their factions.

"Wren, can you get Ansel ready for another session?" She needed to break something, someone, anything really to remind her of who the hell she was and who she never wanted to be.

"Didn't we just use him yesterday? He'll still be heal—"

"I said get him ready for another session," Sloane snapped as she released Jessi from her hold. "And Jessi, tell your sire I need him to be ready for dinner tonight with the Romanian Delegation. No doubt they're going to want to see with their own eyes that their beloved brethren is truly on the side of monsters."

Jessi stretched her arms behind her back, shaking off Sloane's magic. "He's training this afternoon with his men."

"I don't give a shit. Tell him he'll be there on my arm with a fucking smile on his face. Otherwise, not only will I take it out on his precious little wolf, but I'll make a spectacle in front of his people and remind him why he chose me over her."

"Oookay." Jessi took a step back and excused herself from the room.

"Was that necessary?" Wren stood with her hands on her hips, her lips twisted in a sneer.

Sloane narrowed her gaze. "I'm pretty sure I told you what I needed."

Her second's eyes widened, and she shook her head. "You know you can be a downright bitch sometimes."

"And yet you know I'm the winning hand."

Wren hesitated, and chewed the inside of her cheek. For a split second, Sloane thought this might be the moment she challenged her. It wouldn't surprise her, but it would be a shame to have to train a new second.

Thinking better of it, Wren blinked and huffed a sigh. "I'll have the wolf ready in ten minutes."

"Thank you," Sloane spat.

Sloane stared at the door for ten long seconds after Wren exited the suite, trying to steady herself. There was no need to take out her anger on Wren and Jessi, especially when Wren was no doubt close to questioning her logic. She needed to remind herself and them of the power she held, and the goals she'd yet to reach.

From behind her, a slow clap echoed, and she whipped around to see Dal striding from her bathroom.

Fucking hell.

The god was the epitome of handsome, with striking features that defied logic. Women no doubt told stories of the way his dark hair fell to his shoulders and how the line of his jaw felt caressing the skin of their thighs.

She should know. He had defiled her in the best possible ways. It made sense that he knew his way around a woman, considering he was the God of Death and women would do anything to defy his coming.

"That was some show for a queen," he taunted.

Sloane scoffed and turned back to the book in front of her. "What are you doing here?"

Dal rounded the desk, sliding his fingers across the slick wood and over the pages of the grimoire. "I would think you would welcome your benefactor more warmly, considering I am the reason you stand with a throne at your back at all."

Sloane looked up, narrowing her gaze. "You are nothing but a silent contributor who has yet to do more than serenade me with long-winded monologues and vague musings of what I should consider in order to achieve our goal."

Dal's eyes darkened, and his lips twisted into a sardonic grin. "You and I both know we have the same goal. This world cannot exist as it does. You are the key to bending it in my favor."

"And yet you haven't lifted a finger." She slammed the grimoire closed and pushed her chair out so she could stand.

Dal followed her as she crossed the room, but stopped short when she dipped behind a privacy screen. "We have been over this. My brethren and I are not allowed to intervene."

Sloane huffed as she tugged off her sweater and leggings. "No, but you're allowed to use me."

"And you love every minute of it," he mused.

She did. Dal was just as ruthless in bed as he was calculating in everyday life. He took what he wanted, and didn't leave room for requests. Dal was who Sloane should have wanted at her side, but the small, weak-minded human side of her still craved warmth in a man.

It was pathetic, and she knew it.

"Is that why you're here?" Sloane stepped out from behind the screen to where Dal stood. She ran her fingers across his chest. Rounding his shoulders, she caressed his earlobe before heading into the washroom. "My pussy must be worth it if you are making late night house calls."

Dal turned and followed her silently. He turned on the bathtub and poured in a generous amount of bubbles while she grabbed a towel and her robe from the cupboard. "While I would love nothing more than to defile your cunt and hear you curse my name, I'm here to motivate you to break the mate bonds. Without them broken, we will not succeed in breaking this realm from its mate."

Sloane tilted her head. She hadn't planned on soaking, but maybe she would take her time and keep Ansel's wolf on edge while he waited. She also wanted to know more about the mate of the realm as it was the first time she was hearing of it. "So that's your end game. To break this realm of its mate."

"In a way." Dal extended his hand and when Sloane placed hers in his, he pulled her against his broad chest. His fingers curled beneath her chin and lifted it so she met his gaze. "All you need to worry about is ending your sister and the plans she has for mates. That will be enough to shift the balance in my favor."

Sloane sucked in a breath, struck by his devilish charm. "And you'll provide me with the life source I need to balance myself in this realm?"

Dal chuckled. "Yes, little necromancer. Although I suggest you stop pulling from the dead; my people are none too happy with you."

His hands dropped to her waist. He splayed his palms on her sides and ran them up her torso, his thumbs brushing over the lace of her bra, causing her nipples to tighten.

Sloane clenched her thighs together like he wasn't affecting her and shrugged. "They'll survive."

A low growl rumbled in his chest and Dal dragged his fingers down her stomach to the top of her panties where he hooked them in the waistband. "Do you want me to continue?"

She shouldn't, but she did. Sloane stepped forward,

lifted herself up on tiptoe and sucked his lower lip between her teeth. "I want you to tell me how to break the bonds."

His eyes flared with heat, but Dal didn't move. "The fates forbid it, but I can tell you it's not in the words you see, but in those you don't."

"Are you always so damn cryptic?"

Dal shrugged. "Death is never what it seems."

"So, the answer is yes." She reached up and with a flick of her fingers unsnapped the clasp of her bra, letting it fall to the floor.

"You're trying my patience."

"You can go, then." Sloane stepped back and tugged down her panties. When she stood back up, Dal's eyes narrowed on the swell of her breasts.

"So be it," he said with a shrug and turned for the door, as if her denying him was no big deal.

He wanted to make her a queen, but it was clear to Sloane he'd never see her as more than a pawn. That knowledge only spurred Sloane to prove him wrong. One day she'd be what he needed, not just a plaything he visited when the timing suited him. There would come a day when he would beg to stand at her side, and she would relish denying him.

Dal looked over his shoulder as Sloane slid beneath the bubbles, a hint of regret in his features. "Don't wait too long. There are monsters being born in darkness where there was only light before."

"It's a good thing I'm not afraid of the dark, then."

Dal's lips pulled into a tight line, and he shook his head. "It's the light you need to worry about, little queen."

"Don't worry about coming for me, Death," she mocked, "I'm not going to perish in its radiance."

"This would be so much easier if you held your sister's blood," Dal muttered so low that Sloane almost didn't think she heard him correctly.

What did Emery's blood have to do with the spell?

Dal's words should have worried her, but she meant what she said. The light could come for her, but it couldn't break her. Not when there was nothing left to fracture. Emery wasn't the sister destined for royalty. She was.

"Read the damn book again," he muttered before disappearing through the doorway.

She knew that even if she ran into the bedroom, he'd be gone. He may have been a cryptic bastard, but Dal had been useful before in helping her find the ways to strengthen her magic and form her army. If he said the answer was there, then it was.

Sloane soaked for an hour, clearing her head of Dal and the wants her heart had tempted her with. When she was pruny and back to feeling more like herself, she wrapped herself in the black-on-black power suit she favored when she knew she'd be visiting the dungeons.

Before she left, she examined the book one more time, Dal's words echoing in her mind.

It's not the words you see, it's the ones you don't.

Sloane called on her magic and let the inky purple pool in her hands, hovering above the page. The iridescent light from her magic radiated over the pages, acting like a black light.

"That sneaky bitch," she whispered.

Between the lines of written words, penned in invisible ink, were Runa's keys to breaking the spells her sister magicked into existence. It seemed she could only break one bond at a time, but one was all she needed to set an example.

A wicked smile tipped her lips.

Dal was right when he said monsters were being born, but it wasn't those of the light they should be worried about.

Chapter Thirty-Two

EMERY

Malcolm's face paled as blood dripped from his eyes, nose, and ears. His entire body shook as he fought to remain standing.

"Keep going," he spoke through gritted teeth at the same time Dorian ordered her to stop.

Things were still tense between the two of them despite the numerous times Emery tried to apologize. She was pretty sure nothing short of bringing Ansel home and getting them the hell out of Enchanth was going to bring her friend back to her. This realization was enough to drive her to perfect her magic.

Sweat pooled in the notch at the base of her throat as she tried to focus. Feeling the magic in the blood of those around her had become second nature, making them bleed was as easy as flicking her wrist, but pulling it toward her was proving to be a fucking bitch.

That wasn't true. It's just what she continuously told Nico, Dorian, and now Malcolm. The truth was she wasn't ready to give into the blood. She didn't want to pull it to her and lose herself in the darkness. Every time she made them bleed, Emery felt the wicked magic of her soul grow stronger.

"This isn't working," Emery huffed, lowering her hands and calling back her magic. "I can only make him bleed. I can't pull it toward me." *Lie.* "Not to mention we still have no idea how the hell I'm supposed to funnel the blood back into him once I've taken it."

Malcom fell to his knees, a heap of worn-out limbs, and Lily rushed to his side, offering her wrist. He latched on and groaned, pulling his mate tight against him.

Emery's heart constricted, but she shoved the pain down. She didn't have time to think about her mate or how her soul ached for him the longer she was in Enchanth. There was no room to consider how he was publicly denouncing her or that he was on Sloane's arm at every event she hosted. She had to stay focused. They were a few weeks out from Heil, which was the day they wanted to be ready to attack. Sloane would know they were coming, but they planned to have the upper hand now that August was their man on the inside. As long as Emery could get her shit together and master her magic, all this would be worth it.

"It's too bad you can't fill blood bags on the battlefield," Flora offered, hopping off the arena fence.

Wouldn't that be nice, Emery thought. She wiped the sweat from her brow and walked over to where Cosmina sat holding Lina along with Bronwyn and Braxton. Watching her mother pull blood from her uncle probably wasn't conducive to a healthy upbringing, but thankfully she was still only a few months old and wouldn't remember any of this.

Lina's eyes sparkled when she saw Emery, who pulled

the baby into her arms and snuggled her nose into the crook of her neck.

"I love you," Emery whispered and Lina squealed.

"But what if she could?" Bronwyn murmured, before getting a far-off look in her eyes that Emery knew all too well. It was the look that told her that fun Bronwyn had left the building and had been replaced by the scholarly Bronwyn who always came up with the most hare-brained ideas. The last suggestion she'd made after a look like that ended with Brax wrapped in cellophane so Bronwyn could test the effects of certain lotions on a turned vampire's skin in sunlight.

A smile tugged at one side of her lips, and she nodded her head like it was all coming together. "Okay, hear me out. What if once you pulled the blood from a person or beast, you wrapped it in magic? Light magic would probably be better, considering that is what they are made of, but dark likely wouldn't hurt them. You'd have to be fast on a battlefield, but the magic would create a barrier, keeping the liquid inside. Distributing them might be a problem, but once a vampire got it, they could tear through the magic and consume both the magic and the blood, in theory giving them the power boost Nico intended."

"So, it's basically a supercharged juice box," Brax offered.

"It's not a bad idea," Lily added.

Emery rolled her eyes. "There's an awful lot of what ifs and theoreticals in that plan."

"Do you have a better one?"

"No."

Bronwyn shrugged, "It's a good plan in theory, then."

Emery swung her head to see Callum leaning against

the fence about halfway down the arena. He pushed off and started toward where they all sat.

"You're back!" Emery walked toward him and tugged him against her, squishing Lina between them.

Callum was spending more and more time away from Enchanth. Partly because he still had a kingdom to run, but unlike everyone else, Emery knew that wasn't the only reason. It was the same reason she hid in her room most nights with Lina. Being around other mates was hard when yours was gone. She couldn't imagine how Callum felt, knowing he didn't have one at all.

Callum pulled back and smiled, searching her eyes. "How are you?"

"I'm fine." He gave her a half-hearted smile but it didn't reach his eyes. He leaned down and whispered, his voice low enough the other vampires wouldn't hear. "I have news, but you're not going to like it."

Emery's smile faltered.

"Do you want me to wait to tell you?"

Callum didn't give options. He did what he thought was best and only what he thought was best. It was as if it was his world to control and the rest of them were just living in it. If he was giving her the option, then it really wasn't good and likely had to do with her mate.

"Is he okay?" Emery asked, needing to know before she could decide.

"He's fine. So is Ansel."

"Okay." Emery swallowed hard and nodded. "Tell us all, together."

It should lessen the chance of her absolutely losing it. With Lina in her arms and her friends surrounding her, she wanted to believe she could handle whatever news Callum had. She hoped she could, anyway.

Callum followed a few steps behind her to where everyone sat, and when she turned to face him, she didn't like the way his lips pulled in a grim line.

"I don't like that look." Malcolm said. "Take it back. We were just onto something good and you're here to ruin it."

"For once, I agree with him," Bronwyn muttered.

"I wish I came bearing better news, but Sloane says she's figured out how to break mate bonds." He announced this with absolutely no lead up and no softening the blow. "She's decided to make a spectacle of it and host a ball to mark the occasion." His gaze drifted to Emery. "August's bond will be the first to be broken."

"No." Emery sucked in a gasp, but the noise was drowned out by the ringing in her ears. She shook her head as if somehow disagreeing would make the truth less real. Lina cooed in her arms, waving her little baby hands. Emery narrowed her gaze on the silver mark on her daughter's arm. Out there somewhere, she had a mate waiting to change her life the way August had changed Emery's. Tears blurred her vision as she considered that it could all be taken away with one spell. Her daughter's future could be stripped from her with one fucking spell. It wasn't fair.

She instinctively reached for her mate bond, searching for the emotions of her mate and sending him every ounce of love and devotion she felt in her heart, but she came up empty. There was nothing but a vast desert of space and time between them with only the flicker of a presence at the opposite end. The only hint he was alive and living in the realm they called home.

Was he feeling the same thing? Did he still reach for her? Weeks had passed, and Emery had no way of knowing how August was feeling. She might house a piece of his soul, but little good it did her. Beyond what Callum reported back to her, which wasn't much at all, she didn't really have any indication of where his head was at. For all she knew, he might have grown to see things the way Sloane did. He'd been the one to side with Aberforth in favor of exploring what could be done for those who didn't want their mates. What if he wanted this?

Emery choked on a sob, but before anyone could move to comfort her, before any words of action or encouragement could be spoken, a soft pop sounded and Nico stood in front of her.

His eyes were wide and his usually pristine hair disheveled behind his horns. Blood trickled from the corner of his mouth. "I need you to come with me," he panted.

"No," Emery shook her head. "I can't. I have to get to August. I have to stop this. Sloane is going to take him from me."

Nico's hand shot out and grasped her bicep, his nails digging into her flesh through her top. "I'm calling in my favor, Emery. You owe me this. Your precious mate will survive, but mine won't if you don't help me."

Emery yanked her arm back and Lina started to cry, startled by the jostling. "Your timing is shit, Nico. I can't go right now."

"Then you can get the hell out of my realm, and take all your people with you." Rage filled his voice. "You owe me this, Emery."

Her eyes darted to where Callum and Dorian stood.

They both nodded, and Callum stepped forward and extended his arms to take Lina. "We can't leave here yet. We aren't ready. Go. For once, time is on our side. We have about twelve hours in Enchanth before we have to go back to the human realm. I already have someone reaching out to August to meet us. We'll come up with a plan while you're gone."

Emery hesitated. The last thing she wanted to do was whatever the hell Nico had planned for her, but this was one of those shit moments where being a queen came before her own needs. Her people needed her to fulfill her end of the bargain to keep them safe.

She turned and narrowed her eyes at Nico, "You have twelve hours."

"If you can control your magic, it will take one, tops." He extended his hand, and Emery didn't miss the slight tremor. His eyes flicked up to Dorian. "You're coming too."

"The hell I—"

"Dorian, I need you at my side," Nico snapped.

Dorian seethed, but nodded reluctantly.

She placed her hand in his and turned to her friends. Some had tears in their eyes while others showed the kind of fire and determination that lifted a weight from her soul. This was another lesson in not going at it alone and trusting those around her.

"We'll be back in one hour," she assured them, but it was as much for her as it was for them.

Lina giggled in Callum's arms, and offered her a gummy smile right before the world vortexed around her and she was thrust into darkness.

Chapter Thirty Three

EMERY

"Where are we?" Emery blinked her eyes a few times in an attempt to adjust her sight to the darkness. They were in an enclosed space, but the cragged stone edges paired with the damp air made her think it was less of a room and more of a cave. The space was empty, though, lit only by two torches that didn't give off enough light to say for sure.

Torches.

Where the hell were they that they used torches instead of electricity?

"The northern mountains of the unseelie court," Nico muttered, grabbing one of the torches from the wall and handing it to her.

Emery wrapped her hand around the wood base and held it up in front of her. "And that is where?"

"The Feywilde."

"You brought me to the Feywilde?" Her eyes grew wide and her voice wavered. The ramifications of her being there filtered through her mind. "Am I even allowed to be here?'

"Technically no, so stay quiet and don't talk to anyone." Without another word, Nico turned on his heel and headed down the nearest corridor.

Dorian looked over at her and jerked his head in the same direction. "Come on. You don't want to be caught alone in these mountains."

She didn't want to be caught there, period.

Light on her feet, Emery followed the two fae through a winding maze of tunnels, having to speed walk to keep up with their long strides. Magic licked at her skin like it did in Enchanth, but it felt more alive here than it did in the pocket realm and definitely more so than in the mortal realm. It beckoned to her own, alive in every molecule of air.

Finally, they reached their destination, the tunnel opening up into a cavern larger than the one they'd sieved into. What she assumed was moonlight shone from above through a crack in the mountain's surface, bathing the space in a soft blue glow. Her breath hitched when she noticed the crystal altar in the center, much like the one August had fucked her on in Scotland. Upon it laid a woman dressed in leathers and fur. She looked as if she belonged not only in a different world but a different time altogether. A time where torches were perfectly acceptable. The woman's blood red hair was fastened in three braids close to her crown before falling in waves over the edge of the altar. Beside her lay a broadsword, and fastened to her thigh were three small daggers. Dirt covered her ivory skin, and if it weren't for the slow rise of her chest, Emery might think she was witnessing a wake.

"Did you bring her?" A woman stepped out from the shadows on the opposite side of the cavern. She wore a dark cloak over her shoulders with a hood that hid her features.

"Yes, she's here. Did Trine make it?"

"I'm here. I'm here." Emery turned around to see the old crone enter from the same tunnel they had. "Can we get this over with? Just being in this realm has my hair standing on end."

Emery felt it too. While her magic reveled in it, her instincts had her wanting to run.

"I see you haven't changed one bit, crone," the cloaked woman taunted.

"At least I don't pretend to fight for a realm that wants me dead."

"Stop it, both of you," Nico snapped, his eyes narrowing on the hooded woman. "She's right, Addia. We need to be quick before Thorne realizes I have her and what I intend to do."

"Yeah, stealing your bonded from her betrothed is frowned upon," Dorian muttered low enough that Emery barely heard him, though she was sure Nico did, based on the way his lip curled in a snarl.

This wasn't what she signed up for. Emery didn't know who the hell Thorne was, but it seemed Nico had made her an accomplice in kidnapping this woman and whatever the hell he had planned next. But what could she do? She didn't even know how the hell to get back to Enchanth. Could they even portal between realms?

Addia stepped into the moonlit center of the cavern, reached up and tugged down the hood of her cloak. Her hair was a beautiful array of silver and gold, woven in crown-like braids. Her eyes were the lightest blue, looking almost silver in the moonlight as they roamed over Emery.

"So, this is the Queen of Light and Dark, the balance of the moral realm. She doesn't seem that special."

Well, wasn't she lovely?

"If I wasn't, I'm sure Nico wouldn't need me, yet here I am," Emery sneered, already not liking the woman.

"Silence!" Nico snapped. "Addia, place the bloodstone on her chest; Emery, go with Trine and stay by her head."

His voice was angry, but Emery didn't miss the sweat on his brow or the panic in his eyes. She'd never seen Nico anything but calm, cool, and collected, but right then he was anything but.

"And where would you like me, Your Highness?" Dorian quipped.

"You know damn well where I need you."

Emery rounded the top of the altar and slid next to Trine. She looked down at the woman, taking in the scars along her collarbone. "Who is she?"

"Kenna," Trine whispered at the same time Nico snapped, "It doesn't matter who the hell she is."

Emery's eyes widened and she threw her hands up in surrender. "Okay, it doesn't matter. What exactly do you need me to do?"

"She's in danger in this realm. I'm going to hide her in yours, but first I need to make her human and ensure she doesn't remember the Feywilde. The latter is where you come in. I need you to pull forth her memories while Trine alters them."

"I don't know that—" Emery began to protest, but Nico cut her off.

"I don't care. This is the deal."

She swallowed her opposition and nodded before glaring at Trine.

This had been the plan all along. It had been the reason she'd met Trine at all in Enchanth, the reason she'd gained Emery's trust and taught her about her magic, the reason she'd pushed her into examining the past instead of focusing only on the future. Emery's sight was a tool for them to exploit. They needed more than one sight-touched witch, and she was the only one available.

Her gaze fell to the girl on the table. She didn't look much older than Emery, and despite the blood and dirt, she looked almost innocent laying there. Like she was a pawn in the game of those around her. Emery could relate, which only made the sinking feeling in her stomach double. This woman might be Nico's bonded, but that didn't mean she deserved to have her memories taken. The choices she'd make from this moment forward would no longer be her own. They'd be based on something that never happened.

And there was nothing Emery could do about it.

Addia brandished a knife from beneath her cloak, and Emery gasped when she made a shallow slice on the woman's chest and placed a blood red stone with silver and gold swirls on top of the wound. The swirls began to glow, taking on a life of their own as they moved rhythmically over the stone's surface.

Emery's gaze narrowed on the stone, and her magic hummed, yearning to caress the blood inside. It wasn't dark like Dorian's, Nico's or even Malcolm's as a turned vampire. This blood hummed with a magic all of its own. Light, but not the same as hers. It was ancient like Nico, but ethereal in its presence.

Addia's eyes whipped to Emery, narrowing, but when she spoke it was to Nico. "You've got fifteen minutes of healing."

Nico nodded. He stepped forward and took the woman's hand in his while Dorian rounded the altar and mirrored his actions on the opposite side.

Dorian dropped his glamour for only the third time since Emery had met him. Her gaze drifted from the dark ribbed horns that curled away from his forehead and past the points of his ears, landing on the painted obsidian of his hands, which matched Nico's. The two of them were unlike any fae she'd ever seen, not that she'd seen a remarkable number in her lifetime. Enchanth was where her knowledge ended and began. But there was something different about them. In fact, the entire cavern was filled with fae who were more than otherworldly. She got the feeling they were the silent monsters that echoed throughout their history, conforming the future to their wills. They were on par with the gods and the stars, and she wasn't sure how it made her feel that she was in the same room as them.

Nico inhaled slowly and, on his exhale, instructed, "On my go."

Trine huffed beside her, murmuring something so low under her breath that Emery couldn't hear.

Nico lifted his gaze to Dorian, whose jaw tightened, and Emery wished, not for the first time, that she knew the whole story between them instead of only the bits and pieces they'd each offered up.

The two of them tipped their heads back and closed their eyes, bathing in the moonlight. In unison they murmured words Emery didn't understand in what she could only assume was the language of the fae. It was beautiful and ancient, and sounded almost like it was only meant to be whispered between lovers.

The light in the cavern intensified with each word they uttered, until Emery found herself squinting to see. Light erupted around them once they finished, and when Nico and Dorian opened their eyes, they wore matching obsidian gazes with faint blue specks that almost looked like stars in the night sky.

"Begin," Nico said, but his voice was low and gravelly instead of his usual smooth tone.

Addia stood opposite Emery and Trine at the woman's feet, her eyes widening when shadows like wisps of smoke wafted from Dorian and Nico's hands and crisscrossed up the woman's arms. The two of them moved in unison, using their fingers to trace rune-like marks on her skin, shadows clinging to where they'd marked them, darkening the woman's complexion.

The swirls on the stone Addia placed on her chest glowed brighter and the red color slowly drained from the stone.

When Emery glanced up, she met Nico's narrowed glare. "Now, Emery," he growled.

She stepped back and Trine's hand was there to steady her.

"They're really something aren't they?" Trine whispered before sliding her arm around Emery's elbow. "But we best get on with it. I wouldn't want to be on the receiving end of their wrath."

What the hell were they?

They were more than fae. And there was no doubt Trine was right, the last place she wanted to be was on the receiving end of their magic.

Not that she wanted to do what came next, either.

Emery looked to Trine for support, but only found the

crone's lips tightened into a thin line. She nodded and entwined the fingers of one hand in Emery's, bringing the other to Kenna's temple. Emery mirrored her actions and waited for guidance. It wasn't like she knew what the hell she was doing; she was flying by the seat of her pants and was in way over her head.

"Look into her past just as we've practiced before with your own. Feel for her soul and pull forth her memories in small clusters. Once they are there, I'll alter them."

Emery hated what she was about to do. It made her feel slimy and unworthy of the gifts she'd been given. There was no way this is what the stars had in mind when they bestowed her with the sight. Still, she'd do what she had to in order to protect her people, and right then that meant getting her hands dirty.

Magic hummed around her, a palpable force in the air, brushing against her flesh, begging her to tap into it. The rush that came when she called her magic nearly knocked her off her feet, but she managed to stay upright. Gold and ink pooled in her hands, and she touched her fingers to Kenna's temples.

Emery sucked in a breath the moment she entered the clusterfuck of Kenna's mind. It was cold and desolate. Images of war and famine plagued her recent past, each one forming a fortified wall that stopped Emery from going any further. A literal wall of memory bricks towered in front of her, taunting the wisps of her magic.

This wasn't the first number done on this woman's mind, and whoever built these barriers didn't want anyone to break her. Or maybe they were of her own doing, and if that was the case, this woman was a damn warrior.

"Dig deeper. She's a strong one," Trine whispered.

Strong was an understatement. Emery's magic caressed the edges of Kenna's, and Emery recoiled.

She was like her.

Light and dark magic coursed in her veins. But it wasn't magic of the earth, and she wasn't a witch. It resembled magic more akin to Dorian's and Nico's, more intense and emanating from her soul instead of the world around her.

A flicker of black dusted in opalescence caught her eye in a memory at the cornerstone of the barrier. Emery zeroed in on it and concentrated her magic on that memory, wrapping her tendrils around it and pulling it forward.

"That's it," Trine encouraged.

The memory thrust forward and filled their sight.

Kenna was standing beside Nico, facing another male fae with silky blonde hair and emerald eyes. His jaw was all angles while his smile curved up wickedly.

Kenna slowly walked over to stand beside the other fae and turned to face Nico. Her eyes were vacant, but Emery didn't think Nico noticed. Not with the way his expression faltered like his world had been stripped from him. It only lasted a second before he steeled his features and lifted his chin.

"So be it," he whispered.

Emery waited to see more of what came next, but the next moment never came. Tendrils of Trine's orange magic filtered through the memory, and in seconds the entire scene was altered. No longer did the three of them stand at odds with one another; instead, the men's faces had been blurred and replaced by nameless humans, while the beautiful Feywilde landscape had been replaced with a cobblestone boulevard in a quaint little town.

They were pulled back from the memory to the barrier, and Emery watched the ripple effect of changing this core memory. Every single one that followed in succession changed as well. The death and destruction fell away, replaced by mundane happenings on an average street in what looked to be a college town.

Emery's heart constricted. These memories were likely a cakewalk compared to the battles she'd seen, but they weren't Kenna's, and that felt so damn wrong. Emery was nothing without the shittiest parts of her past. She thought back to the moment she'd learned Sloane died, or the dungeon after Chelsea died. The lost moments where she cried for the mate who didn't want her and the moment he gave his soul for hers. Even in some of the darkest moments in her life, there was always a silver lining that had helped her grow.

Kenna would never have those moments and that just didn't sit right with her.

Once the barrier was no longer in their way, the memories flowed, and Trine worked quickly to pick out the most important and alter them slightly to build a past in the human realm. But each memory only served to make Emery feel worse.

She watched the most important moments of Kenna's life fly by. The loving family who raised her, the discovery of her magic, the moment she met Nico and the other fae. The love they shared.

Bile rose in Emery's throat each time Trine's orange tendrils grasped the memories and tore them from Kenna's mind.

This was so fucking wrong.

Still, she kept pulling memory after memory because

every time she thought of her options she fell back to her people. *I'm a queen,* she told herself. *Their queen. They need me.*

But so did Kenna. Emery could feel it in her bones.

Without thinking, she waited until Trine was focused on altering a large batch of memories and pulled a handful toward her. She wrapped them in her own darkness and managed to shove them into the recesses of Kenna's mind with the memories that had been altered. There was no telling what the repercussions of her actions would be, and Emery had no way of knowing if what she'd saved would be of any use to Kenna, but they would be there if she ever needed them. All Emery could do was send a prayer to the stars that they would be the right memories.

They finished quickly, and even though it felt like ages had passed, when Emery opened her eyes, the stone on Kenna's chest was a quarter of the way red, indicating they still had time. Emery's eyes widened when she took in Dorian and Nico's progress. Runes lined Kenna's arms, chest, and face. Her features had grown lackluster and less otherworldly, and her ears no longer poked through her hair, but were rounded beneath the waves.

She was an ordinary human with boring features, just like Emery.

Nico's fingers paused mid-rune, and his gaze darted to Emery. "Is it done?"

Dorian looked up, studying her, and she was sure her voice would give her away if she spoke. Emery's lips pulled into a grim line, and she nodded.

"Good. Back away from the altar and don't move."

Emery and Trine did as he instructed. She watched as Nico and Dorian finished the last three runes that she assumed would magically seal Kenna's fae nature away, finishing her transformation.

Upon completion of the last rune, Emery expected something magical; a burst of light or the sky to open up, but nothing happened. Nico and Dorian's smoke-like magic slithered back into their palms, and Kenna remained still on the altar.

"Dorian will take you and Trine back to Enchanth," Nico murmured, his eyes still transfixed on Kenna. "If you breathe a word of this to anyone, I will end your entire kingdom."

The malice in his words was enough to ensure she'd never breathe a word of this to anyone. Not even August. Not that she wanted to. It's not like she was proud of what transpired in the cave.

"I won't."

Emery stepped toward Dorian, who looked a little worse for wear. His eyes were sunken in like when he'd shown up from talking with Nico all those months ago. She'd assumed being in the Feywilde would replenish him, but assumption with him had gotten her into trouble before.

"Do you need to feed?" She lifted her wrist.

"No. I'll be fine, let's just get out of here," he said, offering her his arm.

Emery nodded and placed her hand in the crook of his elbow before turning to Nico.

"She loved you," Emery whispered just before Dorian sieved them from the cavern, but she didn't miss the faint lingering of his response.

"Sometimes love isn't enough."

Chapter Thirty-Four

AUGUST

THE CAULDRON ON THE DAIS TAUNTED HIM. IT WAS OVER THE top and all for show. Sloane didn't need more than a few ounces of the components for the spell, but this wasn't about the actual spell. This was about making a spectacle of him and Emery. It was her chance to prove she was stronger than the bond between them—her chance to break apart the mates destined by the stars to usher in the future of the supernatural world.

August kept his eyes zeroed in on Sloane as he slipped through the ballroom. She wore a gaudy purple gown that matched his family's tartan and ruffles that fell to the floor. It looked like a damned cupcake had exploded on her hips. He forced a smile at the witches and vampires who lifted their glasses in his direction, always with the arm that held the mark they wished to banish. As if he needed the reminder.

Bile rose in the back of his throat, and he forced it back down. Everything about this was wrong. August was all for examining mate bonds for those of his people who didn't want to follow through, but it should be a choice. As for him, the last thing he wanted to do was sever his bond to his mate. Emery was his life. His passion. She was his future. Unfortunately for him, his people now believed that she was nothing to him, and he was stuck playing the part.

It seemed like this had been all he'd been doing. Faking it till he made it. Pretending the lies weren't breaking him. Every moment since he'd become Sloane's lap dog was spent in dishonesty. Weeks of meetings and balls where he was the spectacle. The savior of his people, leading them into a world of darkness with Sloane at the helm. What was worse was he'd yet to find out anything specific about her plans, aside from her need to end Emery's reign. The celebration at Heil would be an ambush, Sloane's and Emery's, with both armies ready and waiting to fight. Sloane was aware she had not only the weight of her magic behind her, but his army as well, and that was enough to make her believe she'd win. His army had proven they'd follow him anywhere, even if they didn't agree. August didn't dare give them any inkling that he would ask them to flip, but he was happy to hear the grumblings behind his back.

Only a bit longer, he reminded himself.

When he reached the doors, the sentinel standing guard narrowed his gaze. "You aren't to leave the ballroom, Your Majesty."

"I understand, I just needed some fresh air."

"I'll have to ask—"

"Don't worry, I've got eyes on him." Another sentinel interrupted and stepped in front of August, holding the door open for him.

August eyed the caplets on his shoulders, the sign of a general, but they were blue instead of purple, signifying this sentinel was not one of his. The laurel across the coat of arms had him guessing it might belong to Graves, but August hadn't seen his traitor-in-arms in attendance. Graves generally tried to steer clear of anything that wasn't strictly mandatory, so Sloane didn't catch on that his kingdom was playing both sides.

August stepped into the balmy summer air and followed the general to the deck railing.

"It's a nice night, wouldn't you say, Your Majesty?"

"Indeed," August murmured, but his gaze was already searching for the opportunity to lose the sentinel.

"If you dart off, I won't go after you," the general mused, tipping his head up to look at the clear evening sky. "I know your mate is waiting, but I was hoping for a moment of your time."

August's gaze whipped to the sentinel, and he studied him for the first time. His features were familiar, his strong jawline that looked like it could take a punch and a nose that had likely taken more than a few. They were common to any sentinel in his army, but then the general turned and August got a look at him head on.

It was his eyes. He'd know those eyes anywhere. They were the color of pine when the sun hit its needles. More importantly, they were eyes he'd stared into countless times in the heat of battle.

"Rex?" August whispered. The features were subtle, but the resemblance was there.

"He was my father." The general straightened and offered his hand. "I'm General Cody of the Greek detachment. I serve under Graves, but if you'll have us, me and my men will gladly fight at your side."

"You're a vampire." August placed his hand in Cody's and pulled him forward into a hug. "Your father looked for you for centuries, hoping my father had been enough of a bastard to turn you."

August couldn't count the number of times he'd pored over maps with Rex in the hopes they'd find where his father had stashed away his general's family. He hated the way the king used them against Rex, holding them over him as a way to keep him in line. Then, before they could find them, his father had sent Rex and his men on a mission without August, and they had all been killed at the hands of Sloane's zombie vampires. Dorian had been the only survivor, which now made sense. August vowed to honor Rex's kin as his own if he ever found them, but it seemed they'd found him first.

Cody returned the embrace and clutched the back of August's shirt.

"He was a good man," August swore, his voice catching in his throat. "He loved you and your sisters more than life itself."

"I know." Cody nodded into August's shoulder. "Dorian found me and gave me the letters."

"Holy shit. He did?" That bloody fucking fae and his secrets were going to be the end of him. He was in the running to be worse than Callum.

Cody pulled back and met August's gaze. "I'm here to kill her, to avenge my father's death, but I'm also here to meet the man my father would have given his life for. He believed in you, and what you stand for. I needed to see for myself."

His eyes brimmed with tears. What he'd seen so far had been nothing but August's undying loyalty to Sloane.

"Cody, I...what you've seen from me here—"

"I know." Cody's smile reaffirmed his words. "Graves sent me to ensure you got out of the party tonight. I know where your loyalties lie. I can see it in your eyes every time they say you're going to forsake your mate."

August looked down to Cody's left arm and the silver laurels wrapped around it, intertwined with poppies.

"I know you are doing what you have to do, Your Majesty. But know that there are those of us who are fighting for the love you share."

August pressed his lips together and nodded, afraid to allow himself to be overcome with emotion if he spoke. Rex would have been so proud of the man Cody had become.

The sound of the string quartet starting up inside filtered through the door. It wouldn't be long before the toasts and the main show.

"You need to go. I'll keep the guards busy looking for you."

August looked toward the path that led to Lily's cottage and back at Cody, torn. "I wish we had more time to talk."

"We will." Cody smiled. "But first you need to get the hell out of here."

"You could come with me," August offered. He truly didn't want this moment to end. He wanted Cody at his back just as Rex had been all those years.

"No," Cody shook his head, the same glint in his eye as his father. "I need to stay here and continue my mission."

August cocked a brow.

"Who do you think is going to inform the army you aren't actually a backstabbing traitor to your mate?"

August cracked a smile. "Thank you."

"Go."

August swung his legs over the edge of the banister and dropped from the terrace to the gravel below. Keeping to the shadows, he sped across to the safety of the forest and the dirt path leading to his mate.

What once was a bustling village filled with hopeful witches had been reduced to a ghost town. It had been ransacked by Sloane's followers for supplies, but they wouldn't congregate there, claiming they were above the witches who would squander in desperation waiting for their mates.

What they didn't know was the earth was rich in magic because of the ley lines Lily hid with her wards.

His gaze fell to the cottage where he was supposed to meet Emery. Anticipation fluttered in his gut. He reached for their bond, hoping to feel her before he saw her, but Sloane's magic prevailed.

When he reached the door, he hesitated, his hand hovering over the doorknob. They'd reconnected just that one time, in their dream realm, but since then he'd been nothing but a traitor to their bond. It didn't matter that he'd been disgusted by every single one of his actions, even if they were in the name of saving their kingdom.

What if she felt the same way? If he were Emery, he had no doubt he'd feel betrayed, even if logically it was all part of their plan.

The doorknob twisted beneath his fingers, and the door flew inward without him having opened it.

His gaze was cast down, but he'd know those boots anywhere. He'd seen them littering their suite more times than he could count.

Time stood still as he slowly drifted his sight upward, taking in every inch of his mate. The subtle curve of her hips beneath her leather pants and the swell of her breasts against her shirt. His cock twitched with need. She wore a smile, her lower lip caught between her teeth, and tears trailed from her amber depths.

She was bloody fucking beautiful. The woman of August's dreams who had once walked into his club and stolen his damn heart.

Emery gasped and thrust her hand out, tangling it in the front of his dress shirt. She yanked him forward over the threshold and crashed her lips against his.

The moment August was inside the cottage, he was overwhelmed by the strength of their bond and the emotions freed once Sloane's magic was neutralized. This was what love was. The sea of need and want churning in all-encompassing desire, leaving him stranded and desperate for more. He let out a growl, one hand tangling in her hair while the other dipped beneath her shirt and dug at the flesh of her hip.

He wanted more.

Needed more.

Emery moaned, which he all too willingly used as an opportunity to slip his tongue between her lips and tangle his essence with her own. Being this close to her, tasting her, was like taking a breath of fresh air after drowning for weeks on end.

I love you, she echoed down their bond, like a prayer, clawing at his chest as she tried to get closer.

Before he could answer her, a short "ahem" filled the air, and he reluctantly pulled his face from hers to see Dorian standing behind her.

"While typically voyeurism does it for me, I don't particularly want to see my king and queen going at it."

August cocked a brow and a smile tipped his lips before he untangled himself from Emery and stepped toward Dorian, pulling him into a hug. He'd never been so happy to see his second.

Dorian stiffened against him, but relaxed after a moment.

"I'm sorry about having to use you as our decoy. I didn't want to put any strain on you and Ansel, but…"

Dorian grimaced. "It was for the good of the kingdom."

"That doesn't mean—"

"Let's not focus on that right now," Dorian snapped, but August could see it was taking everything the fae had not to worry about his wolf just by the way his jaw tensed. He stepped away from August and glanced at Emery. "We should get going before she knows we're here."

It was August's turn to hesitate, his gut churning as he strayed from their plan. "I'm not leaving without Ansel."

It might just be the craziest thing they'd ever attempted, but there was no way August was leaving without at least attempting to get Ansel out. He'd been the one keeping August sane all those weeks in the dungeon. The things they'd been put through together were enough to bond them for life in the most fucked-up way.

Plus, he could see how much Ansel needed Dorian. Even if he did believe that Dorian was hitched to Emery at the moment, he'd no doubt forgive him as soon as they got him free. That's what mates did. And even if they weren't technically mates, he wasn't sure Ansel's wolf realized that. Or maybe wolves could have more than one? He wasn't sure, but the one thing August did know was the fates had given them to one another for a reason, and they were due their moment in the sun.

"If we go after him, we risk Sloane knowing we've taken you as well," Dorian gritted out through clenched teeth, but August could tell he was mulling over the idea and trying to find a way to make it work.

"I am not leaving without him," August said, accentuating each word as if it were law.

Emery's eyes softened, and she reached out, tangling her fingers in his. "August, we can't. You don't think we've discussed this at length? We don't know where he's being kept, and even if we did, it's a huge risk to send any of us in there."

"I know where he is. I can tell you exactly how to get to him. I can't—" August choked on his words. He'd only ever lost it where Emery or Lina were concerned, but he couldn't lose Ansel either. Not after the bullshit they'd faced. "We are going after him."

"So, what's your plan then?" Dorian asked. "You do have a plan, right?"

Not even in the slightest, but it can't be that hard. August mentally pictured the castle and the layout of the dungeons. "We pop into the dungeon and get him out. There shouldn't be too many guards, considering the majority of them are working the ballroom. In and out."

Emery looked to Dorian, who chewed his lip before letting out a deep sigh and nodding. "In and out."

August's lips curled upward and he tugged Emery against him, kissing the top of her head. His family was finally going to be together again. He could finally taste the beginning of their victory.

"Then let's do this."

Chapter Thirty-Five

EMERY

If she had never returned to the castle dungeons it would have been too soon.

The dank smell hit her full force the moment Dorian popped them into the hallway, and the memories of waking up there after Chelsea's death under the cloud of August's betrayal wracked her mind. If it hadn't been for his hand in hers and the steady hum of love down their mate bond, the panic gripping her spine would have overtaken her.

She hadn't expected it to hit her so hard. Maybe it was the fact Sloane was trying to take away what they had fought so hard for or maybe it was simply that nothing good could come from this place.

Despite her attempt to block her thoughts, August managed to read her mind and spoke softly down their soul bond.

I'm here. We're getting out of here together. All of us. Just focus a little longer, princess, and then I'm going to remind you of all the ways I love you.

Emery swallowed hard, but nodded silently and gave his hand a squeeze. She could do this. For Ansel. For August.

Snarls and growls echoed down the hallway, but it didn't seem to bother August, so Emery tried to put it out of her mind and focus on their mission.

"He's in the fourth cell on the left," August whispered.

She peered down the dimly lit hallway and counted the cells. They pressed forward, treading lightly so as not to make a sound.

The cells were a mess of dirt and human waste. None of them were currently occupied, but it was clear at one point they each housed someone tortured by her sister.

This is where she kept you? Emery asked softly down their soul bond.

For a time.

Fuck, August. I'm sorry we didn't come sooner.

We did what we had to survive, August growled.

But—

Her thoughts were cut off by footsteps behind them. The three of them froze for a second as they grew closer, and August leapt into action, shoving Dorian and her into an open cell.

"Stop right there!" Someone yelled behind them.

August threw his hands up, his eyes locked on Dorian and Emery, pleading with them to stay put.

Stay silent.

Fat chance of that happening. She wasn't letting him get caught again. Hands wrapped around her waist and covered her mouth before she could move, and she cursed Dorian for his betrayal.

August put his hands up and turned toward the voice. "I'm only here to visit my friend."

"You aren't supposed to be down here, Your Majesty. The Mistress is looking for you."

"I'm sorry." August stepped toward the guard, his voice steady and diplomatic. "I just needed to see that he was okay."

"I can't let you do that." The sentinel's footsteps grew closer, and August took another step toward him so he wouldn't be able to see Dorian and Emery from where he stood. "Orders are to return you to her as soon as you are located."

"Let's go, then."

No! Emery shouted in his mind. *You don't get to sacrifice yourself again.*

August's footsteps continued toward the exit of the dungeon.

Get Ansel out and then have Dorian meet me in the royal suite off the ballroom dais. Sloane doesn't like to use it since it reminds her of my father. I will get there as soon as I can.

Please don't do this. I can kill him.

I have no doubt you can, little witch. But can you take on a castle full of vampires, witches, and beasts if they discover you are here?

Emery remained silent for a breath, his footsteps so faint they were nearly gone.

I love you, Emery. Know that I am leaving with you tonight, but I need to ensure we do so alive. Get Ansel out. He needs you more than I do right now.

Be safe.

I love you.

Always.

Emery relaxed in Dorian's arms, and he lowered her so her feet reached the ground.

"He said to get Ansel out and meet him at the royal suite off the ballroom dais."

Dorian nodded. "He's going to be fine."

"You don't know that."

"He didn't become King without knowing how to play the game."

"Sloane doesn't play by our rules," Emery scoffed. If anyone should understand that, it was Dorian.

Dorian pressed his lips together and nodded. "Let's be quick, then."

He stepped around her and peeked out of the cell, ensuring the hallway was clear, and silently waved his hand for her to follow.

The snarls and growls grew louder the further they went into the dungeon, and Emery couldn't help but wonder what kind of creatures Sloane kept down there. No matter what they were, they didn't deserve this sort of life.

"Stay behind me," Dorian whispered as they approached Ansel's cell, apprehension in his voice.

A menacing growl filled the air. As she reached the bars of his cell, Dorian only just managed to wrap his hand around her arm and yank her away before she was mauled by a clawed hand.

Emery fell against Dorian, her eyes wide and jaw dropped.

"Betrayer," Ansel snarled through foam and fangs. His partially shifted hands gripped the bars of his cell, and his muscles tensed as if he'd be able to pull them apart to reach them.

The man before her was not her beloved bestie. He was a feral wolf trapped in the body of a man. His eyes were blown and there was no doubt she was looking at the wolf and not Ansel.

"We're here to get you out," Emery squeaked.

"After you betrayed your mate and stole mine for yourself? How fucking noble of you, Emery," he growled, stalking the length of his cell.

"It's Your Majesty, you fucking fool." Dorian shook his head and broadened his stance to protect Emery. "And it was all an act so we could get August closer to Sloane and plan to get you both out."

"You expect me to believe that bullshit? I may be a prisoner, but I hear things. Did you think I would come with you willingly? I would rather rot in this cell than watch my mate with the woman I swore to protect. That's a worse hell than what I'm forced to endure here. At least here I can tear shit apart until I can forget who I was." Ansel's eyes narrowed. "Maybe I can even forget who you are."

Dorian's shoulders sagged briefly, the weight of Ansel's insult hitting its mark. Deep down, Emery knew Dorian would do anything for Ansel, and somewhere inside him, Ansel knew that too. But Sloane had broken him beyond realizing that and there was no way of knowing if or when the Ansel they knew would come back to them.

"We don't have time for this shit, Ansel." Dorian stepped toward him, but Ansel took another swipe, this time only barely missing him. "I swear to the gods, *gaol*, if you don't calm your feral ass down, I am going to tear you a new one."

Ansel paused at the term of endearment, his eyes flashing back to their normal size for just a fraction of a second. Emery didn't know what it meant, but it had worked.

Emery took a step forward, her hands raised, but Ansel's gaze instantly tracked her movement, and he released a sharp snarl.

"I think you should take him, Dorian."

"What about you?"

"I know a passageway I can take to outside the ballroom. Find Nico and drop him there to get us."

"But—"

Emery shook her head and pleaded with Dorian to listen. "He needs you. Don't fuck this up because of me."

Dorian's eyes softened, and he nodded, conceding. Even though he didn't say a word, she understood his gratitude. They deserved this, and she was all too willing to give them this moment to start healing.

"This is going to suck, but try not to hurl on me," Dorian whispered as he snatched Ansel's arm through the bars and disappeared.

Emery let out a small huff and smiled. Sieving was not for the faint of stomach.

She turned on her heel and prayed the guard was still preoccupied with returning August to her sister.

The castle was empty, and except for a few sentinels, Emery could have likely roamed the halls and made her way to the royal suite undetected. Still, she opted to keep to the hidden passageways August made her memorize in case there was ever another attack on the castle. She never thought she'd be using them to sneak in and get her mate back.

By the time she made it to the royal suite, there was no doubt August had been returned to Sloane.

Emery cracked the door to the royal suite enough to see August with one of her sister's hands gripping the back of his neck while the other lifted the arm that wore his mate mark. The crowded ballroom cheered, hailing their king and queen.

Emery's stomach rolled.

August's eyes were wide, glaring out over the ballroom, but he didn't move.

I'm here.

Don't, little witch. She's got me under her magic, and she knows you're here. That's why we can talk in our minds outside the cottage. She dropped the magic that separated us to taunt you.

Why would she do that? Why would she let them enter and do nothing about it? It didn't make any sense.

It doesn't matter, August. We are getting you out of there. As soon as Nico gets here, we'll get you out.

No. You need to get out of here on your own. Don't face her. Not now. Not here with an army of witches and vampires who will rip you to shreds. They won't hurt me. Please, Emery. I don't want you here for this.

There was no way she was leaving him behind again. She might not be as strong as her sister, but she wasn't helpless. Not anymore.

Her magic hummed in agreement, both dark and light itching to take on Sloane and bring her to her knees. If it weren't for the fact she had no backup, she probably would have charged headfirst into the ballroom if it meant saving August.

Sloane called her magic to the surface, and it charged the air around them. A wicked smile tipped her lips as the ballroom fell silent.

"This is the moment you've all been waiting for," she announced, and the crowd cheered.

"No," Emery whispered. She turned and looked behind her, only to see the royal suite was still empty. "Come on, Dorian. Where the hell is Nico?"

Her eyes darted back to August and Sloane, and her heart beat wildly against her rib cage. There was no way she could win if she stepped onto the dais. Maybe if she were facing Sloane alone, she'd stand a chance, but even then, Emery wasn't convinced. This was the throne room all over again. If she dared to try, Sloane could kill them both, potentially leaving Lina all alone.

Emery closed her eyes and forced a vision, focusing first on August and then herself. Again and again, she did so, while Sloane prattled on to their followers about how their king was going to lead the way into the future. It didn't matter how many times she tried, every vision ended the same. If she intervened, they both died, and the future of the realm became unclear.

"Fuck," she cursed the stars. "What good is this gift if I can't change a damn thing?"

Emery, please go.

I am not leaving you, August, Emery snapped, trying to hide the pain in her voice. *We said forever. She doesn't get to take that from us. It doesn't matter what happens next.*

But it did. This was a core part of who they were.

Emery racked her brain for an answer but only came up

with shitty outcomes: let Sloane tear them apart, or force her daughter to grow up without her parents.

Desperation to do something clawed in her chest, but there wasn't a right answer.

"And now, we cut the binds that tie."

Sloane took the nail of her pointer finger, sharpened into a claw, and sliced into August's wrist. At the same time, her hand dropped from his neck, and she pulled out a vial filled with a dark crimson liquid that Emery could only assume was her own blood. Sloane murmured something under her breath, and the cauldron began to bubble and waft a wispy purple smoke.

No matter what happens, I love you, little witch. With every breath, I am yours.

August let out a grunt as Sloane forced him forward, plunging his hand into the cauldron. She muttered the incantation beneath the roar of the cheers.

The moment his hand hit the liquid inside, August threw back his head and the noise that came from his mouth could only be described as one of all-consuming pain. Sweat dripped from his brow as he struggled to stay upright, his body draped over the cauldron.

With nothing to support her, Emery crashed to the tile floor and her hand flew to her chest, clutching the fabric as if it could stop the growing pain tearing her in two. Her skin vibrated the way it had all those months ago when she'd seen him for the first time. Her magic's way of calling to her mate, only this time it was protesting his departure.

Emery clamped her eyes shut as if it would hide the images of the two of them that flitted through her mind, but it didn't. The spell continued to show her exactly what it was taking from her. The night at the club. The first time he touched his lips to hers in the hotel. His venom in the gardens. Scotland. The hunt. Their suite. All the moments they'd come together as one in their bond, even when they didn't know it.

Sobs racked her body as her teeth started to chatter once the mark on Emery's arm grew cold. She pulled it to her chest and curled up in the fetal position, protecting the mark from the world around her. As if that could stop the spell that had already taken root in their bond.

Forever.

August's words echoed in her mind as the final strand of their mate bond snapped, and with it went every ounce of control left in Emery's soul.

Her ears rang, and a soul-piercing scream from Sloane filled the ballroom. Emery's gaze slid to where August lay prone, trying to right himself. Beside him, Sloane was weak on her feet and being rushed away by two of her beasts.

No. She didn't get to slink off and lick her wounds. She didn't get to get away with this.

Emery's darkness took over, pushing down the pain and overwhelming sorrow, erupting from her like a dormant volcano determined to decimate everything in its path.

On a path of ultimate destruction, Emery took a step forward only to be yanked back by a strong force wrapped around her bicep.

She whipped a murderous glare at the offender to find Nico in full fae form, snarling at her.

"Let go." Emery demanded. "I can take her."

"No. This is not the time," Nico growled, his eyes the same dark obsidian they had been when she last saw him at Kenna's side.

Her lips curled back, and she bared her teeth. "She took him from me."

It had left her whole and broken at the same time. Her heart was hers once again, but she didn't want it. There was no way Nico could ever understand the turmoil inside her. His bonded might not know who he was, but she was still his.

August wasn't, and might not ever be again.

"So, take him back, but if you go after her now, she'll kill you." Nico growled as if it were the simplest thing in the world.

And she supposed it was to him. That's exactly what he'd done with Kenna. But it wasn't so simple with her and August. What were they without their bond?

Her gaze slid back to where August now stood, looking at her as if he didn't know who the hell she was anymore. What was worse, the same sentiment echoed in her own soul.

Instinctively, she reached for the mate bond and felt... nothing.

No emotion. No tug to him.

Nothing.

She still housed a piece of his soul, but it was his heart that had been snatched away from her.

August raced toward her, ignoring the crowd cheering his name, and once he was inside the room pulled her against his chest.

Everything in her wanted to pull away, but his arms kept her firmly in place while she tried to reconcile what she felt when she looked at him. How he felt the same but different. The way she loved him but couldn't feel him.

It was isolating and lonely, and came on all at once.

Like losing a limb she didn't know she had because it felt as though it had always just existed.

Her darkness protected her from the worst of the agony, but it couldn't fully take it from her. Not when she was breaking on such a visceral level.

Give into the blood. It will heal you, her magic pleaded in her soul, but as much as Emery wanted to get lost in the haze of blood and rage, she couldn't. She had enough logic to reason that if she did, she might not come back.

"We need to get the hell out of here," Nico said and, placing his hand on their shoulders, sieved them out of there.

The castle fell away and when they appeared at the archway, Emery tried to pry herself from August's arms, but his grip tightened.

"I'm not losing you again, little witch," he whispered.

She tipped her head back and met his icy blue stare. They were the ocean depths she'd fallen in love with and gotten lost in time and time again. The tides of her soul recognized them, but even though she felt every ounce of love, something about it wasn't right.

"Lina needs us."

"And I need you," he pleaded, as he ran his hands down her arms and entwined his fingers in hers.

Emery nodded and allowed him to lead her to where Nico stood waiting for them.

"You must be Nico. It's nice to officially meet you."

Nico nodded, but his gaze never left Emery. A sign that his loyalty was to the queen and not the king. She might even think he was checking to see if she was alright, but that wasn't like him. Nico didn't give a shit about anyone except himself.

Emery was the farthest thing from okay, but she gave him a slight nod anyway and pressed forward through the arch.

"Emery," August whispered.

Tears welled in her eyes when she looked up at him. He was still the same man, and she still had so much love for him, but when she looked at him, she only felt the edges of it. Emery had never felt more alone. Not during the Culling. Not in New Orleans. Not in Enchanth.

His soul gave her life, but his heart filled it with meaning.

That meaning was gone.

"August," she squeezed his hands and untangled her fingers from his. "I don't know what all of this means, but I need a minute to reconcile my heart and my mind."

August nodded and stepped away.

I will grant you that, he started in her head but went silent, then continued, *But I'm not going anywhere.*

Emery pressed her lips together and nodded. A single tear fell down her cheek, and when he didn't move to catch it, she felt the chasm in her heart deepen a little further. She sent up a silent prayer that she was doing the right thing, but deep in her heart she knew there was no one listening to her plea.

Chapter Thirty Six

AUGUST

Lina bounced on his lap and August tugged her against his chest, kissing her forehead. She had gotten so big while they'd been apart. When he'd last seen her, she was only just beginning to coo and smile, now she was laughing and babbling, bringing constant joy to every room she entered. There was no doubt his daughter was the light of not only his life but the entirety of Enchanth. He loved watching the curious way she took in the world around her.

And Enchanth was a lot to take in. Between the fantastical sceneries and the way his people, witch and vampire alike, had taken not only to each other but the fae, the hidden realm was no doubt magical.

Not that he was actually absorbing any of it, considering his thoughts kept drifting to the woman beside him.

Emery wouldn't look at him, and when she did, it was as if she was seeing right through him. What was worse was he understood, because looking at her was like exploring a trench in the depths of the ocean. The love he felt for her was still there in the current surrounding them, but he couldn't find the bedrock where it took root. Their cornerstone had been torn from their hearts and they were left bleeding.

They needed to talk about it, but as always, the kingdom came first.

Let me in, Emery, he whispered, more to himself than her.

Later. We can't do this right now.

August's lips pressed together in a line, and he ran his hand through his tousled hair.

This was so bloody fucked.

A firing squad made up of Callum, Malcolm, Lily, Bronwyn, Draven, Flora, and Brax had spent the better part of four hours grilling him about Sloane and the castle. They'd drilled him and tested him, ensuring there was nothing he missed or any way Sloane could be using him as a spy. He understood their concern, but he was a bloody king. He wouldn't have put his kingdom in danger if he thought he was a threat.

He played his vow to Sloane over and over in his head. Neither of them could act out against each other or against Emery. Nowhere did he say that he had to be in her presence for it to remain intact. As long as he didn't actively make plans against her, he should be fine, and the magic of the vow wouldn't react and smite him.

"Are you sure there is nothing else you remember?" Malcolm asked, his eyes drifting to the spot where August no longer wore Emery's mark.

They couldn't help it. Every single one of them, with the exception of Callum, had allowed their eyes to linger a moment too long on his arm before darting to Emery's and then looking away.

The two of them were supposed to be the hope for their kingdom, and now it was as if they were somehow less than the other vampires and witches.

It didn't help that they weren't a united front; something they needed to rectify before they appeared in front of their people.

"I assure you, I am not a threat," August sighed. "Now if it's all the same to you, I'd like to spend some time with my family and maybe take a bloody shower."

Malcolm nodded and took his seat at the long table beside Lily.

"Actually," Emery spoke beside him, and he didn't like the disapproval in her voice. "I was hoping you could take Lina and get her fed. Your mother can help you."

August narrowed his gaze on his mate and bit back the snarl that threatened to surface at her dismissal. "And where will you be?"

"Here, planning our attack." Emery answered, meeting his gaze with her own inky swirls and queenly defiance. "Sloane was weakened by the spell. She was practically unconscious when she was carried off by two of her beasts. Time is on our side here, so if we can plan an attack that will end in our favor, we have to take the opportunity."

"Then I'll stay."

"You can't," Emery winced. "The vow you made extends to you planning to hurt Sloane, remember?"

The pain was seared in his memory. The one time Emery had seen him get sucker-punched when he'd made the vow was nothing against the crippling agony he'd experienced every time he threatened her life while she tortured Ansel.

"I'll find you after." Emery reassured him.

His gaze shifted to the rest of their family and friends, who all offered sympathetic smiles. The dismissal hurt worse than the pain he was avoiding.

August nodded. "Okay. I'll meet you later, then."

Emery gave him a half smile and allowed him to press a kiss to her temple before he saw his way out.

I'm sorry, she whispered down their bond.

Don't be. Do what you need to do, my love.

She didn't look back in his direction, as if she hadn't heard his reassurance, and that hurt worse than the fact she felt she needed to apologize for being the queen their kingdom needed.

He didn't need help feeding his daughter. Finding the kitchen to get her milk was another story.

Lina fussed in his arms, and he smiled down at her.

"I will get you your milk as soon as I can," he cooed before reaching up and pricking his finger, offering her his blood. Lina settled immediately, sucking on it. It wouldn't keep her happy forever, but it was a start.

August searched the barren walls for any sort of indication to where he was, but nothing stood out to him. There was a good chance he was traveling in circles.

"You look a little lost," a familiar voice washed over him, bringing a smile to his face.

He turned around to find his mother and Thea standing behind him.

A smile tipped his lips. "Aren't you a sight for sore eyes."

His mother crossed the space in two strides and wrapped her arms around him and Lina, while Thea did the same to his legs.

"I was so worried," she whispered into his chest.

"You know I always come back."

"Yeah, but I'm your mother. Also, your brother and you always had a penchant for coming back worse than you left. Though I don't see any life-threatening injuries."

August straightened his spine and sucked in a sharp breath.

Life threatening, no, but he wasn't returning unscathed.

His mother pulled back and searched his eyes. "What is it?"

August averted his gaze down to Thea and gave her a full smile. "It's nothing, Mother. Can you show me where the kitchen is?"

"Augustine Robert Finlay Nicholson." Her eyes narrowed, and she chastised him in the way only a mother could. "If you think I can't see past your bullshit, you're not as smart as I thought. Now tell me what happened."

He sighed. Silently, he promised Lina he wouldn't push her until she was ready to talk when she was older.

His mother was going to find out as soon as the others were done with their meeting, so the news of his severed mate bond might as well come from him. Pulling his finger from Lina's mouth, August lifted his arm and allowed his shirt to slink toward his elbow, revealing his bare forearm.

"Oh, no." His mother's hands flew to her mouth and tears welled in her eyes. "She didn't."

August's eyes fell to the mark that coiled around his mother's arm, and his heart swelled.

Despite feeling like shit about the loss of his own mark, seeing the hope of a future for his mother that wasn't steeped in the shadows of his father healed a sliver of his heart. It reminded him that there was more to be fought for than his own relationship. There were vampires and witches out there, like his mother, like Thea someday, who had only just been afforded their happily ever afters.

"Do you want to talk about it?" his mother asked, but he knew damn well it wasn't negotiable. He'd been on the receiving end of that tone more than once.

Her hand dropped to the small of his back, and she led him toward an open door that he assumed must be the way to the kitchen.

She signed to Thea where they were going, and his sister led the way, bouncing along.

After winding through more hallways he was sure he'd seen before, and through a doorway that was hidden behind a staircase, they made it to the kitchen. It wasn't what he expected for a castle kitchen. Where theirs was set up to host elaborate delegation dinners, this was cozy, with clean lines and stainless-steel appliances that should have looked out of place against the fantasy vibe the rest of the castle gave off. If he had to guess, he'd bet Nico took some liberties with the technology of the human realm, mashing it with the magic of his home.

His mother rounded the large island, pulled cookies from a large jar, and handed Thea two.

"Why don't you take these and go find Haven?" She signed at the younger royal.

"But I want to stay with August." Thea protested.

August stepped forward and handed Lina to his mother. He dropped to one knee in front of his sister and smiled. *"I promise that as soon as we are done, I'll come find you and we'll draw mustaches on all of Malcolm's mirrors."*

"Promise?"

"I promise."

A beautiful grin stretched across her face before she leapt forward and wrapped her arms around his neck, placing a kiss on his cheek. She then turned around and raced toward the door.

"Haven has been good for her."

"I can see that." August snatched a cookie from the jar for himself and one for his mother. "She looks good. Both of you do."

"It hasn't been without growing pains, but for the first time in a long time, I think we are going to be okay."

His mother had seen more than her fair share of wars and hardships on the arm of his father.

After he finished his snack, August crossed the space, opened the fridge and pulled out a bottle for Lina. He went about finding a pot and, like he had so many times before, filled it with water and brought the bottle to temperature on the stove.

His mother watched him with a knowing look, but she didn't interrupt. He was convinced that was her super power, the uncanny ability to use her silence to force her children to speak their mind.

But what was he supposed to say?

Over the last month, August had watched a man, his friend, be tortured into creating an army of monsters. Ones he felt with every breath. He himself had been forced to create a fledgling who was nothing more than a spoiled bitch who chose the wrong side, and yet a part of him was forced to care about her well-being as her sire. Then, in order to save his kingdom, he had to pretend to betray them and his mate and play the part of a good little puppet to their enemy, which had arguably been worse than the torture, only for his mate bond to be stripped from his soul.

No.

His mother didn't need to know the details. She didn't need to know how lost he felt coming back only to be shunned from a meeting to save his kingdom. He was a king without a throne all because Sloane had stolen it from him in every way imaginable.

No.

For the first time maybe in his entire life he didn't want her kind words because he didn't deserve them.

"August, the milk."

"Huh?" He looked down to see the water boiling around the bottle. "Shit," he murmured and pulled the bottle from the pot before testing the liquid on his wrist and handing it to his mother.

Her eyes searched his before she situated Lina in her arms to eat.

August slid onto the stool across from her and rested his elbows on the island, his head in his hands.

"I won't bother asking if you're okay, anyone can see you're not. But I'm not just anyone. I'm your mother, and I know more than most about the struggles you've faced."

"Mother, I—"

"No, August. Listen to me." He looked up, meeting his mother's loving gaze. "You need to let someone in. If not me, then your mate."

"Except she's not mine anymore." His words were

laced with desperation and venom, and he was unable to decide if they were truth or lies.

His mother cocked a brow. "Do you really believe it is the mark that makes the mate? That Emery isn't yours in every way?"

"You didn't see the way she looked at me after. Like she was lost at sea, and I was no longer the light that guided her. Like my shores were no longer a safe haven for her heart." August swallowed hard, pushing back the ache in his chest. "It's like my heart has been ripped in two, and yet it's still whole. It's just wholly mine now, and I don't know how to reconcile that."

He hated what that said about their bond and about him. He wanted what was rightfully theirs, but a small part of him didn't think it was possible, and it scared him that that same part of him could live with that outcome. They'd fought so hard and yet he was so confused as to what came next for them. Shouldn't this be easy? They were meant to be together, the stars had dictated it, but then why did having his heart back also feel so right?

"Have you considered that neither does she? The weight of the loss of your bond is as much hers as it is yours. And more than that, she's been keeping this kingdom together all on her own. Between the inflow of every supernatural faction, including hybrids, and trying to master her own magic, Emery has been carrying everything on her shoulders and doing it with more grace than I ever could. Even now, she is fighting for our future when you can't."

Bloody hell.

August's shoulders slumped forward, feeling the weight of his selfishness. He'd made it about him, about what he needed, and hadn't considered what she'd been going through during her time in Enchanth. Since becoming his mate, she'd been his silent strength, believing in him even when he didn't believe in himself. She'd given life to their daughter, all the while handling the things the castle threw at her so he could be the diplomatic front and strength of the kingdom. Then, he'd sacrificed himself and left her with a kingdom and no castle. And Emery hadn't thought twice before stepping up and becoming the ruler their people needed.

He might need her in ways she didn't understand, but she needed him too. They'd both been through the ringer these last months and being stripped of their mate bond was just another hurdle they'd have to overcome.

"She's incredible," he whispered, wishing Emery was there to hear the words.

"She is, but she's exhausted. Not that she'd ever tell anyone. That woman is more stubborn than you."

"Believe me, I know."

"Then maybe you can get your head out of your ass and don't give up on her."

August growled. "I promise you, giving up was never in my plans."

"I know." She smiled and reached out her hand, palm up. August placed his hand in hers and she gave it a gentle squeeze. "That's not to say your feelings aren't valid. You've been through more than any man or vampire should at the hands of that wicked bitch. All I'm saying is, you aren't alone in your tribulations. Find your future in each other so Sloane doesn't succeed."

"Thank you."

"What are mothers for?"

August shrugged and the corner of one side of his mouth turned upward. "I don't know, I think most blow steam up their sons' asses and make them believe they are the gods' gift to the world."

She grinned. "Eh, sounds like a lot of work."

He was damn lucky to have this woman not only as his mother but as a sounding board in his corner. He returned her smile and cocked a brow. "Now, are we going to talk about the mark on your forearm?"

He'd never seen his mother blush, but it was a good look on her. "Not until I know for sure someone out there wears its match."

"I'm happy for you," August offered sincerely. "You deserve the world, after everything he put you through."

"He's right. You do, Mother."

They both turned toward the door to see Malcolm leaning against the kitchen door frame.

He pushed off and rounded the island, pressing a kiss to the top of their mother's head. "I am the errand boy sent to fetch you, August."

He cocked a brow and scoffed playfully. "Am I allowed to come to the meeting now that all the fun's been had?"

"The opposite, actually. The gods have decided to grace us with their presence, and they want the leaders of each faction to appear."

Bloody hell.

Could anything ever be easy?

Chapter Thirty Seven

EMERY

She searched their futures but consistently came up empty-handed. There were futures where they were standing next to each other and those where they were alone, but none of them gave her a clear view of the mark that had been stripped from them.

Emery cursed under her breath and reluctantly opened her eyes in time to see August walking with Malcolm toward where she stood with their advisors.

Her heart beat against her rib cage at the sight of him, and ached at the knowledge that any other day she would have felt him coming.

"What's the plan?" Malcolm asked as he settled in beside Lily, sliding his hand in hers.

August rounded Callum's side and took his place beside her.

His place.

It was where he belonged. But then why did everything about it feel off? She loved this man, but it was as if everything had been rotated one-hundred-and-eighty degrees and she wasn't sure if it was him, or her, or their missing bond, but they were not a cohesive unit. Which only further perpetuated the fact that with this uncertainty between them, the last thing they should be doing was facing the gods.

But as the fates had proven time and time again, turmoil was handed out like candy on Halloween, and it didn't matter if you were on a diet. Especially for them. As king and queen, August and Emery were the ones to pay the ultimate price, and they were expected to do so with a smile on their faces.

She felt August's soul nudge at their bond, and she reluctantly opened it to him. He didn't look down at her, but the corner of his lips upturned slightly.

They may be gods, but we are—.

We are what?

August didn't look back at her, nor did he finish his statement.

"August?" She tilted her head and looked up at him, a little annoyed. "We are what?"

"You didn't hear me?"

"No," Emery shook her head and crossed her arms over her chest. "You didn't finish your thought."

"I did." His brow furrowed, creating deep lines across his forehead she didn't remember being there before. "I said, they may be gods, but we are intended."

Emery sucked in a breath and tears welled in her eyes, but she blinked them back. She wished she could believe him, but she'd seen where they could end up, and without their bond, she feared his words were just that. Words.

What worried her more was she couldn't hear the words in her head.

"You couldn't hear him?" Malcolm asked.

"That's unfortunate." Octavian chimed from beyond the circle.

Everyone turned and looked at him, but only August spoke. "Why is that?"

Octavian pinched his chin between his thumb and forefinger and mused almost lazily. Like his words were of no consequence and he was stuck between lucid and off his rocker. "I fear it means the soul bond is weakening?"

"What the bloody hell does that mean?" August growled, taking a step toward the older vampire.

"Well, in theory, the only reason you have the soul bond is because you were mates. It's why you could give a piece of yourself to Emery in the first place. If your mate bond is gone, there is nothing to tether your souls."

"So, what you're saying is I could be dying?" Emery said, her voice barely a whisper. Not that everyone in the tight circle didn't hear her. They did, and each of their jaws dropped in unison.

"That's not going to happen, little witch." August promised and wrapped an arm around her.

"I don't know." Octavian replied honestly. "This has never happened before, but it's possible."

"Emery, we'll—" August started, but Emery cut him off. This was too much to worry about right now.

"No." She pressed her lips together and shook her head before stepping forward out of August's grasp. Her darkness reared in her chest, echoing her need to compartmentalize this information for the time being. "We will worry about the glitch in our bond later. Right now, we need to address the gods in our midst. The plan is we go out there and see what the hell they want, then we will figure out what comes next. Sloane is weakened, we need to strike while we can."

They all nodded, and when Emery took a step forward, August didn't hesitate. He stayed at her side, a united front while the others filed in behind them.

"Emery," he whispered.

"Not now." She swallowed hard past the need to fall into his arms. They were the king and queen of their kingdom. They didn't get to fall apart. Not when their people were counting on them to ensure their future.

The cliffs were lit with the setting double suns, bouncing soft golden light across the mossy ground. Standing stoically in a semi-circle were six figures, three male and three female, all draped in white as if they were angelic hosts. But Emery knew better.

As if to prove her point, a low growl came from behind her. Emery looked over her shoulder to see Draven's eyes narrowed on the goddess with silver waist-length hair and eyes that glowed like the moon.

"It's nice to see you too, my child," the Goddess mused.

Draven scoffed. "Yours is the last thing I would call us, Rieka."

Rieka's eyes widened, but a playful smile tugged at her lips. "Is that how you treat the goddess who gave your mate life?"

"That's not exactly how I remember it," Flora muttered.

Ah, so this was the Goddess of the Moon who trapped them in a pocket realm and ultimately killed her best friend, making her a hybrid. She expected more from the lithe goddess, but as with everyone there, looks were often deceiving.

The god who stood at the center of the celestial beings stepped forward, his eerily pale eyes locked on Emery. "Thank you fo—"

"What the stars fucking hell is the meaning of this?" Nico burst into the clearing, stepping between Emery and the pale-eyed god.

"Hello, Nicodranas," the god said dryly.

"Don't 'hello' me, Mikael. You and I both know you aren't supposed to interfere, and I'm pretty sure the last we spoke I told you in no uncertain terms that you were not welcome in my realm."

Mikael tsked. "You were granted this realm by my sisters; I suggest you remember who you are speaking to."

"Speak plainly, what are you doing here?" Nico ordered.

Emery rolled her eyes. He was one to talk.

"Dal has sided with the dark one. We are here to offer insight."

"More like cryptic bullshit, I'm sure," Nico muttered, and Flora snorted.

This whole interaction was going to hell quickly, and Emery wasn't having it. She shook her head, exhausted and losing her patience. "Nico, stand down. At this point, if they are willing to help, I need to hear them out and you," she narrowed her gaze on Mikael, "need to get to the point quickly because we don't have the time to put up with your godly bullshit otherwise."

"Oh, I think I like you." The tall, dark-haired god beside Mikael crossed the space in three long strides. He picked up Emery's hand and brought it to his lips. "I'm Gallant, God of Passion."

Emery snatched her hand back at the same time August snarled. She pinned a glare in his direction.

Down boy, she thought, unsure if he would hear her.

You are mine.

Well, it seemed their words went through that time. Emery reached for the soul bond between them and was satisfied to find it still intact, though there was something about the way it pulsed that had her worried. Maybe Octavian had been right, something wasn't right with their bond.

"Spoken for, I see," Gallant said with a lopsided smile. "That's too bad."

Emery gave a shrug. "I don't think so."

Rieka rolled her eyes. "Stop thinking with your dick, Gal. We've got more important things to discuss."

"She's right," Mikael echoed and stepped forward, offering Emery his hand. "I'm Mikael, God of the Heavens. You must be the little Queen of Light and Dark."

She placed her hand in his and shook it. "Emery will do."

He nodded. "You have impressed us with your ability to bring the factions together. We didn't believe we'd ever see the day, but as always, the fates have proven to be right."

"Finicky bitches, if you ask me," Emery huffed.

He tipped his head back and laughed. "You aren't wrong about that. But that doesn't mean that we haven't managed to circumvent their plans a time or two. How do you think these realms came to be?"

"I'm sure I've heard a creation story or two, but you're going to tell me a new one, aren't you?"

"Indeed," he nodded. "Only mine is written in the stars and expands thousands of realms and millennia, while yours are the wayward tellings of man's need to make sense of his place in the universe."

Mikael folded his hands together in front of him and inhaled deeply. "The realm of the gods is built at the core of all realms, or it was when they existed. Like a house of cards, they each held their own weight and distributed magic in a never-ending loop. We didn't understand the depth of what we had created, only that it was our playground to rule. As time went on, we created beings for each of our realms, some magnificent while others," his lips tugged into a grimace and he shrugged, "not so much. The only thing that mattered to us was they existed and were ours to manipulate within the parameters of fate."

"So, you created the worlds we live in."

"Aye. We did, yours and so many others. Over time, realms died out, usually due to destruction at our hands, but we didn't care. There were plenty of others."

"Until there weren't," the god on the other side of Mikael chided.

"And you are...?" August asked.

"Kasen," he lifted his hand in a sort of half wave. "God of Trickery."

"Makes sense," Callum snorted.

Kasen shrugged and winked. "Don't hate the player, hate the game, little vampire. I only guided you to where we are now."

"What the hell is he talking about, Callum?" August growled.

Callum sighed. "This is the man who has delivered every ounce of information we've needed when we've needed it. He told me about mates, about the books I needed to find. He had me send Malcolm to Octavian and the flower, and pointed me in the direction of the hybrid camp. I've been his pawn."

Everyone's mouth dropped except for Emery's. She'd been given a heads-up about Callum's little rendezvous with the gods.

"And you didn't think to ask questions?" Malcolm snapped at Callum.

"Oh, he did," Kasen chuckled. "I vaguely remember threats as well."

Callum snarled. "Cheeky bastard."

Draven threw up his hands and paced a circle beside Flora. "So, to hell with fate, you've been pulling the strings all along?"

Mikael stepped forward and raised his hands up. "Enough. We did what we had to do in order to save the realms."

Emery cocked a brow. "Save them?"

"Yes. As you know, your realm is symbiotic with the Feywilde. Consequently, they are also the only two realms holding up the deck."

"You said there were thousands."

"Once upon a time, there were. Now there are four. Ours, yours, and the afterlife. If yours fall, ours will as well."

"A union to stop the darkness of the fall." Emery whispered the line from the prophecy Agatha had recited to her all those months ago. "All this time we thought it was in reference to Sloane's magic, but it wasn't, was it?"

Mikael's lips twitched upward, and he nodded. "It was. You and Sloane house the darkest magic in your realm. You are the balance needed to keep it stable. But she isn't alone in her quest for power. My brother is feeding her lies to fulfill his needs. If she wins this war, her darkness spreads, and eventually this realm will fall. When it does, Dal will be there, waiting to claim what's his."

"Why the hell are we just learning all this now?" August questioned, with the same edge in his voice that Emery felt in her chest.

It was a lot to reconcile on top of everything else going on around them.

Mikael steepled his fingers together in front of his stomach and proceeded to talk to them like they were five and couldn't possibly comprehend the reasoning of the gods. "We cannot directly intervene; the fates will not allow it. We can gently suggest and lure you in the directions we believe will provide the most favorable outcome, but we cannot give you the answers."

"Then I'll ask again," Nico growled. "Why the fuck are you here?"

"Because your realms are running out of time and we don't want our own realm to crumble because some insignificant humans and fae could not silence one witch," Gallant offered, his annoyance evident.

Nico huffed a sardonic laugh, "So, just like always, you are no help. Let me guess, you're just here to tell us to figure it out so we can save your asses even though we've been fighting for centuries to fix your mistakes."

"This isn't about you, Nico," Mikael's eyes hardened, and he narrowed his gaze on the dark fae leader. "Your deal with Dal is yours to own. This is about our damn existence. Yours, mine, and the mortals'. Now is the time to strike while Sloane is weakened. We've preoccupied Dal, but it won't be long before he tries to restore her magic."

"Wait, if you created this realm and others, why don't you just build more?" Lily asked, and Emery wondered the same thing. Why was this all such a big deal to gods who could literally create something from nothing?

"We can't," the smallest goddess, a woman with light blue hair and deep emerald eyes squeaked from the far end of the line.

Mikael sighed. "What Odelle means is that with the loss of influxed magic to our realm, and the fact we haven't had a god of realms in nearly a millennium, we are unable to create more than pocket realms that live in the spaces between, such as this one."

"Bloody hell," Callum and August muttered in unison.

"You are the answer, Emery," Mikael continued, "With the witches, wolves, and vampires united, along with your magic, you are ready for the fight ahead."

Emery shook her head. "I still haven't mastered it."

"Your blood is a part of you. All you have to do is trust. I've seen it written in the stars."

So had she. But she'd also seen every way they'd lost and the way darkness would descend on their realm like a never-ending night.

"Is that all you're here to offer us? Words of encouragement and a history lesson?" Emery's patience was wearing thin, and she got the feeling she wasn't the only one. She fidgeted with the ring on her third finger, a reminder she still had other problems to fix.

Mikael's eyes met hers, and for a split second, Emery

swore he saw a flicker of sadness in them. "When the time comes, I need you to be sure you can end your sister's life."

No reason, just a sentence admitting she'd been factored into whatever Mikael had seen in the stars and the inexplicable emotion in his eyes.

Emery's lips fell into a grim line and she nodded. "That won't be a problem."

Except it would be, because they had no idea how to kill her. It was what they were arguing about before they were informed of the gods' arrival. Sloane wasn't entirely a witch or human any longer. When Flora killed her and she was brought back through necromancy and dark magic, Sloane changed. She had enough life in her to thrive, but what would stop her from coming back again and again?

Mikael nodded. "Ask the question, young witch."

"How do you kill a witch who has been brought back by necromancy?"

"I cannot say too much—that would be interfering—however, if one were to take the parts of the body that govern logic and magic, she wouldn't be able to use either. It might be the answer you seek. Then again," the leader of the gods tipped his head and shrugged, "you may also take her toes. Just be careful to avoid transferring the darkness to a magicked soul."

"Another cryptic load," Nico snarled.

But Emery nodded, following along completely. They would need to take Sloane's head and heart. Logic of the brain, magic of the heart. As long as no witch took on the magic, there would be no way for Sloane to return.

A few months ago, she might have felt a gut-wrenching sorrow at the thought of killing Sloane, but now she was ready. She had the tools to end her sister, especially since she had proven there was nothing left in her but darkness. She couldn't come back from the things she'd done. And if what the gods had said was true, she was making deals with the literal equivalent of the devil, all in the name of power.

Mikael clapped his hands together and nodded. "Then we will leave you to your planning. Oh, and tell Octavian that Celeste is waiting."

"I'm right here, you overgrown cloud dweller." Octavian hobbled out from behind a bush off to the side of the clearing. "Tell my wife I'm not letting go until our youngest ancestor is safe."

Emery whipped her head toward Octavian. "What the hell does that mean? Is Lina in danger?"

"Oh no, that sweet child isn't in any danger. She is meant for great things; I just want to be around to see them. And the others. So many others."

Others?

Emery looked to August, then to Malcolm, and finally to Lily, whose cheeks had turned bright pink.

"Is there something you want to tell us?"

The clearing got very quiet, and Emery knew each of the vampires was listening in to hear if there were any additional heartbeats present.

Malcolm's shoulders relaxed, and he pressed a kiss to Lily's temple. "Soon, my love."

Octavian clapped his hands together and snickered excitedly.

Emery didn't even know they were hoping for children, but she supposed it made sense they would want some of their own.

"On that note," Mikael interrupted, "We will be on our way. Best strike under the harvest moon."

If her calculations were correct, that was in a manner of days in the mortal realm.

One by one, the gods disappeared until only Kasen and Mikael remained.

"Wait," August interrupted before the final two disappeared. "Everything has been about balance. Light and dark. If we kill Sloane, won't that upset the balance of magic housed by her and Emery?"

Kasen chuckled. "You are much smarter than you seem."

"Balance will remain in your queen's lineage. Her descendants will carry both light and dark. As long as they remain as neutral as she is, the blood in their veins will be enough to anchor the realm in both magicks."

"No pressure," August whispered, and Emery couldn't help but smile.

They were the key to balancing the realms. It would take all of the heirs to fight and win against Sloane as the prophecies predicted, a united front of every faction, but it was Emery's line that would bring balance. Lina and any other future children with August.

If he would still have her.

If they could figure out what the hell happened between them and why their ability to communicate telepathically was on the fritz.

He's still your soul, a voice sounded in her head. Not August's, but it was still familiar. One she'd heard before, telling her to embrace her darkness. Her eyes darted across the clearing to where Mikael stood. His eyes softened, and he bowed his head.

It was him. She didn't know what he meant, only that he wasn't wrong. August was still lodged in her soul, at least for the time being.

Does this mean I live?

You ask questions I couldn't possibly know the answers to, young witch. But I can tell you that things are how they are meant to be.

Callum was right, you lot are a bunch of cheeky bastards.

A smile tipped Mikael's lips.

"Callum," Kasen called out. "May we have a word?"

Callum mumbled under his breath too low for Emery to hear but Malcolm, Draven, and August chuckled.

She craned her neck and looked up at the Nicholson men. "What was that about?"

"Nothing. Just Callum being Callum," Draven offered.

Emery shook her head, but she didn't take her eyes off of where Callum stood talking in hushed tones with the gods.

"Can you hear what they're saying?"

"No," August leaned in, but shook his head. "They've put up some sort of wall around them."

"Sneaky bastards," Malcolm grunted.

"Do you believe them?" Draven asked.

"I have come to realize the stars like to fuck with us, but too much makes sense for this to be one of those times."

"She's right," Nico interjected, running a hand through his hair. "They don't show up unless it's dire. Trust me. If they are trying to help it's because shit is about to go sideways."

"So, what do we do?"

"We plan for war, and make sure we're on the winning side."

"You can bloody well fuck off!" Callum yelled and stormed off toward the path that led to the beach below the cliffs.

The hairs on the back of her neck rose like they did before a vision, but her sight didn't overtake her. Instead, it nudged her in Callum's direction.

Emery looked to the rest of her friends and family, kings and queens in their own rights. "Get some dinner and let's meet in the war room in an hour."

They all nodded and turned for the castle.

"And where would you like me?"

Emery turned and faced August. Her gaze trailed up his wrinkled shirt and lingered on his lips. Lips she wanted to feel against hers, even though a part of her felt like she had no right to them. Soul or not, the loss of their mate bond was a mindfuck she didn't have time to dissect. Still, she found comfort in his presence, and deep down knew they weren't finished.

"I need to go talk to Callum."

August nodded.

"I'm sorry you can't plan with us. I...it should be you leading them."

August stepped forward, invading her space, and despite everything, the drunk bees in her belly took flight being near him. He lowered his head and pressed a kiss to her forehead.

"My sweet little witch, you are as much a queen as I am a king, and I trust no one else to lead our people."

Emery blinked back the tears that threatened to fall. There was still so much unsaid between them, but for the first time since being stripped of their marks, she felt something akin to hope for their future.

"I have to go," she whispered, her voice slightly wavering.

"I'll be waiting," August stated, nothing but confidence in his words.

Then, just as she turned to walk away, she heard the whisper of his voice on the wind.

"Always."

Chapter Thirty Eight

CALLUM

He didn't always do the right thing, or whatever was right by society's standards, but that wasn't his fault. He wasn't wired to be their puppet. From the moment he was born, he always knew he was destined for something more. Something greater than the mundane life of a vampire prince.

Still, Callum did his time, paid his dues. He played the game that was expected of him. He'd learned to rule a kingdom and lost a woman and a child whom he'd loved deeply. He would have been happy with his life if it weren't for the persistent nagging in his soul that told him he was meant for more.

It was the same bloody fucking nagging that was there now.

Only this time, he didn't want it.

He wanted what was promised to him when he started this. A mate. His happily ever after. A family to love and cherish for the rest of his days.

There was no doubt in his mind that he could go

through this world alone, but he didn't want to. Callum wanted the epic love and mundane Sunday mornings.

When Kasen first appeared to him, all those centuries ago, he knew there was something ethereal about him. The bastard never came out and said he was a god, but it wasn't hard for Callum to imagine where he stood in the hierarchy of life.

He picked up a rock from the beach and chucked it into the sea. The waves that had calmed him since he'd arrived in Enchanth now only served as a metaphor for the ache in his chest, upturning the sediment of his dreams and leaving him with more questions than answers.

"Callum?"

His shoulders sagged and he dropped his chin to his chest. He didn't want to talk about it, but if the way she was walking toward him was any indication, he knew Emery wasn't going to let it be. Not after she'd already seen him fall apart after finding out he didn't have a mate. At least the stars had sent her and not someone like Malcolm, who would try to find the silver lining.

There was none, and Emery understood that. She knew better than most the pain of the fates and the way they could upend everything you ever dreamed of. She was living the same lie he was, forced to make decisions for the good of a kingdom, a realm, literally everyone else but herself.

She stepped up beside him and nudged his shoulder. "Do you want to talk about it?"

He didn't bother looking up at her. Instead, he locked his gaze on the tumultuous sea. "If I said no, would you leave it alone?"

"Psshhh." Emery scoffed. "With the fucking gods

involved? Not a chance in hell. But I'm also avoiding talking to August about what the hell comes next for us, so it's not like I have any moral authority to judge your avoidance."

A small smile quirked at the corner of his lips. "Is it bad that I don't envy you?"

"I get the feeling I won't envy you either." Emery huffed a laugh. "Now, what's going on? And take your time. I need every moment you can spare."

Callum shook his head as he replayed Kasen's words in his mind. Emery wouldn't envy him. In fact, he had no doubt Emery was going to be outraged for him when he told her.

If he told her.

He sighed and turned his back on the sea. A mistake in any other circumstance, but he had nothing left to lose. He made his way to the jagged rocks that lined the beach at the base of the cliffs and leaned against its smooth side.

Emery followed him, and the two of them sat in silence with nothing but the lull of the waves to comfort them.

"Whatever it is, Callum, you don't have to face it alone," Emery whispered.

He ran a hand through his hair before exhaling a weighted breath. "I've known Kasen for centuries."

"So you said." She let her voice linger, but when he didn't continue, she guided his story. He could hear the hint of irritation in her voice as she added, "He's the one who enabled you to be the sneaky bastard we all know and love."

Callum chuckled. She never could hide how she felt, but it was something he admired about her. He kept things close to his chest. Always. It's what kept him alive all these years. He had more enemies than any of them could imagine, but he'd always managed to leave them guessing. With Emery, there was never a doubt where she stood or what she was thinking or feeling.

"Essentially, yes. He came to me and gave me a book, one that I now know belonged to Celeste. He was the one who set this all in motion. But his arrival in my life wasn't the first time I felt like I was made for something more."

"What do you mean?" Emery said with a tilt of her head.

Callum shifted his weight against the rock so he was facing her. He searched her eyes and silently begged her to understand that he didn't ask for any of this. "Do you ever feel like something is guiding you, but you don't know what? Not fate or destiny, but like you're a part of something bigger?"

"Every damn day, but I know it's fate and destiny because I can see what comes next."

"And what do you see when you search for me?"

Emery shut her eyes and looked to her sight while Callum held his breath. He'd never asked her a more important question. What she said next would no doubt change his future. It was a long shot, but maybe she would have the answers he needed. The right path he was supposed to tread.

Emery's brow furrowed, and her jaw tightened.

"I can't..." Her frustrated tone matched the furrow in her brow. "There isn't a clear path. It's hazy and the only thing I can see is that it forks in two directions." Emery opened her eyes and turned toward him. "I've never seen anything like that. It's almost as if it's not predestined but rather an active choice."

"Bloody gods," he whispered under his breath. "Thanks for trying, lass. I'm not surprised, though."

Emery reached out and placed her hand on top of his. Her thumb gently moved in a circle. "What did Kasen tell you? Was it something that will help us?"

Callum inhaled and slowly exhaled as he scrubbed his face with his free hand. "No. He told me I'm not my mother's son."

Emery's jaw dropped. "What?"

Tears pricked at his eyes, but he blinked them back, staring out at the sea. Saying the words out loud made them real, and Callum wasn't sure he was ready for it to be true. What Kasen told him defied logic, something he relied on to make sense of the world. People assumed he was mysterious because he knew more than them or had access to a witch. Bloody hell, now they knew he had access to the gods. But that's not how he defied everyone. His mysterious nature was due to the logic of the world around him. He took the time to consider all sides and never right or wrong, only what came next. Even with all the magic and fate in his life, he always seemed to find the underlying logic to make it all make sense. Which was bloody fucking frustrating, since the more he considered Kasen's words, the more they made sense.

Constantly feeling out of place. The urge to find the bigger picture. The nagging weight that if he did, maybe he would find the answers his soul needed.

"It's no surprise my father liked to sleep around. I mean, that's how we have Draven and likely a plethora of other half-siblings on this earth. What I didn't know was that my supposed mother was infertile. She couldn't carry a child to term., and when she couldn't, my father attempted to produce an heir at any cost. Of course, the gods took it upon themselves to try and fix things without the help of fate."

Emery cocked a brow in question, but didn't say anything. She was smart, but there was no way she could string together the events that transpired. Even he struggled to believe them.

"Remember how Mikael said that there was no longer a god who could build realms?"

Emery nodded.

"The goddess who could was my grandmother."

Emery's mouth fell open. She closed it again, then opened it like a fish gasping for oxygen. "That would make you…You're a god."

Callum shrugged and kicked a rock, hating the way it sounded out loud. "At least half of me is. Mostly. Sort of. I don't even know. That's the fucked-up part."

"What do you mean?"

"I'm still me. Still a vampire."

Emery chuckled, and ran a finger along her neck where he'd bitten her when they first met. "I can attest to that."

"Leave it to you to make a joke when my entire world has just been ripped out from underneath me."

"You're saying you wouldn't have done the same?"

His gaze narrowed, and she smiled.

"Continue. No more commentary, I promise."

He highly doubted that but still he continued. "My grandmother built thousands of realms, and then one day disappeared. The gods have searched for her, but most believe she is dead. When my mother didn't inherit her mother's abilities and became the goddess of secrets instead, with her firstborn following in her footsteps, they decided they had to do something. The realms were disappearing slowly, and they had no way of replenishing them. So, I became a result of their experiments."

"Demigods," Emery whispered, following along.

Callum pursed his lips and nodded. "Only I was born a royal vampire, or at least that's what they thought. I don't know exactly how it works. Kasen and Mikael weren't exactly forthcoming. All they said was the reason I don't have a mate is because I must choose if that is my path, or if I want to give up my vampirism and become a god. If I stay a vampire, I will have a mate, but if I choose to become a god, I will have…well, I have no fucking clue because I don't even know if gods have mates. I mean, obviously they can procreate because I exist."

Emery's eyes widened. "Holy hell."

"I know."

She let out a cackle. "Your mother is the Goddess of Secrets. Do you know how perfect that is?"

Callum blinked at her and scoffed. "That's what you took away from all that?"

"Listen, don't knock my coping mechanism. I've already got a ton of shit going on up here." She pointed to her temple and chuckled, which garnered a smile from him. Emery was just trying to do the same as him. Keep it together. Her eyes met his. "What are you going to do?"

Wasn't that the million-dollar question?

"I don't know." He ran his fingers through his hair again, tugging on the strands he usually kept perfectly maintained. "Emery, all I have ever wanted was my mate. From the moment Kasen told me about them, and I read the texts, I knew that I was made for her. This mystery woman who would complete me in every way. She is who I've been fighting for. Who I sacrificed everything for."

"So go find her," Emery said as if it was the easiest thing in the world. "Forsake your god-ness and find your mate. We're going to stabilize the realms and everything will be fine. They won't need you or your grandmother's powers anymore. You have given up so much, Callum, you deserve to find your happiness too."

He wanted that more than anything. When August and Emery found each other, and then Malcolm and Lily, and Draven and Flora, Callum was ecstatic for them. The way that they completed each other so wholly was greater than any of the magic he'd seen performed to date. They all saw him as this secretive bastard who played on logic, and they weren't wrong, but more than that, he was still a child hoping and praying that someday he would find the love that had never been shown to him. Bloody hell, he was a gods-damned mess.

And yet, he wanted what Kasen offered him, too. Because deep down there was a side of him that was drawn to life as a god. In all his years fighting for mates and the possibility of happiness for his kind, Callum had developed a need for adventure and conquering the unknown. It was more than wanderlust. It fed a part of him he hadn't known existed. And while he thought he was ready to give that all up and settle down with his mate, a part of him was sad to let it go.

Then he discovered he didn't have a mate, and that was all he had left—this need to fix things, to find the next problem and whittle away at it while exploring the world around him.

He was left with the burning question: why did giving that up feel so much harder now than before?

Emery's gaze softened, and her brow furrowed. "Why do you look like I did when I realized our bond was severed?"

Callum blinked and met her gaze. Did he? The weight in his chest certainly felt like he was being stripped of everything he'd ever wanted.

"I dunno, lass."

"Why are you questioning it?" she asked. "I would give anything to have my bond with August returned to me."

"But what if there was a part of you that you'd never get to know because of it?"

"Do you want to be a god?"

"A pretentious asshole?" It wasn't as simple as she made it seem. "I'm pretty sure you called me worse when I bit you and delivered you to your mate."

Emery sucked in a breath. "He's not my mate."

"He's yours, Emery." Callum growled. "Mark be damned, we all know it."

She dropped her gaze to the sand, all the confidence she held while pushing him gone. "It doesn't feel the same anymore, and even our soul bond is on the fritz. Hell, I could be dying."

"Don't be dramatic, lass." Callum tsked. "I don't know why your souls are misaligned, but August would never let you die. That man would go to the depths of hell to bring you back. My question for you is, does your mate bond need to be the same? Is there not beauty in the unknown?"

He watched her mull over his question and knew the

moment she came to the realization everyone else already had.

"It doesn't," she whispered, but Callum still heard the trepidation in her voice. "I just...I miss it. The connection to him and the ability to feel his emotions were something I took for granted. I still love him, he's still the man I want to spend my life with because of who he is and all that he's done for me and Lina. Not to mention everything he has overcome for himself. He's my other half even without the mark. But it just feels...off. Not only that, but what kind of leaders are we if we aren't mated? What if the soul bond is next? What if she tainted that too?"

"Your mate bond doesn't make you leaders. The question remains, would you rather not have his love at all?"

Emery's gaze connected with his, and she reached out and took his hand in hers and gave it a squeeze. "I'm sorry. This must seem so juvenile to you while you're over here wrestling with not having your mate at all and the fact your entire identity is at stake."

"Thanks for putting it lightly." Callum smiled and squeezed her hand back. "Surprisingly, it doesn't. Your feelings are valid, even if I have nothing to compare them to, and my life is falling apart. If there's anything I've learned about pain it's that it doesn't discriminate, and it loves company."

"So, what are we going to do about it?" Emery looked up at him and smiled. "You never did answer my question. What are *you* going to do?"

"*We* are going to make plans to save our realm from collapsing into darkness." Callum clapped his other hand on top of hers. "And then *you* are going to go talk with your mate."

"And *you*?"

Callum stood and tugged Emery up from the rocks, pulling her into a hug. She was the sister he'd always wanted. The ruler this realm deserved. "I'm going to stand with my friends and family because I would do anything for them. Then, I'll worry about what comes next for me."

Emery wrapped her arms around him and whispered into his chest. "You deserve love, Callum."

"I...Thank you. So do you." He'd been about to tell her that he wasn't sure he did, but she didn't need to worry about his insecurities. Emery had much bigger concerns at the moment, and Callum did too, for that matter. The fate of multiple realms was on their shoulders. He needed to focus on what he could control, and at the moment, his future wasn't one of those things. It would be there when they'd righted the wrongs and ushered in a new world.

Then he could worry about his own beginning.

Chapter Thirty Nine

EMERY

EMERY STARED AT THE PLANS STRETCHED OUT ON THE WAR room table, her mind racing. Between the revelations about Callum's heritage and everything the gods had thrown at them, there was little room left for anything else. She didn't like the way Callum considered the gods' offer. He might have been born of them, but he belonged to her family, not theirs. Gods or not, they didn't get to take him away.

If that weren't enough to drive her to the brink of insanity, there was the fact that there were too many what ifs in their plan for Emery's liking. Despite the fact that they'd accounted for as many as possible, she didn't like the sinking feeling in the pit of her stomach that something was about to go wrong. Which most likely stemmed from the notion that every time they'd faced Sloane, she'd been five steps ahead of them and six times stronger.

Emery leaned forward and pressed her head against the cold wood of the table. She was the last one in the room after sending everyone to get some sleep. They'd spent all night planning, and while they had a plan, there was one glaring reality that settled in her chest like an icy dagger.

She was the weakest link.

Nico argued she just needed more training, and Malcolm argued she didn't need to use her blood. They'd initially planned to attack at the time of the witches' Heil celebration, but the timeline now had to change in order for them to stand a chance. Sloane was weak now, not weeks from now. And Emery wore the pressure of that fact like it was a second skin.

It didn't matter that they had a solid army. Their strength came from the fact that, in theory, Emery should be able to give them a magic power boost on the battlefield. Which they needed, because as it stood, their army would tire and fall far faster than Sloane's beasts. But, in order to do that, Emery needed to figure out how to master her blood and gift it to her army. Without it, their advantage decreased exponentially.

Emery lifted her head, and her gaze drifted over the maps one more time, the lines on their plan blurring. Her mind hummed with the need for action, but her body couldn't take much more. Still, she went over the plan two more times in her head before finally calling it quits.

The early rays of dawn broke through the windows on her walk back to her suite, and she savored the eerie silence of the castle.

Stepping into her suite, she was fully ready to strip down and sink into the oversized tub, but froze the moment her eyes landed on the bed.

It was occupied by the very large, very naked body of her mate, her sheets draped at his waist. Ex-mate. She'd never get used to him not being her mate.

Her eyes lingered on his handsome face, the way sleep made him look younger. Without the darkness of his stare, she could almost believe he was innocent of all the crimes he'd committed. The simple bow of his lips couldn't possibly be that of a killer, and there was no way a man with cheekbones like his could be anything but stoic.

And yet, there was the stubble on his jaw that gave him just a hint of a bad boy persona. One that left Emery clenching her thighs with need. Especially since she knew what it felt like to feel his roughness against the soft flesh between her legs.

She sucked her bottom lip between her teeth as she traced the hollow of his throat to his collarbone, where she liked to bite him as they made love. The same spot he often sank his fangs into on her body, lighting her up with his venom.

Damn this man.

Her eyes dipped to his abs, and she recalled vividly what it felt like to trace her tongue between each ridge and valley, down to the trail of hair that dipped beneath the sheet.

"I can feel you staring, little witch," August mumbled, his voice thick with sleep.

Emery sucked in a breath, and her cheeks flushed. "I'm sorry. I didn't mean to wake you. I'm just...I needed to change before I head to the arena."

She took a step forward and shrugged off the oversized sweater she wore, leaving her in her camisole and leggings.

One of August's ocean eyes peeked open, and his gaze drifted lazily over her, pausing on the swell of her breasts before continuing on. Heat flooded her core. "It's nearly morning and you've been at it all night. Come to bed."

"Don't you think we should talk before I come climbing into bed with you?" she whispered as she kept moving toward the closet. The question was more for herself than him, considering her body wanted nothing more than to follow his command.

"I think you should come regardless," August muttered lazily.

She narrowed her gaze, and he smirked.

"Fine," he mused sarcastically. August rolled over quickly, and his hand darted out and clutched her wrist when she passed the bed.

Emery's eyes zeroed in on his hand so she would focus on something other than the way the sheet fell, revealing the round of his sculpted ass.

"I'll go first. Has anything changed, princess?"

Emery cocked a brow and lifted her free arm, her bare flesh evidence enough.

"While I will never tire of your sass and my need to tan your ass because of it, you knew damn well what I meant."

Oh, he was feisty this morning. She loved this side of him. And there was no denying the way his words added fuel to the growing inferno inside her. The mark on her arm didn't matter, this man only needed to whisper her name or any variation or nickname and she was a damn puddle of need.

Still, the mark was a big part of them. A big missing part that they'd yet to address, and she wasn't sure she was ready to. She knew how she felt, and she could assume, based on his actions, he felt the same way, but without the words, it was just an assumption, and she knew all too well how those could backfire.

She opened her mouth to speak, but before she could,

August tugged her down onto the bed. Emery stumbled forward, landing on his chest. She tried to back away, but August wrapped his arms around her and forced her legs on either side of him. Slowly, he rolled his hips so he was sitting up, and she was sitting in his lap, face to face with him, their breath mingling together.

August's eyes flitted to her lips, and for a split second she thought he was going to kiss her, and damn did she want to feel his lips on hers, but instead his tongue darted out, wetting his own. When he lifted his gaze and met hers, Emery saw nothing but heat in his swirling blue depths.

"You want to talk, little witch? Nothing has changed for me. If anything, seeing the way you have become a queen in your own right has driven me to love you more than I did before. While I still want to slay dragons in your name and lay siege to their hoards, more than that, I want to stand at your side while you lay waste to your own demons."

Relief flooded her, and the tension in her spine relaxed.

August reached up to tuck a stray strand of her hair behind her ear and his hand lingered. Emery leaned into him as he cupped her cheek. "When I look at you, I see the woman of my dreams. Mark or not, you are my mate. I may not be able to feel your every emotion, and my ability to know your thoughts might be waning, but make no mistake: I know you, Emery Montgomery. I know the way your eye twitches when you're trying to hold back a smart-ass comment, and that when you blush in the middle of a conversation," He swiped his thumb across her trembling lower lip and rolled his hips again, his lengthened cock sliding against her needy core, "it's usually because your mind is in the gutter."

Emery sucked her lower lip between her teeth in a manic attempt to stifle the moan that worked its way up her throat. August's lips pulled back into a wicked grin, and he leaned forward and pressed a chaste kiss to the corner of her lips. Close, but not at all what she wanted from him.

August pulled away, and allowed his hand to fall from her face, racing the outline of her collarbone before falling to her hand. He intertwined their fingers and continued. "I love the glint in your eye when you talk about killing our enemies, and the twinkle that replaces it when you look at our daughter. You are more than a mark to me. I love every bloody thing about you, and I'm sorry if I let it seem like that had changed for even a second."

Tears stained her cheeks, and when she opened her mouth, she nearly choked on a sob, but managed to swallow past it. "I love you too. You are mine, and as much as I miss having you intertwined in my magic, I want you by my side more. But what if we lose? What if I'm dying and Lina—"

August's smile widened, reaching his eyes and revealing the dimple that seldom found its way to the surface. Then, like a man possessed, he crashed his lips against hers, swallowing the whimper of a woman in love.

"No ifs. No buts." He groaned against her lips. "Leave all those worries behind for just one moment. Just let me love you, that will be enough."

"August, we—"

"No, Emery," he growled. Pulling away so she could see his eyes wide with anger and lust. "Fuck them all to hell. Fuck this empty feeling. There is no discussion. We are meant to be. Fuck the stars. Fuck the nobles. Fuck anyone who stands in the way of us. For us, there will never be any other way. You. Are. Mine. Just as I am yours. I will fight until my dying breath for this. You and me. Together. United."

She wanted to fight him. To yell that they had to think about more than just themselves and consider what this meant for their people, who were either lost in the idea of mates or completely against it. She wanted to argue that if their mate bond tainted the tether in their souls, in time she could wither away into nothing. But she couldn't fight against this. Him. Even without the bond, he was right. They belonged to one another.

"Okay." She whispered.

"Okay," his lips tipped upward. "Now, let me worship you like the queen you are. Let me be your throne."

August hooked his fingers beneath her thighs and in one fluid motion lifted her, sliding his body beneath her until she hovered over his face.

She glanced between her legs, the heat of his breath greater than the thin fabric of her leggings. "August, what are you doing?" she breathed.

"Exactly what I suggested." He smiled wickedly, bringing his fingers to the waist of her leggings and gripping them along with the lace of her panties.

The sound of fabric ripping echoed through the room and August's breath tickled the sensitive flesh of her pussy, no longer hidden by clothing. Emery squirmed, trying to slide herself down his chest, but August's fingers dug into the flesh of her hips and held her in place.

"Now, little witch, the only squirming I want to feel from you is when you ride my face into your first orgasm. I want to taste your cum as it drips from your delicate pussy and feeds my addiction. I have gone far too long without you, and I don't intend to leave a single inch of your cunt unexplored. And once I am sure you are satisfied, I am going to fuck you so hard you'll never forget that we are made for one another."

Emery's thighs clenched at the same moment her stomach dropped. Damn this man and his filthy promises. She should have known the moment she found him naked in her bed that this was exactly where they would end up.

August pulled her down to meet his mouth and slid his tongue through her slick folds, exploring every inch like he promised, until he reached her clit. He sucked the tiny bud between his lips and growled.

"Holy shit," Emery moaned and her hands shot out to grip the headboard for balance. His vibrations settled into a steady hum and sent a bolt of carnal lightning shooting through her. "Please, August."

She wasn't going to last. Not with his fangs grazing her clit and his tongue, a literal treasure, working magic with its delving strokes.

Her magic hummed in her chest, recognizing the man beneath her as its mate even without the mark. It fought against her, wanting to wrap around him and make him theirs, but Emery wanted this moment for them.

No magic.

No bonds.

This was about reconnecting. A man and a woman, defying the stars and finding their love in the darkness.

"Hmmmmm," August hummed, driving her wild. "I need to taste you. All of you. Your essence and your pleasure."

"Please." Emery begged. "Take me over the edge."

August's lips pulled back, revealing his fangs, and it sent a shiver down her spine. "Yes, my queen."

His fingers dug further into her thighs, pinning her against his mouth as he began to tongue her pussy more aggressively.

Emery cried out, his name on her lips followed by a string of praises he'd absolutely earned. She should have been in control, seeing as she was riding his face, but August proved yet again that he would always take care of her. The stubble on his chin left a delicious burn on her flesh, and she wouldn't dare tell him to stop. Her stomach tightened, and despite the fact she wanted to hold on longer and ride out the pleasure only August could bring, she couldn't. The tell-tale tingle started in the depths of her core and sparked through her, straight to her clit.

"Oh. My. Gods." Emery struggled to form words, let alone breathe. "I…August, I'm so close."

"Mmhmmmm," was his only reply before he went back to worshiping at the altar between her legs. He didn't let up until Emery was on the edge, fighting for the last bit of control.

As if he could read her mind, August sucked her clit hard and sank his fangs into the soft flesh of her mons.

Emery arched her back and her strangled cry echoed throughout the suite as August simultaneously sucked her blood and rolled his tongue over her clit. His venom flooded her, heightening her pleasure. Stars and circles swam in her vision, and her fingers dug into the headboard as her body trembled through each bliss-filled wave.

When it finally crested, Emery slackened, and August lifted her from his face. He gently slid her down his body and rolled her so she was beneath him. His fingers tugged at the hem of her camisole, and he lifted it over her head.

Exposed, she looked up at him with what she was sure was a struck-stupid smile on her face, and August returned the sentiment. Only his fang-filled grin was coated in a mixture of her blood and arousal. "Watching you come will never not be my favorite thing."

"You really know how to make a girl's heart go pitter-patter."

He shrugged. "I try."

His eyes raked over her naked flesh, and the remnants of his venom had her body reacting instantly and of its own accord. Her flesh pebbled and her nipples tightened into hardened peaks. It was like her body was demanding more, as if she hadn't just experienced a mind-blowing orgasm at his tongue.

"I need you inside me," she panted, desperation lacing her voice. "Fill me."

"Bloody hell."

In seconds, he had her flipped over onto her stomach, ass presented in the air.

"You bring me to my knees. Do you know that?" He ran his palm over her supple flesh, and Emery half expected him to rear back and smack her ass. She wanted him to.

But he didn't. This wasn't about punishment. It was about ownership, and she wanted him to own every aspect of her. Her heart. Her mind. Her future. It all belonged to him.

August ran his fingers down her spine. "Arch your back for me, princess."

Emery looked over her shoulder and did as he said, the

carnal look in his eyes making her bite back the smart-ass remark on her tongue. Usually, the bond would be flooded with his need, but she didn't need it to know exactly how much he wanted her.

"Fuck, Emery. You are exquisite."

He was one to talk. The sheet had slid from his torso, leaving Emery with a delicious view of his naked form. Her eyes trailed from his glistening lips to where his cock bounced against his abdomen.

August growled and pressed one hand between her shoulder blades, forcing her onto the mattress while the other dipped between her legs. He slipped two fingers inside her, the delicious stretch forcing a guttural moan from her.

"I wanted to take my time. To worship every inch of you until you're writhing under me, but I need you too, Em." August removed his fingers from her and slid his cock through her folds, his head teasing her clit and making her pussy clench and tighten with need.

"Please, August."

"Tell me I'm yours," he growled.

"You're mine," she moaned.

"For how long?"

"Forever."

In one swift motion, August entered her, seating himself completely within her. He fell forward, wrapping his body around hers. His breath tickled her ear and he whispered. "That's right. This tight pussy is mine, forever. This body is mine to claim. And you, little witch, are my queen until our dying breaths."

"Yes. Always. Forever." Emery clenched around him. "Now, fuck me."

He grunted, and while one hand tangled in her hair, pulling her back so she was arched at a nearly impossible angle, his other wrapped around her hip with bruising force.

He pulled out until only the tip of his cock remained notched inside her then pistoned forward.

Emery fisted the sheets and felt him everywhere with every thrust.

Marking her.

Branding her.

She was already all in with him, but again and again he was proving to her they didn't need the marks reassuring them. They would always have the memory of what had been, but what they had now was still special. Maybe even more so. It wasn't driven by magic or by fate. They were choosing to be together. A happily ever after that they willingly had to fight for every day.

August growled and pulled her up against him, one hand wrapping around her throat while the other slipped between her legs. He didn't slow his merciless pace, thrusting upward and hitting the spot within her that made her toes curl. Emery panted with the need for release as his fingers danced over her clit.

"Come for me, little witch."

His command was her undoing. The world tilted, and she exploded with pleasure all at once. Emery's muscles squeezed, clenching tightly around him, and August let out a hiss that transformed into a guttural moan as he followed her with his own release. The magic she'd been holding back erupted and, just as before in their studio, wrapped around them, this time recognizing what had been stolen from them.

Emery sagged against him, the most delicious spent feeling taking over her limbs. He slipped from her and gently turned her to face him.

"Bloody hell, I love you, Emery," August purred, pressing his forehead to hers.

She sighed, still breathless, and cupped both sides of his face. "I love you too."

August leaned down, pressing his lips to hers. The remnants of her blood and arousal flitted over her tongue, and Emery clenched her thighs, more turned on by it than she should be.

August let out a low growl. "If you keep flooding your pussy with arousal, I won't be able to stop myself from fucking you again, and you need to sleep."

Emery was about to snap about how sleep was for the weak, but her traitorous body gave her away when her mouth dropped into a long yawn.

"I need to go practice making blood juice boxes," she muttered, sleep threatening to take her.

"Do I even want to know?"

"I can't tell you, even if you did."

August sighed and lowered her to the pillow, situating himself behind her. Emery hated that she had to keep things from him. They had just found each other again, and yet in some ways, they were forced to remain miles apart.

August propped himself on one elbow and pressed a kiss to her temple. "Sleep and then I'll personally deliver you to the arena."

Emery frowned. He'd take her, and then he'd leave because of her fucking sister.

"What's that look for?"

"I hate that you aren't part of our planning." She

snuggled her back against him. "This is as much my fight as it is yours. I want you at my side."

"Then I'll be there."

"August you can't, the vow—"

August tsked. "She can't control me when I'm in this realm, and the vow only harms me if it's me who plans to hurt her. Even if it does, if you want me to be there, I'll be there, little witch."

"Are you sure?"

"More than my next breath." August tightened his hold on her before he nuzzled his nose into his favorite spot on her neck. "Now close your eyes, you need to sleep."

For the first time in a long time, her brain quieted, even though there was so much uncertainty and plenty to be done to prepare for the battle ahead. It could wait. Right then, she wanted to bask in the warmth of August behind her and the love that they shared. Her eyes grew heavy and she let sleep take her. There would be time for all their plans later, but moments like these were few and far between.

Chapter Forty

AUGUST

He knew before his eyes opened that Emery was gone. Still, August reached out beside him, hoping he was wrong.

He wasn't.

August tested their bond, asking where she was, but an answer never came. He wasn't sure if it was because she'd closed her side of the soul bond or if it was on the fritz again.

The sheets were cold, indicating she'd been gone for a while. He'd never known her to disappear on him, but he'd also never known her as a queen in charge. It was both admirable and infuriating. It was supposed to be him leading. It was what he'd been born to do. And yet, he couldn't deny he loved her commitment to their people. Emery was everything his kingdom needed and more. Selfishly, though, he wished they'd had more time to reconnect.

Coming together and finding their love stronger than

ever had been a dream come true. If he'd had it his way, she never would have left the bed, and they'd be going for another round. Or maybe five. Hell, he'd keep her tangled in his sheets for the next year if he thought it was feasible. But war waited for no one, and Emery was in the thick of it. He might not know the extent of their plans yet, but there was no doubt she was their saving grace, and she took the responsibility seriously.

That didn't change the fact that a part of him was scared shitless by the revelations about their soul bond. He'd done his best to keep a brave face, but the thought that he could be losing her again made his heart constrict with fear. He wasn't lying when he said he'd go to hell for her. Just as she'd save their kingdom, he'd do everything in his power to ensure she lived beside him until his last breath.

August's stomach rumbled. After pulling himself from the bed, he took a quick shower before dressing and going in search of food and his mate.

Fiancée.

No. Mate.

Even without the mark that was the only way to describe Emery. She was his match in every possible way.

After a few wrong turns, he finally found the kitchen again.

He was eyeing the array of muffins and blood bags on the island when a tiny sprite with wings popped out of the mountain of suds in the sink.

"Help yourself, Your Majesty," she squeaked.

"Thank you." August smiled and picked up a blueberry muffin.

The sprite turned around and dove back into the suds.

He wasn't sure he would ever get used to the fact that the fae existed. It was one thing to have Dorian around, he blended in well with them most of the time. You'd never guess he was fae. But in Enchanth, there were fae of every species: sprites, nymphs, goblins, selkies, and pixies. And those were just the ones he'd recognized. There were plenty he couldn't classify that roamed the halls. Yet, they all lived harmoniously with one another.

It was impressive.

He flipped the muffin in the air and caught it before heading out toward the common area he'd passed on the way down, hoping to find some of his people there to figure out where exactly Emery was.

The sound of people laughing echoed from the room, and August recognized the guttural chuckle of one as Roland's.

Perfect.

August rounded the last corner to the entrance of the room, and stopped in his tracks at the sight laid before him.

Roland was sitting naked from the waist up at a table surrounded by three young witches, a nymph, and a dryad, playing what looked to be a game of poker.

August's mouth fell open, trying to process what he was seeing.

Roland hadn't ever been as openly against the witches like Aberforth, but he'd made it known that he wasn't on board with their plan to integrate the other factions into their kingdom. He'd even gone so far as to suggest they should have their own camps to live in under their rule, like they were supernatural inferiors.

Emery had suggested during their time in the dream

realm that the nobles of their court that had chosen to stay were coming around to the idea of mates, but seeing the shift with his own eyes forced hope to bloom in his chest.

His gaze drifted around the room to where other noble vampires interacted with witches, chatting and laughing like they were old friends. The last he'd seen many of them, they'd all been too happy to be a faction ready to war not only against their enemies, but against each other.

"Your Majesty!" Roland hollered and waved August over. "Come join us. I could use another male to even the score. These ladies are taking me for everything I'm worth."

"Are they now?" August crossed the room, the lively energy infectious. "What's the game?"

One of the witches giggled. "Strip poker, Your Majesty."

August pressed his lips together in an attempt to hold back his laughter but failed miserably. "Now how did you get this crotchety old bastard to agree to that?"

"It's simple, really. He thought he was the only one who knew how to actually play. What he didn't know was we witches ran all the underground games in New Orleans."

"A miscalculation on my part," Roland mused, but the hint of a smile tugging on his lips told August he was enjoying every minute of their game. "I assure you, though, I will be victorious."

Yeah, at getting one, or maybe even all three of these women in his bed. They batted their eyelashes at the vampire like he was their next snack.

"While I would love to help you even the score, I am actually looking for my bride-to-be. Have you seen her this afternoon?"

"She's usually at the arena at this time of day, working with the sentinels from every faction. We are set to join them later to learn our parts in the attack."

"Your parts?" He was certain Roland hadn't lifted a finger in the last three skirmishes their kingdom had participated in, and the last one had been nearly two centuries prior.

"Well, yes. It's our kingdom as much as it is yours, there is no reason for us not to help in some capacity."

August's eyes widened and he chewed the inside of his cheek to stop his jaw from dropping. Who the hell was this guy and what happened to the Roland he'd fought in his war room because he wouldn't recognize Emery as his wife?

"Thank you," August replied. "I'm going to go find Emery, but I'll see you out there."

"Absolutely," Roland chuckled. "Hopefully I won't have lost every stitch of clothing by then."

"Hopefully he will," one of the witches muttered under her breath.

August chuckled and turned on his heel, pleasantly surprised at the twilight zone he'd woken up to.

The halls were quiet as he made his way to the arena. It wasn't something he thought he'd ever get used to. He missed the hustle and bustle of home. Animosity may have filled his halls as of late, but it was better than the quiet.

He rounded the corner and nearly ran into Draven, having a conversation with a woman he didn't recognize.

His brow furrowed momentarily, and then he raised a brow at the wolf. There wasn't a chance in hell that he would ever step out on Flora, so what business did he have whispering with this woman in an abandoned corridor?

As if he knew the thoughts in August's mind, Draven lifted his hand in his direction. "August, this is Nina. She is the leader of the hybrid compound that joined us in Enchanth."

Nina eyed him with suspicion, but extended her hand and bowed her head. "It's nice to officially meet you, Your Majesty."

August hesitated for a moment when he saw her mate mark, but quickly took her hand in his and nodded. "You as well."

He didn't need to ask what type of hybrid she was. There was only one combination she could be, considering Draven was the only royal hybrid wolf and his daughter was the only witch vampire. Nina had to be a hybrid wolf witch, as were all the others in Enchanth.

Nina stepped back and turned to Draven, smiling uneasily. "We should be going. The others will be waiting for us at the arena."

It was clear she was trying to get away from August, but he wasn't sure why.

"I'm heading that way myself," August interjected more forcefully than he should have. "Do you mind showing me the way?"

He didn't want to waste time getting lost, but he was also interested in talking more with Nina. She was the leader of the people his daughter would find kinship in. As much as he would always love and accept her, Nina and the other hybrids were more like Lina than August would ever be.

"Absolutely," Draven replied with a sympathetic smile. He gestured in the direction they were heading, and the three of them walked side by side. "Nina and I were just talking about finding a way to help hybrids adjust in our kingdoms."

"I think that's a fantastic idea," August offered. "What are your thoughts, Nina?"

The small woman pursed her lips for a moment and then exhaled, "May I speak candidly, Your Majesty?"

"Please, call me August."

"Okay, August. I do not trust you. Callum found us and brought us into the fold of your kingdoms. Your mate has proven herself in her ability to unite the factions. Draven and Lily have stepped up and ensured we were welcome in Enchanth. All I have seen from you is someone who gave himself up to the enemy and turned his back on his mate. Now you are back and expect us to welcome you as our king. A king who is the successor to a tyrant who would have seen my kind killed."

August's jaw dropped and he stopped walking. He expected honesty, but Nina was brutal in her assessment.

Draven's fist clenched at his sides, and he released a low growl. "That's not exactly how it happened, Nina."

August put up his hand to stop his cousin from saying anything more. "It's okay, Draven. She's right. She's only seen me as an absent king. She doesn't know the nuances of what I've been through or how I came to be at Sloane's side." He turned his gaze to Nina. "I may not be the king you expected, but I am Emery's king nonetheless. Together, we rule our kingdom, and if you have a problem with me, then we may need to rethink your compound's place within our ranks. That being said, I am not my father, and I vow with every breath to try to be the king your people deserve. My daughter is among your ranks, as is every child born from the vampire-witch mates to come. I assure you that I value every hybrid life."

Nina's gaze raked him over, and she turned up her nose at him. "We shall see. Until then, I reserve the right to withhold judgment."

The hybrid leader turned on her heel, striding down the hallway and out of sight.

August huffed and ran his fingers through his hair. "She's intense."

"You don't know the half of it," Draven chuckled. "You should have seen when she first met Emery. She tried offering to take Lina and raise her with the other hybrids."

"She did what?" August growled and charged in the direction Nina had taken off in.

He would tolerate a lot of things, but he wouldn't allow for anyone to insinuate that his daughter belonged with anyone other than her parents.

Draven's hand caught his shoulder and halted him before he took a handful of steps. "Whoa. Settle down. She didn't know where Emery stood in terms of hybrids. Her compound has been through a lot. They've lost everything, to our peoples and their prejudices. More than once."

The rage that bubbled in his chest simmered, but didn't dissipate completely. Nina had every right to be wary of him and his motivations, but she didn't get to question his or Emery's place in Lina's life. Not even the gods would separate him from his daughter. August inhaled a breath to steady himself.

"I am going to prove her wrong."

"Of that I have no doubt," Draven agreed. "They need us to show them. When it comes to the hybrids, actions speak louder than words. It was the same for me when I came clean to the packs. Seeing them welcome me meant more than the words of my father."

"What can I do?"

Draven turned to follow Nina "Fight for them, August. And never stop. They need to know they have a place here."

August tightened his jaw, upset that Draven would even have to ask him to do so. His people were wrong in the role they'd played thus far, but there was no way he would sit by and let history repeat itself.

"That won't be a problem," August promised.

Chapter Forty One

AUGUST

The arena was a madhouse of people wielding magic and various weapons. Swords glinted in the setting suns, and the sound of flesh hitting flesh followed by growls and grunts echoed off the surrounding tree line. On one end, wolves and hybrids trained with Flora leading them. In both human and canine forms, they battled witches lobbing offensive elemental magic and illusions of daggers and spears that he was sure packed a hell of a punch. The few sentinels who had escaped to Enchanth took up a section in the middle with Brax and trained the vampires who'd sought refuge.

Every single person there trained with fire in their eyes. They had skin in the game, fighting for the future they wanted to see in their realm.

August trailed his eyes over the arena until he found who he was looking for. The wind whipped her pink hair against the sweat that pooled on her face as she concentrated on Dorian, who bled from his nose and mouth.

August bit back the growl in his chest. Dorian wasn't supposed to be training with Emery. If there was anywhere he needed to be, it was at Ansel's side. Considering his wolf friend was nowhere to be seen, he couldn't help but wonder what the fuck Dorian was doing there.

He stormed toward the end of the arena and opened his mouth to yell at the fae, but Nico's voice carried across the arena.

"This isn't a fucking game, Emery, you need to concentrate," Nico yelled over the fighting going on around them. "Pool the blood and bend it to your whim."

August clenched his fists at his sides, his rage building. This fae may be the one who saved his people and provided them a safe haven, but he'd be damned if he was going to let him speak to her that way.

"I wouldn't if I were you."

August whipped his gaze around to find Malcolm standing beside him.

"He is disrespecting my mate."

Malcolm raised a brow. "And if you storm out there like a damn barbarian, she's going to eat you alive."

"But—"

"Just watch," Malcolm cautioned, leading August to lean against the rickety arena fence. "His communication skills are shit, I'll give you that, but Nico knows what he's doing. Emery needs the tough love."

August ground his teeth and reluctantly watched as Emery continued to pull blood from Dorian only for it to fall to the ground at his feet.

"It doesn't seem to be working," he growled.

"Just wait."

With each passing moment, he could see Emery growing more frustrated. She managed to pull a drop of blood from Dorian, but the liquid only floated several feet before falling to the ground.

He knew she thrived under pressure, but she needed more than just tough love. He'd witnessed it himself. Hell, he'd been the one to force her hand when it came to growing the flower that saved Thea. What Emery needed was someone to believe in her, but more than that, she needed someone to piss her the fuck off. And Nico wasn't doing that. He was pushing her down with no intention of building up the fire inside of her.

"Bloody hell, I'm done waiting." August pushed off the fence and stormed toward Emery.

Malcolm called out behind him. "What are you going to do?"

"She needs someone to light a fire under her ass."

"And you think Nico can't do that?" Malcolm laughed.

"Oh, I know he can," August muttered under his breath, "but he isn't and damn the fucking stars if I'm going to let him."

August headed straight for where Emery stood, chest heaving as she struggled to recover. He knew the moment she saw him because her hands fell to her side.

"Hello, little witch," August growled.

Emery shook her head and sighed, looking up at him. "What are you doing here?"

"Watching you train."

She looked up at him, defeat in her gaze, and shook her head. "You can't be here."

"I can and I will."

"Please, August," she whispered.

"I told you, Emery, I'd rather be at your side writhing in pain than anywhere else."

"She doesn't need a distraction, she needs to focus," Nico chided.

"And you know what she needs?" August snapped, seeing red. "You're pushing her, but she's been here for weeks and she's no closer to honing the blood. And you," he whipped his gaze to where Dorian stood, wiping the blood from his eyes. "You should be with Ansel."

"August..." Emery sighed.

"No, Emery." He threw up his hand silencing her, his eyes returning to Nico, who stared at him with one brow raised. "You yell at her like that's somehow going to make her better, as if by doing so her magic will bend to your will. But that's not how it works. You may be some high and mighty fae, but that isn't how you get things done."

He should know. His father was the yell-first-and-ask-questions-later type. Hell, he'd been that man for a time too, too proud to see what was right in front of him. But this woman, this beautiful, capable witch had shown him there was more to being a leader than simply yelling and demanding. Sometimes it was about playing to the person's strengths or, in Emery's case, her insecurities.

She was likely going to hate him for what he was about to do, but it would make for great sex later, so he wasn't going to complain.

Nico smirked and lifted his hand, gesturing at Emery. "If you think you've got what it takes to get her out of her damn head, then be my guest. She's been a pain in my ass for weeks fighting what she has already proven is inside her."

August looked across the way to Dorian. "You staying or going where you should be?"

Dorian winced but didn't make a move to leave. He wiped the blood from his nose and mouth, and nodded.

Fucking fae. He had no doubt Dorian needed to have his head pulled from his ass, but he'd worry about that later.

August moved to stand behind Emery. When he was situated, he whispered. "Let's see it then, little witch. Impress me."

She rolled her eyes.

Oh, she was in for it.

August slid closer to her, pressing his chest to her back. He lowered his mouth to the shell of her ear and whispered, "I'll remember that for later."

Emery shivered against him, and he was sure if he inhaled, he'd taste her arousal in the air.

Gods, he loved this woman.

"Now what?" she whispered.

Now the fun could begin. August smiled wickedly to himself and trailed his fingers down the length of her arms until he reached her hips. He then slid his hands around her waist and tugged her so her back pressed into his thickening cock.

"You have no idea what seeing you wield your darkness does to me."

Emery sucked in a breath and rolled her hips. "I think I have *some* idea, but I'd rather not give everyone here a show."

"Oh, little witch, I think a show is exactly what they need." August dug his fingers beneath her shirt and into the soft curves of her hips. "Now make him bleed."

August felt sorry for Dorian for a split second, but then he peered across the arena and saw the fire in Dorian's gaze, confirming he was ready to go again.

"I would bleed a thousand more times if it meant helping you defeat that sadistic bitch."

"Can't Nico take his place?" Emery jerked her head to the side and whined. "He should be with Ansel."

"He will be with Ansel as soon as you do this correctly. "August promised. "You just want to see Nico bleed."

"I'm not opposed to the idea."

"Focus, princess, because you aren't going to like what happens if you can't harness his blood."

Dorian widened his stance, preparing for the onslaught of Emery's magic, which would no doubt sting.

August watched in awe as Emery lifted her hands and called her magic. Inky black tendrils, flecked with gold, slithered down her arms and pooled in her palms. Her ability to control her darkness had increased tenfold during the time they'd been apart. It was the sexiest damn thing he'd ever seen.

Her magic swirled and evaporated like smoke in the wind, and he knew the moment she called on her blood magic, not because blood pooled at the corners of Dorian's eyes but because Emery's entire body went rigid against him.

"That's it, little witch. Take what you want from him," he encouraged.

The tension in her shoulders relaxed slightly as she leaned into him, and he relished the way she used him. Emery was one of the strongest people he'd ever met, but even the strong needed support.

She obeyed, pulling Dorian's blood into a bigger drop than before and allowing it to hover in front of him.

"That's it. More." August urged.

Her arms shook with fatigue as she pulled more, only managing to extract another few drops.

"I can't," she whimpered

August growled softly. "Yes, you can."

Emery shook her head and her voice fell to a whisper only he could hear. "What if it consumes me? Pulling blood and controlling it are two different things. This isn't just harnessing my darkness, this is finding the darkness in my soul and owning it. It's allowing it to take over and giving myself into the same magic that broke my sister."

The fear in her words sliced through his heart, but where she fell prey to it, August didn't. He had seen darkness in his own soul, and at the hands of Sloane, and even if she wielded it, he had no doubt she wouldn't succumb to it.

"I will be your light. I will bring you back."

Sweat dripped from her brow, and her elemental magic whipped around them as she clenched her fists, visibly trying to grasp for more. She managed to hold on a few seconds longer before her hands fell to her sides, and she slackened against him.

"Again."

"I can't, August."

"I watched you bring a field of witches to their knees. Don't tell me you can't."

"That was out of rage, and I wasn't trying to control it and infuse my own magic or my will on it," Emery sobbed. "There is no controlling it, August. There is only yielding to it."

"Then fucking rage, Emery. If there is anyone who should be angry, it's you. Sloane has taken so much from us. Bloody hell, she took our son from us. Give in and let your darkness do what needs to be done."

Emery scoffed and pushed away from him, shooting daggers in his direction. "You don't think I know that? A part of me wants to let go and damn the consequences. I know what's riding on this, you insensitive prick. I have been here running this damn kingdom, keeping our people safe while you got to play the lovable bad guy with my sister."

August cocked a brow. He hated baiting her, but Emery needed to get out of her head and get angry. "Then why are you lost in your fears? It looks to me like you've been pretending to be a leader. Playing war games you can't possibly win because you've got your head so wrapped up in what you should be, not who you are."

"Stop."

"No. He's right." Dorian crossed the space between them and gave August a subtle nod before sliding in next to him. "We need you to do this, and you just can't seem to follow through. Maybe you aren't the queen we need."

"Who the fuck do you think you are? Both of you are way out of line." Her eyes blackened, and August kept pushing.

Dorian stepped forward until he was standing toe to toe with Emery, and August silently thanked him for recognizing his plan and taking the brunt of Emery's anger. "You know she wants your daughter, and it's clear she wants your mate. Maybe she'll spare his life despite the fact that he betrayed her. Mostly because she wants to fuck him and really make sure everyone knows he belongs to her. Either way, your daughter will have one parent, because as it stands, you won't survive the fight. None of us will."

"Take it back." Her fists clenched at her sides and her jaw tightened to the point August was worried she'd crack her teeth.

"No. Ansel is a shell of the man he used to be, and you are going to let her win. I won't let you allow his sacrifice to be in vain. If you can't do this, you might as well kill him now because there is no hope of him coming back from a life in that castle. In fact, you can sign over Flora and her children to her as well. I'm sure she'd love another hybrid in her dungeon to build her army."

"Stop it," Emery sobbed, tears streaming down her face.

Prove him wrong. Prove me wrong. Be their queen.

August knew she heard his passion-filled plea when Emery unfurled her fists, and blasted Dorian with a gust of magic. August reacted, side-stepping, so the magic that landed Dorian on his ass missed him, but just barely. Her tendrils wrapped around Dorian, a web of darkness against his pale skin. Blood flowed from every orifice, and his muscles shook as he tried to right himself.

I will follow you into the dark. I will be your light.

If Emery heard him, there was no indication. Her obsidian eyes were locked on Dorian, blood pooling at the rims.

"Rage isn't who I am, and darkness isn't who I want to be." Her voice was gruff, but held a weight to it that demanded respect. She blinked, and slowly shifted her gaze around the arena. Everyone had stopped training to watch this momentous occasion. When her eyes finally landed on August, her lips turned down into a frown. "Remember you asked for this."

The ominous words slithered down his spine, but August didn't have a moment to think about it before Emery cried out and lifted her hands to the sky. Wind whipped around them and the ground quaked. A strangled moan bubbled from Dorian's throat as her magic pulled his body, chest first, from the ground. His blood flowed in streams that spiraled around his limp form, pooling below his feet.

Emery flicked her wrist and the blood split into three equal spheres. She pulled them toward her, as Dorian fell to the ground in a heap. Malcolm rushed over and offered him his wrist, replenishing the life force Emery had taken from him.

August's eyes flicked back to his mate, who was lost in the blood before her. She manipulated the spheres in a triangle, weaving her golden black magic between them. With each pass, her magic further wrapped itself around the blood, sealing it within.

The wind around her settled, and her lips tipped upward in a grin he'd been on the receiving end of too many times to count. It was one filled with smug satisfaction that signified she'd proven herself. What worried him was the cold glare in her eyes, pinned directly on him. Usually, once she was finished, her darkness relinquished control, but this time her eyes remained void of the amber he loved.

Emery floated the wrapped blood across the arena and set each of them down in front of the men she sought to prove wrong: one to Nico, one to Dorian, and the other to him.

"There's your blood, you heartless pricks."

August reached out and took the makeshift blood bag in his hand. Her magic hummed in his hand the way their bond once had.

"Well done," Nico commended her while August couldn't help the feeling in the pit of his stomach that continued to grow.

Malcolm brought the sphere to his mouth and tore through the magic with his fangs as the fae continued to feed from his wrist.

August sucked in a breath, and he wasn't the only one. From the corner of his eye, he saw Lily flinch and Bronwyn's eyes widen as they waited to see what would happen next. This was the test—to see if the dark blood's power would enhance the vampires' abilities.

Dorian's blood brimmed with dark magic, and while it wasn't exactly the same as Sloane's or her monsters', it was the closest thing they had for Emery to practice with. Malcolm's pupils dilated and a shiver racked his body before he turned to Dorian and chuckled. "Holy shit, Dorian. You've been holding out on us. I feel like I could run a marathon and then tear through an entire fucking army. I want to rage and go to war and fuck. Bloody hell, do I want to fuck."

A few of the sentinels let out a few whoops, and when August looked over at Lily, her cheeks were bright pink. She covered her eyes and shook her head, but no one missed the way her thighs clenched together.

"So, it worked?" Bronwyn asked. "Aside from the raging hard-on as a side effect."

"That might be because he's fae," Nico offered, still

examining the blood ball in his hand. "I wouldn't expect that reaction from Sloane's beasts' blood."

"Well, that's shitty, but I'm not complaining. It most definitely worked, though. I am so juiced up right now it's not even funny." Malcolm tugged his wrist from Dorian and hopped to his feet, crossing the space between him and Lily in the blink of an eye. He squatted down and picked up his mate. Lily squeaked but didn't protest. "Now if you'll excuse me, I think I'm going to go take care of a few things."

Everyone in the arena chuckled, but once Malcolm and Lily were gone, their focus fell back to where Emery stood, silent and void of any emotion.

She was a queen. Strong. Ruthless. Everything Emery wasn't. And yet it suited her. It was the side she'd fought to keep at bay. It was fucking gorgeous.

"If that's all, then I suggest we get back to training; we leave at dusk tomorrow for the mortal realm."

August adjusted himself in his pants and asked. "Do you think they're ready?"

He really meant to ask if she was ready.

Emery let out a sardonic laugh. Paired with her obsidian eyes, it was unsettling. "Do you hear this? Your king wants to know if we are ready? What do you say?"

The arena erupted in cheers and claims they were born ready for this battle.

August narrowed his gaze on Emery, but she was lost in the excitement of the war ahead.

"We've been ousted from our homes, branded as the outcasts by a witch who desires only power. And why? Because we want something greater for our future. She doesn't give two shits about us or our mates. All she wants is to control us, to take everything we hold dear and sacrifice it for what she deems is the proper path. But it's not. I've seen the future. A future in which we are allowed to hold love in our hearts and stand united as a formidable force in our world. She wants to take that from us. What we've built here goes beyond her vision. Our worlds are on the verge of destruction if we don't take back what is rightfully ours.

"We've trained for months. Overcome our differences. Faced horrors we should never have had to suffer through. And now is the time to fight for what is our star-given right. Our mates. Our families. Our realm." Emery paused, her dark gaze slowly drifting over every set of eyes staring back at her, witch, hybrid, wolf, and vampire alike. "You know your roles and what must be done, so let us take back our home and usher in the new era of supernaturals."

Her army replied with thunderous cheers and calls for blood. The blood of their enemy.

Even Bronwyn and Flora cheered on their friend, lost in the promise of their future.

August stood silently, his eyes locked on Emery. She was magnificent, embracing her role as queen and leader like he always knew she would. Only the woman standing before her wasn't the same as the one who had stepped into the arena this morning. She wasn't the woman he made love to for hours the night before.

No. The woman before him was all strength fueled by the darkness in her soul, and he was afraid he'd made a grave mistake pushing her to become the woman their army needed.

"Hug your loved ones tight tonight, because at dawn we fight!" she cried.

More cheers erupted and everyone began to crowd around Emery, chatting about the battle ahead. A few of the witches managed to conjure bottles of champagne and barrels of mead, and a celebration quickly took hold around them.

August pushed forward but lost sight of Emery in the commotion.

Nico appeared beside him and tugged him to the edges of the fray. "You know you're going to have to help her find her balance," he said, his expression serious.

August nodded, guilt gnawing at his heart. He'd never meant to push her this far. He's assumed it would be like learning to use her earth magic with the flower. He should have known nothing with dark magic was that simple.

"I'd hoped it wouldn't come to this. She is no doubt the future of your realm, but it is a fine line she must walk to maintain balance in her soul. If she were still your mate, I would suggest feeding the bond, but without it, I'm not sure how you can balance her."

"You wanted her to give in to this," August growled. "You pushed her as much as we did."

"Yes, but I wanted her to learn to separate the magic from the darkness that is rooted in her soul."

August pried his eyes from his mate and looked at Nico. "There's a difference?"

"Yes," Nico nodded, sincerity in his eyes. "And it will be different for your daughter too. So, I suggest you find out who her mate is because they will help her as you do Emery."

"How do you know all this?"

"When you've lived as long as I have, you pick up a thing or two." Nico pressed the magic sphere into August's hands alongside the one Emery had given to him and walked away, leaving him to stew on his words.

Bloody hell.

He'd done this. She wasn't like him when he was younger. She never wanted to be this person. Emery wanted to rule with compassion and grace, and yet he'd pushed her to wholly welcome her darkness in order to save their kingdom. She wanted their daughter to live in the light, but if Nico was right, this was something every one of their children would face. A call to the dark and a need for the light.

The Queen of Light and Dark. Their descendants would forever be locked in a war to balance themselves.

Blonde and pink hair caught his eye as Emery emerged from the fray, and August had to stifle the groan that bubbled in the back of his throat. She had her shoulders pinned back and her chin held high, the epitome of a regal queen and war general wrapped in the sexiest little body.

She peered up at him, her confidence unwavering even if her obsidian eyes were a smack in the face. He couldn't deny there was a part of him that found this part of her just as bloody intoxicating as her compassion, but as much as he would love to ravish her darkness into submission, that wasn't the answer. He could lead her there and be her tool, but Emery would ultimately need to find the will to balance both sides of herself.

Her lips turned up into a seductive smile, and in three swift steps she was in front of him, arms wrapped around his neck and lips clashing against his. Her hands gripped the front of his shirt, pulling him closer so their chests were flush, their stomachs, their hips, their— bloody hell, the heat radiating from her pussy was enough to make him rock hard.

And her mouth, gods, her mouth was exhilarating. Her tongue worked against his, tasting and accepting everything he had to give. A body-wide shudder ran through him, and his breath caught somewhere between his lungs and his mouth, drawing a moan from his throat.

His head spun as Emery's hands roamed up his chest and linked behind his neck.

More. She echoed in his head. *I need more.*

There were so many things they needed to discuss, but August was caught helpless by her whims. She could ask him for anything, and he'd give it to her.

Yes, take what you need. He replied, thankful for their soul bond's cooperation. There was nothing quite like hearing her in his head in the midst of carnal desire.

His hands slipped from her waist to the round of her ass and lifted her against him, dragging her pussy up the length of his cock.

Fuck, I need you.

"Ahem."

August registered the noise, but was too focused on giving Emery exactly what she needed.

"Ahem." The voice interrupted again, this time louder, and August tore his swollen lips from Emery's.

He turned his head slightly and locked eyes with Callum while Emery continued to pepper his chin and neck with kisses.

"This better be important," he growled.

"As much as I'd love to see where this," he waved his hand at the two of them tangled in each other, "is going to go, your mother wanted to make sure you got to see Lina before we leave in the morning."

Instantly, the need to fuck Emery senseless was doused like he'd been hit with a bucket of ice water.

"Thanks."

Callum smirked and shook his head.

Emery groaned and buried her face in his neck. "He's never going to let me live that down. Is everyone staring?"

August peered down at her, loving the heat in her cheeks. "Does it matter if they are?"

"We're their king and queen."

A wicked smile tipped his lips. "And as such, we should set an example for how to prepare for battle."

August looked around and chuckled. Not surprisingly, he found they weren't the only ones in a compromising state. "No, it seems the brink of war has lowered everyone's inhibitions. Not that they were high to begin with."

He slid Emery down his body and once she was firmly on the ground, tangled his fingers in her hair and tipped her head back so he could see her eyes.

August let out a sigh of relief when he saw they were no longer wholly obsidian. Around her iris, a small ring of amber pulsed.

There was hope.

"Rain check?" she smiled.

"If you think I'm going to war without fucking you senseless beforehand then you don't know me very well, little witch."

Emery's eyes vibrated with darkness, but a smile flitted across her lips. "Okay then—let's go see our daughter."

Chapter Forty-Two

EMERY

There was something to be said for darkness. It was the absence of light, the place where evil lurked and monsters thrived. But it was also the entity that allowed the stars to shine. The dark doesn't destroy the light in the night sky; it defines it. August hadn't been wrong when he'd said Emery had every reason to let go and give in to the demons in the dark. It understood the part of her in constant agony that craved vengeance. Holding back had been hard, but giving in... holy hell, giving in had been like taking a breath of fresh mountain air for the first time.

It was intoxicating.

The minute she gave into her darkness and allowed herself to wield the blood like it was her own, the whole world fell into place. It no longer mattered who she wanted to be; this was about who she was meant to be. The potent rush filled her chest to the point nothing else mattered. This was who she was.

Except it wasn't. Not anymore. Maybe at one time it

was who she was supposed to be, but that woman died months ago, slain on the veranda of the castle she was destined to rule.

Emery didn't give that woman enough credit; she was still learning who she was and where she belonged in this world. That woman would have been lost in the dark. Even with her mate at her side and a healthy fear of her dark magic, that version of herself didn't yet know what it meant to be a queen. She didn't understand that sacrifice brings its own darkness and stains the soul, allowing resentment to grow and monsters to be made. She didn't know how far her heart could break and still find the light. She didn't know...

The woman she became after death harbored all those same fears and fallacies, but she had something that would make all the difference.

Emery blinked back tears and squeezed the hand of the man next to her. The man who had given her life.

August didn't flinch, just squeezed back and kept walking toward the looming obsidian castle where their daughter waited.

Lina was their heart, but August was her life.

When she gave into the darkness and pulled Dorian's blood, wrapping it in her magic, she'd felt nothing but pure power. Most would assume that necromancy was the darker of the two black magicks, but they would be wrong. Blood was greater than death. It was the essence of mortality. Its most basic function was to deliver nutrients and do away with waste, but in their world, blood was the beginning and end of a being. It not only fed vampires but more than that it was the basis of their connections. Sires forever linked to their fledglings and mates bonded through exchange. Blood was at the center of it all.

But blood could also be used to their detriment. Emery hadn't realized just how deep blood ran in their world. There was a reason history books didn't talk about this magic. When you dabbled in blood, you ran the risk of forming connections with those you pulled it from.

She hadn't known what was happening at first. When she'd pulled blood from all those witches, it had been a minimal amount from each of them, and so there wasn't a thread formed between them. But when she'd drained Dorian, it became obvious that had she wanted to, she could have tethered him to her. In the same way Sloane used necromancy, Emery could control the living through their blood. She could forge and break them. In him, she saw the frayed ends left behind by the death of his bonded. She saw the growth of a thread that she assumed would tie him to Ansel. She saw the inner workings of everything that made Dorian who he was.

The cruel part was that she wanted to touch them. Her darkness urged her to break him—to make him theirs. To use him as a puppet to do her bidding. If it wasn't for the niggling piece of her soul that didn't belong to her, Emery might have given in to the darkest parts of herself.

She hadn't, because she wasn't that person anymore. She was Emery, August's mate, his queen and keeper of his soul.

"Are you mad at me?" August's voice pulled her from her thoughts. He stopped walking and tugged her hand, pulling her against him just outside the castle doors.

Emery scrunched her face and tilted her head. "Did that kiss say I was mad at you?"

"No, it's just..." August ran his hand through his hair nervously and looked at the ground beside them. "I pushed you to give into your darkness. I wanted you to face your fears but, your eyes...they're still dark. You're still fighting it."

She was. Now that she'd tasted the darkness, a part of her wanted to live in the heady realm of that magic, but more than that, she wanted the life she'd built.

Emery reached up and cupped his face, forcing him to look at her. "You pushed me to accept a part of me I was afraid to give into, and while it was both incredible and terrifying, I'm glad you did. I needed to know what I was up against, and if I could withstand the magic that made my sister go crazy. And while I will likely always fight the pull of the darkness, I know now that I will always be able to find my way back to the light."

"You will?" The hope in his voice made her smile, and she nodded.

He had no idea what he did for her. Just his presence in her world made staying in the light worth it. Sloane didn't have what she did, and she would forever pay the price.

Emery nodded. "Yes."

"It was the kiss, wasn't it?" August smirked.

"No." Emery chuckled and August cocked a brow. "Okay, the kiss helped. It grounded me, but it was your soul that kept me from falling into the deepest pits of my magic. My connection to you, to our daughter, to our kingdom—that's what brought me back initially. Even then, I was still in its grasp, fighting not to give into the need for more of the blend of blood and darkness. Finding you was all I could think about. Our soul bond may be dwindling, but it is still strong for the time being. That kiss, your hands on my body, the delicious way your body needs mine like it needs blood to survive, it's more intoxicating than any magic. So, while there are many things in our lives that keep me grounded in the light, it's you that makes me want to stay there."

August spun her and pressed her against the cool obsidian wall of the castle, burying his face in the crook of her neck. He dragged his fangs over his favorite spot, one hand tangling in her hair while the other dipped below her shirt and dug into the flesh at her hip. "Do you know how incredibly sexy that is, knowing that my touch is enough to bring you back from the brink of darkness?"

Emery let out a strangled moan as he ground his hips against her core. "About as sexy as it is knowing you are more than my darkness. You are my light."

"You need to stop saying things like that or we are never going to make it to our daughter," August rumbled.

Emery pressed against his chest and pushed him back so she could see his eyes. "Later then."

His lips tipped up into a fang-filled smirk. "I am going to wreck you, so no matter how much the darkness pulls at you in the heat of battle, you remember who you belong to."

"I wouldn't have it any other way."

They managed to make it up to the common room with only one more minor distraction. Emery mentioned that she wanted to test some theories about her magic while tasting August's blood and that sent him over the edge. He'd pressed her into an alcove and slipped his fingers into her pussy, bringing her to the cusp of an orgasm mumbling something about how it was unfair for her to mention his blood in her veins after losing their bond. Then, he walked away.

Her mind reeled with all the ways she was going to exact her revenge on him for leaving her a needy ball of arousal. At the same time, she didn't blame him one bit. Since the loss of their bond, she'd missed the connection they had whenever he shared his blood with her. She no longer felt the pull to consume it when they climaxed, which was a damn shame because his venom just didn't hit the same way as his blood.

Emery smiled as she pushed open the door, promising herself to be present instead of counting down the moments until she could get August back to their room, but stopped instantly when she saw that Cosmina and Lina weren't alone.

Ansel was stretched out on the floor, rolling over from his stomach to his back over and over, laughing as he mimicked Lina doing the same thing. The bottom of his shirt rose up from the waist of his sweats with every twist and turn, revealing faint white scars and yellow, healing bruises.

Emery brought her hand to her mouth and choked back a sob, alerting Ansel to their presence. He looked over his shoulder to see them standing in the doorway and a broad smile etched across his face.

Ansel looked down at Lina and then back up at her and August, and when he did, tears lined his eyes. "She's more perfect than I could ever imagine."

She'd envisioned this moment so many times. Before he was taken by Sloane, she'd always pictured Ansel being the fun uncle to her daughter. The one who taught her how to love fiercely, but also how to escape her room when she'd been put on timeout unjustly. Then he was taken and her only hope was that someday he'd get to meet the little girl that brought him into her life. He was her protector, but more than that, Ansel had become one of her closest friends.

Emery ran across the room, dropped to her knees, and pulled Ansel into a hug. He wrapped his arms around her, and she felt his tears mingle with hers on the side of her cheek.

"I am so sorry," Emery whispered. "You...I..."

She had planned what she would tell him so many times, but now that the time had come, no words seemed to convey how sorry she was that he had to endure Sloane's torture.

"Hey," Ansel pulled back and wiped his thumb across her cheek. "I am here. I am fucked up beyond belief, but I am here and that is thanks to you."

Emery gave a half-hearted chuckle and nodded. "You were already fucked up."

"You aren't wrong." A half smile tipped his lips and he looked up at August. "I really hated you, bloodsucker."

"I know, guard dog," August said with a smirk and offered Ansel his hand. He pulled the wolf from the ground into a hug, both patting each other on the back. "I'm sorry I had to make you believe I was a traitor. It was the only way."

"I know that now, but let me tell you, there were more than a few times I imagined all the ways I was going to rip your body from your head and deliver it at Emery's feet."

"If I ever betray my queen, I would expect nothing less."

Emery gathered up Lina and hugged her to her chest before sliding onto one of the oversized sofas across from Cosmina while Ansel and August poured themselves a drink. Before they could sit down, Flora and Draven joined them with Kade and Mateo not far behind. Tears streamed down her face as August snuggled in beside her and Lina, and they witnessed each of the wolves welcome their pack mate home.

By the time everyone settled in, Bronwyn and Brax had also joined them, along with Malcolm and Lily, who stumbled in wearing wide smiles and looking more than a little disheveled.

Emery glanced around the room, her heart full, but there were still two missing from their little family.

As if conjured by her thoughts, Callum and Dorian stepped through the doorway.

Now they were complete.

Unsurprisingly, Callum made a beeline for the bar cart, pouring himself two fingers, while Dorian only had eyes for Ansel, who sat on the floor against the couch Emery shared with August.

In two swift steps, Dorian closed the distance and knelt before him, pressing a kiss to Ansel's forehead. "Are you sure you are well enough to be here?"

Ansel reached up and placed a chaste kiss on his lips. "There is no place I would rather be than with our family."

Emery's heart swelled in her chest and her magic hummed. She looked down at Lina, and then up at every person present in the room. This was what the light was. This was what kept her grounded and made it possible to fight another day. It didn't matter what bloodline or pack they came from; it was the smiles on each of their faces, the loyalty in their blood, but most importantly, the love in their hearts that mattered.

Emery unlaced her fingers from August's and stood with Lina on her hip. Then she picked up her glass from the table beside her and lifted it into the air. "I'd like to propose a toast."

Everyone in the room grew silent, all eyes on her.

"Tomorrow, we go to war."

"I'm pretty sure we've already heard this speech," Bronwyn snorted, and everyone chuckled.

Emery rolled her eyes.

"I didn't," Malcolm offered.

"That's because you were too busy nailing your mate," Callum muttered from behind his whiskey, before taking a long sip.

Malcolm snarled, but offered Callum a half smile after Lily smacked his arm. "I'm not the one who dishonored your name."

Lily raised a brow as if to say he'd done plenty of dishonoring, and Emery couldn't help but smile.

"Alright, alright. Enough of that, this one is different," Emery continued. "This one is short and sweet. It's to you. My family. There is no one I would rather have at my side, protecting my daughter and our kingdom."

A chorus of, "Hear, hear!" and "To family!" filled the room.

Callum cleared his throat, and everyone turned and looked in his direction. His eyes locked on Emery and for the first time she realized they were bloodshot. She wanted to ask if he was okay, if something had happened, but how could she? She was the only one who knew the choice he had to make.

Callum nodded and lifted his glass. "To August and Emery. The king and queen our world deserves."

Everyone cheered again, and August wrapped his arm around her and Lina and tugged them against his side. Emery looked up at him and smiled.

"Your eyes. They're amber again."

"This is my light. You and Lina and all of them."

He pressed a kiss to her forehead. "As you are mine."

This was their moment. She could feel it. They were on the cusp of something great. Something new. And now that her family was complete again, all they had to do was win. Which was exactly what she planned to do.

Chapter Forty Three

EMERY

THE WORLD FELL AWAY FROM HER AS THE VISION GRIPPED HER spine.

Bodies everywhere. Covered in sheets, blood seeping through the white fabric. Sloane looking out the window of the bedroom they used to share. The pyres. So many pyres. One in particular caught her eye. The crest of the sword on top glinted in the setting sun. The Nicholson crest. Eyes. Amber. Blue. Purple. Black. Silver vines etched on flesh. An obsidian haze. A heart rolling from blackened fingers. The sun rising over their castle.

Her heart pounded in her chest to the steady beat of an imaginary war drum, and the dark magic coursing through her veins begged to be unleashed as she came back to the present.

Emery inhaled a steadying breath in an attempt to calm the raging swell of darkness inside her. The vision wasn't anything helpful, but it was something. She felt it at her core. The problem was she didn't have the time to decipher what it meant.

Her magic swirled, and Emery silently reminded herself it was almost time and she would be able to unleash this newfound weapon on their enemies. A fact she shouldn't like as much as she did.

She peered through the front gates, across the manicured lawn. The castle was quiet. Too quiet. But that didn't mean that they'd been discovered. It was likely its occupants were still hungover from the ball at which her mate bond had been stripped from her.

Thank the gods the time difference in Enchanth worked in their favor, giving them triple the time to prepare for this attack. Still, Emery was left with mixed feelings about the battle ahead.

The light of dusk danced across the sky and bounced off the intricate stone castle in an array of yellows and oranges. Emery exhaled a deep sigh, remembering the first time she'd laid eyes on the structure.

She hadn't known it then but she'd been a lost woman with no purpose, no direction other than to keep her throat free of fangs and stay in line with what she'd been told.

"Everyone is in position," Dorian whispered beside her.

Emery nodded and managed a half smile, grateful for supernatural metabolisms.

Their army had celebrated life into the early hours of the Enchanth suns while she'd spent the night and most of the day with her mate doing their own celebrating. He'd offered to heal her when she woke to sound the alarm to gather their troops, but Emery liked having the delicious ache between her legs. It was another reminder of who and what she was fighting for.

She glanced to her right and took her time allowing her eyes to travel over August's war-ready form. He was dressed like her and the other sentinels and witches in all-black tactical gear made from thick Kevlar and spelled to repel magic. While the uniform had the ability to make anyone look like a badass, it also made August downright mouthwatering.

His eyes didn't leave the castle, but August tipped his head so she could see his lips upturned slightly at the sides. "If you keep looking at me like that, I'll have you riding my cock instead of marching into battle."

"I might like that."

"Don't tempt me, little witch. I'm already on edge letting you anywhere near your sister."

Emery's lips twitched and she tried not to smile at his sweet sentiment. "You know I have to—"

"I know," he growled, his ocean eyes finding hers. "But knowing and watching you walk away from me are two different things. Especially when I can't feel you and I can only hear you in my head fifty percent of the time."

He was right to be worried. She was too, but not because of their bond. After feeling the way he pulled her back from the darkness, Emery was confident it was strong enough to get them through the battle. She'd worry about what it meant that they couldn't hear each other after this was over. She couldn't think about the fact that she could be forced to leave them behind. Not when war waited for them with their next breath.

She went up on tiptoe and pressed a kiss to his cheek before whispering, "I promise to come back to you."

August wrapped his arm around her waist and held her against him. "You wouldn't be here if I didn't think you would come back. I'd have tied your ass to our bed and left you in Enchanth if I thought I might lose you. But you are our greatest asset. You are why we are going to be victorious. We won't make it out unscathed, but I have no doubt we are going to see the light of tomorrow."

Emery's mouth fell open, and he used the opportunity to press his lips to hers, his tongue sweeping in languid strokes against hers. It was more than a kiss—it was a promise that he believed in her more than his next breath, which shocked the hell out of Emery.

When they finally let him in on the plan earlier that morning, August nearly tore apart the solid oak table of their makeshift war room. There'd been no easy way to tell him she'd be going after Sloane alone.

August twisted the braid at the nape of her neck around his fist and forcefully ended their kiss, pulling her back so she could meet his gaze, "Give them hell, little witch."

Emery's chest heaved, out of breath, but she managed to nod.

The plan was simple. Their strongest witches, including Lily and Bronwyn, would lead a team of witches and sentinels through her cottage and bring down the wards in designated spots around the castle for their sentinels to enter. Once they were down, Emery and August would lead the charge through the front of the castle. Malcolm and Callum would head for the barracks to rendezvous with Cody and the sentinels still loyal to them inside. Draven and Flora would lead a team from the west, with Nina and Brax meeting Lily and Bronwyn on the east side. The goal was to take the castle and thin Sloane's ranks while getting out as many innocent bystanders as they could.

There would no doubt be losses, but the hope was to

take the castle with as few casualties as possible. Dorian would be their go-between, relaying information to each of them, allowing him to be kept out of the fray so as not to upset the balance of fae involvement in their realm.

Dorian chuckled huskily. "If you're done flooding the battlefield with your arousal, I suggest we get moving before we give ourselves away."

Emery rolled her eyes, and August let out a low snarl. "What happened to my agreeable second-in-command?"

"Ansel's mad at him and now we're all being punished," Emery snorted.

Ansel had begrudgingly agreed to stay behind and watch over the women and children in Enchanth who were not prepared for battle. Many of the witches did their part beforehand, supplying those who had magic that could be wielded as a weapon with extra spells and components to be used on the battlefield. Dorian deemed Ansel one of those who needed to stay behind, and Emery got the impression it was for his benefit and not Ansel's. The exact words he used were, "I forbid you from going near that sadistic witch bitch again," before storming off through Emery's portal to the castle.

"Just apologize and offer him your dick," August offered.

Dorian cocked a brow. "Because that works so well for you?"

"While his dick game is on point, his groveling could use some work," Emery smirked. "Seriously though, I think Ansel will forgive you. I'd be pissed if I'd been forced to stay back too."

"I should spank your pretty ass for that."

"Don't worry, I'll teach you the art of groveling," Emery winked at him.

"As long as you're on your knees, I'll allow it," August muttered through his teeth.

"If you two are done, I'm leaving to go tell Lily to bring down the wards."

Dorian popped out of existence at the same time movement caught her eye, and Emery turned to see a single figure standing in the middle of the veranda at the front of the castle. She'd recognize the witch anywhere. It was the woman she'd called her best friend for so many years. The one who had betrayed her and sided with her sister in the name of power.

Wren looked straight out and Emery could feel her eyes on them, even though their army hid behind the tree line. She tipped her head back and opened her palms, her magic humming in the air. It was dark but not as dark as what would come from a witch born in darkness. Still, there was a malice behind it that left Emery wondering if they really stood a chance.

Emery sucked in a breath and waited for Wren's next move. She ignored the way her heart wanted to weep for her friend and the path she'd chosen, while the inky magic in her chest had no problem condemning Wren to death.

Wren called her magic to her palms and green sparks erupted. Two mirror portals opened on either side of the grand staircase leading down to the lawn, and an army of beasts and sentinels marched through with weapons strapped to their backs and a fire in their stare. A wicked smile stretched across Wren's face before turning back into the castle, leaving Sloane's army to fight a battle they believed they'd already won.

"Fuck," Emery whispered. So much for having the element of surprise.

Sadness bloomed in her chest as she looked over the sea of beasts and sentinels that flooded the space between them and the castle. The beasts might be controlled by Sloane, but the men and women weren't. They were supposed to be their people, but they had chosen to fight for her sister. Whether it be because they wanted the option to stick with tradition and deny their mates or because they thought Sloane was the logical choice, they were now their enemies.

Nausea rolled through her and her magicks warred in her. Nothing about this was right. They were supposed to unite the kingdom, not kill those who opposed them. And yet, it was kill or be killed. Her darkness understood that, so reluctantly, Emery followed. Her light retreated, allowing the tendrils of obsidian to take the helm.

Emery looked up, meeting August's ocean eyes for what she hoped wasn't the last time.

"Let's take back our kingdom, little witch."

"Gladly."

Emery opened her palms and, using her wind to propel her magic into the air, sent orbs high above the castle where they exploded into shimmering gold and black flecks and fell like embers to the ground. It was their signal that the battle had begun, a sign meant to unify them as they entered the darkest moment of their lives.

She inhaled the air not yet stale with blood and sent a silent prayer to the gods or the fates, really whoever was listening, that they be seen and protected. Her mind itched with the fact that if they lost this battle, they would lose everything, but she refused to scratch it. She needed to be present.

August's knuckles brushed against hers and she turned, noticing how he was no longer smiling. "I love you," he whispered.

"Always," she replied.

Emery stretched up on tiptoe and pressed a kiss to his cheek before turning to face the army marching toward her. She stepped out of the trees and up to the gate of the castle, flicking it open with her magic. Crossing the threshold with ease, she smiled at the marvelous job her witches had done taking down the wards. When she reached the edge of the grass, she paused.

She closed her eyes and breathed slowly, feeling the magic in her chest. It swirled with anticipation, as if it could taste the blood and mayhem that would be hers momentarily.

This was their final stand.

All around her, creatures, friend and foe, held their breath waiting for her next move. Sweat dripped from her brow under the waning sun. She tipped her head back, relishing its last rays of warmth. In moments, there would be nothing but shadows and blood. Emery then stretched her fingers wide and called her magic to her palms.

"Attack!"

She heard the cry from the heart of Sloane's army, but it was already too late for them.

The wind picked up around her, the elemental witches at her back setting the stage. The once cloudless sky rolled with ominous waves of gray and rumbled with the sounds of war. Rain poured like waterfalls and pooled at her feet, begging to be tainted with the blood of their enemy.

Emery lifted her arms wide, feeling for the pulse of the beasts before her. They beat as one, more magic than man. These beasts had once been human before Sloane twisted them in death to be hers, and yet there was no hope for them. She grasped the darkness and a gasp fell from her throat. She dropped her chin and met their gaze, the blackest depths, and yet there was light buried in their essence. Her light. The blood Sloane used to keep them alive was Emery's.

Like called to like.

Nico's words echoed in her ears as she latched on to the light, and intertwined it with her darkness. Her soul warred, mourning the loss of life, while her magic cackled with delight as it pulled the essence from every last beast. One by one, they began to howl to the sky above, but there was no one to hear their cries or intercede on their behalf. She was their deliverance and executioner, and none would be spared.

Her dark magic cheered her on as one by one each of the monsters fell under her spell. It wanted her to own them, to make them hers, but Emery fought against it. She remembered that they were once alive. They were once her people. Dorian's people. August's people. Then she remembered what young Haven had told her all those weeks ago. She'd said the dead didn't like to be controlled.

So, Emery gave the dead their peace. Blood pooled at the corner of her eyes, washed away by the rain as she pulled their blood toward her, forming tiny spheres above the beasts. Their army started to drop one by one, hitting the wet ground with resounding thuds.

Magic hummed around her and she felt the weight of

her army approaching behind her. The earth quaked and split apart as the bodies fell to their final resting place.

The coppery smell of blood filled the air, and Sloane's sentinels stood with their eyes wide and jaws open. It was poetic, and Emery wished she had a damn camera to document the moment they realized they had chosen the wrong side.

She worked the tendrils of her magic through the blood, turning the spheres into the power-packed juice boxes to fuel her sentinels when a flash of movement moved toward her. A second blur crossed her path and blood splattered in a fine mist toward her, revealing August, chest heaving and face covered in the blood of the sentinels who dared charge her.

"I think it's time to wrap this up, princess," August muttered against her ear. "Those sentinels aren't going to stand there looking stupid for long."

Emery nodded and flicked her wrist, wrapping the last of the blood in her magic and pulling them toward her so they sat in a line on either side of her.

"Eat up, boys," she hollered, and all hell broke loose.

Chapter Forty-Four

EMERY

In the blink of an eye, it all became real.

It was one thing to take out the beasts. Even though they had once been human, they were never supposed to exist. They died the moment they became beasts. But the blood at her feet now was not from those who needed to find peace in death.

August withdrew the sword from his back, and sliced clean through the sentinel who thought to engage him. He turned and looked at Emery with a wicked grin on his face that told her just how much he enjoyed being on the battlefield again. "Emery! Our witches!"

Emery hesitated for a beat, before his words registered. Right. She needed to boost their power so they'd last through the battle.

Light magic. Give them only the light, she reminded herself. She couldn't subject them to the rage in her veins. Not if she wanted them to survive this.

Rubbing her hands together, Emery pulled all the light

she'd taken from the beasts and a fraction of her own until a ball of gold formed between her fingers. She then threw it up into the air and pushed her hands apart, willing her magic to find its like and boost her witches in battle.

Sparks of gold flew like embers, refracting off the rain and shimmering down until they found the bodies of each of their witches.

Emery watched as their magic grew brighter and more powerful. Blasts of magic not only hit, but obliterated their marks. Her lips curled up into a smile as she huffed a laugh of disbelief, even though she felt as though she might fall over from the loss of the light.

It worked.

Sure, the dark filled in the cracks where her light once resided, but what mattered was it worked.

The clank of a sword next to her ear brought her back to the moment, and Emery stumbled away from the attack. She locked eyes with a murderous sentinel and followed the cross of swords to the hilt of August's.

"That's twice I've saved you," he grunted, swinging the blades away from her and lunging forward to impale the sentinel.

"Are we keeping score now?" she asked, blasting a sentinel that moved to take a swing at August from behind. "Because I'm pretty sure that between this and my epic castle rescue, we're even now."

"We'll see." He grinned and winked. "Now go, the rest of our army needs your little power boost."

She nodded and sarcastically blew him a kiss before opening a portal to the east side of the castle where Lily and Bronwyn had met up with Nina and Brax and were waiting for her.

Her hair whipped around her face as she stepped through, and a wall of wind magic hit her. Emery screamed as her knees hit the dirt and she ducked below a stream of teal magic being hurled in her direction.

"Sorry!" Bronwyn shouted from across the clearing by the stables. "I didn't know if you were with us or them."

"Who the hell else do you know with gold magic?" she grunted and pushed to her feet.

The clearing between the forest and castle was lit with magic of every color mixed, and the clang of swords filled the air. Bodies littered the ground, and at a glance it was hard to tell if they belonged to them or their enemies.

Fuck war.

Emery pushed a wall of air in front of her, using it not only to part the battlefield but also to protect herself from any attackers. With every step, her feet squished into the blood and rain-soaked ground, and the darkness in her chest itched to be set free so it could contribute to the bloodshed. On the edges of her sight, her magic sent visions of every way it would enjoy dismembering their enemies.

Not now. You'll have your chance. First, we help our people, then you can destroy their queen.

It hummed in agreement, but Emery sensed its underlying reluctance. The darkness she'd pulled from the beasts on the front lawn nearly filled her wells, and she was about to test the capacity three more times before she faced Sloane. Worried about the darkness simmering in the back of her mind, Emery struggled to concentrate. Unleashing the darkness on her people wasn't an option; the darkness wasn't a part of them, and it would rip them apart. She didn't feel as though she had enough control over it to only target their enemies.

"Cover me," she shouted to Bronwyn and Lily, who fought back-to-back against a frothy-fanged beast that had a few tufts of hair missing from its chest and a deep wound across its eye and down its snout. It snarled and lunged toward Lily, who only narrowly jumped back in time to avoid its clawed hand.

"A little busy here, lass," Lily snapped.

Bronwyn shot a blast of teal magic that swirled into a flail at the last minute and lodged its spiked ball into the skull of the beast. After sinking into his flesh, the weapon disappeared, leaving behind a gaping wound. The beast staggered on its feet but didn't go down.

"Of course you couldn't use daggers," Emery huffed a laugh.

Bronwyn grunted. "Where's the fun in that?"

"Just make sure I don't get hit."

Bronwyn nodded and turned her focus back to the snarling beast. Emery didn't waste a second and got to work, letting her darkness reach for the blood of the beasts. She focused again on the smidge of her light magic in each of them and wrapped their blood into pools as it poured from their faces. While the light bent to her will, the dark dug its claws in her chest, taking root in its new home.

Emery fell to her knees, swallowing painfully past the narrowing in her throat. She tried to focus on the task at hand, but it was growing harder and harder for her to ignore the call of the malice in her soul. She reached out for August to ground her, but found only the empty place where their mate bond used to reside. Their soul bond was still there, but she didn't want to distract him from his own battle and risk something happening to him.

When she completed the balls of blood, she scattered them for their sentinels to grab. They did so greedily.

A shiver racked Bronwyn's body, and she shook her head. "I will never get used to seeing that."

"Well, hang on because your power boost is coming next."

The sound of steel striking steel echoed around her in time with the darkness sloshing in her chest. She was filled to the brim now. It was a stupid idea to try and push herself; she needed to expel some of the darkness, but that magic was meant for one thing and one thing only. It was the only way she was going to defeat Sloane.

She tuned out the battle around her and harnessed the small well of golden magic, calling it to the surface. The warmth of the light spread through her, vibrating under her skin and wrapping her in its embrace. It wasn't cunning or malicious like the dark, but it held power in its own right.

The tendrils of gold left her palms. It trickled over the battlefield, steering clear of the dark, tainted magic that vibrated from Sloane's witches, and once again finding her people. Her magic filled their wells, giving them a second wind against their enemies.

"Fuck," Emery cried out and fell forward, the weight of the dark magic in her chest taking its toll.

"Emery, are you okay?" Lily yelled, pushing forward and knocking a sentinel sideways with a blast of magic while another witch used her elemental fire to torch the vampire where he stood.

"I'll be fine," she growled and lifted her hand to wipe the sweat from her brow.

A small gasp fell from her mouth as she looked down and saw the tips of her fingers were completely black, much like Dorian's and Nico's in their fae form. Like Sloane's.

Her hand shook and a wave of anxiety gripped her spine as she took in the visceral representation of the darkness taking over. She needed a release.

The glint of steel caught her eye as a sentinel lifted his blade behind Bronwyn. Emery lifted her hand and instinctively shot a blast of magic at the enemy, but what came from her was not the light magic she'd pulled. Instead, an obsidian sphere flew from her hands and the vampire exploded upon impact, covering them both in entrails.

Bronwyn's eyes shifted to Emery, wide with either fear or admiration, it was hard for her to tell.

"I think you have intestines in your hair," she chuckled, and turned to blast another sentinel, ignoring the fact Emery had used her dark magic as a weapon for the first time.

"Better than the ear on your shoulder."

Bronwyn looked down and shuttered. "Ew, gross." She flicked it off and jumped back into the fray.

As Emery pulled herself from the ground, a witch moved to attack her, snarling as orange light filled her palms. "You will never enslave us to fucking vampires."

The witch thrust her magic toward Emery, muttering an incantation under her breath that turned the light into spinning circular blades.

Emery lifted her hands, and a wall of darkness formed

in front of her, blocking them. What happened next only confirmed why she shouldn't have allowed this magic out to play. The wall dissipated into a thick black smoke as if it had a mind of its own and wrapped its tendrils around the offending witch. Her eyes widened, and she flailed against the magic that cinched around her throat and lifted her off the ground. She screamed as blood oozed from her mouth and lips until the magic cut through her flesh and severed her head from her body.

Blood spattered against Emery's face, but before she could register the weight of what had happened, she felt a tug on her shoulder. She spun on her heel and was hit square in the stomach with a blast of magic. She winced and looked down, and it wasn't until she saw the damage the blade magic had done that she cried out and fell to her knees.

She sucked in a breath, tasting copper on her tongue and peered up at her attacker. Wren stood with magic in her hands and a menacing grin etched on her face.

"You didn't think you were going to win, did you? Even with your little parlor trick taking out our first wave of beasts and taking your traitorous sentinels back. We are backed by the God of Death. There is no hope for you."

Emery spit the blood from her mouth and focused on the tiny twitch at the corner of Wren's eye as she lied through her teeth. To anyone else, Wren's confidence would have inspired fear and hesitancy, but this woman had once been Emery's best friend. At one point she knew Wren better than anyone in the world, or so she'd thought. That twitch was Wren's ultimate tell.

They weren't losing at all. In fact, glancing beyond

where Wren was standing, Emery could see the way her people were easily taking down Sloane's forces.

That wouldn't help her, though. Blood poured from Emery's abdomen, and if she didn't get help soon, she wouldn't live to see their victory.

Lily and Bronwyn started toward her, but Wren flicked her wrist and smoke surrounded them. In the depths of the mist, Emery could see the illusions woven to distract her would-be saviors.

Emery coughed and pain shot through her. She lifted her hand to try to shoot a ball of darkness at Wren, but no magic came. It was more focused on trying to keep her from dying on the battlefield, creating a barrier between her organs and the outside world.

Tears formed in her eyes. This couldn't be how it ended for her. She still had so many people to help. So many moments to share with August and Lina.

Wren stepped forward, the light in her hands brightening. "I'll make sure to tell Lina you loved her," she sneered.

Emery looked up from the ground and opened her mouth to respond, but before she could, Wren winced and blood dripped from her lips. She wheezed before her body crumpled to the ground. revealing Ansel standing behind her, Wren's heart in his clawed hand.

His chest heaved, and he shot her a menacing grin that matched his feral gaze. "You didn't really think I'd let you guys have all the fun, did you?"

A laugh bubbled in her throat but came out a strangled mess. "How?" she whispered, her eyes drifting to where the illusions around them dissipated. They'd stopped Lily and Bronwyn from reaching her, but somehow Ansel managed to make it through.

"I've been to hell at her hands. The illusions don't scare me anymore." Ansel scooped her up, careful of her wound. "Now let's get you to August."

Emery winced and glanced down at her stomach to where obsidian wisps of magic knitted against her skin, trying to stop the bleeding, but only managing to slow it to a trickle.

Ansel turned to take a step toward the castle, but his path was blocked when Dorian popped into existence in front of them. He landed behind an unsuspecting sentinel who was eyeing her and Ansel. Reaching up, he snapped the neck of their enemy, rambling on before he registered whose arms she was in. "What the hell happened, Emery? August said he felt your soul begin to diminish."

His eyes went wide when he saw her in Ansel's arms. "What the fuck are you doing here?"

Before Ansel could answer, Dorian stepped forward, wrapped his arms around the two of them, and the world tilted. The battlefield around them faded away, replaced by the golden walls of the throne room.

If she wasn't trying to keep a grip on the world around her, she might have cared that the floor was littered with the bodies of beasts and sentinels, many of them ripped into pieces.

Ansel set her down on the dais, and Dorian glared at him. "I'll deal with you in a minute," he growled and knelt in front of Emery. He pulled out a small vial of a vibrant red liquid that swirled with gold and silver. It looked familiar to her.

"Don't ask questions, just drink this."

She suspected it was the same liquid that was in the rock Addia placed on Kenna's chest.

Emery cocked a brow. "Is this you and Nico not getting involved?"

"Precisely."

Emery drank it down, and then gaped at the way her magic reabsorbed into her flesh, repairing the damage in seconds. Soon, there were nothing but three angry red lines where Wren's dagger magic had torn into her. Dorian smiled as Emery lifted her head and nodded her thanks.

His smile didn't last as he shifted his gaze to Ansel, surely ready to berate him.

But Ansel wasn't having any of it. He crossed the short distance between them and crashed his lips to Dorian's, stunning him into silence.

When Ansel pulled away, Dorian looked at him wide-eyed and breathless.

"I'm not leaving," Ansel declared. "This is as much my fight as it is yours and Emery's. So, yell all you want or have my back, either way I'm not going anywhere."

Dorian's jaw tightened, and he slid his hand into Ansel's and gave it a squeeze. "Fine, but you stay with me. I'm not losing you again."

Ansel snarled, but reluctantly nodded. "Deal."

"Where is everyone?" Emery asked, her eyes darting around the throne room.

"Every team except Lily's and Bronwyn's have made it to the castle, but they didn't look far behind."

"Casualties?"

"Too many to count." Dorian replied, his gaze consistently drifting back to Ansel like he expected him to disappear. "Kade took a pretty severe blade to the neck, but other than that, all of our family is accounted for."

Emery nodded. "Has anyone seen Sloane?"

Dorian's lips pressed together. "No."

Emery knew the answer before he said it. One part of her vision filtered through her mind, and a wicked smile stretched across her lips. She knew exactly where Sloane was hiding.

Emery stretched her arms up and out, the skin of her abdomen still tight. "Where is August?"

"The great hall." Dorian stood and offered her his hand to help her up. "There was a situation."

"What does that mean?" Emery took his hand, and he tugged her to standing, but she didn't miss the way Dorian avoided her gaze.

"Jessi."

His fledgling.

"Take me there now," Emery snarled.

Dorian nodded and placed a hand on her and Ansel's shoulders, sieving them to the great hall.

They landed at the top of the stairs. The same stairs she'd walked down all those months ago when she'd chosen August. Before he knew she was a witch. Before they were intended. When they were just two beings fighting a love they didn't understand.

The walls of the room were lined with a few sentinels, along with Draven, Flora, and Callum. Their eyes were trained on the center of the room and the tense look on their faces told her just how much they wanted to jump in and end the fight.

Jessi zoomed across the ballroom, her fist connecting with August's jaw. Emery tightened her hands into fists at her sides at the same time her magic flared in her chest. She didn't need the darkness to know that Jessi was not long for this realm. The only thing stopping her from blasting her with the magic that itched to take her life was the fact that August had allowed her to take that punch. He was allowing her to live.

This woman was his fledgling, and that meant that she had a bond with August that Emery would never understand. It clearly meant something to August, too, otherwise she would be dead.

That was the only thing stopping Emery from smiting the woman with her darkness and ending her existence.

August recovered quickly. Spinning with the punch and sweeping his leg out, he tripped Jessi, who went tumbling toward the ground.

"Give up," August growled but it sounded more like a plea.

Jessi tipped her head back, laughing. "Like hell. I am not going back to what I was before. I am not second to her. I am not going to bow to you."

"But you'll bow to Sloane?" August quirked a brow, and set himself for another blow.

Jessi's eyes softened for a split second, and Emery saw what she was sure August did. A girl broken by their world. "She sees my worth."

"She used you to get to me." August's voice was less growl this time and more diplomatic.

"And?" Jessi scoffed. "That's more than you ever did."

August slowly walked toward her, careful not to spook her into running or another blow to his head. "So, you would rather be used. Used by my father. Used by Sloane. Is that what you aspire to be?"

Tears welled in Jessi's eyes, and she bared her fangs in his direction. "What I aspire to be is none of your business."

Emery's heart broke for her. This woman had no say in being thrust into the supernatural world. She was a grade A cunt, but how much of that was because she felt she had to be? The whole thing was a mess, but for the first time Emery was looking at her with different eyes.

"Then how does this end then, Jessi?"

A scathing grin stretched across Jessi's face as she nodded in Emery's direction. "With her dead."

It was the final nail in her coffin.

Jessi darted toward the stairs where Emery stood, but she didn't make it more than three steps before August was on her, his hand in her chest.

"I'm sorry I failed you as a sire," August whispered.

"Long live the Mistress." The words fell from her trembling lips as August pulled her heart from her chest.

Emery choked back a sob, and hot tears burned in her eyes. Not because Jessi was dead, but because of the look of utter defeat on August's face.

She raced down the stairs and wrapped her arms around his waist. Jessi's heart fell to the floor beside her body, and August shook against her.

"I'm sorry," she whispered into his chest, and he slumped into her.

Time stood still, and she didn't know how many moments passed before August spoke.

"Don't be." His body quieted, the moment to mourn her over. "I was foolish to believe she'd ever change. She betrayed us over and over again. It's better she's dead."

That didn't mean it was okay. Jessi never deserved

August, not as a king and certainly not as a sire, but that didn't change the fact that she belonged to him, and her death took a part of him. The sadness in his tone ignited her own, and she mourned for a woman she hated.

Emery was opening her mouth to soothe him when a wave of magic rolled over them. Emery's stomach turned, her sister's darkness seeping through the deepest parts of her as if it were searching for something.

"What the hell is that?" Flora asked, stumbling off the wall toward where she stood with August.

Callum and Draven helped her stay upright, their own expressions twisted in pain.

Sweat dripped from Emery's brow as she focused on pulling her sister's magic away from her family and forcing it into Jessi's lifeless corpse. Around her, a few of the sentinels behind August bent over and vomited their guts out. Emery pulled the magic from them as well.

"It's Sloane," Emery ground out, focusing on Jessi's body and easing the magic from around them into it.

And then it twitched.

Emery blinked, trying to ascertain if she'd really seen Jessi's arm move or if her own magic was playing tricks on her. Then the ground began to quake, and her leg jerked from lying to bent at the knee.

"Did her leg just…?"

"Yeah." August nodded.

The door to the great hall burst open, banging against the wall as Malcolm, Lily, and Bronwyn slid to a stop at the top of the staircase, covered in blood and debris.

"We have a problem," Malcolm announced.

The once lifeless corpse at her feet grunted, and

Emery's gaze snapped back down to where Jessi's eyes popped back open, glowing and silver.

"She's reanimating the dead," Emery whispered, defeat staining her voice. They couldn't fight this battle again. If she gave their army every ounce of dark magic in her veins, then she couldn't stop Sloane. There was only one answer: they had to find her and face her *now*.

"We need to find her and end this," Callum whispered beside her, putting her thoughts into words.

Emery nodded. "I know where she is."

August slid his hand into hers and gave it a gentle squeeze. "Then let's do this, little witch."

Chapter Forty Five

EMERY

EMERY STARED AT THE DOOR. IT WAS POETIC, REALLY, THAT Sloane had chosen to hole herself up in the room they'd both used as women of the Culling. The room had once made her feel close to her twin, and then it only reminded her of how vastly different they were. Now...she considered the emotions racking her mind and body. It might have been seeing the countless dead on their way through the castle, or the look on Ansel's face when she'd found him. Or maybe everything changed when she'd taken August away from her by stripping them of their bond. It could also have been the well of darkness brimming in her chest, but looking at the door, Emery felt nothing for her sister.

"Are you ready for this?" August asked, his voice filled with concern.

No.

Yes.

Maybe.

She couldn't tell him that. He needed to believe she was ready or he wouldn't let her cross the threshold and face the one woman who had the power to end her and bring her back ten times over just for her sadistic pleasure.

The truth was, her sister needed to die. Their realm was in danger because of her. Their people would never have the option to know their mates. But most importantly, Emery knew Sloane's tyranny would know no bounds. She'd tasted the darkness and knew what it was capable of. And if what the gods said was true and Dal was guiding her, then there would be no end to the destruction they could cause.

That didn't mean Emery didn't still mourn the loss of what could have been with Sloane.

"I'm as ready as I'm ever going to be."

"I know you need to do this on your own, but I'm here."

"Always. I know." Emery looked up at him and closed her eyes as he leaned in and pressed a kiss to her forehead.

August stayed behind her as she pushed open the door and stepped into the familiar space. Nothing in the room had changed. She expected it to be completely different after her departure from the castle to New Orleans, but it wasn't. She knew August used to go there when they were apart, but she'd figured he'd at least had the reminders of her removed when he was Augustine. He hadn't. Or maybe he'd put everything back, because everything was the same, down to the picture of her, Chelsea, and Flora on the nightstand.

Her gaze slid to the window where Sloane stood staring out through the glass at what Emery knew was the west lawn that led around to the gardens. The cries of battle ramping up again faintly echoed below, and Emery's heart sank.

Her sister turned slightly and Emery could see her profile. Sloane's eyes were hollowed, and dark purple circles marred the area under them. Her cheeks were carved out, cavernous and empty. In the twenty-four hours since she'd broken August and Emery's mate bond, it seemed she'd aged at least twenty years.

"If you're wondering if it was worth it, it absolutely was," Sloane sneered.

"I don't wonder anything about you, Sloane. Not anymore."

Sloane turned around so Emery could see the stuffed green dragon she held.

Sage.

It was the twin to Emery's Copper. They had been gifted to both of them when they were two or three. One of Emery's earliest memories was of Sloane and her lifting the dragons in the air to make them fly around the tiny home they'd shared with Ada. It was one of the memories she held dear. A memory of simpler times when they had no idea what the world had in store for them. They were just Sloane and Emery. Sisters. Best friends.

"You're here to kill me," Sloane said, flicking the ear of her dragon with her obsidian fingers. It wasn't a question; she knew as well as Emery did that only one of them would be leaving that room.

Emery lifted a brow, watching every move Sloane made. "Do you think you deserve to live?"

"I deserve to thrive." Sloane stepped toward the bed and set the dragon down in the exact same place where Copper had sat each day she'd been a part of the Culling.

"So does this world. We just have two very different ideas of what that looks like."

Emery couldn't help but shake her head. Sloane didn't get it. Her eyes softened and she tried. One last-ditch effort to make her sister see. "You would put your trust in a god who wants to destroy our realm for his own benefit. You would deny vampires and witches their mates."

"No," Sloane sneered, "I would deny you your mate. I don't care about the rest of the world."

"Why do you hate me so. damn. much?" Her lips spat out the words.

Sloane chuckled, and Emery watched her with a blank stare as it grew to a full laugh. "You really don't get it, do you?"

Sloane clearly wanted an answer, but Emery just waited for her to continue. When she did, her eyes darkened. The amber in Sloane's eyes—a color that once matched Emery's—grew black, much like Emery's own did when her darkness took hold. Only Sloane's glowed with a purple hue as she snarled, "You got everything I wanted, and you did nothing to deserve it. Because of that, yours and August's life will never be easy. I won't allow it. Even after I'm gone, you will feel my reach."

Sloane flicked her wrist, and Emery felt the familiar ward fall over the room. She knew that if she reached for August, she'd feel nothing but his presence in their soul bond, the ward preventing any sort of communication. It was only her and Sloane in this fight. As it should be.

"How can you say that?" Emery called her magic to the surface, but kept it beneath her skin, ready and waiting. She knew what came next, but damn if there wasn't still a part of her that wished it could be different. "I would have defied the stars for you. I would have jeopardized this realm and found a way to keep you at my side, because you are my sister. You are the light to my dark, but you consistently chose the dark over me. Power is nothing without loved ones beside you. You chose this, Sloane."

"And I'd choose it again in every lifetime. You know the draw of the dark now, I can see it in your eyes. The way they pulse, growing darker with every word I speak. There will be a moment where you let go, and that may be my end in this realm, but it is only the beginning of my legacy."

A shiver gripped Emery's spine. Sloane wasn't wrong. Like called to like, and Sloane's darkness was no different from hers. Now that she'd tapped into it and given it life in her chest, it wanted to be set free. Only Sloane thought Emery's magic was like hers. For the first time, she realized it wasn't. It wanted to vanquish Sloane, to be the only darkness in the room. It might push Emery beyond her comfort zone, but that night in the arena they'd come to an agreement, her magic and her. They were fighting the same fight, even if it was through different means. Her darkness would still have her rule through darkness, while her light would see her do it through compassion and grace, but at the end of the day, they wanted the same thing.

It wasn't until that moment she realized how much her magic supported her. Even her darkness.

"I won't deny the allure of the dark, but mine is nothing like yours," Emery hissed, glaring at Sloane. "I will ensure you will not have a legacy. Look at what you've done to this realm. You've devastated people and forced them to do your bidding for your own twisted agenda. How could you not see that your plan would fail? Your future would always end in the destruction of our realm." Emery shook her head, her breath heaving as she tried to make Sloane see. It had always been a losing battle.

"From death comes new life. Remember that, Emery."

"Not this time."

Emery called her magic to the surface, the inky gold tendrils vibrating against her skin, ready for a fight. She was ready to end this.

"So be it." Sloane stretched out her hands, her inky purple magic mirroring Emery's.

Emery didn't hesitate any longer; she wanted this to be over. She closed her eyes and inhaled a steadying breath. Sloane used the moment to allow her magic to fill the space.

She thinks she can sneak up on us and overtake us, Emery's darkness echoed in her mind. *We are not weak. Let us free.*

A single tear fell down her cheek, and Emery could feel the power she held rattling through her. Her body trembled, but she'd never felt more confident in her magic. She wondered if the stars had always planned for her to end up there, or if she'd somehow managed to change the spinning coin of fate, knocking it off balance. Her sight told her this was her moment, it showed her taking Sloane's head, but it also revealed that there was truth in Sloane's words. She saw her kingdom at peace, but a purple smokey haze filtered through the gates and over their castle: two almost-transparent green eyes rimmed with silver.

But those eyes were a problem for another day. Right then, Emery needed to fight for the promised peace.

So, she let go.

Magic burned through her, and when she opened her

eyes, she saw that her darkness had taken control. Her hands were outstretched, and beams of gold tangled with Sloane's purple in the middle of the room.

Emery sucked in a sharp breath and stepped forward, her body shaking as the power ripped itself free of her and dominated the room. Papers and trinkets flew around them and the glass in the window shuddered against the frame.

Sloane's hair whipped around her face, which was contorted into a grimace beneath her wide eyes.

Joy bloomed in Emery's chest at the fear in her sister's eyes. "You didn't think I was going to come unprepared, did you?"

"How?" Sloane's lip quivered. "I am supposed to be stronger than you. I am death incarnate. I am the darker half."

A wicked grin stretched across Emery's face. "Blood may be thicker than water, but blood is also the essence of life, and life is far greater than the death that rots in your veins."

Her heart beat like a war drum in her chest, carrying the tune of promised victory. Emery took another step forward and then another, urging her well of magic through her darkened fingertips. She built an enormous storm of magic around her. Her power was immense, a roaring flame that might never go out.

Sloane's fingers trembled as she strained, willing her magic to meet Emery's strength. But with every step forward, the obsidian-purple tendrils retreated, until Emery's own wrapped around her sister's wrists.

"I loved you," Emery whispered the last ache of her heart as she forced her magic to bind Sloane.

Her sister locked eyes with her, the obsidian swirls that matched her own receding until all that was left were matching amber depths. "Love is a weakness. You'll see that someday."

Emery tasted the lie in her words and forced her magic to wrap around her sister's neck. "Rest in peace, Sloane."

"See you in hell, Emery."

Emery wallowed past the last of her conflicting emotions and clenched her fists at her side. She wanted to look away, but forced herself to watch as her magic mirrored her actions and sliced through Sloane's neck, sending her head and body to the floor in slow motion.

She'd done it. She'd killed her sister. All that was left to do was take her heart so she couldn't come back again.

Emery stepped forward, but the moment Sloane's head hit the floor, something blasted through the room and everything went black.

Emery wasn't sure if it had been magic or if she had blacked out, but when she blinked, she could hardly make anything out through the dust and debris. All she knew was she shouldn't be able to see the night sky, but there, staring back where a wall had once been, were the stars that dictated their lives.

"Emery!" August shouted, free from the wards that separated them.

"I'm here," she cried, pain ripping through her. She peered down to see two holes in her armor, one just below her right shoulder and the other in her left thigh. Blood poured from each of the wounds, but particularly the one on her leg.

Fuck. If she didn't get help soon, she'd bleed out.

August fell to his knees in front of her, his eyes

immediately taking stock of her injuries and widening once he saw the holes in her flesh. He immediately leaned over and bit into her thigh, sending his venom to heal her. He did the same to her shoulder, and even though she could see her wounds healing physically, she still felt weak.

"We need to take her heart." Emery's speech slurred, and she tried to blink away the darkness clouding her vision. "She can come back."

"Callum is taking care of it."

"NO!" Emery shrieked.

She pulled herself up, screaming in pain as her wounds protested the movement.

The fucking bastard. What the hell was he thinking? He couldn't take on her darkness, and he knew it. The gods told them it had to be a magicked soul. She had to do it. She had to take on Sloane's darkness because she was the only one who could hold on to it. It would kill anyone else. This was her burden to carry, and she was ready for it. She had August and Lina to keep her balanced.

If Callum touched her sister's heart, it would end him.

Vampires might be glued together with the magic of her ancestors, but they weren't made to be a vessel like witches were.

August's eyes went wide. "What's wrong?"

"Get me to Callum. We have to stop him."

August picked Emery up and the two of them navigated the debris field that had once been a bedroom toward where Sloane's body fell.

She froze when the dust cleared and she saw Callum looking up at her, his hand wrist deep in Sloane's chest, wrapped around her heart.

"Don't!" Emery shrieked.

"This is my choice," he said, his voice even and calm, like he'd known this was how things would end all along.

Callum yanked his arm up and pulled the blackened life-giving organ from Sloane's chest, crumbling to the floor beside her.

"No!" Emery yelled and scrambled from August's arms, clawing her way through pieces of wood and stone to his body.

She tugged him to her, cradling his head in her lap. She looked up at August and pleaded. "Bite him."

August's mouth formed a grim line and he shook his head as he walked over and knelt on the other side of Callum. They both knew his venom couldn't overcome death. That didn't mean Emery wasn't willing to try.

"Please," she begged.

Her eyes flitted to Sloane's heart, still clutched in Callum's hand. The black that stained the organ mere seconds before had filtered itself into Callum's hand. It snaked its way up his arm and under his shirt like a tree taking root in fertile ground.

Emery snatched the heart away and tangled her fingers in his. She tipped her head back and pleaded to whatever god would listen. "Give it to me. It's mine to bear."

Callum coughed, and Emery bowed her head to meet his gaze. "I know this will hurt, but you'll see it's for everyone. And for me. I need to see what comes of this."

"But your mate?" Emery pleaded. All Callum wanted was a family of his own. A woman to love who'd return his love.

"What was once mine is yours now. Your soul is no longer in jeopardy" His eyes flicked to August. "Mates should never be torn apart. Take care of her."

"Always with the cryptic answers." Tears stained Emery's cheeks, and she forced her light into him. "Please. Don't leave us. You didn't have to do this. Why is the magic staying in you?"

"I'm no longer a vampire. Everything's different now." His lips tipped up slightly, and he wheezed. I'm not going anywhere. I'm only a prayer away."

No. The gods couldn't have him. She wouldn't allow it.

"No. No, no, no," Emery sobbed. "Please. You weren't supposed to do this. It was my darkness to bear."

"You've already got enough darkness. Go live in the light, lass." Callum coughed and blood trickled from his lips before he closed his eyes, his lips twitching as he took his final breath. Emery leaned over his body, shaking with each sob that racked her chest. For Callum and Miles, and for every member of their kingdom who had given their lives to secure a future ripe with possibility.

At some point, August rounded Callum's body and tugged her against his chest, holding her as she wept.

When there were no more emotions left to purge, Emery tipped her head and looked up at August. She saw a mix of pride and sorrow in his eyes when he reached up and wiped the tears from her cheeks before pressing a kiss to her lips.

"He asked me not to tell you," she whispered.

August tightened his hold on her. "I didn't say anything."

Emery shrugged. "I know, but I can see the hurt in your eyes."

August was quiet for some time, likely piecing everything together. "He's a god, isn't he?"

Emery nodded against him. "Your uncle liked to get around, it seems."

"That explains a lot."

Emery pulled away and placed her hands in his. "I'm sorry I didn't tell you. I didn't think...I didn't know he'd—"

But that wasn't true. Her sight hadn't shown him giving his life, but it had shown her the sheet with the Nicholson crest. It had warned her, but she hadn't had a clue. If she would have, she'd have stopped him.

Fucking fates.

"It's not your fault, Emery." August tucked her tangled matted hair behind her ear, his cerulean eyes filled with nothing but love. "Callum was a sneaky bastard. If he didn't want you to know, you wouldn't. And as much as I'd love to punish you, I'm just glad you are okay. It seems like this is what Callum wanted."

Emery nodded, unsure if she was convinced.

"Is it really over?"

"I think so."

Chapter Forty Six

EMERY

Dawn was supposed to bring a new beginning, but before they could start anew, they had to say goodbye.

The stark white sheets glimmered in the sunlight that filtered through the skylights in the great hall. Emery blinked and counted the columns and rows again as if it would somehow change the number of lives lost. Ten across and nineteen deep. Her eyes always came back to the one body in the center of the front row.

The sword placed atop his body announced his royalty, and the crest in the hilt denoted he belonged to them.

But to her, Callum was so much more than that. He was her friend, and at times her confidant. He was the driving force for peace and a visionary for the future. He wasn't supposed to be gone.

Tears pricked the back of her eyes, and she swallowed hard when she felt August's presence beside her. He slid his hand across the small of her back and tugged her against him so he could press a kiss to her temple.

"Are you ready?"

Emery glanced up at his face, still covered in blood and dirt. Neither of them had taken the time to clean themselves. They'd been too busy helping to recover their dead and take account of the living. And that was before the calls started pouring in. Now that Sloane had been defeated, leaders from every faction, vampires, wolves, and witches wanted to announce their support of August and Emery's vision for the future.

If you asked her, it was too little, too late, but August pointed out that they would need support from all sides if they were going to change the way the supernatural world thought about mates and their hybrid children. He was right, and she knew it. That didn't stop her darkness providing her with some very gruesome images of how it would like her to remind them that they should have played their part in stopping Sloane from the beginning.

Her mind flitted back to his question, whether she was ready to stand before their people, declare the war over, and share their plans for the future. The problem was admitting it was over out loud meant moving on from everything they'd lost. It was easy to push it to the back of her mind when they were focused on the war ahead, but now that there wasn't a looming battle, the losses felt so much bigger.

Miles.

Agatha.

Her mate bond.

Callum.

Not to mention the lives of the nameless sentinels she'd never get to meet, because they'd given up their lives to secure the future of their kingdom.

Still, she nodded and replied, "As ready as I'm ever going to be." Because that's all she could say.

This wasn't about her, or the dead. It was about the hundreds of vampires, wolves, witches, and hybrids that lined the walls and stairs of the hall, looking to her and August to lead.

A shriek-filled laugh filled the space and Emery turned to see Cosmina walking onto the dais with Lina. She handed her to Emery, and their daughter gazed up at her and August with her gummy smile and mismatched eyes. If there was any reason for Emery to press forward, it was this little girl.

"Ahem, if I could have your attention, please." August's voice reverberated over the idle conversations, causing everyone to pause and take notice.

"Today we mourn the loss of so many who gave their lives selflessly so we might live in a world where love is celebrated, and everyone is welcome. Grief doesn't have a time limit, and we will continue to feel these losses every day, but as we step forward, we must celebrate their lives and ensure that we continue striving for the future they fought to—."

The ornate doors at the top of the stairs swung open and banged loudly against the walls of the hall, drowning out August's last words. Emery whipped her gaze to the top of the stairs where people groaned and shuffled until they could see the face of Mikael gazing down on them as the other gods who'd spoken to them in Enchanth fanned out around him.

"I see we're a tad late."

August's jaw ticked, but he plastered a smile on his face

and greeted the god. "Welcome, Mikael. To what do we owe the visit?"

Emery wasn't sure if their people knew who he was, but with the way they skittered out of his way as he descended the stairs, it was clear they felt the power rolling off him in waves.

The room was so silent you could hear the clicks of the gods' shoes on the tile floors as they walked down the center aisle of the dead. Mikael's lips moved, and he opened his palms as he passed each row of bodies. Emery was sure she heard the faint mutterings of a protection spell.

Where the hell had that been before they died?

When he reached the dais, Mikael stopped and the other gods arched around him. He looked up at them and smiled.

Emery bit the side of her cheek to stop herself from blurting out the questions burning a hole in her chest. Was Callum okay? Was he going to become a god? Could they see him?

"I can see you are dying to ask questions, little queen, and I promise you will have answers." Mikael folded his hands across his abdomen and threaded his fingers. "First, I would like to thank you and your army for protecting this realm. Because of you, life will continue to thrive here and in the Feywilde for centuries to come."

"We will always fight for our home."

"I know you will. Which is why the fates have sent me here. To bear witness to the titles they would like to bestow upon you and the other intended." Mikael looked to the side of the dais where Lily and Draven stood. "Please, come forward with your mates."

Lily, Malcolm, Flora, and Draven stepped forward, one couple on either side of August and Emery.

"The six of you are the future of your world. The stars have aligned and given you the power to make this realm one of the greatest ever created, if you so choose to take on the titles bestowed upon you. With these titles, you will be bonded together in every sense of the word. There will be no higher honor."

The six of them swiveled their heads, looking to one another for confirmation before each one of them nodded. There was no question they would do what was asked of them, even if the gods' involvement made their stomach turn. They were the intended. United, they would rule.

Mikael stepped in front of Draven and Flora first and stretched out his hands for the two of them to place theirs in his. When they did, he wrapped them around each other and said, "Draven and Flora, you are the first hybrids of royal blood. You fight not only for your hybrid brethren but for what is right and just. As such, the fates would bestow upon you the titles of High Alpha and Luna of Hybrids."

Around the room, wolves began to howl and the hybrids, led by Nina, pressed their hands to their chests and bowed to their leaders.

Stoically, Flora and Draven bowed their heads, accepting their titles, and when they raised them again, they each wore elegant crowns made from the deep purple wood of the trees in Enchanth.

Emery bit back a smile. Flora was going to love that. She hated those damn trees.

Mikael then passed August and Emery and stood before Lily and Malcolm. His smile stretched wide as he entwined their hands. "Lily and Malcolm, you both believe in the fight for love and understand what it means to put the world first. The fates believe you will lead your people in this time of healing and rebirth, which is why you are being bestowed with the titles High King and Queen of the New Realm. You will lead the vampires and witches of this realm into their new future."

Cheers erupted as Lily and Malcolm bowed and accepted their titles, and crowns of silver and emerald appeared on their heads.

Tears leaked from Emery's eyes. She couldn't imagine two better people to lead their people on the path of healing. It might have taken them some time to get to their happily ever after, but Lily and Malcolm were ideal mates in every way.

That left August and Emery without titles, though. If they weren't to be the King and Queen of vampires and witches, then what was their purpose in all this?

Flora reached out and took Lina from Emery's arms as Mikael stepped in front of her and August and extended his hands for theirs. His lips stretched into a smile, and Emery could have sworn his eyes went a bit misty. "August and Emery. From the beginning, the two of you defied the odds. The stars weren't always kind to you, but you continued to believe the fates had a plan for your future, and you were right to do so. Which is why I am happy to bestow upon you the titles of High King and High Queen of Light and Dark, Rulers of the Realm."

The great hall erupted with deafening cheers and hollers from every faction present, but Emery's mind went blank as she tried to reconcile what that meant.

Rulers of the realm.

The entire freakin' realm.

She looked up at August, who seemed as dumbfounded as she was. What did that even mean?

Mikael spoke softly, but somehow, she could still hear him over the thunderous response of their people. "I have no doubt that you two will figure out the best way to reign, but there are no two I trust more to ensure that the balance of the realm remains intact."

August peered over at her and smiled. "As long as I'm with you, I'll accept whatever comes our way."

Emery nodded and smiled at him through her joyous tears.

The two of them bowed their heads and waited for their crowns to appear, but she didn't feel the weight of anything atop her head.

"I have one more gift to give, before I give you your crowns." Mikael said as he slid his fingers from their hands and wrapped them around their forearms. He looked up and met Emery's gaze. "This isn't from me; it was given freely by a mysterious vampire. He's alive and well, and told me to tell you to live like he would, with no regrets."

Callum.

Heat seared in the place Mikael touched their arms, and Emery choked on a sob as her magic surfaced and entwined its gold tendrils over their flesh. It grew brighter and brighter until she was forced to close her eyes or be blinded by its light.

In the darkness of her mind, a vision played like a movie at triple speed. She watched all of the moments, good and bad, that she'd shared with August throughout their relationship. The ups and downs, joys and sorrows, they had all brought them to this moment.

Love radiated in her chest for the man beside her, and in the deepest part of her soul she knew he felt the same way. It was almost as if she was sharing this moment with him not only physically. She could feel him beside her... she could...

Emery froze.

Little witch, I can feel you. Your love. Your fear. I feel it too. I don't want to open my eyes and find it's not real. Please tell me I'm not imagining this.

Emery opened her eyes and saw silver vines etched on her forearm, along with four perfect flowers.

"It's real," she whispered in disbelief.

Callum did this for them. He gave them the gift of their mate bond with his death. He repaired the damage done to their soul bond in its absence. Everyone thought he was self-serving and mysterious, but not for the first time, he proved he'd done everything with great thought and even greater love.

August dropped her hand and pulled her against his chest, hitting her with every emotion in his chest. Love. Pride. Joy. Lust. The last one sent a bolt of lightning down her spine that landed straight in her clit, causing her to let out a faint mewl. August captured it with his lips, and as he did, she felt the weight of the crown on her head.

When she pulled back and looked up at her mate, a circlet of gold and black sat upon his head encrusted with deep red stones. Light, dark, and blood. The foundations of their realm.

August reached out and took Lina from Flora, holding her between the two of them. When they turned, Mikael had disappeared, and all that was left was their people cheering for them and their future.

When Emery entered the castle, she hadn't believed she was meant for greatness, but now she knew that greatness was meant for her. For all of them.

She glanced across the dais at the family she'd found. Each of them held a special place in her heart and would forever be the reason she fought for their realm. When her gaze finally landed on her mate, he smiled.

"This is our beginning, little witch."

"No, this is our happily ever after."

Epilogue

AUGUST

He wasn't sure he'd ever willingly step foot back in New Orleans, let alone the bayou, but living there made sense for Malcolm and Lily.

August pressed his hand to the small of Emery's back as they walked up the expansive lawn that led to his brother's house. If it could even be called that. Considering it was a centuries-old mansion and sat on the edge of the swamp with sprawling trees and canopies that were draped in Spanish moss, it was more estate than house. It was regal in an old-world kind of way, and yet it still managed to hold an air of whimsy. It was perfect for the new King and Queen of the New Realm, and gave them a place to call their own outside the rebuilt witches' compound in New Orleans.

He and Emery were fashionably late, although as the High King and Queen of Light and Dark, Rulers of the Realm, they could argue everyone else was early.

Not that Malcolm would see it that way. He'd called no

less than a dozen times to make sure they remembered Talamh Heil and that everything was in place so it was perfect for Lily.

The way he doted on that woman was bloody fucking adorable.

Lina cooed in Emery's arms, her eyes wide as she stared at the bulbed lights strung from the trees.

"Lily is going to kill us for being late." Emery hitched her step, but the dress she'd opted to wear didn't allow for her to widen her stride, unless she wanted to flash the entire world.

Not that he was complaining.

August dragged his eyes over his mate and willed his blood to remain in the head that would remember they had to be present at the Heil celebration.

He might not want the world seeing what was his, but he absolutely planned on sampling every bit of skin Emery had on display.

When Bronwyn dropped off the dress and declared it was time for Emery to embrace her sexuality through her witch heritage, his mate nearly declined the invitation to the Heil celebration altogether. The dress dripped with sexual tension. The way the deep navy panels draped over her shoulders and across her breasts, leaving her skin exposed to her navel, left August wanting to sink his fangs into her supple flesh.

The silver vines wrapped around her waist, kept the panels in place, and accentuated her curves. From her waist, the material fell in waves between her legs as she walked, with slits that exposed the soft flesh of her hips.

She was a walking dream.

His dream.

August had never appreciated the witches' need to flaunt their sexuality, but after seeing Emery like that, he completely understood the allure. He both loved and hated that everyone would get to see Emery in all her witch glory, but was happy to be at her side for the celebration of her magic.

A sting on his arm pulled him back to the present, and he found himself on the receiving end of a wicked glare from Emery.

He reached up and rubbed the spot she'd just pinched. "What the bloody hell was that for?"

"Keep staring at me like that and I'll be portaling Lina inside while we christen that rowboat we saw on the way in."

August huffed a laugh. "We both know Malcolm and Lily have already christened every surface on the property."

It wasn't a surprise they'd announced they were pregnant a week after they moved to the estate. If they were anything like August and Emery, they were using every free moment alone to bask in their bond now that the war was over.

Before Emery could respond, Malcolm and Lily appeared at the entrance to the house.

"There you guys are!"

I guess we'll never know what it's like for you to ride me to the rhythm of the bayou.

Emery's cheeks flushed and her lips twitched, but she didn't look in his direction. Instead, she flooded their mate bond with arousal, and August let out a growl.

"Seriously, you two. Act like the rulers you are."

Malcolm chided for the sake of his mate, but August didn't miss the way he attempted to hide his smile.

"Nope," Emery shook her head. "Tonight is your night. We may be the rulers of the realm, but this is your shindig, and I for one plan to enjoy not being in charge."

Lily cocked a brow. "You do know you still have to help lead the charging of the ley lines."

"Oh absolutely," Emery said, handing Lina to August, where the baby squirmed in his arms. "But this is the first time since we had Lina and the war ended that I get to enjoy myself, so I plan on doing that."

She wasn't wrong. They'd been busy every moment of every day getting the kingdoms in order and establishing what the supernatural world in their realm would look like. It wasn't perfect, and Emery hated the endless requests and trials of those witches and vampires who wanted to forsake their mate bonds, but somehow, they managed. She handled each request with grace and compassion, and August had never been more proud. They were creating a world their children could thrive in.

August laughed as Emery pushed her way past his brother and Lily, heading straight for the bar in the other room where he also saw Dorian and Ansel.

A smile tugged at his lips, despite the pang in his heart. The two of them were huddled close whispering, and Ansel wore a rare smile on his face. The mortal realm still proved to be too much for Ansel, so the two of them had been spending most of their time in Enchanth, much to Dorian's dismay. It was good for Ansel, though, who, like August and the rest of the kingdom, was slowly healing from what happened.

Ansel had Dorian.

August had Emery.

The stars knew exactly what they were doing when they gave them their mates.

Lily tsked and called after Emery. "Five minutes, Em. You have five minutes."

"I'm glad to see her back to being herself," Malcolm said softly, even though there was no way Emery could hear him from across the room.

"She has her good days and bad days, but more often than not, she's learning to heal."

While her presence was enough to keep the memories of his time with Sloane at bay, Callum's death had hit Emery hard. Even though she knew he wasn't really dead, his absence was enough to enliven her darkness. There were days where she woke up with obsidian eyes, and only Lina and August could coax her back into the light. But she always came back to them.

"And how are you?"

August hesitated, looking at Lina in his arms, her gummy smile enough to keep his own darkness from creeping in. "I'm healing too."

There were nights he woke up in cold sweats shivering like he used to on the dungeon floor. But every time, Emery was there. She wrapped herself around him and flooded their bond with love. He still couldn't bring himself to go down into the deepest parts of his castle; there would be time for that, though. Every aspect of their healing was done in baby steps, but they were doing it together.

A waiter walked by them with glasses of champagne, and August grabbed one with his free hand and handed it to Malcolm before grabbing one from himself.

"I love you, brother." Malcolm took his and tipped his head, suggesting they should join the rest of the celebration in the main room.

"Bloody hell, don't get sappy on me," August grumbled, but if he was honest, he loved being there with his brother and their family.

The party was in full swing, witches and hybrids everywhere with the occasional vampire there to support their mate, or those who were curious about the celebration. It was the first time since the final battle at their castle that members of all three factions from around the world had gathered. August couldn't help the smile that was permanently plastered on his face.

It was a beautiful thing to witness. He hated that so many had given their lives for it to become a reality, but this was no doubt the start of a bright future of unity.

The clinking of metal on glass echoed over the crowd, and everyone silently turned to where Lily stood with Emery. "If everyone could please head outside, the Heil ceremony is about to begin."

August followed Malcolm and Emery slid beside him, her head held high. She was beautiful in her confidence.

Stay by my side? she asked as she took Lina into her arms.

He loved that she wanted him there. Even though this was her defining moment, she wanted him there.

Always, little witch.

Under the canopy of the bayou and the stars and moon above, the witches gathered in a circle. Emery and Lily stood beside one another, with Lina in Emery's arms.

August slid behind Emery and Malcolm did the same behind Lily.

Magic hummed around them. Aside from when Emery wielded her magic at him in the bedroom, he'd never felt it in such a tangible way. Like the earth had come alive around them, naming this place sacred.

Lily threaded her fingers with Emery's, and the two of them raised their united hands. Their magic, obsidian-gold and teal, wove its way down their forearms and charged in their palms.

August watched in awe as they began to chant in the ancient language of their ancestors. One by one, the witches in the circle joined in, calling their magic and pushing it forward until a rainbow of colors filled the space above them. The tendrils intertwined from a singular point and formed a pillar of magic into the earth. From that point in the center, silver-glittering magic erupted in every direction, finding its way back to the witches.

As they continued to chant and commune with the earth, the witches tipped their heads back so their eyes could gaze upon the sky above.

August, Emery whispered down their bond, her voice filled with the awe he felt radiating from her. *Come closer.*

He stepped forward until his chest pressed to her back.

Look. Emery nodded to their daughter in her arms.

August looked over her shoulder at Lina, who was looking up at the colorful magic above them, but in her palms, there was a faint blue glow.

Is it her magic?

Emery choked past a sob and nodded.

The sound caught Lina's attention and she looked up at the two of them. She reached up her hands and one of them cupped Emery's cheek, while the other remained outstretched for August.

When he brought his hand around Emery and placed it in his daughter's, the world around them went black, and August's chest was overwhelmed with the onslaught of magic, no doubt the gift from the earth to his mate and daughter. But along with it, there was an almost innocence he couldn't quite grasp.

Unlike when he'd been pulled into Emery's visions before, these were only quick flashes of images.

August and Emery holding a baby boy with Lina bouncing beside them. A blonde little girl with two colored eyes, Lina, riding a bike through the halls of the castle. She was beautiful. Lina studying with Lily and Emery. Lina and her brother tossing magic between them. August and Emery chasing twins across the gardens toward Lina. Haven and Thea, sneaking a teenage Lina into the castle. Lina running toward an ethereal Callum and getting swept up into a big hug. Lina, standing on the dais, a crown on her head, with magic tendrils of blue and black snaked around her arms, and a man with indistinguishable features by her side.

Black tendrils crowded the edges of his vision, but August tried in vain to cling to the images the stars granted them. His eyes burned as he tried to keep them open, focusing on the visage of his daughter, but finally he couldn't keep them open any longer. When he blinked open his eyes, they met his mate's, and his breath caught in his chest.

The ceremony carried on around them, but it was no longer the highlight of his night.

Was that...?

Emery shook her head. *Those weren't my visions.*

They were hers?

Emery nodded, tears falling down her cheeks. *Did you see? He's alive. Somewhere out there, he's alive.*

August nodded, tears welling in his own eyes. Callum was the reason he had Emery in his arms. He was the one who sparked the fire in this realm and started their quest for a better future.

The two of them shifted their gaze to the tiny witch in Emery's arms.

Their daughter.

She had the sight, and if the visions were correct, his daughter held an aspect of darkness in her just like her mother.

What if she's like Sloane? Emery voiced the concern that plagued his soul, but ultimately, he felt at peace knowing that even with the darkness, Lina would always have them.

She may be a child of the dark, she may have the ability to raise the dead, but our daughter will never be like Sloane, August reassured her. *Lina has you to guide her and me to scare away the darkness. She is so incredibly loved. Even if she does carry the same magic that was in your sister's veins, I have no doubt she will be the light our world needs.* August reached over and ran his finger across Lina's cheek. "Isn't that right, *gealiach bhig?*"

Lina cooed, and Emery melted into him, the back of her head resting against his shoulder.

Lily concluded the ceremony and each of the witches walked a little taller as they headed back into the mansion.

He followed his mate, grabbing them each a glass of champagne as they mingled with the witches present.

"That was incredible."

He hadn't noticed Flora and Draven saddle up beside them. Kade wasn't far behind them, an ever-present guardian looming over his Alpha and Luna. What surprised him was Mateo was nowhere to be found.

"He's in Ambersey." Draven offered after seeing August's eyes wander behind them. "After the war ended, his uncle wasn't keen on giving up his quest for power. Mateo is seeing to his removal."

"Ah, I see." August's eyes drifted to Kade, who chewed his lower lip but remained silent. He'd have to ask Draven later about why Kade was still at his side when there was no doubt he was worried about his second.

Draven raised a brow and nodded before sliding his hand into Flora's. August smiled. He loved the united force between the intended heirs and their commanders. There was never a question as to whether they supported one another; it was a given—a constant that strengthened their realm.

August flagged down a waiter and grabbed another two champagne flutes for the pair.

"None for me," Flora whispered, and a flush filled her cheeks.

Emery tilted her head and scoffed. "What do you mean by 'none for you?'"

August narrowed his gaze and, on a whim, opened his senses to listen carefully to the world around him.

The steady beat of a second heart echoed from Flora's midsection.

Emery's gaze bounced between August, Draven, and Flora, and when she finally put together what was going on, her jaw dropped.

"You're pregnant!" Emery screeched.

A sheepish smile stretched across Flora's face, and tears lined her eyes. Emery pulled her into a hug, and the two of them whispered excitedly with one another.

"Congratulations." August clinked his drink with Draven as the two of them watched their mates.

You're next. August whispered down their bond, already loving the image of Emery swollen with their next child.

Emery's gaze slid toward him over Flora's shoulder and a knowing smile tipped her lips. *Maybe we should test out that boat theory.*

Lead the way, little witch.

But before he could pawn his daughter off on his brother for the night, he caught a commotion across the room in his periphery. Bronwyn wove her way through the crowd toward them, panic etched across her face. When she reached August and Draven, she latched on to each of their free hands and dug her nails in. "Oh, thank the stars, you are both here."

August brow furrowed, and Draven's gaze darted around the room. "Are you okay?"

"Tell me what it felt like?" She stumbled over her words like an excited child. "When you met your mate? What did it feel like?"

"My entire body vibrated in her presence and I was drawn to her." August glanced at Draven. "You?"

"Same, and my wolf told me she was mine. There was no one else in this realm that could have pulled me away from Flora." His eyes drifted to his mate, and August knew he was feeling the same thing he was. It was the same way he looked at Emery. Like he was the bloody luckiest damn man in the world.

Bronwyn practically bounced in front of them. "She's here." Her eyes flicked across the room.

"Who's here?" Emery asked, her and Flora joining their circle.

"My mate. I saw her. She's a hybrid. And she's fucking beautiful."

"Then what are you doing talking to us?" Emery asked, sliding up next to August.

He wrapped his arm around her, loving the way she fit perfectly against him.

"Her wolf is probably going crazy." Flora worried and glanced in the direction Bronwyn was looking. "You should probably go introduce yourself."

Bronwyn's eyes widened and for the first time since August met her, pink tinged her cheeks. "I…what if…what if she doesn't want me?"

"Then she's a damn fool."

"Go." Emery placed her hand on Bronwyn's shoulder and gave it an encouraging squeeze. "That's what tonight was about. Celebrating life and magic. This is your beginning and I wouldn't be surprised if it was the beginning for others, too."

"Okay." Bronwyn nodded. "I'm going to go talk to her."

The four of them watched as Bronwyn crossed the room and cautiously approached a tall redhead at the bar. She twisted her hands in front of her nervously, something Bronwyn never did. The two spoke softly and the collective group of them watching held their breath.

When the redhead reached out and tangled her hand in Bronwyn's hair and crashed their lips together, Emery let out a small gasp.

THE UNITED

This was what they were striving for. This celebration of life. Of love. The unity between two people who were meant to be together.

Emery let out a whimsical smile. "I am so glad we had this party."

"It's actually a really good idea," August mused.

"What is?"

"A mate gala." Draven, Flora, and Emery tipped their heads in his direction, clearly not following his thought process. "If we held a gala every year and invited those in the supernatural world who were looking for their mates, it would provide them with the opportunity to find one another. We could host them around the world, not just here."

Emery looked at him like he'd hung the damn moon before she launched herself at him. "You are a damn genius."

"I like to think so."

"That is seriously brilliant," Flora agreed.

"We'll host one in Scotland." Draven offered, since he'd taken over Callum's position as the only heir to the Scottish throne.

"And I bet Graves would host for Eastern Europe." Emery offered.

It was all coming together. Everything they'd fought for. What Callum had given his life for.

Emery tipped her head back and looked up at August.

I love you.

Always.

THANK YOU FOR READING

Thank you for Reading The United!!

I still can't believe this is the end of August and Emery's story! But don't you fret, I still have so much in store for the other characters in this world!

If you enjoyed TheUnited, or even if you hated it, I would so appreciate you hopping over to leave a review on Amazon and/or Goodreads. Reviews help tiny self published authors like me to gain new readers and get my books on fancy lists some day.

Thank you to everyone who reviews, recommends and posts about this series. I couldn't do this without you!

If you are interested in what happens next for our newest God, flip to the next page for information on his book!

REALMS OF RUIN

REALMS OF RUIN BOOK ONE

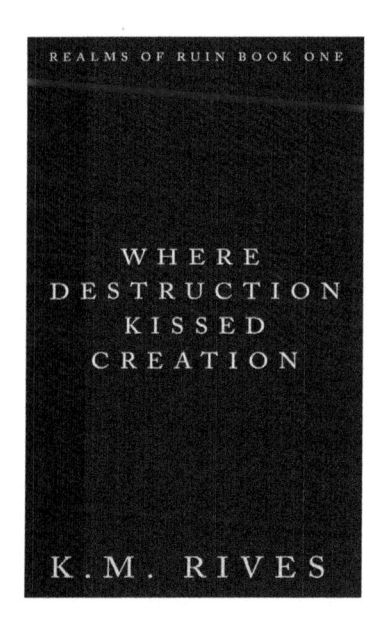

WHERE DESTRUCTION KISSED CREATION

K.M. RIVES

I gave up everything.

My life.

My identity.

I am the Architect.

The God of Realms.

I am their savior and she is my demise.

Check out Amazon to Pre-Order Callum's book.

ACKNOWLEDGMENTS

Holy hell! I cannot believe this is the end of August and Emery's story!

This story was my first book baby. It was what launched me into this crazy beautiful book world and ignited my passion after many years of doubting I could do it. August and Emery taught me so much along the way and I will forever love their story. They were the bane of my existence, but also the greatest gift.

But they weren't alone in dragging me through this series. I had an amazing team behind me cheering me on and inspiring me to keep going. Without them this story wouldn't be where it is, in your hands today.

To my husband, my rock, my home: Thank you from the bottom of my heart. You allowed me to dream of becoming a writer and encouraged me to make it a reality. Even when you were gone for work you never stopped cheering me on and helping me plot through the holes the story presented. Your fresh perspective is one I cherish immensely!! I love you forever and always.

To my daughters who remind me everyone needs a brain break and cuddles. You guys are my world. #betheromance

To my extended family: I love the way you believe in me. Thank you for always pushing me to follow my dreams and consistently supporting me in everything I do. I am so lucky to have you.

To the book community:

Holy hell, I must say I am blown away by the kindness and support of authors, bookstagrammers and readers who have promoted my books. Every single time I get tagged in a gorgeous photo or video I get a giddy smile on my face and it restores a bit of my faith in humanity. You seriously make my day and inspire me to keep writing worlds you love.

To Sienna Varrone: How the hell did I get so lucky to find you? Writing a book can be a lonely journey, but even from half a world away you are always there for spicy conversations and drooling over covers. You are my sounding board and mushball. I can't imagine doing life without you!

To Melissa Ivers: We have been in this together from day one and it's been a wild ass ride! But you are my ride or die and without you I wouldn't be where I am today. Thank you for listening to my drama llama ass every single day and reminding me that I know my story best, keeping me on task and cheering me on even though you have a million other things on your plate.

To Amy Dodson: I'm not even sure you understand how grateful I am that you've come into my life let alone become my PA. Seriously this release would have been dead on arrival if it weren't for you and your meticulous organizing and making sure we are on track. Not to mention you are the best cheerleader ever, make me laugh with incredibly accurate TikToks and you're the best sounding board when I am doubting myself. Thank you for your friendship and everything you do.

To Christiana: This series would be nowhere without you. From the day we met you have always believed in my story and these characters. You gave them life when I was unsure and for that I am forever grateful. Thank you for your insight and delicious comments throughout. Writing wouldn't be the same without you!

To Leticia: Oh my goodness woman, you are incredible. You came in at the final hour and blew me away with your skills and proofreading and ability to enhance this story and make it shine. Your love of this story radiates on the pages. Thank you for being on this journey with me.

To Nana Logan: The one who started this crazy journey with me. I couldn't ask for a better mentor and friend. This past year has been one of the most trying in our lives and I can't imagine having battled it with anyone else but you. You have helped me craft a solid foundation in not only my writing but my life. Thank you for standing by me and encouraging me every step of the way. For teaching me endless photoshop tricks when I stubbornly wanted to make all my own graphics. For reminding me the pool is fun, but the ocean is deep. Love you to the fucking stars and back woman.

To Amy: You are an editing queen. I am so glad to have found you. You accept me even though I am shit at commas and I couldn't ask for a better person to work with and bounce ideas off of. You single handedly gave Callum death and life again. I can't wait for the plans we have inshore for him. Thank you for everything you do and for believing in me and my story.

And finally, thank you to my readers.

Every. Single. One of you.

I can't believe how much love this series has gotten or the overall support I've received as an author. I am so grateful I get to do this job. Thank you for every sentence you read, every review you leave, every post you make. I see you. Thank you for taking a chance on me and my stories. You guys are magic.

— K.M.

ABOUT THE AUTHOR

Krista is a California girl living in a North Carolina world…for now. After all, home is where the Army tells her husband they're moving next. She's a lover of dungeons and dragons, singing at the top of her lungs, ice cold beer and all things dessert. Most days you can find her wrangling her two young daughters and finding any moment she can to sneak away into the worlds she writes. Check out her website kmrives.com to sign up for her newsletter and to find all the ways to stalk her.

THE CULLING OF BLOOD AND MAGIC SERIES

The Replacement

The Intended

The United

Hybrid Moon Rising - Companion Novel

Printed in Great Britain
by Amazon